I0822144

SHADOWSPHERE

Published by Silvettica 2022

FIRST EDITION

www.bewildernessseries.com

SHADOWSPHERE

BEWILDERNESS
BOOK TWO

KEVIN COX

PROLOGUE

SHE ROSE FROM the chair, uncertain if she had strayed from the boundaries of reality into a dream. Her numbing senses rendered a surreal quality to the moment. His eyes narrowed in recognition as a smile slowly spread across his face. As he began to move toward her, she shifted her feet, attempting to maintain her balance.

"I've been looking everywhere for you," he said, a degree of uncertainty in his voice.

Her surroundings returned as Ms. Bracklin loudly cleared her throat.

"Let's go sit in the corner . . ." she managed to whisper. "We can talk better over there."

She picked up the books, and he followed as she led him to a table where two large windows met, revealing a small pond among the swaying trees outside. Pressing her lips together tightly, she tried to restrain the variance of emotions threatening to cross the precipice.

"We can't be too loud," she told him.

"Is something wrong?" he inquired as he set his things on one of the chairs at the table.

"No, but we can't disturb the others." She slid a chair out and gingerly lowered herself into it.

"Okay, I'll be as quiet as I can," he said, grabbing another chair and sliding it beside her to sit.

"I can't believe you're actually—" she said. "How did you get here?"

"It's a long story." He leaned toward her. "First, there's something I came to tell you—something you need to know."

CHAPTER 1

WHISPERS FLICKERED LIKE the forked tongue of a serpent through the dark recesses of Tavarian's mind. He shuddered as he snapped out of the daydream, leaning against the wooden fence for stability. The words, so clear for a moment, quickly faded from memory as trepidation boiled within.

Nearby, standing as if he owned the world, Dexius ruined the serenity of the view with another boring hunting story. Beneath the mountain, a drifting dark haze split through the rolls of soft billowy clouds. A bulging distortion, like a droplet of water magnifying the surface of a leaf, seeped across the churning cloudscape.

Tavarian pointed at the strange object. "There's something down there!"

Gray mist moved across the white blanket of the lower atmosphere. The shifting of wind allowed for a rare glimpse of something darker beneath the layers of mist, perhaps revealing the bottom of the world for the first time.

"Where?" Lirah stared out across the skies. "I don't see anything."

"That spot over there." Tavarian recalibrated his finger to point again toward the separation between the clouds. "Around that line of sulos clouds."

Dexius and Lirah squinted their eyes, searching the layers of white and gray over the side of steep cliffs. The unusual object vanished. Lirah had been too focused on Dexius's endless boasting to see it in time. Tavarian scanned the blanket of white, hoping it would reappear.

"I can't ever remember the difference between sulos and tenus," Lirah said, turning to face Tavarian.

"How can you not remember?" Tavarian's head twitched. "Sulos clouds are those gray puffy clouds scattered above the flat white band of the—"

"There's nothing there." Dexius threw a rock over the edge of the plateau. It vanished into the roaring falls that cascaded into the opaque clouds below. "He's lying."

Lying? As bad as Dexius's constant crowing about his stupid accomplishments and talking over him had been, calling him a liar was a new low. Tavarian waited for Lirah to come to his defense.

Lirah played with the curls of her white hair with her palms, bouncing them up and down. "What did you see, Tav?"

That's her response? As much as she criticizes me for any mistake, she says nothing to Dexius for calling me a liar? Tavarian lowered his head, staring out across the misty cloudscape. "It was . . . I guess it was nothing."

Apparently, she cared more about Dexius than she did him.

They came to this spot often, spending hours after school, staring out over the lower atmosphere. They had grown up together dreaming about what mysteries lay at the bottom of the world beneath the clouds. Lirah believed that one day they both would discover all the wonders of the surface world of Rootcore, bringing their amazing finds back to Rethia.

Rootcore remained a mystery to all Rethians. No one had any reliable information on it. Most Rethians were unable to breathe the air below the dense clouds.

Those days of dreaming with Lirah were over now. For reasons that Tavarian did not understand, she had become friends with Dexius. It made no sense at all. Nearly everyone who talked to Dexius disliked him. His rude arrogance, stubbornness, and the way he ordered people around did not attract many companions. He only talked about himself, never listening to what anyone else had to say. Tavarian had only a few encounters with Dexius at school, but none were pleasant. Dexius had made it clear that he didn't like Tavarian, and in turn, Tavarian did not care for him.

Everything he tried to say in front of Dexius either got mocked or interrupted. Lirah's judgment had to be called into question. Why would she want to spend time with Dexius? As the only person to truly understand Tavarian, Lirah actually listened to what he had to say and respected him. His mother only had time for the new baby these days and his father only told him what he should or shouldn't do. He would no longer be able to share his thoughts and feelings with Lirah with this obnoxious person around all the time.

"You should have been there yesterday—I killed this huge borhend," Dexius said. "Everyone else was scared of it charging them, but I stood, keeping my aim, took a deep breath, and released . . . hit it right between its eyes."

Tavarian groaned silently. Instead of sharing his ideas and dreams with Lirah, he now had to listen to Dexius brag about himself every day. He couldn't do this anymore. Tavarian backed away from the fence and ambled back into the forest.

"Wait up, Tav!" Lirah called out.

He stopped without turning around, allowing her to catch up to him. It gave him a glimmer of hope that she called after him so quickly. He needed that reassurance.

He heard Lirah say goodbye to Dexius, and then she came up alongside him. "Where are you going?"

Tavarian resumed his path through the trees and underbrush. "Why do you hang out with him?"

"He's a really good friend," Lirah said. "He's different when—"

"When what?" he said. "When I'm not around?"

"Give him a chance," she said. "He's just . . . he feels like he has to compete with you for attention, I guess. It's nothing against you. He's like that with everyone."

"And that's supposed to make me want to be around him?" Tavarian lifted a low hanging branch while Lirah passed under it.

"He's getting better. He has a lot of insecurities. Give him some time," she said.

They came out of the forest near one of the main roads leading to town. The pleasant smells of dry grass and sweet blooms reached them as they approached the Plentyfield farming region. A cletine orchard stretched far into the distance, and fields of planted grains and leafy vegetables were spread out in front of them. Tavarian surveyed the road for any peace control officers. They didn't like anyone in the Plentyfield region without good reason.

"I prefer to be with people I like," Tavarian said. With no sign of officers, he stepped out onto the dirt road. "I don't want to spend time with some jerk and take his abuse until he decides to change. People like that don't change anyway."

"So, I'm the only person you like?" Lirah giggled. "You never hang out with anyone else. I would have thought that you, if anyone, would understand."

"What do you mean by that?" he asked as they headed toward the Deralawn district.

"You used to be very insecure, Tav, even more than Dexius. You still are in a lot of ways. That's why we are friends; you needed someone to help you."

"Dexius isn't insecure—he's full of himself. And I thought we were friends because we liked being around each other." Tavarian kicked a loose rock in his path, sending it tumbling through a sandy part of the road.

"We are." Lirah placed her hand on his arm as she walked beside him. "But it wasn't that way in the beginning. You were impossible."

Tavarian didn't want to continue this conversation. He would just as soon forget those days when he first started classes. No one wanted to be seen with him if they hoped to have other friends—no one except Lirah. Her popularity among the students and teachers made her immune to the adverse social effects of being around him.

They walked past the old farmhouses in silence. The hilly land was marked with dry patchy weeds among its beautiful green grass. Tavarian wanted to lie down on one of the hills to watch the birds tend to their nests as quecks swam in the ponds beneath.

"What happened in your calculations group?" Lirah inquired, breaking the peaceful ambience of the fields around them.

"What do you mean?" he said, replaying events from the class in his head.

"I overheard Serak and Jespa say something about how annoying you are." Lirah eyed him, waiting for his reaction.

"They said that? They didn't say anything about it to me." Tavarian tried to remain calm and wait to see what point she was trying to make.

"People don't often criticize others directly," Lirah said. "They're more likely to mock you than tell you straightforward."

"If they had a problem with me, they should have said something." Tavarian clasped his hands behind his neck. "I could have reminded them how bad they are at trapedish equations."

"That's probably why they didn't say anything." Lirah sped up to stay beside him. "If you could take a little criticism, a little joking, instead of getting so defensive, then people wouldn't do it so much."

"I would be giving them some criticism in return." Tavarian got a whiff of the animal pens over the hill and attempted to squeeze his nostrils together.

"I don't think that's how it's supposed to work." Lirah buried her nose in the collar of her dress. "Criticism shouldn't be a retaliation."

He turned toward her. "But you're okay with them saying it about me?"

"Tav, just tell me what happened." Lirah came to a stop, her hands firmly on her hips.

Tavarian paused, and then resumed walking. "The teacher said my answer to this problem we were working on was wrong."

"Okay. What's so bad about that?" Lirah caught up to him again.

"It wasn't my mistake. The issue was the way the problem was worded. If you say *the* three hundred eighty-two infleks, that implies there are more infleks that are unaccounted for, so—"

"Tav . . . just admit you made a mistake." Lirah sighed. "I've told you this is the type of thing that makes people dislike you. You're almost always right about everything as it is, but then when you do get something wrong, you won't admit it!"

"I want to be the best. How can I be the best if I mess up?"

"I've told you this so many times, it should be burned onto your forehead by now. Everyone makes mistakes, even the best. If you own up to them, people will forget. If you never admit it, they remember the mistakes more than all the smart answers you've had. It's okay to laugh at yourself sometimes. It can be quite endearing, actually. Endearment is one thing you are sorely lacking in right now."

Tavarian couldn't listen to Lirah's scolding. If there was one thing he disliked about her, it was how she sometimes talked down to others, lecturing everyone on what they should and shouldn't do. Although she was friendly and helpful, she sometimes acted superior to those she tried to help. Tavarian's feet dug into the grit beneath them. He had heard this speech too many times.

"Don't you want them to forget about the bird incident?" she said.

Tavarian's attention suddenly focused. "Why are you bringing that up again?"

"Because people still associate that with you," Lirah said as the clang of something metal hanging on the trees sounded nearby. "Carrying that dead bird around all day from class to class."

Tavarian's head began to burn. "I was just a kid. I didn't know any better."

"I know." Lirah walked close, brushing up against him. "You thought you could fix it. I think it's sweet. But you're missing the point I'm trying to make."

Tavarian's head began to cool, and his neck relaxed. "And what is your point?"

"I was going to say that the bird incident is the only reason that some people think you are . . ." Lirah stopped as if trying to find the right word.

"Stupid?" Tavarian speculated.

"Weird," said Lirah. "What I'm trying to say is that if you show people the real Tavarian more often, they will forget about the bird thing and won't be hesitant to talk to you."

"They're a lot weirder than I am," muttered Tavarian.

"Tav," said Lirah, "must you always be defensive?"

Lirah had been the only one to come over and talk to him when they were both kids first starting classes. She only asked a few questions at first, but gradually she came over more often. As they grew up and wore down each other's barriers, they began to share their honest thoughts and feelings about everything. Those few minutes a day turned into hours and before long they had become best friends, even after the bird incident. Admittedly, she helped him become comfortable around the other kids. He had a few acquaintances now because of her, but none that he would call real friends.

He didn't like how she brought it up every chance she got, though. He wondered sometimes if she wanted to hold it over him and keep him beneath her, always needing her help. At the same time, he appreciated her reaching out to him and he usually heeded her advice. Most people would not have done something like that. She was the friendliest Rethian he had ever met. Though taught not to value one person's physical appearance over another, he couldn't help it. Lirah shined above all the rest.

"What's wrong, Tav?" she asked as they passed the farm region and turned onto a side road into the Deralawn district.

"It's nothing." Tavarian kicked through a pile of leaves on the road, scattering them into the air to quickly fall back to the ground. If she didn't know by now, it wasn't worth telling her. She had heard what Dexius said.

"You always do this," she grumbled. "Now tell me what is wrong."

He didn't want to engage in this right now. There were some things even she wouldn't understand. He would be better off getting through this in his head, and then everything would be fine again.

"You don't like Dex being around?" Lirah said, eyeing him. "You're going to have to get over that."

Her comments were only making this worse.

"It's not just that," he said. "I miss being able to talk to you without someone butting in every time."

"I'm not going to stop being friends with him." Lirah said, "You should try being friends with him too."

"I can't. I don't want to be friends with him."

"Well, if you're going to be friends with me, you're going to have to deal with Dex being around. You and Dex are not as different as you think."

"Maybe I'll just walk home alone from school every day."

Lirah sighed and they walked in silence until they got to Lirah's house. The house had a plain, boxy design like most of the houses in Rethia. The roof slanted to keep the rain and leaves from collecting on it, which gave Lirah's room a low ceiling on the inside. The white paint peeled off around the windows. He had offered to help paint it, but the council wouldn't approve it for a few more years.

She stopped at the gate in front of the house.

"Well with, Tav. I hope you are in a better mood tomorrow," Lirah said as she opened the gate.

"Well with," he said as it closed behind her.

Tavarian turned around, heading down the road toward his house. He saw a pair of peace control officers on the road ahead.

"Run along home, boy," said one of the officers as they passed by him. "It's getting close to curfew."

"Yes, sir," said Tavarian, drawing his lips inward. "Well with you."

"Well with," said each of the officers. Their steel armor and swords clanged together as they continued their patrol through Deralawn.

As he walked through the door of the house, the smells of cooked meat and fresh topagani greeted him. His older sister, Valea, cooked while his mother sat in her chair feeding his baby brother. Tavarian tried to walk quickly to his room before anyone noticed.

"Tav, why don't you help your sister?" said Elina, his mother.

Tavarian grumbled as he turned back toward the room where Valea shook a mixture of seasonings onto small cuts of meat. He didn't want to do this right now—there was too much on his mind.

There were some vegetables on the counter that needed to be diced up, so he pulled a blade from the rack. Chopping up kichain and topagani wasn't so bad; he didn't mind doing that.

"This is all we have tonight?" he asked.

"Yes—they cut back on what everyone gets on the food voucher this week," said Valea.

"Again? This isn't going to be enough."

"Maybe it will go up next week. They have to make sure there's enough to go around for everyone."

"I'm just tired of going to bed hungry every night."

"You along with everyone else."

Valea finished kneading the seasoning into the meat and turned toward him. "Don't worry about the Descent, Tav—you're not going to get chosen."

"Who says I'm worried?" Tavarian began slicing the oblong red kichain into rows.

She grinned. "You worry about everything."

"I do not," he replied, slicing the rows into squares.

"Oh, of course you don't," said Valea sarcastically. "You never worry about class, never about that girl, Lirah." She smiled as she placed the cuts of meat on the metal griddle over the fire in the circular stone pit in the middle of the room.

"Will you be quiet?" Tavarian huffed.

"Why don't you just admit it?" She laughed. "She's a sweet girl—nothing wrong with liking her."

"She's a friend," Tavarian continued cutting the kichain into smaller bits. "I don't like her any more than that."

In truth, his sister was right. He had been enamored with Lirah ever since he first met her. Her blue eyes glowed like the full moon, and her white curly hair was as lovely as the fresh blossoms that grew in the school garden. Lirah had to be aware of his adoration, but she never brought it up. She had a knack for telling people's emotions by their expressions and mannerisms. He often wondered if she used his affection to her advantage. He shouldn't focus so much on her flaws, but her associating with Dexius had made him mistrust her intentions.

"Do you think you will get picked?" Tavarian asked as he scraped the diced kichain into a metal pan.

"I have a better chance than last year," she said. "I have more survival skills, but I don't really want to go."

"Why wouldn't you want to go?" Tavarian started chopping the topagani. "It would be a huge honor."

"I want to be around to see our little brother grow up." Velea turned over the pieces of meat to cook the other side. "I would miss everyone here."

"There are so many things in Rootcore," he said. "It would be incredible."

"You don't know that," Valea said. "No one who has been to the bottom world comes back. Rootcore is probably dangerous."

"It's probably because they have rokenstones; they can use machines to plant and harvest more food," Tavarian said.

"Yeah, so they say," she said, cutting a slice out of a piece of meat to check the inside. "If anyone ever came back with the stones, we could produce more here."

"If someone does bring them here, I want to build new machines that can use them."

"I'd be too afraid to go down there. I think something bad happened to them."

"Remember how there was one year the Descenders were told to go to the bottom and immediately return so they could tell them what was down there? They still didn't come back. Nothing bad would have happened that fast."

"You actually want to go?" she asked.

"Maybe . . . I want to find out what is down there."

"What if you couldn't find any food and water for a while?"

"Then I would come back, but there must be plenty of food or someone would have returned," he said.

"What if there are wild animals?"

"I would build a shelter. I can build things."

"Maybe one day you'll be ready," she said, "but don't get your hopes up about going soon. Take some survival classes. That would help you get picked."

"What about your friend, Deavin?" Tavarian said as he finished cutting the topagani, and then scraped it into the pan. "She never knew much about survival."

"Yeah, I don't know how she got chosen," Valea said. "She must have had some hidden talents they liked aside from being able to breathe the air in the lower atmosphere."

The door opened loudly as Hathan, their father, came inside, tossing his bag of equipment into the corner of the room. Valea rushed by Tavarian to put some of the food on the table and Tavarian brought in another plate behind her. Their mother set the baby on his bed and came back to sit down. Once they all settled into their chairs, they began taking the food from the serving plates. Their father, being the oldest, got his portion first, and then their mother, Valea, and Tavarian took theirs. Soon, he wouldn't be the youngest at the table anymore.

"How did things go with you two today?"

"Pretty good, Dad," said Valea. "I learned how to clean fish for cooking."

"Excellent," he said. "That's the kind of thing you should be learning, Tav."

"I've learned some of that stuff," Tavarian said, "but I mostly just want to build and figure out how to improve things."

"You can do that later," Hathan said. "Right now, you should be learning how to survive out there in case you get chosen."

"Would they choose someone who doesn't have survival skills?" Valea asked.

"Who knows what their criteria are?" Hathan said, cutting into a piece of meat. "Surviving in those toxic clouds is the main thing."

"If it's just that, why did they take Deavin last time and not all the other times we were tested?" Valea asked.

"Hathan, pass the topagani, would you?" their mother said.

"She must not have been able to breathe it before. As your lungs grow stronger, you can build up some resistance too," he said, handing Elina the bowl of topagani. "Very few pass the test the first time."

"Could I get picked this year?" Tavarian asked.

"If you pass all the tests," said Hathan.

"Tav, you really need to start taking those classes," Elina said. "Just in case you are picked."

"He only takes classes that Lirah takes," said Valea, grinning.

"That's not true!" Tavarian shouted, realizing too late that he let the volume of his voice get away from him. "She doesn't even take carpentry."

"Whoa, hold on there," said Hathan, "if it's not true, there's no need to get so defensive."

"Fine—I guess I'll start taking the classes," Tavarian mumbled.

After dinner, Tavarian took a walk outside to sit in the gentle breeze. It whispered through the tall trees glowing with the blue light of the full moon. All seemed calm out here in the night. He could think clearly without the annoyances of his family inside. Though he loved his sister and parents, he could only listen to so much to their lectures and criticism. They always had different plans for him than what he wanted.

They held up Valea as the example of what he should be. They enjoyed laughing at things he said, never taking him seriously. If he shared his ideas about Rootcore or the things he dreamed of building, they would probably tease him even more.

He could open up to Lirah, except for when it came to his feelings about her. She was the only person he could tell anything without it being taken as a joke. She enjoyed dreaming too, and liked hearing about his ideas of things he could build.

Lirah knew firsthand that he could create things. After a lot of trial and error, he had built the gate for the small fence around Lirah's house. It would swing closed automatically so that the frabbies Lirah kept as pets wouldn't get out. That had been one of his best ideas that worked out. Others didn't work nearly as well, but he had little to experiment with. Eager to learn all that he could about both carpentry and blacksmithing, he hoped to one day be able to make all his ideas a reality.

Now Lirah's friendship with Dexius threatened everything Tavarian planned for the future. Each day, she got closer to Dexius and further away from him. He would end up alone again with no one he knew how to connect with.

Thousands of stars twinkled in the canopy of darkness above. Tavarian wondered if there were any other worlds out there like Isodonia. Perhaps it was too crazy to imagine this mystery that could never be revealed. His focus remained on the secrets of Rootcore, a place so close and yet so unreachable. He fantasized he had more in common with the people living at the bottom of the world than the ones in Rethia. What if he ever did get chosen? Would he really be able to survive whatever lay at the bottom of the world on his own?

The next morning, Tavarian ate breakfast and got ready for his classes. The dry road dusted the legs of his trousers as he strolled toward Lirah's house. He wondered when it might rain again.

For the first time, Lirah was late. Every morning, she usually waited for him by the gate.

"She already left, Tavarian," her mother said from the doorway. "Dexius came by just a bit ago and they went on ahead."

"Oh . . . okay, thanks," he said.

His heart dropped into his stomach. As much as he expected this, he didn't think it would be this quick. What should he do when he got to class? How would he act around Lirah without making a fool of himself? He would pretend they didn't exist. Dexius would no doubt gloat if he appeared to be hurt by this. Hopefully, Lirah would just let him be and not try to talk to him. It would be easier for both of them that way.

Tavarian decided that he would ignore everyone in class from now on. He would keep his head down and focus on learning as much as he could. With no distractions, he would become better than the rest of the kids that wasted their time with friends and socializing. Once he became the greatest builder Rethia had ever seen, they would all want to be friends with him. He'd be welcomed anywhere by anyone.

A few kids and one of the instructors stood outside the building for metalworking lessons when he walked up to the old wooden building.

"Tavarian, come join us please," said Ms. Parrow, one of the class administrators. "I was just telling everyone that the council has made a decision to cut the number of students for this class. We have too many metalworkers right now and do not need any more. So please choose another class for this hour. You are also taking carpentry, and the same goes for that class. So, now you have two spots in your class schedule that you will need to fill."

"But I don't want to do anything else," he said.

"Oh, of course you do," Ms. Parrow said. "What's most important is your contribution to the community. None is any more valuable than another, and they all earn you the same voucher."

Tavarian walked over and sat on top of the wooden fence. This had to be one of the worst days of his life—first Lirah and now this. What was left for him? Whatever he had to take now, he refused to care about it. He decided he wouldn't even choose new classes. The teachers would have to choose for him. It no longer mattered to him.

"Hey Tav!" Lirah walked briskly toward him, with Dexius not far behind. "We were going to wait for you this morning, but I didn't feel well last night, and my mom kept scolding me about my chores this morning, so I went ahead and left."

"Okay," said Tavarian.

Lirah's expression changed as she narrowed her eyes. "Okay?" she said. "That's all you have to say?"

"What do you want me to say?" Tavarian's head began to grow warm.

"Well, I thought you might wonder how I am feeling now," Lirah said, the volume of her voice rising a bit.

"Why don't you tell Dexius about it? You can have him help you with chores and running your errands too," Tavarian said.

"What's gotten into you lately?" she said, her forehead wrinkling.

"Let's go, Lirah. He's a loser," said Dexius.

"Shut your stupid face!" Tavarian shouted without thinking.

"Oh, real tough words there, loser," Dexius said. "What are you going to do? Nothing."

"Both of you, stop it!" Lirah yelled.

Tavarian's internal debating process raced to catch up to the explosions going off inside him. Tavarian shoved Dexius as hard as he could. Caught off guard, Dexius stumbled backward, nearly falling to the ground.

Dexius punched Tavarian across the cheek, but as the adrenalin surged though him, he barely noticed. Tavarian launched himself into Dexius. He wrapped his arms around Dexius's chest, taking him to the ground.

"Stop!" Lirah continued to yell.

Pinned to the turf, Dexius couldn't do anything but claw his fingers into Tavarian's back. Every time he did so, Tavarian increased the pressure of his hold. Two peace control officers came over, prying Tavarian away from Dexius.

At the end of the day, Tavarian and Dexius had to stay and do chores in the class buildings as punishment. They cleaned the chairs, walls, and floors until they were finally dismissed. Lirah had gone home by the time Tavarian started on the road. As he passed by her house, he wondered if he should go talk to her and find out the degree of her anger.

He needed to speak to her about it, not as someone involved, but as an objective friend. She probably liked him even less now, and Dexius even more. Maybe it was better to give her some time before trying to talk to her again. Besides, he needed to stop caring anyway.

Once he made it back to his house, he found his sister setting food on the table. Tavarian turned the crank on the pipe enough to pump some water and scrub his hands clean. He returned as the family sat down to eat.

"Tavarian, what is that bruise on your eye?" his mother asked.

He froze as he reached for a piece of meat to put on his plate. He had completely forgotten about Dexius hitting him. Putting a hand to his face, he touched the puffy skin under his right eye.

"Don't even think about lying to your mother," his father advised.

"This guy hit me. It's not a big deal," Tavarian answered.

"I never thought I would have to worry about you getting in fights. What has gotten into you?" she asked.

"Someone hit me and it's my fault?" Tavarian said. "What does it take for someone to be on my side for once?"

"We're all on your side, Tavarian," said his father. "We're just trying to get to the bottom of this."

"He kept calling me a loser and getting in my face. I shoved him out of the way and he hit me."

"Was that it?" his father asked.

"We wrestled on the ground until the officers came over."

"I suppose that's why you are late coming home," his father said, "because you were being punished?"

Tavarian nodded.

"I can't imagine what you would need to be fighting about," said his mother.

"Probably a girl," Valea said. "Must have been Lirah."

Tavarian slammed his wooden fork down on the table. "Okay, I have an announcement to make! Everyone . . . I like Lirah!" he yelled, turning to his sister. "You happy now?"

Valea stopped mid-chew, her eyes growing wider by the moment.

"Well, that's nice, Tav, but don't fight over her," his mother said. "If she likes you, there's no need to worry about the other guys."

"She doesn't like me, so it doesn't matter," he said.

"So why were you fighting with this boy?" said his mother.

"It sounds like he was standing up for himself," his father said. "Something he needs to do more often, if you ask me."

"I hate him," Tavarian said. "I don't get what she sees in him."

"So, she likes him?" his mother asked.

"Apparently so."

After dinner, Tavarian went to his room and sat down on the bed. He leaned his back against the wall, replaying the day's events over and over in his mind. What did Lirah think about what he did? He had never reacted in any kind of aggressive manner toward anyone, especially not around her.

Valea stood in the doorway, raising her eyebrows as if asking if she could come in. Tavarian gave her a quick nod of approval.

"Hey," she said, "I was just thinking . . ."

"Yeah? Don't worry, it gets easier after the first time," he joked.

"I'm trying to be serious, Tav," she said. "I realized that you're not the little kid you used to be."

"What gave it away? When I started putting my shoes on all by myself?" He didn't know quite how to react. The only response that he could be comfortable with was to maintain the same level of sarcasm.

"You've always been my little brother. I guess being around you every day . . . you're not supposed to be this close to being an adult."

"Does that make you feel old?"

Valea laughed. "No, it's just . . . I forget sometimes. I tease you about Lirah as if it's a little childhood crush, but I don't always think about how I was at your age, which wasn't that long ago, by the way. I just wanted to say that I'm sorry for making fun of that."

What made her say all this? They always picked on each other but never apologized for it. They knew exactly how to press each other's buttons, but usually not going too far. Although they had made each other miserable at times. Valea knew how to get under his skin better than he did hers. Could this be some kind of trick?

"It's fine," he said, "I mean, it does get a bit tiresome. Today was just . . . it was a bad day."

"Okay, it won't happen again," she said. "There's so many other things to make fun of you about."

He pressed his lips together into a mocking smile as she turned back toward the hallway.

CHAPTER 2

"SHE WALKED TO class by herself today," said Lirah's mother as Tavarian strolled by the house.

He waved and continued through the long morning shadows of trees stretched out over the dirt road. He didn't expect her to be there, but it surprised him that she didn't go with Dexius.

As he arrived on the campus grounds, Ms. Parrow sat on a stone wall watching him as he walked up. She stood up as he got close. "Tavarian, you'll need to choose another profession class. I hope that a night's sleep has made you more willing to move on to something else."

"I don't care," he said. "Like you said, it doesn't matter."

"Oh, now, surely there is something else you will enjoy. Cooking, tailoring, shoemaking, masonry, and hunting are a few that are available. I'll get you a list."

"Which ones are Dexius in?" Tavarian asked.

"I think he's in hunting and cooking. I'm not sure about the rest," Ms. Parrow said.

"Okay, I'll scratch those off the list."

"Why were you two fighting?"

"Just don't like each other, I guess," Tavarian said. "He always mocks everything I say and calls me a loser."

"Well, perhaps if you can't get along, it's best that you stay away from him. I don't know why he would say those things. It could be that he is envious of you."

"Why would he be envious of me?"

"Wasn't it you who proved him wrong in one of the metalworking classes? Or it could have something to do with Lirah."

"He has nothing to worry about with her. She always wants to spend time with him."

"Well, she talks about you quite a bit."

Tavarian stared off toward the soft clouds hanging above the surrounding trees. He had been so focused on his discontent for Dexius that he didn't question why Dexius didn't like him. Could the reason be that Dexius thought Lirah liked him more? That couldn't be it; he was always so smug and confident about everything.

"Do any of those classes I mentioned so far sound interesting?" she said.

"Not really."

"Well, you have some time to decide since the trials start tomorrow."

He had forgotten the trials were so close. Everyone in a certain age range would be tested on if they would be able to survive below the dense clouds beneath the mountain. Unsure what types of gases comprised the lower atmosphere, Tavarian only knew that few Rethians could breathe it.

Tavarian spent the next hour going over the list of classes that Ms. Parrow had given him. Nothing interested him. In the middle of town, peace control officers were lining people up to go into the market. Each region had a day to use their voucher to get their assigned foods and supplies for the week.

Bored, he walked toward the town circle, checking if he recognized anyone standing in line. Yevis waved to him from near the back of the line and Tavarian went over to him. "So, this is why you weren't in school today."

"Yep," said Yevis, covering the hole in the left side of his tunic with his hand. "It's Plentyfield Day."

Tavarian averted his eyes, pretending that he didn't notice the tear in his shirt. "I always forget which day it is, only that Deralawn Day is the end of the school week."

Yevis crossed his arms to cover the tear in a more natural way. "That would be the best day for it—not having to come to school on the last day and then having off the next day too."

Tavarian bent down, noticing a shiny object in the loose sand. "I think this is better, divides the week up." Picking up the sparkling stone, he brushed away the remaining dirt with his fingers. It was a jinspar, a translucent rock formation that served no real purpose, usually found in the mines.

"No, two days in a row is much better," Yevis stepped into his place as the line moved forward, bumping into the person ahead of him.

Tavarian turned the jinspar in his hand, watching it glitter in the sunlight. He realized he should probably say something if he was going to continue standing here. He glanced back to Yevis and said, "One of those days is waiting in this line though, and there's more Deralawns than Plentyfields."

"Yeah, I guess that is true."

"They reduced what is listed on the voucher last week. Is it any better this week?"

Yevis checked his family's voucher. "Looks the same as last week. Maybe a little worse."

Tavarian went back to playing with the jinspar. "We're almost out of everything already and still have three days to go."

"Yeah, it's getting bad, but I'm sure it will get back to normal soon."

"Even normal isn't really enough. You're lucky that you don't have any siblings. When my baby brother is older, will we have enough?" Tavarian dug his feet into the sand, frustrated at the thought of further rationing their food.

"You'll be a master carpenter by then, Tav, and getting your own voucher."

"I can't be a carpenter. They have too many—blacksmiths too."

"Well, maybe you can be a farmer and live in Plentyfield."

"Yeah, maybe then I could grow some extra food for myself."

"No, you can't do that, Tav. It's not allowed. You'd get thrown in prison for that."

"Really? Why?"

"That's stealing from the community. We grow all the fruits and vegetables for Rethia. If we ate some of it ourselves before it was brought to market, there wouldn't be enough for everyone else." The line moved forward again and Yevis moved up behind them, using a bit more caution this time.

"I mean some extra." Tavarian lifted his eyes from the stone, realizing that he now stood beside an old woman. He put the jinspar into the pocket of his trousers and took a step toward Yevis.

"You're only allowed to grow what the council says you can grow, for each fruit and each type of vegetable." Yevis stretched his arms, forgetting his shame over the hole in his tunic.

"Why is that?"

"Because the council has to determine how much of each type we need; there's only so much room and it can't be wasted."

"There's room all over the place," Tavarian waved his hands around. "Why can't they use one of the empty lots that doesn't have houses yet?"

"I'm sure there's a reason. They have to plan for everything, Tav. There's more than just the food. Be glad there are people much smarter than us planning all this out. We don't even have to think about it."

Tavarian began to notice some uncomfortable stares from the line of people. "Yeah, I guess, but why can't you grow more vedaros? They're much more filling than topagani."

"The council said people were tired of vedaros and wanted more topagani. If any type of food doesn't get eaten, it's a waste. The food spoils and it hurts all of us. Sometimes what we try to grow dies early or gets eaten by animals and that hurts everyone as well. So they change what we grow according to what they think won't get wasted each week."

"Who would waste anything at a time like this? Does that happen with meat too?"

"I would think so, according to how hunting goes or how much livestock is available."

After chatting with Yevis for a few more minutes, Tavarian walked back to the campus, and saw Lirah and Dexius among some students standing in the shade of the pavilion. He turned around like he hadn't noticed them, and sat on the stone wall to wait for his community class to start. He unfolded the list of classes Ms. Parrow had given him. As he read, someone walked up close to him.

"Are you going to pretend I don't exist now?" said Lirah.

Tavarian lifted his head. "You were mad at me. I was giving you some space."

"I'm not mad at you for that," she said. "He deserved it and I'm glad that you stood up for yourself this time."

"Oh, so you're on my side now?" he asked.

"I've always been on your side," Lirah said, "but that doesn't mean I'm against Dexius. I'm still going to be friends with him."

Tavarian sighed.

"Just because we're best friends," she said, "doesn't mean you get to decide who else I'm friends with."

"I never said that," Tavarian said. "If he wasn't always mocking me, I wouldn't have a problem with it. I don't feel like I can talk to you when he's around."

"So, tell him to shut up, like you did yesterday," she said. "Just without the fighting."

"Why do you always blame me for not getting along with him? You never say anything to him."

"Because you need to say it," she said. "If it comes from me, it's never going to end."

❧

After community class ended, Tavarian followed behind the line of students as they exited the building into the yard. He spotted Lirah, her curly platinum hair catching the breeze. The sunlight outlined her angelic face with its aura.

As he made his way through the tangled mass of students to get to her, Dexius also headed her way. Tavarian stopped, wanting to avoid the confrontation that would occur if he went over there. He started home on his own, but then he remembered what Lirah had said. It was almost cathartic shoving an object of his frustrations to the ground. Just like when he verbalized his annoyance with his sister for picking on him about Lirah so much.

This is how he had always wished he could be and now he had stepped toward it. Now it left him at a crossroad—had he truly changed or was this just a fluke? He could either go back to being the old, awkward Tavarian who always internalized his anger and frustration, or he could choose to continue this newfound bravery.

He found himself moving again, heading straight for Lirah.

"How was class today, Lirah?" he asked.

She beamed at him. "It was great! It's a shame that we won't start back to classes for a few days until the Descension is over."

Dexius clenched his teeth, squinting his eyes, but this time it did not intimidate Tavarian. If anything, it encouraged him.

"Yeah, that's what Ms. Parrow was telling me earlier," Tavarian said. "I have some time to decide on which classes to choose."

"What do you mean?" Lirah asked. "You decided to change classes?"

"It was decided for me," Tavarian said. "The council determined that they had too many blacksmiths and too many carpenters, so I have to pick two new profession classes and start over."

"Oh no!" Lirah said. "I'm sorry, Tav! I know how much that meant to you."

"It's fine," he remarked. "Maybe I'll fit in better with everyone in the new classes."

"If it's any consolation," she said, "you don't have to start all over behind everyone else. When that happens, you get a personal mentor to teach you until you are at the level of the rest of the class."

"That's good, I guess."

"Hey, Lirah," Dexius said. "Let's go to Drakewood—it would be a good day to see the mermaks."

"Why don't we go to the fence behind the mill?" Lirah replied.

"Again? Why do want to go there so much?" said Dexius.

"I like it over there. It's my second favorite place after the waterfall," she said. "It's the only place where I can clear my head and forget about all the problems in the world."

"What problems?" he asked.

"I'm worried about the trials," she said as the sea of students flowed around them. "What if I get chosen? Or what if one of you gets chosen, or any of my other friends?"

They were encompassed by the ephemeral fragrances of flowers that some of the girls wore in their hair as they moved by.

"You don't want to be chosen? All you do is talk about Rootcore," Dexius said. As the last few students walked past, a group of flitterlyns flew by them from the springy palms of a nearby bush. One of them brushed by Dexius's head, making him flinch.

"Hey, Lirah," said a slender blond male walking with a large group of other students. It was Neylin from Tavarian's metalworking class.

"Oh, hey, Neylin! How have you been?" she cheerfully replied.

The excited expression on her face indicated that she liked him, opening a new boil of jealousy. Tavarian mentally scolded himself for not giving up on the fantasy of being coupled with Lirah.

"Tavarian, I heard about you getting dropped from the class," said Neylin.

"Yeah, I have to find something else," he said, stamping down a bit of uprooted grass nearby.

"We'll miss seeing you there, but I guess it happened at a good time now with the trials coming up," Neylin said.

Tavarian's face drooped as the depressing reality hit him again. "It's just so stupid, my whole life's plans have to—"

Lirah elbowed him in the side before he finished. Why shouldn't he be mad? She wouldn't like it either if it happened to her. Though, knowing Lirah, she would still be happy as ever. She rarely got mad about anything—except when he did or said something that she had told him not to.

"But you're right, I guess it will give me more time to find something," Tavarian said as a gust of wind blew his hair awkwardly over his eyes.

"I'm sure whatever you do, you will do it well," said Neylin. "Whatever class you end up in will be lucky to have you."

Though Neylin probably said this just to make Tavarian feel better, it actually did have some effect. Tavarian had always liked Neylin. He thought they could be friends if he ever talked to him. Whenever he tried, he never could think of anything they had in common to talk about for any length of time. After Neylin talked to Dexius a little, he ran ahead to catch up with his group. Lirah, still smiling, headed toward the mill, with Tavarian and Dexius following.

The other mountain gleamed in the distance, like an island in a sea of clouds. Not far across the cloudscape, some dark patches parted the clouds beneath them. Flashes of lightning glowed on nearby mists, creating random patterns of light. Tavarian always enjoyed this light show provided by storms in the lower atmosphere. He wished it happened more often. When storms occurred in Rethia, it could be a frightening experience, but fortunately, those were not common.

The wind whipped Lirah's hair as she turned into the breeze. "What are you going to do about the lightning when you ever get down there?"

Tavarian made his way to the wooden fence. He ran his hand over the uneven patterns of the cut wood, searching for an answer. "First thing I'm going to do is build a fort."

"We should go up the other mountain." Lirah brushed back her hair as she eased beside him. "Maybe there's another town like Rethia over there like we always talked about."

"I don't get it, who cares what's down there?" Dexius kicked a dried clump of dirt, sending it tumbling between the fence posts, breaking apart before it even reached the edge of the mountain. "Why do they keep sending people every year?"

"We have to do something," Lirah turned to Dexius. "We're running out of food in Rethia, if you haven't noticed," Frustration came out in her tone, and she paused to take another breath, resuming her normal sweet, lifting voice. "There's only so much space for crops. They also need space for trees in the forests for lumber, and fish in thc river. If the population keeps growing, we won't be able to feed everyone. That's what I worry about more than anything."

Tavarian stared at the grooves in the fence. There was a long crack that ran the distance of one of the rails, threatening to split it in two. "Someone has to go and actually bring back some of the stones."

"Does anyone even know what they look like? What if someone picked up a rock and came back saying they found one?" Dexius had that lopsided expression on his face. It was like he knew everything, and everyone else was stupid for not realizing it. Tavarian hated that look.

"What do they look like, Tav?" Lirah's hair waved in front of her enchanting eyes as she turned toward Tavarian. "I'm surprised no one has ever done that."

"Because it's ridiculous," said Tavarian, hoping to indirectly insult Dexius. "I'm sure there's a big difference between a rokenstone and some regular old rock. Like you just said, someone has to bring back the stones. If any of us ever get chosen, it falls on us to do the right thing."

"You're right," Lirah said, "if any of us ever get chosen, we have to promise to resist whatever temptations are down there and bring back the stones."

"Everyone promises that at the ceremony, and no one ever does it." Dexius sat on one of the top rails, propping a foot on the rail below it. He leaned over to pick one of the tall weeds, twirling it to make the leaves fan out.

A flash of lightning below lit up Lirah's face for a moment. "We have to promise each other that if any of us makes the list, we will bring them back for Rethia."

"I promise." Tavarian lifted his body from the fence, standing up straight.

"And I promise too," Lirah said.

Lirah turned to Dexius, waiting for him to say it, while Tavarian hoped that he wouldn't agree to it, and Lirah would experience his selfishness on full display.

"Sure . . . I promise." Dexius stripped the leaves from the weed one by one and tossed them into the wind.

"Okay, hold my hand to make our link complete." Lirah held her hand up for Tavarian to take it. The thought of touching her made him jittery. The soft delicate skin of her palm sent surges through him. Tavarian squeezed a little tighter, and his hand became clammy with sweat. He hoped that she wouldn't be able to tell.

Dexius dropped the stem of the weed and took her other hand, lifting her arm up and poked her in the side with his other hand to tickle her. She bent toward him, bringing her arm back down in defense. "Stop Dex! This is serious," she said, laughing.

Tavarian rolled his eyes and loosened his hold of Lirah's hand.

"Okay, we're linked to the promise now. We have to bring back the stones," she said, and let go of both of their hands. She wiped her hand on her dress. Unfortunately, she must have noticed the sweat.

"I never understood exactly how rokenstones are supposed to help," she said.

"They can absorb lightning and use it to give the city power. Like the wheel at the mill, but you won't need water to make it turn. It can make light at night and heat when it's cold," Tavarian said. "You could have a city with wheels turning on every building to make work faster and easier."

"Is that why there is more lightning down there?" Lirah said.

"Could be," said Tavarian.

"So, lightning could help us produce more food?" she asked.

"Yes, they could power machines to make the harvest faster, and maybe help with planting crops too," Tavarian said.

Strands of clouds blew with the wind, overlaying sheets of mist below them. So soft and puffy, as though you could bounce on top of them if you jumped over the edge. That, of course, wouldn't happen.

"Could they produce more cloth?" Lirah tugged at her lower lip with her fingers as she turned back to Tavarian.

Only vaguely familiar with the cloth making process, Tavarian tried to imagine how rokenstones could make a difference. "Maybe looms could be made into machines so that clothing could be made faster."

Lirah's eyes lit up. "That would be amazing!" She pulled on her long brown dress, causing it to flare as she spun back and forth. "I could have more than two dresses! I want to have a different dress for each day of the week! Can you imagine?"

It was unusual for Lirah to indulge, at least outwardly, in her own material wants. Tavarian longed to make her dream a reality.

"There's no way there's any stone that can do all that." Dexius leaned on the fence, flicking a tiny insect crawling toward him.

"Why would they send people out every year, then?" Tavarian rested his hands on his sides, daring Dexius to come up with an answer.

"One of my teachers said that rokenstones are especially rare and no one has returned because they have yet to find one," said Lirah, smoothing the wrinkles out of her dress with her hands.

"How do they even know about these stones if no one has returned from there?" Dexius made the face again, the one Tavarian hated.

"Good question," Lirah glanced at Tavarian. "Tav?"

"Didn't you guys ever pay attention in class?" Tavarian's head twitched. "There used to be rokenstones in Rethia a long time ago. Over time they were used up. So now we would have to go down to Rootcore to get more."

"How do they get used up?" Lirah moved toward the fence next to Dexius. She placed her forearms on the top rail and propped her chin on top of her raised hands.

"I don't know exactly," Tavarian slowly eased back toward the fence. Seeing Lirah close to Dexius burned him up inside.

"Oh, something he doesn't know. . ." Dexius tapped on the top of the fence post with his fingernails.

Tavarian's face grew warm. He paused, turning toward Dexius. "There's not a lot of solid information." Tavarian sharpened his tone. "But theoretically, the lightning stored in the stones is consumed over time. I believe another lightning strike would be needed to recharge it. Maybe it can only be recharged so many times before the stone is destroyed." He had no idea if that were true or not, but he wasn't about to let Dexius show him up. "There should be more in Rootcore."

"Why do they call it Rootcore?" Dexius asked, seemingly changing the subject.

"Because it's the bottom of the world," Lirah stated confidently.

"Not exactly . . . There's a bit more to it than that," said Tavarian. "It's the roots of the mountain—the roots of everything interwoven, making up the foundations of the world."

"That doesn't make any sense," Dexius sneered, continuing to drum his fingernails on top of the wooden post.

Tavarian took a deep breath. He eyed Lirah, trying to read what she was thinking. For the moment, she stared out over the clouds as if her focus was elsewhere. "No one really knows for sure—that's what makes it fun to talk about."

"It's not fun to talk about." Dexius set his boot down on the lower railing. "It's stupid."

Why did Lirah have to bring Dexius here? It made it pointless to come here to get away from the stresses of school with him around. They sat on the fence, watching smaller clouds drift across the thick layers of the lower atmosphere. One in particular formed a face. Tavarian didn't bother to mention it this time with Dexius here. As the clouds separated, the face vanished as though it was never there.

"I better get back before Mom starts to worry." Lirah moved away from the fence. "Anyone want to walk me home?"

❧

The next morning, Tavarian met Lirah waiting outside at the end of her yard. Dexius had not shown up yet.

"If he doesn't hurry up, we're going to be late." Tavarian paced back and forth, tracing the shadows cast by the branches of the old lerimeg tree.

"Are you nervous?" Lirah wondered as she shifted the tattered book she carried to her other hand.

Tavarian stopped ambling, straightening his shoulders as if displaying a relaxed confidence. "Why would I be nervous?"

"About the trials," she said, glancing up at him. The shadows of the tree speckled across the bright sunshine on her face.

"No, I just don't want to be late." Tavarian kept his arms at his sides, though it felt unnatural.

"We'll leave soon. If Dexius doesn't get here, we'll . . ." Her eyes darted toward the road. "Spoke his name and summoned him," she said with a laugh.

Tavarian pinched his lips together—his hope of walking to school with Lirah alone was now ruined.

"I had to make breakfast for my little sister," Dexius said as he ran up to them. "My mother disappeared—not sure where she went off to."

"Your father couldn't do it?" Lirah asked, her soft perfect eyebrows tilting upward.

"He hasn't been around the last couple days," said Dexius. "I guess my mother is off trying to bring him back home."

What a weird family. This further called into question Lirah's judgment in wanting Dexius around. Now because of her, Tavarian had to be around this guy all the time. Dexius hanging around with them would only lead to trouble, and Lirah would end up caught in the middle of it.

"I'm sorry to hear that, Dex. What do you think could have happened?" Lirah brushed a strand of hair away from her lips, twirling it around her finger.

"It'll be fine," said Dexius. "My mother usually knows where to find him."

"Oh . . ." Lirah said, a confused pout forming on her lips. "Who's watching your sister then?"

"I had to leave her in the closet," Dexius said casually.

"In the closet?" Lirah scoffed, her eyes opening round and large.

"So she doesn't get into anything that could hurt her," Dexius said as if it needed no explanation.

Tavarian tried not to smile. Maybe this would finally show Lirah that Dexius was not a nice person.

"Why didn't you just stay with her?" Lirah questioned.

"I can't miss class. That will get me in big trouble," Dexius said.

"More than putting your sister in the closet?" Lirah asked skeptically.

"My mother does it all the time," Dexius shot back, squinting his eyes as his shoulder stiffened.

"Maybe I should go over there and watch her," said Lirah, turning back toward her house.

"You always think just because other people don't do things the same way you would, there's something wrong with it," Dexius snapped.

"All right . . ." she relented. "I guess it's fine then."

Once they arrived at the campus yard, they joined the lines of students waiting to be taken to through the first round of trials. Valea stood in one of the other lines talking to her friends. She waved to Tavarian, and went back to her conversation. A soft breeze rustled through the white leaves of the ekuwon trees that were scattered about the small campus. As he watched them flitter about, Tavarian began to tune out the noise of the crowd, losing himself in a daydream.

He imagined being in Rootcore, walking with Lirah through a forest of trees growing along the mountain roots that wrapped around each other. Baring leaves of every color, their bowl-shaped treetops held water from the last rain. They overflowed like waterfalls onto the land below. Giant flowers grew everywhere with sweet nectar that dripped onto the lush plants and grass below. They picked some fruit from the plants near the ground, sweetened by the nectar of the flowers above them.

As he tried to imagine what else could be in this paradise, he envisioned the plants fading away. The colors turned to gray as the shadows at the base of the trees grew. They swallowed everything, covering the world in darkness.

"Tav?" Lirah called out.

Tavarian jumped, exhaling loudly.

"I thought you weren't nervous," Lirah said, grinning.

"Just lost in thought I guess," Tavarian said.

"What were you thinking about?" Lirah's blue eyes gleamed.

"Just imaging what Rootcore is like."

"You're not going to get picked." Dexius smirked. "If any of us is chosen, it would be me."

"Why's that, Dex?" Lirah crossed her arms.

"Because I'm the best hunter in my class," he said. "You guys wouldn't survive two days outside Rethia."

"I'd be just fine," Tavarian said, clenching his teeth underneath closed lips. Did this guy ever shut up?

Dexius chuckled. "You wouldn't last two weeks down there."

"I'm sure Tav would be fine, and so would I," Lirah said.

As much as he hated to admit it, what if Dexius was right? Would he really be able to survive down there by himself?

As they waited for their turn, some instructors led Lirah through the gates into the councilor district. Soon after, they came for Tavarian. They started him off on some running and climbing tests. The climbing test involved a vertical wall with only short pegs to stand on and grip—it didn't go as well as he hoped. He wished he had practiced that more. Tavarian then started the intelligence tests and a verbal test on survival skills. He took what they called a loyalty test, answering questions while they went through notes from his teachers.

After the tests were completed, one of the instructors led him around to another building and into a small room. They were all the same tests he did last year. Closing him in the room, they pumped in the same air as the lower atmosphere. The instructor told him to knock if he couldn't breathe.

The smoky air poured into the room. Tavarian braced himself for the gagging it caused him last year. Holding his breath at first, he slowly inhaled. Waiting for something to happen, he exhaled. The air turned out to be fine.

He took in a second breath. Nothing unusual, just like breathing the normal mountain air. Could he really have become immune to the lower atmosphere? Tavarian stayed in the room until the vapor dissipated. The door opened and the instructor motioned for him to come out.

"Very good," he said.

Tavarian's heart raced. If he could breathe the air of the lower atmosphere, he would eventually get chosen for sure. Maybe not this year, but he could improve the physical parts like the agility tests and survival classes, and be chosen next year.

Once the trials ended, they gathered what must have been more than five-hundred students who'd been required to participate. The councilors and instructions gathered to announce those chosen to make this year's descent. Tavarian found Lirah among the crowd of students. She stood beside Dexius, but Tavarian did not care. He eased his way through the other students to join them.

Lirah nervously played with the curls in her hair while bouncing on her tiptoes as they prepared to call out the names. A few of the council members gave speeches, but Tavarian couldn't focus on the words. Passing the lower atmosphere breathing test played repeatedly in his head.

"How did you guys do in the trials?" Lirah whispered.

"I did really well," boasted Dexius. "I passed the breathing test and was perfect on all the agility and survival tests. I'll get picked for sure this year."

Tavarian gazed blankly ahead. How would he cope with Dexius being chosen? They'd have to be stupid to pick him. If the dwellers in Rootcore had rokenstone powered machines down there, Dexius would definitely be selfish enough to stay and enjoy all the resources for himself, like all the other Descenders had done.

"I think I did pretty well on the other tests," Lirah acknowledged, "but I didn't pass the breathing test. I nearly choked on the air from the lower atmosphere, just like last year. What about you, Tavarian?" she inquired.

"Well, I—" Tavarian started.

"Wait . . . they're about to announce the Descenders!" said Lirah anxiously.

Councilor Ravaris stepped up to the front. Though he had nice friendly face, there was an air of intimidation about him. Whenever the councilors were around, Tavarian became overly conscious of himself. What he said, the way he stood, and the mannerisms he had were foreign and strange in this type of company.

Ravaris cleared his throat. "As we gather today, we not only honor these chosen individuals—the bravest among us in Rethia—we also set them on an important journey to find and bring back a gift to make our great city even more prosperous. There are likely many things at the bottom of the world, some that promise great riches and others that present great dangers. That is why these youth are chosen. Our criteria and testing are always evolving to find the right Descenders to hold true to our values, those who are capable of returning to Rethia, and give hope to our community. As you all know, there are many who have descended, but none that have succeeded. We are here today to press upon you to remember this moment, the citizens of Rethia, and your duty to uphold the dream of a better Rethia for all. We strive to make this community the best that we can. The rest of us may not be able to live in the dense air in Rootcore, but we lay our hopes on you, the Descenders, to not only find powerful and wonderful things out there, but to also bring salvation to us who cannot. We have chosen you not only because you can survive there, but also because we believe that you will hold true to that purpose. Do not let us down."

Lirah grabbed Tavarian's hand tightly, but she held Dexius's hand as well, which ruined the moment. Tavarian gave her hand a gentle squeeze in return.

"This year, we have accepted seven Descenders, I will now call the names of the chosen for this most important quest," Revaris said. "Tiagra Fairborne."

Applause erupted from the crowd as a tall blonde girl with short hair made her way through the crowd.

"She's in my calculations class," whispered Lirah as the girl stood beside Councilor Ravaris on the hill.

"I don't remember you talking about her," said Tavarian.

"She's kind of . . . odd. I tried talking to her once, but I don't know . . . she freaks me out."

"Migram Rivercut."

More cheers as a short young boy went over to join Tiagra and Councilor Ravaris.

"Mig? How did they choose Mig?" Dexius shook his head.

"Veras Plentyfield."

A tall dark-haired boy walked up to the hill as the crowd cheered. He pumped his fist as he faced the crowd of students.

"Devia Strongwood."

A petite girl with long brown hair sheepishly began to walk through the people on her way up to the hill.

"Tavarian Deralawn."

Lirah's hand loosened from his as he turned to her. She stared straight through him. Those bright blue eyes conveyed something rare for her, a mix of shock and confusion.

"How did they pick you?" Dexius said. "This whole thing is a sham."

"Dexius, shut up . . ." Tavarian said. "I can't wait to be away from you."

"You won't last a day out there," Dexius told him.

"Tav, you're supposed to go up there." Lirah said.

Tavarian worked his way through the crowd, settling in beside Devia.

"Pilo Rivercut."

What a surreal moment. What would his parents and sister think? He searched for his sister's face in the crowd, but couldn't find her.

"And Dexius Strongwood."

Tavarian's focus snapped back to the moment. Did he just call Dexius?

Tavarian found Lirah in the crowd, but Dexius was no longer next to her. How could the council be so reckless? Tavarian grit his teeth. Dexius was exactly the type of person that would find plentiful resources in Rootcore and never return. The only positive to this was that he wouldn't have to think about Dexius getting closer to Lirah while he was away.

While it lessened his opinion of the council's decision-making, it didn't change the mission. He would travel through Rootcore far away from Dexius. Tavarian studied the rest of the Descenders. They were all the type of kids who would follow their own selfish desires instead of the greater good. It was no wonder that no one had returned with choices like this. Their options must be quite limited, having to pick from the few who can breathe the lower atmosphere. How fortunate that he could breathe the air. He would be the one who put Rethia ahead of himself.

At least, that was the fantasy, but now that this had become reality, the worry and doubt began to eat at him. He had never had to find food on his own because it was provided by the community. Even if there had not been much to go around, it was better than nothing. He should have been chosen next year; he wasn't ready for this now.

CHAPTER 3

AFTER THE ANNOUNCEMENT ended, Tavarian, Lirah, and Dexius trekked down the road toward Lirah's house. "I didn't think either of you would be chosen and now both of you are going. I'm going to miss you guys so much!"

"I'll miss you too, but I'll be back," Tavarian said, his feet sinking into a patch of loose sandy soil.

"No, you won't," said Dexius, grabbing a rock from the dirt and bouncing it ahead of them. "You can't hunt or fish or anything like that. You won't be able to protect yourself."

Lirah grabbed his arm, stepping in front of him. "If you don't think he's going to make it, then you should help him, Dex."

Dexius stopped, straightening his back and hanging his thumbs on the waistline of his pants. Tavarian slowed and turned toward Lirah. He put his palms around his waist until he noticed he had the same stance as Dexius. He quickly dropped his arms to let them rest at his sides.

"I'm not taking care of him," said Dexius. "He was chosen—he should be able to do it himself."

"What makes you think I need him?" Tavarian complained.

"You both should look after each other," Lirah said as Tavarian eyed Dexius. He wrinkled his brow as they turned away from each other.

"Please . . . for me," said Lirah, putting an arm around both of them.

They reached Lirah's house, and Dexius and Tavarian parted ways. Tavarian made it home to his crying baby brother and Valea cooking dinner again.

"We heard the news, Tavarian," his father said. "We're going to miss you, but it's a great honor to be chosen."

"You must have done really well on the tests, Tav," said Valea, "I should never have doubted you."

He hadn't heard much of this kind of praise; he couldn't recall doing anything that special in the trials to deserve this. As he took a seat on his bed, he unwrapped his shoes, realizing how much his life was about to change. A shadow filled his doorway as his mother stuck her head in the room. She sat down next to him on the bed.

"We're really proud of you, Tavarian, but I never planned for this . . . not having you around. And now we may never see you again." On the verge of tears, she held him close, resting her head on his.

"I'll come back. I don't care what there is out there. I'll come back, I promise," he said.

"I hope you're right," she said, brushing her fingers through his hair. "If you don't find any rokenstones, there's no shame in coming back without any."

"But there is some shame in it," he said. "I won't stay away too long if I don't find any. I'll come back."

"I hope you're not just saying that," she said, moving a strand of hair behind his ear. "If there's anything dangerous down there, come back right away."

Tavarian acknowledged this, tilting his head. "I want to find out what Rootcore is like and come back to tell about it. That's all I'm really interested in."

Tavarian spent the rest of the week learning about cooking, sewing, and using a bow from his sister, which she'd learned in class. His dad showed him some carpentry tricks that he hadn't taught him yet. One night, after everyone had gone to bed, his father peeked into his room. The flame that was still alive inside the lantern created diamond shapes of shadow and light.

"Tavarian," his father said quietly from the doorway. "I know your mother has been telling you to come back home quickly, but if things are much better down there . . . if you feel like you can make your own way better than you can here, I say go for it. We'll still be proud of you either way. I'll feel better just knowing that you found something that makes you happy, and we will all love you no matter what."

"Dad, I'm coming back," Tavarian declared. "I want to find out what is out there, but I will come back. I made a promise to the council and to everyone in Rethia that I will find and bring back some rokenstones."

Hathan handed Tavarian a small saw and a knife.

"These might help you survive out there if you don't find civilization right away."

⁂

The next day, Valea came into his room, holding the baby. "Your baby brother wanted to say well with before you leave."

Tavarian took his brother's hand with his forefinger and thumb. "I'm not going to miss him crying every night."

"He does more than that—he laughs a lot too."

"He must save that for when I'm away."

"He's just like you when you were a baby. You cried and fussed all the time."

"Only when you were around," he joked.

She forced a sarcastic laugh. "Tav, you have to come back. I don't want this to be the last time I see you. No matter how good things are down there, at least come back for us."

"I wish I could promise that," Tavarian said.

"Why can't you?" she wondered.

"What if I can't make it on my own? Who knows what is down there?" Tavarian swallowed.

"Tav, you'll be fine." Valea bounced the baby, adjusting her hold on him to put her other arm on Tavarian's shoulder. "You're very resourceful. I've seen some of the things you and Dad built. You may not have the survival knowledge that some do, but you're quite clever. You know how many times I've tried to mess with you, but you see through it almost every time."

"This is different." He glanced at her for a moment before setting his eyes on his hands as he rubbed them together. "I can't hunt. I can't farm. What will I do about food?"

"Tav, don't disparage your weaknesses, rely on your strengths," said Valea as she moved her arm back to help hold the baby.

"Next year is the last year I can go to the trials—the last chance I have to be chosen," she said. "If you aren't back by then, I'm coming to find you. If I have to come down there to bring you back, you are doing all the cooking for the next year."

"I practically already do."

She punched his arm playfully. "You hardly help at all!"

❧

The day before Descension, Tavarian met Lirah at the waterfall, this time without Dexius.

"You're finally getting what you wanted, Tav, I'm glad for you," she said as they stood above the silky white blanket of the lower atmosphere. "I always thought we'd both be going . . . together," she continued. "As unlikely as it was, I pictured you, Dexius, and me going."

"I did too," he said. "Well, not so much with Dexius, but whenever I dreamed about it, you were there."

"You will come back, won't you?" She turned toward him. "Remember our promise. Unfortunately, I don't think Dex will return, but I believe you will."

"I'll be back," he said. "I'll come back to tell you about the bottom of the world, and I'll bring some rokenstones so that you don't have to worry about people starving anymore."

She smiled unnaturally, masking her worry and doubt as she faced the clouds. For a time, they stood in silence watching the waterfall disappear into the mist below. Like the Descenders, these drops of water left Rethia for Rootcore, never to return. Unlike these droplets, he would defy gravity—the pull that kept everyone before him from coming back.

"There was a time, not too long ago, that you liked me. Was there anything to that?" she asked.

Tavarian's face began to burn. "I did like you." He cleared his throat.

"I mean, I do like you. But you didn't seem to want that, so I didn't say anything. Then you started talking to Dexius."

"My friendship with Dexius has nothing to do with us," she said. "I like being friends with him. He's a much better person than he shows people. I just don't feel that way about him."

They stared at each other for a moment, unsure what to say next. Lirah played with the curls in her hair, bouncing them with her fingers. The sun set behind the wispy horizon as a wave of wind washed over them. All his dreams were coming true and yet he could think of nothing worthy of the moment to say. Shadows grew long, preparing to fade into the night.

"I better get home before Mom gets worried," Lirah stated.

"Yeah, I guess I should too," he replied.

After they walked through the woods, past the farms, and to the dirt road in front of her house, Lirah opened the gate to her yard. "I wanted to give you something," she said, reaching into a pocket of her dress. "To remember me and the promise you made to come home."

Lirah handed him a curl of her white hair, tied together with a tiny light blue ribbon.

"Now you have one more reason to come back," she said and leaned over. Her sweet lips caressed his cheek as she kissed him.

As she turned and headed toward the house, Tavarian wanted to call her back to return her kiss, but the moment for that had passed. He regretted not doing it immediately, but the shock of the kiss had rendered him immobile.

❧

The day of the Descension had come. Many townspeople gathered near the road leading down the mountain and into the clouds. The peace control officers wore bright polished armor, and the children of the farmers were there to give them ripened fruit they had saved for their journey. Breg Stillwater, one of the council members, pinned a silver pendant to each of the chosen, showing a raised fist rising above the clouds—the same pendant was worn by the council members. He placed it beside their Rethian Community pendant of two hands coming together.

After saying goodbye again to his family, Lirah gave him and Dexius one last hug before they were about to march down the mountain path.

"Don't forget to watch out for each other," she said. "Remember our promise link. And remember the whole community is with you."

"Well with," Tavarian replied back. He wanted to kiss her, but not in front of Valea, his parents, and everyone else watching. He wasn't sure if he even knew how to kiss properly, and decided it was best not to find out with an audience.

Valea came up to him and handed him a beige colored stone. "It's a flekstone that I got in survival class, you can break it in two and rub them together to make a fire."

He put the stone in the satchel that he carried all his stuff in. He hoped to be carrying rokenstones in it before long.

"Thank you," he said as she hugged him.

After giving hugs and saying goodbye to other friends, their parents, his parents' friends, and his relatives, the group was ready to go. The seven Descenders came together and began walking down the path. The peace control officers normally never allowed anyone to get this far down the path leading down the mountain to Rootcore below.

Tavarian glanced back, finding Lirah among the crowd. She smiled, waved, and blew kisses though it barely hid the sadness in her eyes. The chattering of the crowd grew quieter as they followed the path around the mountain.

Once they were out of range of the shouts and well wishes from the people of Rethia, Tavarian turned back toward the plateau now obscured from view as the road wound around the mountain.

After walking a while farther, they entered the clouds. Tavarian could not make out anything but Dexius in front of him and the top part of his own boots. The thick clouds surrounded him, making it feel like he was walking through a tight hallway. It triggered his reflex to lower his head and tighten his body as if he might bump into something.

"We may be getting close," Veras called to the group as he led them down the sloped path. The sea of colored clouds were even more amazing close up. Swirls of pinks, blues, and violets poured into the smoky white and gray. Veras slowed and faced the group. "Just so you're all aware, Pilo and I are sticking together. Once we reach the bottom, the rest of you can do whatever you like, but don't follow us."

They were treating this like a competition. Even though Tavarian had dreamed of being the one to bring rokenstones back to Rethia, he hadn't considered that others wanted the same for themselves. He began to doubt that he could do this. Veras and Pilo were both a little taller than him, and they were also stronger.

"Oh, you guys think you know where some rokenstones are?" Tiagra cocked her head at Veras.

"Maybe," Pilo turned back toward the road. "Either way, we are going to find them first and bring them back."

"This isn't a race. We should stay together and help each other," Devia wrinkled her nose, scanning the faces of the group as if to see what they thought about this.

"I'm with you—let's work together." Tiagra put her hand on Devia's shoulder.

"What about the rest of you?" Devia's eyebrow began to twitch as she looked over her shoulder.

Migram moved around Tavarian to get closer to Devia. "I'm in," he said.

"Mig, why don't you stay with Tavarian?" said Dexius. "These girls need someone who can protect them."

Tavarian started to turn back toward Dexius, but decided to ignore him instead.

Tiagra and Devia shared a glance. "Dexius, you're as rockheaded as I remember," Devia said. "Migram, you're welcome to join us, but not you, Dexius. I don't trust you at all."

Tavarian brought his hand over his mouth to cover the grin. They must know Dexius well.

"May I please join?" Tavarian asked, hoping it would annoy Dexius if they agreed, but mostly because he wanted to group with someone so that he wouldn't have to make it in Rootcore alone.

"Okay, you can come with us too, Tavarian," Devia peered back at him, but a sudden gust of wind blew her hair into her eyes.

"You didn't bring any dead pets, did you?" Talia asked, making Devia giggle.

It sounded sarcastic, but Tavarian couldn't be sure. This is where Lirah would tell him to go with it and laugh at himself, but he couldn't do it. Too many bad memories came along with that remark.

"No . . ." It was all Tavarian could muster in response.

"Already breaking your promises?" Dexius said behind him.

Tavarian didn't bother to look at him. "What promises?"

"You promised Lirah we would stick together," Dexius said.

"Oh, would you like me to come help you?" Tavarian said, trying to sound as sincere as possible.

"You think I need you? No, go with them," Dexius said. Some loose pebbles rolled past him, making Tavarian wonder if Dexius had kicked them at him.

"I tried," Tavarian teased.

He began to feel better about his chances now that Tiagra, Devia, and Migram were willing to group up with him. Maybe this wouldn't be so bad after all. If he didn't have to worry about surviving on his own, he was sure he would be able to find the stones and be the first one to return with them.

The soft path underneath them transitioned to hard rock. With loose sediment over the smooth stone, it made traction impossible. Tavarian began sliding down the steep slope of the path. He nearly lost his footing and he crouched to keep from losing his balance.

"I can't—I'm losing traction!" Veras shouted as a gritty scratching sound rapidly grew more intense.

"I'm sliding! Grab my hand!" Devia yelled.

"I can't!" Tiagra slid down the path, reaching for anything she could grab, but the side of the mountain on their right was too sheer.

"I can't stop!" Pilo cried out, obscured by the mist.

Devia screamed, her voice decaying as she slid farther away. A series of blunt knocking sounds followed, abruptly silencing her.

"Go back!" Veras yelled. He then screeched, fading until he could no longer be heard.

Pilo tried to turn around, but lost his footing, crying out as he went over the side of the path.

Migram, behind him, tried to crawl up the incline, but lost his grip and went tumbling past the rest of them, colliding with Tiagra. The impact knocked her off the side of the path. She disappeared into the thick vapor without a sound.

"Heeeeeeelp!" Migram shrieked as he fell down the mountainside.

The sound of his desperate plea barely registered to Tavarian as the world spun around him. His senses were in chaos as he clawed at the wall of the mountain beside them with nothing to grab hold of. Large smooth boulders lined the sides of the mountain, but were too obtuse to aid him in slowing down.

Dexius shouted something unintelligible. Tavarian continued to keep his hands scraping along the mountain rock beside him, hoping to find something that he could grip. More screams echoed off the mountain as Tavarian's fingers no longer touched rock.

He fell through the clouds. Brushing against the side of the mountain, he bounced off a round stone and continued falling. The bounce slowed his momentum slightly before he picked up speed again. He crashed on a boulder sticking out from the wall of the mountain.

The boulder gave way and rolled down the mountainside, causing Tavarian to slide down the wall. Blinded in dense clouds, Tavarian banged through leaves and branches until his shirt caught on a limb, jerking him to a stop. He froze, afraid to move. After making the decision to act, he grabbed the limb snagged through his shirt. Tavarian peered through the fog and determined that he was dangling from a tree growing from a small ledge.

Tavarian pulled on the limb and eased toward the trunk of the tree. The shirt ripped loose as he climbed hand over hand across the limb. Once he got to the trunk, he stretched his feet out, searching for another limb below him, but not finding anything.

He couldn't hang on this limb forever. Surely there were more branches on the way down. Tavarian wrapped his legs around the trunk, and then let go of the branch to grab the tree with his arms. He loosened his grip just enough to begin sliding down the trunk.

His foot hit a branch, but he slipped off before he could gain any traction. Reaching with his hand, he caught it as he continued down. He draped his right arm around it, drawing himself to it to catch it with his left. Below him was another limb, reachable but weaker than the others. He stood on its base, hoping it could support his weight.

For the last part of the way down, he would have to jump. The trunk had gotten too wide for Tavarian to wrap his legs around it, and there were no branches beneath him. The ledge below appeared occasionally when the wispy clouds opened. With no space on the ledge surrounding the tree, he would need to jump and stick, without pitching forward or any other direction from the landing.

Taking a deep breath, he let go of the limb and dropped onto the hard stone surface of the ledge at the base of the tree. The slick rock caused his feet to slip out from under him. He slid on his back down the side of the wall until the slope ended. He dropped again. Landing quickly on another rocky ledge, he came to a stop. Tavarian had found the rest of the broken mountain path. Here, the stone path had traction, and he could continue walking down.

As he came out of the thick clouds, he got his first glimpse of the bottom of the world. Scattered groups of trees and clusters of dark green grass as well as large areas of shiny red that he couldn't identify yet dotted the landscape.

Rootcore, the bottom of the world, was nothing like he imagined, but not so different from Rethia. Once he reached the ground, he could get a better view. He passed by a large waterfall cascading from an outcropping of stones overhead as the path moved around behind the falls. Could it be the same waterfall where he and Lirah spent so much time together? A strange smell of wet minerals and rock met him as he passed under it.

Tavarian called out, hoping for a response from someone. Nothing stirred except the wind. Something lying across a group of rocks nearby caught his eye. As soon as he identified the object, he turned away.

The twisted, broken body of one of the Descenders was now burned into his mind. The body was not immediately identifiable, but Tavarian chose not to inspect further. He did not want the memory of their ghostly face to haunt him forever, not even if it were Dexius. He didn't hate him that much.

He called out everyone's names—Devia, Tiagra, Dexius, Pilo, Migram, and Veras—but no one answered. There were no words or groans. Bloodied and battered from his fall, he rubbed his face. With no one to help him, he was doomed. Without a way to climb the broken path up the mountain, no hope remained. He would die out here alone.

Tavarian sat on some white stones covering the area. He held his head in his hands, rocking back and forth. His mind was clouded with an overload of thoughts, the horror he had witnessed, the grief he felt, and the doubt of what to do next.

"Don't disparage your weaknesses, rely on your strengths." He could almost hear Valea's voice.

He had to find the rokenstones. All hope rested on him now. The food situation in Rethia could get much worse before the end of the year. He had that much time to find the stones and figure out a way up the mountain before the next group of Descenders left. He had to make sure they never needed anyone to come down the mountain path again.

Dusting himself off, he stood, setting off on his journey across Rootcore.

The ground below the mountain was mostly reddish-brown dirt with a few spike-leaved trees scattered about. Patches of dark green grass were spread throughout the area, and large red crystallized stones peeked through. The stones shined even in the obscured sunlight.

He found no enormous roots that the mountain grew from, making up the foundations of the world. They had it all wrong. Perhaps even the mountains needed soil to sprout. Their roots must be coiled beneath the dirt he stood on.

The whole world was cast in the shadow of the lower atmosphere above. The sun was reduced to a fuzzy blob of light in the sky, giving off about the same level of brightness as Rethia just before sunset. The air here contained a lot of moisture.

As he wandered around the base of the mountain, taking it all in, he spotted a cylinder-shaped boulder standing upright beside the mountain. It had an odd dark green shell attached to it and a stem that reached all the way up to the canopy of trees above him.

He made his way to the cylinder rock and was startled as it lifted off the ground, floated through the air, and then crashed down in another spot. He heard a loud crunching above him as limbs and leaves from trees fell to the ground near him. Above him, an enormous moving object leaned against the side of the mountain. Tavarian backed away—the huge object above the treetops did not appear stable and seemed like it could fall at any time.

The cylinder rock lifted off the ground again and came back down with a crash. As he ran farther ahead, he realized there were other cylinder rocks moving as well. The cylinder rocks were connecting to the object precariously leaning on the mountain, shaking the trees on the side.

Tavarian moved farther away, and he realized the object was an enormous creature with four legs. Stunned, he stood there staring for a moment before running farther away from it. He watched as the creature feasted on some of the trees growing on the side of the mountain.

He had no idea creatures like this existed. Its huge dark body with hard green armor was covered in moss. It paid no attention to Tavarian, but he wanted to be as far away as possible from the thing.

Tavarian headed across the soft mossy terrain as the monstrous creature bellowed behind him. The occasional thump of its stony legs landing on the ground unnerved him as he hastened his steps. A little while later, he had distanced himself from the creature enough that its crashing sounds were gone.

Moving over across the mossy grass and red crystal covered landscape, the horrid events on the mountain began to play back in his head. Migram's desperate plea for help as he slipped over the side. Tiagra knocked off the path as Migram fell into her. Strong and dedicated, Tiagra should be here instead of him. She had a much better chance to succeed. Pilo and Veras were also perfectly suited for this with their lean, muscular physiques. Admittedly, Dexius had survival skills he did not possess. Tavarian was weaker than everyone but Migram and Devia, yet he survived.

He had to make their deaths worth it now. Tavarian tried to erase the image of the body on the rocks at the foot of the mountain, but he couldn't help but picture each of their faces, mangled and broken, lying alone and forgotten. He should have buried the body he found. How terrible of him to leave it there, but he couldn't do it. He couldn't bear to face the ravaged body. He knew it was a person that he had been talking to just moments earlier. That could have been him. It should have been him. He shuddered from the thought of it.

As he wrestled with his thoughts, he came to an old wooden structure surrounded by strange black plants. The entire area was covered in dark sprawls of grass and trees. Something was very wrong with this vegetation, possibly afflicted with a strange disease. Its appearance was more like rotten flesh than plants, dripping with thick, black ooze.

The building had been crafted by someone with better carpentry skills than his own. Though its general design was not so different from Rethian buildings, the intricacy in the details were a level he had never seen. By comparison, Rethian houses were quite plain.

The windows were torn out, but had frames built around them as if highlighting them. It did not appear to have any practical use. Carvings of tiny vines and flowers had been cut into the wood, adding another dimension of detail. Tavarian wondered why anyone would spend time carving these little details into window frames. There was no purpose to it at all. Wouldn't cutting into the structure weaken the wood, only to make some useless designs in it?

The door of the building leaned over, knocked out of the frame. It also had parts carved out in some square patterns of varying depths. This must have belonged to a strange being. He walked around the building, leading to the remains of a small garden. Other similar buildings surrounded the corrupted garden. This had been a town once.

He searched through the rooms of the building, finding nothing but dust on ruined wooden furnishings. The chairs and tables had similar carved designs in them. The legs of the tables and chairs were oddly cut into curves and shaped deliberately. Again, they would have to cut out a good portion of wood to do that. How could they waste materials like this? No wonder this town had been abandoned.

The vile garden lay in the center of all the buildings. Examining the plants, the sinewy leaves bled a dark liquid. They did not resemble any of the dead plants he had ever laid eyes on before.

Near to the garden stood a stone monument. Tavarian found an engraving in the stone. It read: "Welcome to the town of Muloken."

Attached to the top of the monument was a piece of cloth with more writing: "Left for Strakenbridge. This place is cursed."

Tavarian combed through each building, though very little remained.

In one of the houses, a piece of meat charred to a crisp lay over a fire pit. Rotten, dried fruit sat on some of the tables.

One house with had a fancy bed remained mostly intact. Tavarian could sleep here for the night, but the decay and notes about curses dissuaded him. The bed had a word carved into the footboard. In curvy artistic writing intermingled with flowers was the word *Danessa*. Perhaps a name, but who would be so vain as to have their name carved into the wood on their bed? He couldn't imagine even Lirah having something like this.

There was a set of cabinets beside the bed with several little doors. He opened and closed each one until he found something interesting: a sword hilt with golden metal pieces impressed into the wood. The blade had been broken, but the hilt remained in good condition. It looked strange compared to the weapons the peace control officers in Rethia carried. Precisely carved designs stemmed from the bottom of the handle. A golden metal socket grooved out of the top of the hilt had metal stems leading up to the fractured blade. The remains of the blade contained an odd white steel with a line of golden metal running down its sharp edge. Above the socket, a small metal piece lay inside a groove in the hilt.

If nothing else, it would be a unique item to bring back and show people in Rethia. Tavarian placed it in his pack and continued walking through the other rooms. He passed a pile of bones in one of the shadowy corners on his way outside to investigate some of the other houses. One of the houses had most of the boards torn off its frame, and had been stacked in a pile on the ground. In the one room that remained intact, there were several carvings in the walls. Tavarian couldn't decipher most of them because these carvings were not nearly as elegant as the decorative ones on the other wood items he's seen so far—these were chaotic and hastily made.

One group of scratchings read, "in my head they speak" and "death is a blessing." Others read, "beware The Hollow" and "their minds flow in the blood of the serpent." The people of this town must have gone completely mad. What would have happened to kill all the plants and transform them into the hideous form they took now?

As he started to leave the town, he spotted a pen like those in the farms in Rethia where they kept animals. When he got closer, he saw there were skeletons of some four-legged creatures. The light wind blew the last remaining bits of dried flesh from their bones as though it were ash.

The sight made him leave quickly. Though it was an interesting mystery, he wanted no part of this disturbing place. Not one to believe in curses or superstitions, Tavarian never found any evidence that said otherwise. Even with a scene like this, there had to be a logical explanation. He couldn't blame the townspeople for coming to this conclusion. Perhaps he should seek out the town of Strakenbridge. If the people of this town went there for refuge, it should be a good place to find food and shelter. He could inquire about the rokenstones.

As he walked across the plains, Tavarian wondered what made all the previous Descenders want to stay here. The red crystal stones were interesting, but nothing like the image conjured up of Rootcore. How long had the mountain path been wiped out? Had everyone that ever descended fallen from the mountain and perished? He had to find the stones and somehow get back up the mountain so he could warn everyone. Only a year remained until the next Descension.

Even if the mountain road had been out for a while, there must have been others who would have survived like he had. Why had they never found a way to get back up the mountain to warn them? Maybe he couldn't get back. No—he could not accept that.

CHAPTER 4

AS THE DAY wore on, the obscured glow of the sun began to fade. Tavarian found a pond, and he decided it would make a good place to build a shelter. A small forest surrounded one side of the water. He spent the rest of the gloomy daylight using the saw his father gave him to cut some of the small trees down to build the shelter.

He had sharpened the ends of four parts of two tree trunks and staked them into the ground. Building a frame around the four posts at their base, he tied them together with vines. Tavarian did the same for the upper posts. He laid branches across the top for a roof and stood up leafy limbs around the walls for camouflage.

At the pond, he filled his metal container with water. As he walked along the edge between the water and the woods, he scouted for anything he could use for food. He still had a few pieces of fruit left that his family had given him, but he would need more.

He found a group of ryberry plants and picked as many as he could carry in his bag. Farther into the woods, he spotted some eibregs and made his way over. The eibregs were surrounded by thorny vines as usual, but they had a very good taste.

Tavarian tried to slice through the vines with his knife, but they were too flimsy to easily cut. The thorns on them were hard as rock. He attempted to find a place to hold the vines, but cutting them caused them to bend and the thorns closed together into his hand. You don't often pick eibregs and come away unscathed.

He wondered if he could invent a tool that could do it—maybe if he had a way of putting two knives together on each side of the vine. His fingers bled as he got two eibregs loose and into his satchel.

When he started back, a roaring growl boomed through the trees. He caught a glimpse of a wild beast stalking him. Even though it was smaller in stature than him, it was large enough to be a serious threat. It stood on four legs protruding outward from the animal's sides rather than straight down. It had a black coat of fur with bushy gray stripes of hair down its back and sharp teeth. As Tavarian started backing up, the animal charged. Tavarian ran as fast as he could through the brush. The beast dashed toward him, much faster than he could move.

Dodging trees and underbrush as it raced through the forest, the animal's quick feet pounded over the grassy terrain in pursuit. As Tavarian ran through a group of bushes, a voice called out to him. Soon, he made it out of the forest and back into the mossy plains. The animal had already tired out and stopped pursuit. It watched him from the edge of the forest before heading back into the trees.

Tavarian walked around the forest back to the shelter he had made, setting out a blanket on the grassy floor. He sat and drank half of the water from the container and lay down to rest after the close call he just had.

"Hey! You owe me a treg!" said a voice approaching his shelter. He sat up and peeked out between the limbs and leaves of the shelter walls. Golden eyes peered back at him. Stunned, he tumbled toward the middle of the shelter.

"Nice bit of shade you got here. You build this?" she said.

"Yeah, who are you?" he said.

She crouched lower. Her face was partly shrouded by a black hood. "No one. My name is a mark of death," she said. "I only tell those I intend to kill. It dies in the minds of my prey.

Unsure what to make of her response, Tavarian wondered, "Are you trying to frighten me?"

"Are you not?" the young woman quipped. "Intimidation can be a powerful weapon. Especially when traveling alone through unknown territory."

"Well, I'm Tavarian," he said.

"You don't strike me as someone that would intentionally be alone in the wilderness. Where you headed?" she asked.

"To a place called Strakenbridge," Tavarian said.

"I've heard of it. What are you looking for there?"

"Civilization," he said. "The only town I've found so far was abandoned with a note that said they had left for Strakenbridge."

The girl narrowed her eyes, glaring with intensity. "Abandoned? Nothing left at all?"

"Nothing . . . just empty caved-in buildings."

"What did the note say?"

"Something about a curse. All the plants and animals were dead."

The woman's eyes began to widen. "Did you hear any whispers?"

"No, there was no one around."

"How far away was this place?"

"About a half a day's walk from here."

"Interesting. Do you have any food in there?" she asked.

"A little bit of fruit."

"Do you mind if I come inside? After all, you did scare away the treg I was hunting."

"When was that?"

Moving some of the sticks and brush out of the way, she crawled inside the shelter. "You ran past me like you had seen a kodrack."

"Is that what was chasing me?" Tavarian wondered

"Not even close," she said. "A kodrak is a beast that tears its victims apart with its enormous arms. Fortunately, they only live deep in the Ferizine Burrows."

Tavarian swallowed hard. Rootcore seemed a much more dangerous place than he imagined. Peeking through the cracks in the walls, he surveyed the area. He glanced at her from the corner of his eye. She wore a dark undercoat striped in red designs, tightly fitted leggings, and long black boots. Over that was a thick black overwrapping vest that formed a sort of dress below her waist and covered her legs. Far sleeker and cleaner than what he or anyone in Rethia had. His brown tunic was patched together with bits of fabric, and had worn down from years of use. Her clothing, on the other hand, had no visible stitching at all.

She took a device out of her vest wrapping. It sprung into position when she switched a lever. Setting it on the blanket, she inspected the device, and then let out a frustrated sigh. "My crossbow is broken again," she moaned.

"I can fix things. Do you mind if I look at it?"

She pushed the crossbow toward him. "Have at it."

Tavarian picked it up. It operated like a bow, but with a cylinder that turned and wound the bowstring to create tension. The mechanics of it were unfamiliar to him. He pulled the string back to find a piece where the taut string could catch on to. When he pulled on the catch, it released the pressure that would fire one of the arrows wrapped in her quiver from its chamber. The whole device was more compact than the longbows hunters used in Rethia. With its handle and perfect weight balance, he suspected it could be more accurate.

The tension mechanism may not be as great as the strongest hunters could muster with a longbow. Tavarian imagined it had less range than what a master bowman could achieve, and that may have been its only drawback. Someone with quick hands and a solid aim could put several arrows into their targets quickly from intermediate range. It was not something thrown together or invented through trial and error. It was a weapon perfected by a master craftsman.

"What's wrong with it?" he asked.

"Are you sure you've worked on a crossbow before?"

"I figured out how it works, but it appears functional." Tavarian demonstrated pulling back the catch that would fire an arrow.

The woman sighed. "The trigger is broken. Nothing happens when I pull it."

"Trigger?"

She pointed to a curved metal piece underneath. "Look, if you can't fix it, pass it back over."

"Just give me a second." He checked a metal piece extending down from a square hole at the inside of the handle. Turning the crossbow over, he examined the metal parts of the catch. A piece inside connected to the trigger. It flopped around rather loosely inside the metal chamber of the crossbow.

There must be something to hold it in place. Inside the chamber, a component extended from the catch, holding the taught bowstring in place. If he could get the trigger piece on the other side of it, that may hold it.

He bent the trigger piece to get it around the catch, hoping not to break it. Finally, he worked it around and the trigger piece fit nicely into a latch connected to the catch on top.

Tavarian pulled the trigger, and the catch released the string as it snapped toward the barrel at the front.

"You fixed it!" she said.

"Yeah, told you I would."

"Excellent. So what kind of fruit did you say you have?"

He opened his pack. "Some ryberries."

"Is that all?"

"Pretty much."

She peeked into the satchel. "Oh, eibregs! My favorite!"

"Yeah, those weren't much fun to pick." He lifted his wounded fingers to show her.

"Can I have one, since you ruined my dinner?" the woman asked.

"I suppose so, but I'm saving the other one." As much as he wanted to keep it, Lirah always said that flattery and gifts are the quickest ways to make new friends. He could use some friends in Rootcore.

Before he could grab it and hand to her, she had already reached into the bag and taken it. "I never did like ryberries much."

She removed her hood, revealing bronze colored skin that glowed with a soft delicate texture. Her eyes were bright and golden and adorned with long dark lashes. The devilish curves of her eyebrows contrasted with a kindness to the eyes beneath them. Everything about her defined an amalgamation of beauty and danger—a feral beast with elegant grace.

Her hair, striking and unusual, tapered into thick strands that hung around her face, ending below her jawline. Each piece was black at the roots, fading into red, and then bright orange at the tips where black circles filled with dots of white formed a pattern. Her hair didn't appear to be cut, but formed a natural long bob.

"What are you staring at?" she asked. "My hair?"

"Sorry, it's just . . ." Tavarian blushed "I've never seen anyone like you where I come from."

"Never seen an Arkanthian before?" she said.

The woman appeared to be older than him—maybe be a little older than his sister, Valea. A couple creases around her eyes gave them sense of wisdom.

"No, but I haven't been in Rootcore for long."

"Rootcore? Where do you come from?"

"From Rethia, on the mountain."

"Don't know of it," the young woman said, "but I don't know many places in Nalacea yet."

"Nalacea?" Tavarian asked.

"You know . . ." She squinted her eyes. "This continent we are on now."

"Where do Arkanthians come from?"

"Arkanthis, on the continent of Varkandor," she said. "It's on the other side of Isodonia, across the ocean."

"Ocean? What do you mean?"

"You really don't get off that mountain much do you?"

"Most Rethians can't breathe the air down here."

"Oh, but you can?"

"Yeah, I was tested."

"So, what makes you so special?"

"I guess I developed an immunity to it."

"Does that mean I wouldn't be able to breathe the air on your mountain?"

"I don't know for sure—maybe not."

"What's so different about the air?"

"It's above the lower atmosphere. It's a different chemical content."

"Above the clouds? What's that like?"

"A lot brighter—nothing like the gloom here."

"You can see the sun from there?"

"Yeah, most of the time."

"Tell me, what's it like?"

"It's small and round, orange colored," he said. "Like a glowing ball of fire, and it's very bright—so bright you can hardly look at it."

"That sounds amazing."

"I suppose it is. What is your home like?"

"Nothing like it once was. I haven't been there in so long, and there's no reason to go back." She stared off into space for a moment. "We should get some rest, though. It's getting dark out."

"Oh, yeah, I guess we should."

"Do you have another blanket?"

"I think I do."

"Look! The brightflies are out." The young women's stern face changed to that of an excited little girl.

"Brightflies?"

The flame-haired girl pointed at the dark sky through the trees. Streams of sparkling yellow lights moved together in pathways that split in different directions, like a river of stars.

"It looks like stars!" said Tavarian.

"What are stars? Brightflies are small insects that glow at night. We have them in Arkanthis too. Or we used to anyway. Maybe they moved here."

"So those sparkles are all insects?"

"Yes, they fly in groups like that, lined up one after another. They feed on the nectar of the night blooms to carry back to their hive.

Tavarian opened his bag and found another blanket that his mother had packed for him. He unfolded it and laid it down beside the other one. The girl lay down on the blanket, folding part of it around her. Tavarian curled up on his blanket and soon drifted off to sleep.

❧

As the hazy morning light came into the shelter, Tavarian rolled over, checking to see if the girl had woken. There was no sign of her or the blanket she'd used. He quickly got to his feet and went outside the shelter. He yelled out for her, but never got an answer. Had she left and moved on without saying anything? Or was she coming back?

He found her fascinating and wanted get to know her. They were building a connection in the short amount of time he had been in her company. Tavarian missed her a little already, especially after losing the rest of the Descenders and being so alone out here in the wilderness. It had only been a day, but he enjoyed having someone else around.

Tavarian decided to wait before moving out, in case she came back. He opened his satchel to get the eibreg he was saving for breakfast. It wasn't there. The woman must have taken it. It was her favorite after all. She wasn't coming back. She had taken the blanket and the eibreg and left.

Tavarian ground his teeth together. He thought he finally made a connection with someone other than Lirah. Instead, he merely found someone that used him for a blanket, fruit, and shelter for the night. She left the ryberries at least, so he ate most of those for breakfast.

Gathering up his things into the satchel, he left the shelter and filled up his container with water from the pond. He walked around the other side of the water, this time avoiding the forest and the predators that lived within. Tavarian decided to follow a brook that fed into the pond, hoping it led to Strakenbridge.

He was alone again, but he didn't mind it that much. He rarely felt lonely when he was by himself. It was when he was surrounded by others that the loneliness struck.

As he walked for a while, Tavarian wondered what Lirah was doing right now. Probably in class, studying. He wished she could be out here with him. As fun as it would be to tell her these stories when he returned, it would so much easier if she were here now.

The banks beside the brook rose above the water's edge. Clusters of white wildflowers among the mossy grass added beauty to the wilderness. For the first time, he realized the enormity of Rootcore. Even with all the space in Rethia, it couldn't compare to this.

A group of unfamiliar animals gathered to drink at the brook. The current slowed here as the irregular shapes along the edges trapped water. He counted twenty-one of them, standing on four legs, some of them nearly as tall as him. They had light brown fur with some reddish spots on them and thick bodies but small heads. Their ears stood up and then rested again repeatedly, as if detecting his presence.

Tavarian stopped on the rise to observe them. He lay on his stomach hoping to be unnoticed, so he could watch them unseen. He stayed there for a bit, resting and enjoying the quiet serenity of the meadowlands. Some of the creatures would gather water in their mouths and spit it on the other ones, and then rubbed their heads against them, taking turns bathing each other.

Their ears perked up again. They froze for a moment, and then a few of them darted away from the brook. The rest of them quickly followed. Soon after, a giant, round, almost flat creature came jumping out toward them. The creature did not run. It only jumped as it chased after them. It was dark green with oily reflective skin and light green stripes, and it jumped quite far. Soon enough, it landed on one of the smaller animals. The animal no longer moved, either crushed from the weight or trapped by the predator's strength. The creature began eating it without resistance.

Rootcore could be a dangerous place. Tavarian sunk away from the edge of the rise and reached for his knife, hoping the monstrous creature would not come his way. The girl had not stolen that, at least. He returned to his feet, continuing on his journey, staying out of sight of the brook for the time being. Even though the monstrous creature was preoccupied with its kill, he decided it was best to stay out of its sight.

As he trekked across the hilly, grassy land, he came upon a large flat area where two mounds receded. The strange glassy surface was bright with marbled stripes of various shades of blue and white. The stripes followed an outline around the exposed edge toward its other side where the grass covered it.

A small flow of water trickled down from the groove between the two hills, spilling onto the hard blue stone. Water flowed into a pit eroded through the reflective exterior. Thousands of blue and white crystals glistened inside. The whole area reminded him of the geodes found in the Rethian mines, but far bigger.

After crossing over the blue geode and a large portion of countryside beyond, the rise receded to the same level as the brook. The rolling hills gave way to flat lands. Bushy weeds ahead grew around a tall wooden fence. Droning sounds of insects surrounded him as he cautiously made his way over.

The gate had a long wooden latch that secured it, but it was on the outside facing him—a rather odd thing. How did the residents of this place open the gate from the inside? He knocked on the gate, but no one seemed to be on the other side. Could this be Strakenbridge? At least it was civilization. The residents inside must welcome visitors if they leave the bolt accessible from the outside. Tavarian lifted the long board bolting the gate and pushed it open.

Inside the fence were big messily constructed wooden buildings and a large open cave inside a hill. A small field of planted crops in well-kept rows of soil grew in front of a nearby pen of round fat animals eating grain in the dirt. They bumped into each other as they ate, grunting in protest.

Careful to step around the garden, Tavarian walked toward the closest building. A whistle sounded behind him. He turned around, but found nothing. Motion inside the small building caught his attention. People stood against the window bars waving, beckoning him over.

Why did they not just come outside to greet him? They seemed friendly enough. Warily, Tavarian walked toward the building, his right hand on the knife in his pocket. As he drew closer, a man inside pointed downward. Nothing of interest revealed itself where they pointed, though they continued frantically waving.

A loud commotion of voices drew his focus. He saw others marching through the gate with their feet tied together with vines. They staggered into the yard with the difficulty of walking with bound feet. Two giants that must have been ten to fifteen feet tall shoved those lagging behind. The giants were nearly as wide as they were tall, with muscular arms and stout bellies. Their shoulders were huge and round, with a triangular shape to their heads and little to no necks.

Their faces contained beady eyes, small ears, big noses and mouths, but no hair on their heads.

The two giants' eyes widened at the sight of Tavarian.

"Hey! We got us a new one!" one of them said.

Tavarian backed up as they dashed toward him. He turned to run. Even though the giants' movements appeared sluggish, their long strides and reach allowed them to cover ground quickly. One of them grabbed Tavarian's legs out from under him, picking him up.

The giant held him upside down by the legs while they inspected him.

"You'll do," one of them said, grabbing Tavarian's satchel. He took him over to the small building, lifted the board latching the door, and threw him inside. The door closed behind him, followed by the slam of the door being latched again.

A sour, stale odor punched him in the face. His fuzzy eyesight came into focus. Several unfriendly faces gathered, staring down at him.

"You idiot! Why didn't you open the latch?" one of them yelled.

The others in the room began shouting and kicking dirt at him as he pulled himself up on the boards jutting out from the walls. He backed farther into the corner as they continued shoving him and yelling things at him. As they got in his face, Tavarian slid down the wall into a sitting position on the floor.

"Leave him be!" said a man behind the crowd. "If we had gotten out, they would have run us down."

The man pushed people aside, grabbing some by the collar to pull them away from Tavarian. He leaned down and offered Tavarian a container. He took it as the liquid inside sloshed around. Water, not the cleanest, but it helped quench his thirst.

"What's your name, kid?" the man asked.

"Tavarian."

"Don't blame Tavarian here for the mess we're in; he's one of us now," the man said. "Don't turn your anger on each other. The Grundians are the real enemy."

"Who are the Grundians?" Tavarian asked.

"The thick-headed brutes that threw you in here with us," he said.

"Have you planned any kind of escape?"

"We've found a lot of things that won't work. That's part of the reason some of us are no longer moving." The man gestured toward the far corner of the room.

Tavarian shivered. A mass of shattered bones and decomposing flesh held together by nothing more than its tattered clothing leaned awkwardly against the wall.

"This wood is too thick, and it's reinforced with steel. Getting out of this shack is only part of the problem though."

"How long have you been here?"

"Who can tell anymore? A year at least, some of us longer," the man said. "No one survives more than a few years."

"They're going to kill us?" Tavarian wasn't sure he wanted the answer.

"They forget to feed us sometimes, making us fight each other for scraps. I'm trying to make sure that doesn't happen again, and that we all stick together. On top of that, they sometimes get careless and hit someone too hard."

Tavarian grew more anxious by the moment. He found himself in the worst situation possible. The little he knew about survival in the wild had not prepared him for a scenario like this. He may never get the chance to find a way to get back to Rethia and Lirah again. They took his satchel with everything he had, including the curl of Lirah's hair. He wished he could wake up from this nightmare and be back home. Valea's teasing and annoying him had never seemed so welcoming.

"My name is Cavaros, by the way. I should have given a proper introduction as we try to keep some remnants of civilization in here," said the man.

"Good to meet you, sir," Tavarian responded.

"There's no sir or any other kind of titles here, we are all the same in this place," Cavaros said. "Now, let me introduce everyone to you so we will all know each other. We're on the same side here."

Cavaros stood up and put his hand on the shoulder of a younger man standing nearby, who just minutes ago had shoved Tavarian into the wall.

"This is Tamken. He's one of the newer ones in here, aside from you of course."

Tamken stared at the floor.

"This lovely lady is Reva."

She gave a slight smile when he called her name. Tavarian did not find her lovely, but these weren't the best of circumstances.

"This one is Marvus." Cavaros gestured toward a skinny man with stringy long hair covered in sweat, wearing clothes that were falling off him.

"Dalson, over here." Cavaros motioned to young man with reddish hair and blue eyes with large, pronounced nostrils.

"Varga." He was an older man with a long gray beard but little hair on his head.

"And Selas."

Selas appeared to be a middle-aged man with a scruffy beard and matted hair. He was stronger in appearance than the rest of them, except for Cavaros.

Tavarian glanced past them to a young girl who sat in a corner away from everyone else. Underneath the smears of dirt, she had a remarkably cute face. The messy bangs of her short dark hair covered one of her eyes as she stared down, scrubbing a stack of metal plates. Judging by her size, she must have been a few years younger than him—a fawn in a lion's den.

Cavaros noticed Tavarian's eyes on her. "Oh, that's Darby. She doesn't say much, and we try not to draw attention to her. She's too small to do most of the work here, so she does all the cleaning jobs."

"How long has she been here?" Tavarian asked.

"A few months, I think."

"How did she come to be here?"

Cavaros motioned for him to be quiet. "Don't concern yourself with Darby." He gave Tavarian a stern expression. "We're all very protective of her."

"Understood," Tavarian said. "May I ask how you came to be here, then?"

"We were raided by Grundians," Cavaros said. "I used to live in the town of Dusvier along with Selas. The Grundians attack us occasionally. Sometimes we can fend them off. Sometimes we're less successful. They normally come to steal livestock and crops, things like that. So even when they get in, they only take a few things and leave. This time, though, they grabbed me and a few others and brought us here to do all their work for them."

"Is that what happened to Muloken?" Tavarian asked.

"I haven't heard any news of the world in some time. What of Muloken?"

"All the vegetation and animals are dead, and the buildings are caving in. No one was there at all. There was a message that mentioned a curse and that they had all left because of it."

"Doesn't sound like Grundians," he said. "I've never heard of them wiping out a whole town or destroying the vegetation. Grundians like to leave the town intact. They go in, take some things, and leave. They want the town to keep producing goods so they can come back and take some more."

"What are they going to do with us?"

"Eventually they'll grab some of us for work they want done."

"When does that usually happen?"

"There isn't exactly a schedule, kid. Most often during daylight, if that helps."

Tavarian sat jittery against the wall. His senses were heightened to every sound as he anticipated the door latch opening at any moment and the Grundians grabbing him again. He stood up, pacing around for a time as the others rested on the floor. He glanced over at Darby, who was still sitting in a dark corner, scrubbing metal plates. Oblivious to the world around her, she was solely focused on the work she did with her hands.

A blank expression remained on her face the whole time as if her mind had escaped to another time and place. Her eyes told nothing of the hardship she had surely been through since she had been here. If she could remain calm in this place, perhaps he could too.

"You should get some rest," Cavaros said. "You may need it tomorrow."

Tavarian curled up against the wall, hoping he could get to sleep.

CHAPTER 5

A LOUD BANGING ON the door woke Tavarian just as it sprung open.

"Grab some kips for water duty," said one of the giants outside.

"I know what to do! You don't tell me!" said the other.

A Grundian with a gold ring in his nose entered the building, eyeing everyone inside. He grabbed two people and carried them under his arms out the door. The other one came in and grabbed Cavaros, continuing to study the other prisoners. Tavarian kept his eyes to the floor as they looked him over.

A large hand smacked him bluntly under the chin, forcing him to lift his head. The giant shoved Tavarian back and grabbed Dalson instead. Tavarian sighed with relief.

"No! Get the new one!" said the Grundian with the nose ring.

"I decide which ones I want!" the other Grundian said as he stroked his chin. "Breaking new kips in is fun."

He set Dalson back down. Turning back toward Tavarian, the Grundian grabbed him and tucked him under an arm.

He carried Tavarian in a rather uncomfortable position and dumped him onto the ground along with the other three. One of the Grundians threw some large metal containers toward them and pointed to some trees outside the fenced area. Another Grundian tied vines around their waists, and then took another vine and tied them all to one another.

The two Grundians had them carry the containers and

marched them toward the gate. Walking while tied to three other people grew increasingly difficult. Tavarian tried to match the pace of the others, but they all walked at different speeds. He made sure to keep up with the fastest one so he wouldn't slow the group down. The Grundians grunted loudly at them, seeming to want them to move faster.

One of the giants reached over the tall gate and unlatched it from the outside. They staggered toward the brook as Tavarian struggled to keep from tripping on the vines while carrying the big container. Once they made it to the water, they brought their containers over to the brook, dipping them into the flowing water to fill them. The brook came to a bend here and split off into smaller streams where the water was more shallow, and then met in the deeper water to become one again. Tavarian filled his container and the group began walking back. The containers were much heavier with water in them, which made the walking together even worse as Tavarian had to slow down and speed up to stay on his feet.

When they were halfway back to the fence, Tavarian began to lose his grip on the container. The constant fidgeting and stepping together took its toll. Tavarian stumbled, spilling most of the water from his container. The Grundians laughed. One of the Grundians acted out the way he had fallen and tumbled onto his container. The Grundians roared with more laughter.

"It was like this," said the Grundian mocking Tavarian, "and then *ga-dunk*, right into the bucket!"

"No, no, it was more like this, and then . . . *ga-dunk*," said the other as they roared again.

"We'll call the new kip 'Gadunk,'" one of them said, still laughing. "Yeah, Gadunk! Now you go back and get more."

They made the whole group march back to the brook so Tavarian could fill his container again. He had angered the group now.

"You drop that again, and I'll kill you on the spot," Marvus whispered as Tavarian tilted the bucket under the water.

They started back and Tavarian put all his focus on keeping the container upright. The bucket became heavier and heavier and the pain it took to keep going intensified. Tavarian tried to distract himself from the discomfort as they trudged along slowly toward the fence. Pain is just a feeling. It's not real. It's just a signal from his brain, he told himself.

It didn't completely work, but they finally made it back inside the fence. Tavarian put his container down, and bent over to try and catch his breath. Cavaros pulled Tavarian up, but it was too late—one of the Grundians smacked Tavarian across the back with a wooden stick. The blow knocked out what little air he had left in him.

Struggling to breathe, Tavarian went to his knees. The Grundian whacked him again with the stick. The blow hardly registered to him the second time because all his focus was on regaining air. Finally, he was able to inhale deeply, and his lungs filled. Each prisoner poured their water into a shallow brick pool near the animal pen and prepared to set out to the brook again.

"Gadunk's out of the group," said one of the giants. "We've slowed down because of you. Go feed the tregs!" He cut the vines loose and put Tavarian with another group of prisoners who were feeding the tregs grain and seeds. Some of them were taking water from the pool and watering the plants in the garden.

Before they were done with him, the giants smacked Tavarian a few more times with their sticks, presumably for making them do extra work to change out prisoners. Or maybe they just enjoyed it.

Tavarian had not exactly ingratiated himself with the rest of the prisoners. He had made a bad first impression. He wouldn't have minded watering the garden or feeding the tregs or even working in the mine in the cave as some others did, but each day after that, the Grundians grabbed him to carry water from the brook to the town. Tavarian made sure he never dropped his container again, no matter how heavy it got.

Days turned into weeks, and weeks became months. Carrying the containers full of water made Tavarian much stronger. He had never had to carry anything with much weight to it in Rethia, but his muscles took to this new routine quite well after a while.

The daily water task became easier than they were the day he started, though it was still hard work. Tavarian had become friends with Cavaros and Tamken, but the rest of them were either indifferent or some, like Marvus, didn't like him much. Darby still kept to her dark corner, either cleaning something or staring off into space. They all made sure she had food no matter how scarce. For some reason, she never ate in front of them, always turning her back instead.

One day, as Cavaros, Tamken, Tavarian, and Marvus were brought outside the building, two Grundians, Drin and Glug, wrestled on the ground. When Grack, one of the bigger Grundians spotted them, he dropped Tavarian and Cavaros to the ground and went over to stop the fight. The Grundians fought one another a lot, but some of the leaders didn't allow it during work hours.

"Time to work! Fight later!" Grack fumed.

"He left the gate open again and the tregs got out!" said Drin.

The flimsy gate on the treg pen allowed them to get out into the open often, but they could only go so far because of the main gate surrounding the town, making them fairly easy to round up. This time, however, Glug left the main gate open, allowing the tregs to leave Grunda.

"Go round up the tregs. We've got water to haul," Grack ordered.

"I can fix that gate!" Tavarian shouted, lifting his hands to get their attention.

Grack spun around. He stepped toward Tavarian, bending low to shout in his face. "Shut up, Gadunk! The gate don't need fixing—it need closing."

Tavarian turned away, more from the stench of Grack's breath than fear. He tried to compose himself after a bit of dizziness.

"I can fix it so that it will close by itself," Tavarian said.

The other prisoners glanced at one another, uncertain of what to make of Tavarian's announcement.

A quick gust of air blew across Tavarian's face as Grack swatted his palm at him. "Don't be stupid. Get that container and go."

Though he knew it was unwise to keep pushing, he had been here long enough doing the same work every day that it had either made him a little crazy or tired enough that it was worth the risk. "I can do it, and then you'll never have to worry about the tregs getting out again," he insisted.

"You get in line so we can fetch water!" Grack commanded, poking his huge finger into Tavarian's forehead.

The ground shook as heavy footsteps approached. Cold sweat formed on his hands because Tavarian immediately knew who it was.

"I want a magic gate," said the deep, surly voice of Grunch, regarded by the other Grundians as the leader of Grunda. A giant even among Grundians, Grunch carried a giant tree stump that he used as a club.

Holding the massive trunk as a handle, he rotated the weapon as it rested on his shoulder. The club smelled awful, like a dead animal. Tavarian tried not to think about the destruction the horrid weapon must have wrought.

Grack twisted his mouth, less than pleased with this turn of events. "But Gadunk always fetches water."

"Take another for water. I want to see this gate," Grunch commanded.

Grack's head drooped. "Gadunk, you fix the gate."

"Can I have some supplies and tools to do it?" Tavarian blurted out, too excited to think clearly.

Grunch peered down at him, taking the trunk from his shoulder. The knotted root ball end of the club crashed to the ground. "What you need?" Grunch asked, propping himself on his club.

"Some wood and some metal for the gate, and a saw and hammer and nails," Tavarian said quietly.

Grunch straightened his posture and returned the club to his shoulder. "Gadunk can use supplies, but if you fail, you get beaten."

The black gunk on the end of Grunch's club, strung between the broken roots, served as a warning. Tavarian swallowed hard. There could be no mistakes. At least he had added something like this to a gate before. He went over to the work building and grabbed a saw, a hammer, and some nails. Tavarian found some metal he could use in some piles of scrap. While a Grundian named Plop watched over him, he cut through the long plank that had kept the gate locked from the outside.

"You gonna be in big trouble if this don't work," declared Plop delightfully.

Using a pliable piece of scrap metal, Tavarian bent it to work it into shape for the latch. He hammered some nails through the thin edges of metal into the wooden gate. Testing out the hook, he checked to make sure it would catch the rod. He made it so the rod would hit the latch, and then slide down at an angle into a hook that would hold it into place. The only way to get it back out would be using a handle that lifted the rod up to the level of the of the latch opening.

With a heavy piece of metal on the lower part of the gate, he gave the gate the weight it needed to make it swing back toward the fence. Once he had that done, he loosened the hinges to make sure it would swing freely, and tested and adjusted the alignment of the rod and the hook so they would always line up.

He added a handle that the lift stuck through between two boards, low enough that he could open the gate from the inside as well. Tavarian made it small enough so that it wouldn't be noticed—he hoped not anyway.

After a half day of working, he showed the finished product to Grunch. Tavarian let Plop demonstrate. Plop reached over the tall gate to unlatch it on the other side. He opened it and then let go as the gate swung back into place, locking again.

"Gadunk did it!" Grunch said.

A few other Grundians came over to see the commotion. Once Tavarian showed them how to open the new latch and how the gate closed, they all wanted to try it out. Opening it and letting it go to catch the latch, they tried it over and over again.

"Gadunk knows magic!" Plop said after trying the gate out several times.

Later in the day, the Grundians had rounded up about half of the tregs that had escaped. The water crew had come in for the day, exhausted, while Tavarian sat on the fence watching the Grundians. They were still entertained by the swinging gate. Once it grew dark, they were all led into the prisoner building.

"You left us with a crew of three today," said Tamken as he slid down the wall do the floor. "We're out there working harder than ever while you're up here fixing a gate."

"Sorry, I didn't mean to leave you shorthanded." Tavarian felt something snag on his middle finger. "This is kind of my thing—to take something and improve it."

"You really are an idiot," said Marvus as he took a drink from the trough. "If they leave the gate open sometimes, that would be our way out of here. From now on, if you are on the water crew, you stick with us. Don't be fixing anything for them."

The odors of sweat and unwashed bodies began to fill the room. Tavarian never quite got used to it after being outside in the fresh air all day.

He knew he ought to tell the others about the secret inside latch. "I added something extra—" Tavarian started.

"Do we still have anyone that checks the gate every day?" said Tamken.

"It doesn't matter now." Dalson cocked his thumb toward Tavarian. "Gadunk over here fixed it for them."

"But I—" Tavarian tried again, but then he realized nobody was listening to him.

"Warlin used to . . . until they caught him," Cavaros said. "I don't know if anyone does now."

"I check it whenever I can get close enough, but it's always latched," Tamken said.

Tavarian rubbed the splinter in his finger. He tried to pinch his fingernails together and grab hold of the tiny chip of wood.

"We need more than an open gate to escape this place," Varga reminded them as he paced in a small circle, his weathered shoes clomping on the wooden floor. The repeated sound grated on Tavarian's nerves. How could he last any longer here without going insane?

"He's right," said Cavaros. "We can't just bolt out the gate. The Grundians would run us down in no time."

"I really need to get out of here," Tavarian said as he got hold of the splinter and eased it out of his skin. Removing the splinter hurt, but it was so satisfying. "I should have been back home by now."

Several of the prisoners cackled.

"This is a big inconvenience for you, eh?" said Reva.

A large metal plate with scraps of unsettling meat was shoved through a slot at the base of the wall. The Grundians remembered to feed them today. Cavaros made his way over and picked up the plate.

"I'm supposed to be looking for rokenstones to bring back home," he said.

"Rokenstones?" Marvus said as Cavaros handed him a piece of the meat from the plate. "Who would be looking for those?"

"Up on the mountain," Tavarian said. "We need them."

He continued rubbing the reddened skin on his finger where the wood had been removed. It was weird how something so small could cause so much irritation.

"You part of that cult?" Marvus asked. "I thought they had died out long ago."

"Cult?" Tavarian wondered. "No, we need them to power our machines. We're not growing enough food for everyone."

He examined his portion of meat from Cavaros. It appeared to be a smaller piece than he had handed to the others, making Tavarian wonder if he was being punished.

"You touch a rokenstone," Marvus said, "it's going to burn you, kid. If you see one, you bury it."

Tavarian watched as Cavaros set the plate in front of Darby with the remaining pieces of meat. He patted her on the head as he walked back toward the adults.

"I was sent here to find them," Tavarian said. "You must be talking about a different kind of stone."

As usual, Darby turned around with her back to the rest of them while she ate the scraps of meat.

"Trust me, kid," warned Marvus. "They are too dangerous to touch."

What if that were true? He didn't trust Marvus, or any of the prisoners for that matter. He trusted Cavaros the most, even though uncertainty surrounded him. He decided to keep the secret of the hidden gate latch to himself for now. Too many of them had given up any hope for escape. They would be too likely to trade secrets like that to the Grundians for better treatment. If he told anyone, it would have to be Cavaros, but only when the two of them were alone.

The next morning, the Grundians grabbed Cavaros, Tamken, Dalson, and Marvus for water duty. Then Plop came into the building.

"Gadunk, we need your magic," he said as he motioned for Tavarian to come to him.

As Tavarian followed Plop out of the building, the other prisoners tending to the crops and tregs stared at him. It was a rare sight for a prisoner to be left without constraints of some kind. Plop led Tavarian into the large but sloppily constructed wooden fortress where many of the stronger Grundians lived. To his knowledge, none of the prisoners had been allowed inside before.

They passed through a wide hallway into a big open room. There stood a long, wide bed made with a wooden frame, and animal fur covering a mattress. The stuffing of dried weeds spilled out from a tear in the side of the mattress. The bed's sturdy wooden frame had little in common with the clumsy construction of the Grundians—it must have been stolen. The bed posts were carved with a delicate artistry with curving designs and flowers—as detailed as the carved wood on the house of the abandoned town of Muloken, but with a different style. The odd shapes cut into the bed posts must have taken a lot of time to do. Perhaps the unique designs were a sort of signature—a way a master carpenter showed their skill. Did this mean the carpenters here in Rootcore were vastly more skilled than the ones in Rethia?

Grunch bounded into the room and walked to the headboard of the bed. The huge bed frame was not long enough to accommodate any Grundian, much less one of Grunch's proportions. Tavarian grabbed one of the posts. The bed tilted, knocking against the floor as he did so.

"Gadunk, fix the bed," Grunch demanded.

The legs on the bed proved to be uneven, or perhaps it was the floor. Either way, Tavarian recognized what Grunch wanted him to do.

Mounted on the far wall was the unusual sword hilt he had found in Muloken. The fury he felt toward them for using something that belonged to him for decoration burned inside him. What had they done with the rest of his stuff? He feared that they had discarded Lirah's curl.

Grunch moved away from the bed to let Tavarian go to work. He knew he had to stay focused, or he could be the next bloody stain on the end of that awful club. They already had tools laying on a table in the room, and Tavarian picked out one of the smaller saws and took a block of wood from the table.

He considered fixing this the way he normally did, by putting something underneath the leg not contacting the floor. Though if he fixed it that easily, he may be back to water duty for the rest of the day. He cut some evenly spaced notches into the block of wood with the saw. Kneeling next to one of the legs of the bed, Tavarian used the notched wood to measure the length of the post. Underneath the bed were several boxes and bags, but near the edge, he spotted his satchel.

After measuring each post to the shortest one, he cut a line into the longer posts to mark the length of the shortest post. He cut off the edge of the three longer posts to match the exact level they all needed to be. When he had finished, he got up and shook the bed to prove that the wobble was gone. Grunch came over to test the bed. He sat down and stood up again. He got back on the bed and lay down. Only about half of his body fit on the bed, so his legs rested on the floor. A big smile split across his normally blank face.

❧

That night, after the Grundians took Tavarian back to the prisoner shed, the others spewed their anger about his easy treatment by the Grundians. They cornered him, yelling and shoving him against the wall.

"This is helping us!" he told them. "They're starting to trust me."

"He's on their side now. He's got himself set up nicely for easy work. He doesn't care about us! We can't trust him any longer. He'll be reporting anything we say back to them," Reva grumbled.

"I'm afraid this time I'm not going to be able to help you, kid," Cavaros muttered.

Two of the prisoners slapped him across the face as others held his arms and feet. They picked him up and slammed him into the wall and the floor. Wet droplets of spit rained down on him. Thankfully, their throats were so parched, they didn't have much ammunition. Tavarian brought his arms up to defend against their pounding at his head, twisting his body to attempt to find some cover against their kicks, and keeping the hard bony parts aimed toward the attack.

A clattering rose from the other side of the shack, metal hitting metal. Their attacks stopped as they turned toward the sound. Darby clanged two metal plates together.

"What's the matter, Darby? You hungry?" Reva asked.

Darby affirmed with a nod of her head and the group left Tavarian, checking for scraps of food in their hiding places. Cracks in the walls and floors were places they typically hid things such as bread and pieces of fruit that they rationed in case the Grundians forgot to feed them.

Dalson knelt where Tavarian lay against the wall.

"We're in this together. You sell us out to get friendly with the enemy and you won't be around for long," he warned.

Cavaros handed him a piece of torn cloth, presumably to wipe the spit and blood from his face.

"The next time they ask you to fix something, tell them you can't . . . do a lousy job, or something," said Cavaros. "We've got to stick together—help each other out."

"You think this is going to make me want to help you out?" Tavarian growled.

"It's called teaching a lesson, boy," Selas said.

As they left and went back to their regular spots against the wall, Tavarian glanced over at Darby. Her eyes met his, and then quickly darted back to the bowls in her hands—she had been watching. It was the first time he had seen her look at anything other something in her hands. He snuck a peek at her a few more times before it got too dark, but now she remained focused on cleaning the plates and bowls.

Light crept through the cracked spaces in the wood. As Tavarian opened his eyes, the Grundians barged into the shed, snatching four of them up for water duty and two for tending to the farm. Grack led Tavarian out of the shack toward the cave opening in the hill. He had never been inside the mining area. The strange workers here were short—less than half his height—with long arms and bluish skin. Big yellow eyes and long pointy noses adorned their faces. The creatures dug into the rock and dirt using pickaxes.

As Tavarian followed Grack through the caves, they passed by small encampments where other Grundians lived. There were female Grundians here, smaller than the males but not by much. Just like the males, they had no hair on their heads, but their faces were rounder. One of the females stormed out of a chamber den, yelling and throwing rocks at a male Grundian as he ran away.

The cave ramped downward into layers of Isodonian soil. The walls grew closer the farther they went. Stacks of boulders bracketed them on each side. The blue creatures stood on them to chip away at some of the rock in the sides of the chamber. Lying along the rocks were small bones about the size of the blue creatures.

A few Grundians monitored the work of the blue creatures. Whenever they slowed, the Grundians would whip them with stems of vines until they sped their work up again. One of the creatures had fallen from the stacks of rocks, but made no attempt to get up. A Grundian rushed over, whipping the creature with his vines. The creature moved at first, but then collapsed as if it had given up.

The Grundian threw down his vines, and started pummeling the creature with his fists. The strength of the giant coupled with the size of his hand was enough to kill it in a few blows, but the Grundian either wasn't aware or didn't care. He continued brutally hitting the creature until there wasn't much left resembling its original form. Tavarian closed his eyes to avoid staining his memory with such a sight. The soggy wet sounds and the crunching of bone painted a gruesome enough picture in his mind. Images of the broken body of the one of the Descenders flashed in his head. He tried to shake the memory and focus on the caves.

Tavarian followed Grack over to a cylindrical machine filled with rocks. Grack showed Tavarian a turn crank that had bent and broken loose from a rod coming out the side of the machine.

"Fix the grinder," said Grack.

Tavarian took the turn crank and examined it. The rod and the hollow part of the cylinder were frayed where the crank had broken out.

"I need to bring this machine to the forge, but would anyone be strong enough to carry it?" Tavarian asked, trying to manipulate Grack into carrying it. Grundians loved to show off their strength.

"Grack is strong enough—plenty strong." Grack wrapped his arms around the machine and lifted it, and started walking back toward the cave entrance. He brought it to a dark corner of one of the chambers. There, a metal fire pit lit up the stones bordering it in a circle. A pile of sticks and dark colored stones lay in one end of the pit.

Tavarian took a steel shaft nearby and poked at the fire, moving some of the stones down into the yellow flames at the bottom.

"Can you move that grinder down to the fire so the rod gets in there?" he asked.

Grack lowered the grinder into the fire.

"No! Not that side!" Tavarian motioned for him to pick it back up off the flames. Grack lifted it up with confusion in his eyes because he thought he'd been following the instructions perfectly.

"This part is the only piece that needs to be in the fire." Tavarian said, pointing at the rod.

Grack lowered it again, this time getting the rod into the fire.

"Wait! You're getting too much into the fire! Lift it up, please," Tavarian said.

Grack appeared even more confused.

"Lay it down where only this part is in the fire; the rest of it doesn't need to be in there. You can prop it up in the fire on the rod, so it's tilted like this." Tavarian used his hand for a visual demonstration. This time Grack got it right, for the most part. Tavarian put the end of the crank into the forge and waited for the parts to heat up.

Once both parts were glowing bright orange, Tavarian used a clamp to take the crank piece out of the fire and set it against a rock. He hammered the frayed end out until it was the same shape as the opening. Motioning for Grack to lift the machine upright, he took the crank over to the rod in the machine and set the crank onto it. Still red hot, he hammered the crank opening down onto the inserted rod to fuse them together. He kept the position for a moment while Grack held the grinder as it cooled.

The crank shaft was now welded into the grinder rod as one piece. Tavarian turned the crank, spinning two metal wheels inside that angled until they came together at the bottom. Grack picked up a handful of rocks and dropped them into the grinder, and then grabbed the crank and started turning it. The wheels inside began breaking up the rocks as he continued turning the crank. Dust and small pebbles from the rocks collected at the bottom of the grinder.

Grack wore an expression of true delight, as though a childlike soul lived underneath the rough brutish exterior.

"Gadunk did good," he said.

For the rest of the day, Tavarian sat and watched as a few of the Grundians took turns grinding the stones mined by the small creatures—the Grundians referred to them as Feriglens. Finally, the gloomy light of the sun faded, signaling it was time for lockdown and all prisoners had to return to the shack.

"I don't want to go back in there," Tavarian said. "They'll kill me because I'm helping you."

Grack lifted a palm to his pointed chin. "Gadunk can stay in the caves. Grack will find you a place."

Tavarian followed Grack through a smaller tunnel that led to the chamber where the Feriglens' quarters were in high-walled wooden stables. There were five small stables here; some full of Feriglens and some that were empty. Grack led Tavarian into one of the empty stables, and closed and latched the door behind him.

Even with nothing but dirt and rock to sleep on, it was better than getting beaten by the other prisoners. The yellow eyes of Feriglens in the next stable peered at him through the cracks in the strong but poorly constructed walls. All night there were echoing sounds of Grundians arguing and fighting with one another.

Tavarian wished he could get to sleep and dream of Lirah, but his dreams of late had been anything but peaceful. They were completely chaotic, replaying several days' events scrambled together. What was Lirah's life like now? Who could she be hanging out with since he and Dexius had left? If only he still had the curl of her hair, just to touch the silky strands once more.

CHAPTER 6

FOR THE NEXT few weeks, several Grundians came to retrieve Tavarian from his stable for various jobs. He fixed doors, floors, and some mechanical issues in their stolen machines. The Grundians fought over who could use him next. Grunch stepped in and took Tavarian to stay in a small room inside the Grundian fortress at night. It was one of the few rooms—if not the only one—in the fortress that latched on the outside.

Though they kept him locked in the room at night, Grunch allowed Tavarian mostly free reign of Grunda during the day, though guards still followed him wherever he went because they didn't trust him enough to be completely unsupervised. He could build anything he wanted as long as it would help the Grundians.

Like most of his inventions, some of them were a success while others were not. One of his least successful creations, a long flexible beam with posts on each end, was intended to keep birds away from the seeds in the garden. He copied the tension mechanics of the flame-haired girl's crossbow, using one of the posts as the catch that held a taut rope made of vines. If you turned the post, it released the pressure and allowed the beam to swing out when birds got too close to the crops to scare them off. Though the device worked, it proved far less efficient than simply running at the birds to scare them off.

Many of the Grundians insisted that the invention was a big improvement—they enjoyed scaring the birds off much more with this method. The beam swung out so fast that it occasionally hit some of the birds before they could fly away. This made the Grundians love it even more.

His next project involved digging holes near the wooded area between the town and the brook. The Grundians liked the idea for trapping new tregs because they needed to refill their stock. Tavarian hoped that if it worked, it would keep the Grundians from raiding a nearby town to steal some. To dig the holes, the Grundians had brought Tamken, Reva, Varga, and Selas.

"They need to be deeper!" Tavarian yelled as Tamken and Reva stopped digging.

"This is plenty deep for tregs, " Reva said.

"We may catch something even bigger, so make them deeper," said Tavarian.

"Gadunk said deeper!" commanded a Grundian named Rek.

Though not intent on revenge, Tavarian could not help but relish standing over those who beat and spit on him, staying in the shade while they worked. They deserved this.

Whenever the Grundians weren't watching, the workers would spit in Tavarian's direction while he stood by and watched. Once the holes were dug, they laid small limbs and foliage over the holes to camouflage them. Seeds and dried grasses that tregs like to eat were placed on the leaves covering the pits.

At the end of the day, Tavarian liked to go up to the battlement of the small fortress to enjoy the view over Grunda and the land beyond. Oddly enough, he had gained more respect in this place than he ever had in Rethia. He had a chance to finally do what he always wanted—working as a carpenter, and not only building the same old things, but also trying to create something new and better. He wouldn't have been able to do that in Rethia, but here he could build whatever he wanted, and they loved him for it. If only Lirah could see him now.

He even had assistants to help him. They despised him, but they would have to do it regardless. At this point, why even try to escape? He may be a prisoner here technically, but he had found a civilization. If what Marvus told him turned out to be true—that rokenstones are too dangerous to mess with—maybe this wasn't too bad of an alternative.

The next morning, as Tavarian hammered nails into some new fence posts, a group of five Grundians approached from the countryside in the distance. They had some new people with them. When they came inside the gates, they shoved the three captives to the ground—two males and a female. One of the males was short and stocky, and the female was short and lean. The other male was tall with a solid build and had dusty blond hair. He looked very familiar. Tavarian froze, his heart beating heavy in his chest. He couldn't believe it . . . Dexius! He thought Dexius had died in the fall from the mountain.

He tried to position himself around the fence where Dexius wouldn't see his face, unsure what may happen if Dexius recognized him. Tavarian continued working on the fence, wondering where Dexius had been all this time.

As the day wore on uneventfully, the gray clouds darkened to black with a light pinkish hue. The Grundians took Tavarian back to the fortress.

"I think I'll work in the cave tomorrow, if that's ok," he told Plop.

"What is there to do in the caves?" Plop asked.

"There was something Grack needed," he said.

"You don't work for Grack!" said Plop. "You work for Grunch."

"Okay, is there anything Grunch needs done in here?"

"We'll check tomorrow," Plop said as he led Tavarian into the small room inside the fortress where he now slept.

Tavarian had another sleepless night as the fall from the mountain replayed over and over in his mind. He remembered calling out to see if anyone else had survived, but no one answered. Maybe Dexius didn't want to be found. He had planned to go off on his own anyway. Could any of the other Descenders still be alive?

As the obscured sun rose to light up the clouds again, the giants summoned Tavarian outside.

"We got more wood from last raid." Plop said.

"Build this walking way you talked about," said Grunch.

"Oh, right now?" Tavarian asked.

"Yes, now!" shouted Grunch as he took the club from its resting place on his shoulder.

His voice made Tavarian tremble. Grunch could crush him with little effort. His massive club made from the roots and trunk of a tree was intimidating enough by itself.

"I'll put together a piece of fence and use it to trace out the path," he said.

Tavarian sawed a piece from a wooden beam, and then used it to measure off more pieces of the same size. He then cut some smaller pieces for the vertical parts of the fencing. Once he had everything he needed, he nailed the wood pieces together into a section of fence. He used that to mark off in the dirt where each post would need to go for assembling the fence sections together.

"Gadunk, make more fence," said Plop.

"I'm just using this one to measure," he said.

"Make more and we'll copy," Plop said.

Tavarian returned to the stack of lumber and measured out places to cut to be as close to the other fence section as possible. When he was finished with the second section, a Grundian named Griz went to the worker shack and brought out some of the people from inside.

"Get the new kips!" Plop shouted. "Gotta break them in!"

Griz took the prisoners back and came out with the three new captives, which included Dexius. He tossed each prisoner onto the dirt as he brought them out one at a time.

"Gadunk needs you to build fences," Griz told them.

Tavarian starting walking toward the brook side of the town to mark the start of the fence sections. He hadn't gotten far before a familiar voice caught his attention.

"Tav? Is that you?" said Dexius.

Tavarian should have walked away sooner. He stopped and almost started walking again, but instead, he made the mistake of turning around.

"Ha! I can't believe of all people, you survived."

"I . . . I thought you—" Tavarian started, interrupted by the slap of vines whipping Dexius, who hunched over, shocked from the stinging blow.

"Get to work!" Griz said.

"What work?" Dexius said.

"The work Gadunk needs."

"Who's Gadunk?" Dexius asked.

Griz pointed at Tavarian. "That's Gadunk."

"Tavarian?" Dexius wondered.

"No! Gadunk, tell him what you need done," Griz ordered.

It embarrassed Tavarian a bit, ordering Dexius to do this. "Let's get you two sawing. You do the measuring, and you, Dex, start hammering."

"I'm not working for you," Dexius said.

"Dex, I gave you the easiest job," Tavarian said.

Griz hit Dexius a few times with his stick, making Tavarian want to turn away. Ordinarily, he would have enjoyed having this position of power over Dexius. He always wished one day Dexius would get punished, but not like this. One way or another, Dexius's selfish stubbornness would not last long in this place.

Tavarian had been beaten by the prisoners who were supposed to be his companions, but the Grundians were far more dangerous. They could easily kill a person if they did not hold back their strength enough. Even though the prisoners had not treated him well, none of them deserved to be here, especially not little Darby.

"Tell Gadunk you are sorry and that you will do what he says," Griz told Dexius.

"It's okay." Tavarian objected.

"Tell him!" said Griz.

"Sorry." Dexius mumbled.

"No, crawl over there and tell him."

After a moment of hesitation, Dexius began crawling toward Tavarian.

"It's fine. I need to get started on this," said Tavarian.

"Don't be weak, Gadunk," Griz said.

"Sorry . . . Gadunk?" Dexius said. "I'll do the hammering."

"Thank you," said Tavarian. He began carrying the fence section toward the other end of the town.

"You need to be strong like us, Gadunk," said Griz.

Tavarian marked where the posts needed to be placed as Dexius went over to where the others were building more fence sections. One of the Grundians reached over the fence and opened the gate for Tavarian.

While he worked on the measurements, thoughts of Dexius's arrival distracted him. As much as he disliked him, he didn't want Dexius whipped every day. He'd have to figure out what to do soon. Tavarian finished marking everything and headed toward the cave.

"What you doing, Gadunk?" Plop asked as he walked by.

"I was going to check if there's anything in the mines we could use for the fencing," Tavarian said.

"Don't let Grack get you to do more work. Tell him you'll talk to Grunch if he says anything," Plop said.

"Okay, I'll tell him."

Tavarian walked through the caves and found Grack grinding some stones. "You have any more work for me?" he asked.

"Plenty of work—you don't come back in the caves anymore."

"Plop keeps telling me not to come in here," Tavarian said. "He said that I'm his worker now."

"That's not right. You help all Grundians."

"I had to come in here when he wasn't looking," Tavarian said. "He said if I work for you, he's going to beat you and me both."

Grack roared with laughter. "Plop can't beat me."

"Well, he can beat me, so if you want me to be able to get down here again, you'll have to ask him or something," Tavarian said.

"Grack not asking Plop! I tell him with fists." He displayed his closed fists, demonstrating how he would use them on Plop.

"I better go back and finish this fence work he's making me do. Can I take one of these blades?"

"No, leave blades here," said Grack.

"Can I throw one? Watch this," Tavarian said. "I've been practicing with some metal scraps."

Tavarian picked up a large blade and threw it into a wooden wall nearby. It glanced off the wall and hit the ground. He walked over and picked up the blade from the ground.

"What you doing?" Grack asked.

"It was supposed to stick in the wall like this." Tavarian stabbed the blade into the wall and left it stuck in the wood.

Grack laughed. "Gadunk need more practice!"

Tavarian started to leave, hoping that Grack would forget about the blade stuck in the wall, since it happened to be the outside of one of the Feriglens' stables.

"I'll take care of Plop after work's over," Grack said.

Tavarian made his way out of the caves. He trudged over to where Plop stood watching Dexius and the others continue building a section of fence.

"I'm looking for Grunch," Tavarian announced.

"Grunch ain't here," replied Plop.

"Oh, where's he at?" said Tavarian.

"Grunch's raiding."

Tavarian shuddered at what could be happening to the unfortunate people of the town they were raiding. Grunch's club often returned with a fresh coat of gore.

"Grack wanted me to work in the caves again and I told him I work for you and Grunch," Tavarian said. "But he said he's going to find you after work and beat you up."

"That's what Grack thinks?" said Plop, chuckling. "Grack'll be surprised then!"

Plop went inside the fortress and a few moments later, Tavarian snuck in behind him. Tiptoeing across the creaky wooden floor, he headed toward Grunch's room on the other side of the fort. There were voices coming from a room ahead. Some of the rooms had their doors closed, but others did not. Plop opened one of the doors and went inside the room.

As he approached the first set of doorways on each side of the hallway, Tavarian moved with his back against the wall. Maintaining sight on the room across from him, he made sure he remained hidden. Once he got to the doorframe, he peeked around the corner, but saw no one inside.

Tavarian glanced back at the room across from him once more, and then quickly shuffled past the doorway. He shifted his weight as he moved so as not to put too much pressure down on one foot at a time. He couldn't risk making the wooden floor give away his presence.

"Where's my knuckle rings?" Plop said to someone.

"I don't keep up with your things," said a low female voice as Tavarian crept across the floor to the next set of doorways. Rattling and clunking, Plop rummaged through the room facing him. The female Grundian sat on the bed watching Plop. Tavarian would have to enter her line of sight to peek into the doorway next to him.

While she watched Plop throwing junk around the room, Tavarian slid over to the doorframe beside him and slowly peeked around the corner. To his surprise, a Grundian stood right at the door. He backed away so suddenly that he tripped over his own foot and fell to the floor.

"Hey! Who's out there making noise? We're trying to think over here!" said the female Grundian as she slammed the door shut.

Tavarian got up, relieved he hadn't been caught. He moved closer to the wall with the shut door. The Grundian faced the doorway, using a small stick in his ear as if cleaning something out of it. Tavarian couldn't get past without him noticing. He waited out of sight. Each minute felt like an hour as Tavarian watched, hoping the Grundian would turn around.

Finally, the Grundian finished his ear maintenance and moved farther into the chamber. Tavarian eased by the doorway, heading for Grunch's chambers. As he approached the room at the end of the hall, the Grundian behind him came bounding out of his room. Plop's door swung open, and the female came into the hallway. Tavarian quickly moved into Grunch's room.

"Stop all that noise!" she said from the hallway to the Grundian that had exited his room. Tavarian frantically searched for his bag in Grunch's chamber as the commotion continued in the hall. Peering underneath the bed, he found no satchel like his own. He pulled several other bags and boxes out of the way, but still saw nothing of his. The bag had been there when he fixed Grunch's bed. Tavarian opened the wooden chests near the bed, but couldn't find it anywhere.

On the floor on the other side of the bed lay his blanket. Tavarian grabbed it, moving to the piles of junk on the shelves. After searching through it, he found the flekstone Valea had given him. He put the flekstone into his pocket and then he saw it—amid a group of necklaces, Lirah's white hair hung from a long nail. As soon as he touched the silky strands, he remembered her kiss the night before he descended the mountain. Tavarian longed to be back in that moment again.

What did Grunch want with her hair? Placing it into his pocket, his heart ached, thinking about how he had almost lost it.

The sword hilt he found in Muloken was still mounted on the wall. Tavarian wanted to take it, but had nothing to carry it in, so it was too much of a risk for now. He peeked back into the hallway and the Grundians still stood there arguing. He was trapped.

Moving back inside the room, Tavarian searched for anything that would make a good hiding place if he needed one. A bunch of clothes hung from a rope near the back of the room. He could stand behind them if someone came into the room. Tavarian pushed through the clothes, and was surprised to find another door.

As he opened the door, he saw three walls with piles of what appeared to be robes as well as more boxes and bags, one of which was his satchel. Tavarian took his bag and inspected it. Someone had burned the word *Gadunk* into the material. Tavarian groaned. Now that name would follow him forever. He opened the satchel, finding his hammer and saw inside.

Tavarian closed the closet door and pushed the hanging clothes back in place. He grabbed the sword hilt from the wall—there was no turning back now. With the hilt missing from the wall, Grunch would suspect he had taken it.

Tavarian waited nervously until the argument finished. Soon enough, the male Grundian walked down the hallway and left the fort. The female Grundian moved back into Plop's chamber, and shut the door again. Carefully, Tavarian stepped through the hallway. He passed Plop's chamber and other rooms that appeared empty.

"I'm ready for Grack now!" Plop's door opened as he burst out of the room.

Tavarian ran into one of the empty rooms to hide. Shaking the floor as he ran through the hall, Plop went by him and out the main door. Once he was sure that Plop was out of sight, Tavarian crept from the room. Passing by the main door, he approached his own tiny room.

Tavarian lifted the heavy wooden latch on the outside and entered the room, quickly tucking his bag under the bed. While listening for any further activity in the fort, he moved out and latched the door back. The world outside grew dark as Tavarian checked on Dexius and the others.

If things went as he expected, he could tell Dexius his plan during the distraction.

Plop paced around the yard, hitting his fist into his other palm. Grack and a group of others appeared from the cave.

"You think Plop's afraid of you?" Plop shouted at Grack. He remained still, but Plop kept shouting. "What's Grack waiting for?"

"I'll take care of you after lockdown!" Grack said.

The Grundians were unpredictable. Tavarian would need to be adaptable to make this work. Dexius continued hammering, glancing at Tavarian from the corner of his eye.

Plop ran toward Grack, but Grack didn't move.

"If you think you can beat Plop down, let's go!" Plop declared. "If not, go back in the cave where you belong."

Grack stared at Plop, still not moving.

Tavarian waited for this to play out. Would the lockdown or the fight happen first? He wasn't sure which had the best chance of success. His mind went into overdrive, playing through both possibilities. He remained focused on Grack and Plop.

Something moved toward Tavarian. He noticed it too late as Dexius turned the distraction into a distraction of his own. He tackled Tavarian hard into the dirt. Dexius straddled him, attempting to land some punches to his face, but Tavarian rolled over, taking Dexius with him. Tavarian grabbed Dexius's arms as they wrestled on the ground. Tavarian had become much stronger since leaving Rethia—he had surpassed Dexius's strength.

Plop took a big swing at Grack, who ducked out of the way as Plop lost his balance and fell forward into the dirt. Grack began kicking him in the head. Through the blows, Plop grabbed Grack's leg and pulled him off. Plop stood up, taking another swing, but landed only a glancing blow to the side of Grack's head.

With all the ruckus, many Grundians came out of the caves to watch Plop and Grack fight. Workers tending the crops and feeding the tregs ceased what they were doing. The group working on the fences stopped to watch Dexius and Tavarian. More Grundians came out of the fortress and found Dexius and Tavarian wrestling, then became aware of Plop and Grack.

A group of Grundians approached from outside the fence. Some dragged bundles of lumber while others herded tregs into the gate—Grunch had returned from his raid.

"You're not working? Get the tregs to the pen!" one of the Grundians shouted to the prisoners nearby.

The workers moved away from Dexius and Tavarian, and ran over to move the stolen tregs into their new pen.

Grunch entered the gate. "Get these kips. If they want to beat each other and not work, go on and beat them down and end it." One of the Grundians grabbed both Dexius and Tavarian, and lifted them up, one in each hand. The Grundian stretched his hands apart as though ready to slam them into each other.

"Wait, that's Gadunk—put them down. Fight him, Gadunk!" Grunch shouted.

Plop and Grack traded blows. Plop swung fast but blindly while Grack took a more measured approach, making his shots count. Enraged, one of Plop's punches connected and sent Grack tumbling to the ground. Plop ran over and began kicking Grack as he lay on the ground. After a couple swift kicks from Plop, Grack knocked Plop off of him. Plop lost his balance and fell to the ground.

"Dex, stop." Tavarian whispered as they rolled on the ground. "You're ruining everything."

"You're a loser," Dexius replied. "I'm not working for you. I'm only doing what they make me do."

"Who cares about that?" Tavarian rasped. "We need to get out of here."

Dexius rolled on top again. He tried to pin Tavarian's arms so he couldn't stop his punches. As he lifted his lower body to gain leverage, Tavarian kicked Dexius off of him, launching to his feet. Dexius stood and threw another punch at Tavarian. Tavarian swiped Dexius's arm away and landed a punch to his cheek and nose.

Plop lay on the ground as Grack and two other Grundians kicked him. Swinging his fists wildly, Plop tried to fight them off. Grunch's attention turned from Tavarian to Plop.

"Get off of Plop! This ain't fighting time!" Grunch shouted as he ran over to them. "Get the kips back inside! It's past lockdown time!"

Grack and his friends backed away from Plop, who was now bloodied and bruised. Grunch pulled Plop to his feet. Grack and the others gathered up the workers, herding them into the shack.

On his hands and knees, Dexius seemed dazed from the blow to his nose. His eyes watered as he turned toward Tavarian, trying to ready himself to fend off the next attack. Tavarian rushed over and grabbed hold of Dexius and hoisted him up on his feet. His hold trapped one of Dexius's arms while the other tried reaching for Tavarian.

Tavarian jerked him to the side every time he tried to grab or swing at him. He walked Dexius toward the worker shack as the rest of the prisoners were being tossed inside by the Grundians.

"We should end that one," said one of the Grundians.

"No, let me have this one, I'll break him in," said Tavarian

The Grundians laughed.

"Gadunk gets tough," one of them said as Grunch and the others led Tavarian back into the fort to his tiny room.

CHAPTER 7

THE SKY DARKENED as the patch of light behind the clouds settled under the distant trees. The Grundians gathered outside around a bonfire with their usual loud reverie. They typically took a treg from the pen and one of the giants would knock it over the head with his large fists. Then they would roast it over a fire and eat it.

This night was no different. The Grundians drank their stolen rum. Talking and laughing, they told stories of their latest raid. Rummaging through all the goods they'd acquired, they tried to figure out what the kips used them for.

Tavarian forced himself to stay awake as things started to quiet down. Many of the Grundians were drunk and had fallen asleep on the ground. Some of them had come inside the fortress to sleep in their chambers.

Tavarian reached under his bed for his satchel. Thankfully, Grunch must have been too drunk to notice his missing wall decoration. Tavarian pulled out the saw and slid it between the crack of the door and the frame. Loud snoring from one of the rooms across the hall broke up the otherwise silent darkness.

The saw blade found the wooden door latch. Tavarian started a small cut in the latch as he prepared to begin. As the sawing began, it made a jarring sound, but as he drew deeper into the wood, it turned into a nice fast vibration.

He timed his sawing to the snoring coming down the hall. The sounds were quite similar as they made a grinding harmony together. Once the blade had reached the end, and the last splintering piece of wood was cut through, the latch shifted and fell to the floor with a clunk.

The rhythmic snoring stopped for a moment. Tavarian froze—his own breathing was deafening in the quiet. Finally, the snoring resumed. Exhaling a sigh of relief, Tavarian placed the saw back in the bag as he swung it around his shoulder.

Pushing on the door as quietly as he could, he snuck into the dark hall. Prying up the latch on the main door made it scrape and squeak against the doorframe. When he made it outside, the darkness was broken only by the last glowing embers of the fire.

Several Grundians lay around the remains of the fire—some were flat on the ground while others were propped up against objects laying in the dirt. Being careful where he walked, Tavarian took a wide path around the Grundians toward the prisoner shack.

After lifting the large wooden latch, Tavarian silently opened the door.

"Guys . . . " he whispered, "they're all asleep—let's go."

He could see only darkness in the shack except for someone's foot caught by the ember light from outside.

He reached out to shake the foot, and they stirred. "Wha—who's there?"

More of them began to move inside the shack.

"Keep your voice down," Tavarian whispered.

"Grab him!" someone in the back said. "It's Gadunk!"

Tavarian moved back from the doorway as they piled in around him. "Listen, this is our chance to escape; they are asleep."

"I'd rather wring your neck," said Varga.

"We can't climb the fence," said Cavaros. "And we can't open that gate."

"I've got that taken care of—c'mon!" Tavarian said.

"Why would we trust you?" said Dalson.

"Yeah, why don't you come in here for a while, Tav?" Dexius teased.

"Okay, fine, stay if you want," Tavarian said. "I'll leave the door open. It's your choice."

As he turned to leave, something brushed against his arm. Darby had come out of the shack. She wanted to leave this place.

"Darby! Come back in here!" Reva shrieked.

"We can't protect you if you leave us!" Cavaros said.

"If Darby is going, then I'm going," Marvus said.

Tavarian started toward the fence, creeping past the sleeping Grundians as Darby followed. He made it past the treg pen and to the outside gate. Using the hidden lever on the latch, he released it and opened the gate. He let Darby through as he held it open. Marvus and all the prisoners were now coming across the field toward them.

The sound of all the footsteps awakened one of the Grundians. He got up and rubbed his eyes as all the prisoners ran across the grounds in front of him. "Get up! The kips are out!"

Several of the Grundians groggily got to their feet. Tavarian ran back to the garden to the bird chasers he had built.

As the rest of the prisoners made it to the small farm near the treg pens, Tavarian triggered the release. The metal beams sprung out, slamming hard into the rampaging group of Grundians, tripping the ones in front. The Grundians behind them fell over their large falling bodies, while others had time to change course.

Running to the gate, Tavarian realized that everyone had scattered in different directions. Darby stood at the gate waiting for him.

"Guys, this way!" He pointed toward the brook.

The prisoners redirected to the brook. The Grundians appeared slow and awkward when they ran, but had such huge strides, they covered ground quickly.

Tavarian led Darby and the rest past the small, wooded area as the Grundians gained on them. They ran past the deep holes dug to trap tregs. Fortunately, the prisoners remembered where the camouflaged traps were since they had spent so much time and effort digging them. The Grundians, however, did not. The rest of the Grundians chasing them fell through the traps one by one. Even the ones behind those piled into the holes in the ground were unable to stop their momentum. The group continued running along the edge of the brook as it curved away from Grunda.

They ran until they were out of breath. No sound of any Grundians running after them remained. Taking a rest, Cavaros leaned against the peeling bark of an old tree.

"Was this . . ." Cavaros attempted to catch his breath. "Was this your plan all along?"

"Not exactly," said Tavarian, kneeling in the spongy grass. "It took me a while to find a way to deal with all the variables, and then the timing had to be right."

"You're more capable than I gave you credit for," Cavaros said. "Please accept my apology."

"We thought you had betrayed us." Reva sat down in the soft grass, "I'm sorry. Tavarian, we are in your debt."

"Why didn't you tell us?" Selas wondered.

"Why? I tried to," Tavarian said, "but you wouldn't listen, and I didn't want to get beaten up again."

"I guess that's fair," said Varga.

"Thank you," said Reva.

"Yes, thank you, Tavarian," Cavaros said.

"I'm just glad we all got out alive," Tavarian stated.

As their heavy breaths quieted, the sounds of the burbling stream brought some tranquility to a chaotic night. The swooshing of the wind through the leaves reminded Tavarian that the world outside Grunda could be beautiful. He laid his head in the grass, amazed at how good it felt to be free again.

"We're going to head back to Delancin," said Cavaros as he tightened the straps of his shoes, "Selas, Tamken, and I will help fortify against any future Grundian raids."

"We know more about them now. That should help," Selas said.

"Dalson and I will be heading back to Samavere," said Reva. "You can come with us, Darby. You'll have a place with my family."

Darby's eyes moved toward her, but she said nothing.

"What about you, Marvus?" said Cavaros.

Marvus swept his sweaty hair from his eyes. "I think I'm leaving these lands and heading north," he said. "Get far out of the range of these Grundians."

"There are more Grundian camps to the south." Cavaros scratched the hair on his chin. "For all we know, there could be Grundians up north as well."

Marvus stared toward the line of trees on the horizon. "I'll take that chance."

"And you three new folks?" Cavaros crossed his arms as he faced Dexius and the two people who were brought into Grunda with him. "You have a place to go back to?"

"No," said the girl. "Before the Grundians found us, we were looking for a place to settle."

"Come with us." Cavaros extended his hand toward them. "We'll find work for you in Delancin. It's a small town, but it's growing, despite the Grundians."

"We'll take you up on that," said the boy as the girl put her arms around him.

"Dexius?" Cavaros raised his bushy eyebrows. Anxious to get moving, Tavarian contemplated leaving. He cared little about where Dexius would choose to go, but it seemed impolite to everyone for him to walk away right now.

Dexius lifted his hands and shrugged. "I'm not sure what I'm going to do yet, but the offer is appreciated."

Darby sat playing with the grass, eyeing each person as they spoke. Even through the smoky dirt smeared across her cheeks, she bore the sweetest face a person could have. She was the only one Tavarian would miss as they went their separate ways.

"I wish all of you well, if we ever meet again, may it be under much better circumstances," said Cavaros. "If any of you end up in Delancin, come visit."

Reva adjusted her worn dress, moving the many rips and tears to more strategic locations. "Same goes for you all in Samavere."

"Tavarian, if you don't have a place to go, we would be honored to have you." Cavaros saluted with a hand across his chest. "We'll make sure you get a hero's welcome in Delancin."

A chill went through Tavarian. It was everything he thought he wanted. He shouldn't forsake Rethia, but that wasn't really it. It was Lirah—the chance to be her hero overshadowed anything else. "Thank you, but I must get to Strakenbridge," he said.

"Very well." Cavaros took a deep breath as if finally relishing the sweet air of freedom. "Keep following this side of the stream until you reach Vallohal River," he said. "From there, follow the river until you come to the bridge.

Marvus gently slapped Tavarian on the shoulder as he passed by. "Don't waste your time on rokenstones."

Tavarian hesitated. "I'll keep that in mind."

"Come with us, Darby." Reva opened her hand, welcoming her to take it.

Darby turned to Tavarian and then back to Reva as if not wanting to leave either of them.

"They protected you, Darby. You should go with them," Tavarian said, hoping to make it easier on her.

Darby glanced at Tavarian again, her lower lip trembling.

"You coming, Darby?" Reva crouched to look Darby in the eye, but Darby turned to Tavarian. With her head down, she walked toward him.

Reva came over and took Darby's hand, leading her away from Tavarian. She glanced up at Reva and then toward Dalson. Pulling her hand loose from Reva's, she ran back to Tavarian.

Reva walked back over to Darby, kneeling again to get eye level with her. "I thought of you as a daughter ever since you were brought to Grunda. I always wanted to get you out of there and raise you as my own."

Reva gave her a hug, and Darby wrapped one arm around her in return. Reva took her hand again, but Darby pulled away, tears now coming down her cheeks.

"I guess she likes you, Tavarian," said Reva.

"Darby, I can't take care of anyone," Tavarian told her. "I can barely take care of myself."

Darby did not budge. Dejected, Reva forced a smile.

"I suppose we only remind her of the worst part of her life. She needs a new start. Take care of her, Tavarian. Take her with you to Strakenbridge," said Reva. "I'm sure you'll find a good home for her there."

As the group separated, Tavarian and Darby stood looking at the path ahead as the brook wound back and forth into the distance. Dexius rubbed his knuckles as he watched the others head in different directions.

"You waiting until everyone is out of sight so you can hit me again?" Tavarian said.

"No, just thinking," Dexius replied.

"You find any rokenstones yet?" Tavarian asked.

Dexius exhaled loudly. "What do you think?"

"Me either."

"Where was it you were going?"

"Strakenbridge," said Tavarian. "There are people taking refuge there, so it must be a big city. Maybe they have some information on the rokenstones."

"I've heard of it," Dexius said. "I was thinking about going there eventually."

Tavarian gritted his teeth. Lirah's voice echoed in his head. She wanted them to stay together. "I suppose we could both go there if you want to. But if you try to hit me again . . ."

Dexius grinned. "As long as I don't have to take orders from Gadunk."

Tavarian rolled his eyes as he turned and began walking. The three of them tread along the banks of the brook. The brook widened as they got farther along, and the water moved faster. Tavarian stopped to fill his container with water, and they each stopped and had a drink before moving further on. Tavarian was so relieved to have his satchel and all of its contents with him again.

"I thought you were dead," Tavarian said to break up the awkward silence.

"I thought *you* were," said Dexius. "How did you make it?"

"I barely remember what happened," said Tavarian. "I slid down the mountainside part of the way, and ended up landing in a tree. Eventually, I found the road again. What happened with you?"

"Woke up on a tiny ledge," Dexius said. "I didn't have anywhere to go so I tried to climb down."

"Tried?"

"Fell," Dexius said, "but I landed on some rocks that weren't too far down."

"I called out to everyone for a while, but no one ever answered."

"I think I was knocked out for a while."

"I wonder if anyone else made it."

"I don't think so. I found Pilo, Veras, and Tiagra—they were . . . dead."

"Oh . . . I wish they could have been here with us," Tavarian said.

Even though Tavarian had known that the others must have died, the confirmation hit hard. It could have just as easily been him. He came so close to the end of it all. Shuddering, he tried to focus on something else. Tavarian hoped the Feriglens in the mine could use the knife he stuck into the outside wall of one of the stables. Maybe they could cut through the locking board and make an escape.

A patch of trees away from the brook made a nice place to camp because it was hidden from the sight of other travelers. Tavarian had only one blanket now—the three of them used it as a pillow. Tavarian slept off and on until the light from the sun penetrated the swirling mix of clouds above. Eventually, the bright sunlight made it impossible to sleep.

They went down to the brook, washing away the stench of Grunda. They may not have had any food, but they had plenty of water. They drank enough to make their stomachs a bit less empty.

As they hiked across the countryside, Dexius seemed intent on getting Darby to talk. He tried showing her how fast he could run, but mostly just tired himself out. He talked about how well they could hunt and live off the land. She watched him as he talked, appearing to be listening, but never commenting.

Dexius tried to display his jumping abilities, showing how far he could jump, but he landed wrong and fell on his face. Darby covered her mouth as her eyes squinted and her head shook.

"Are you laughing?" Dexius asked.

Tavarian chuckled. "I think she is."

"Well, now we know what makes her laugh," said Dexius, now laughing too.

"Yeah, keep hurting yourself, Dex," Tavarian joked. "It's hilarious."

They continued through fields of tall grass sloping over a group of hills. Bright red wildflowers bloomed on a rise near the banks of the brook. As they reached the last hill, clusters of red, white, and gold flowers filled the meadow stretching out before them.

Darby exposed the dimples in her cheeks as she beamed over the bright, colorful landscape. It was the first time she had let her smile show. Her weary, pained eyes lit up. Moments like this made Tavarian forget all the troubles and suffering that existed. For a moment, he didn't feel so out of place. He belonged. They journeyed toward hope and beyond that . . . glory.

Dexius surprised him by doing so well with Darby. With her around, he became a normal person. Along the way, Dexius sometimes ran off to fetch a flower with a new shade of color to show Darby, and she would usually take it from his hand and inspect it. Dexius seemed addicted to making her smile. Tavarian enjoyed seeing her happy too, but he wished he knew how other than copying what Dexius did.

Regardless, she stayed closest to Tavarian. What had he done to deserve her trust? Whatever it was, he felt honored to have it, vowing to never do anything to break it.

Darkness fell over the landscape and the sparkling bands of glowing insects returned to crisscross the skies. They came across the borders of a thick forest and made their camp under a group of trees. The evening rolled on quietly. It had been a good day. Songs of night birds and insects lulled them into a peaceful sleep.

A sharp sting awakened Tavarian as he suddenly stirred. There were creatures standing over him, large and furry with big round black eyes. Bushy, unkempt hair covered the heads of the creatures. They poked at Tavarian with gnarled sticks sharpened to points.

Darby and Dexius woke up, slowly recognizing that they were surrounded.

"What are you doing in our woods?" said one, still holding the weapon to Tavarian's chest.

"I—I didn't know these were your woods," said Tavarian.

"We just stopped here to sleep. We were about to move on," Dexius stated.

"They don't appear to be crazed," said another of the creatures.

"It doesn't matter; we can't let them go. They could return," the first one said.

"We won't come back," said Tavarian. "If we had known this was your territory, we wouldn't have stayed here."

"They appear to be rational, Kamikal. I don't think they have been affected," said the second one.

"I'm not taking any chances," said Kamikal. He poked Tavarian again with the sharp stick.

"Ow!" yelped Tavarian. "What do you want me to do?"

"I'm not sure yet," Kamikal said. "We'll have to keep you until we can be sure."

"Be sure of what?" Dexius said.

"Take them back to the burrows," Kamikal ordered.

Tavarian, Dexius, and Darby were pulled onto their feet and led deeper into the woods. They walked at the ends of pointed sticks until reaching an enormous old tree. Some of the tree's roots started above ground and twisted erratically around one another before burying themselves beneath the moss-covered dirt.

A deep burrow appeared among the roots, and the creatures crawled into it. One of them picked Darby up and she began kicking violently. "This little one has a lot of fight," said the creature as it helped the other restrain Darby and carry her into the hole that led beneath the tree roots.

He couldn't allow this. She had trusted him more than anyone to take care of her and protect her. An uncommon rage burst through Tavarian's fears, doubts, and general self-preservation. He spun around, grabbing the sharpened tree limb that had been poking his back. The creature holding it shoved him to the ground against the roots of the old tree. Two of the furry creatures lifted him to his feet, surrounding him with their spears.

Dexius and Tavarian were prodded to climb down the hole by a ladder of roots. The creatures led them into a dark tunnel until they reached a larger chamber. Several more creatures sat around an amber-colored crystal formation rising out of the floor of the chamber.

They were surrounded by root limbs of all sizes. The roots reached through the chamber and continued into the ground beneath.

"We found these intruders in our woods," Kamikal announced.

A female sat on a chair made of tree limbs and dried mud. White flowers decorated her mass of grayish green hair.

"And you brought them here?" she said.

"So you could decide what to do with them," said Kamikal.

"This is your task, Kamikal. I appointed you to defend the woods so that I can attend to other matters."

"Makilee, I only brought them because we disagreed among ourselves on what to do with them," Kamikal said. "I would have killed them, but my fellow huntsmen did not believe they were infected."

"So, kill them if you like," Makilee said, "but it seems it is *you* who has doubts."

"Wait, don't kill us!" Tavarian started.

"We were just passing through," said Dexius. "We didn't know these woods were claimed."

"Where do you come from?" Makilee asked.

"From Rethia." Tavarian said.

"Rethia . . ." Makilee propped up the side of her face with a gnarled fist. "I have not heard of such a place, but we are new to this land."

"If you are new here," Dexius asserted, "then what claim do you have on these woods?"

"There was no one here when we came, so we took them," said Kamikal.

Makilee pounded her fist on the knotted armrest of her moss-covered throne. "We were driven from our birthland! We needed a new home and found this place." Her voice began to calm. "It's not much, but it reminds us of home."

"We will not be driven out again!" Kamikal pressed his spear to Dexius's chest.

Dexius's face contorted in discomfort. "We don't want to drive you out. We only want you to let us go so that we can be on our way."

"What drove you out of your home?" Tavarian hoped to distract Kamikal, if nothing else.

Makilee's chest heaved as she exhaled a deep breath. "The Whisperers . . ."

"Whisperers?" Tavarian squinted his eyes. "What do you mean?"

Kamikal lowered his spear, backing away from Dexius to give Makilee a clear view of them both.

"Dark spirits, wraiths." Deep wrinkles formed around Makilee's eyes as her face tightened. "The Whisperers lurk just beyond the light . . . in the shadows. They call to you, command you. They plant seeds of corruption that bloom within your mind."

Tavarian hardly blinked as he stared back at her. "And they threw you out?"

"The Whisperers turned the creatures of the woods against us; they turned us against each other," Makilee's mouth drooped, making her face look longer. "We fought many battles until we were all that was left of our dray. Our birthland was destroyed. The spirits of the trees had left the forest. There was nothing to go back to."

Dexius cocked his head. "Spirits?"

"What do you mean the spirits had left?" Tavarian softly inquired.

Makilee leaned her head back against the seat. "The trees changed, corrupted with rot and decay." She closed her eyes. "What was once green has turned to death."

Tavarian's eyes opened wider. "I've seen a place like that. Do you know a place called Muloken?"

Kamikal ground the end of his spear into the dirt. "We do not."

"All the plants rotted and died there too," said Tavarian. "There were writings on the walls inside one of the houses. It said something like 'Beware . . . Beware The Hollow.'"

Makilee's features twisted. "Do not utter the cursed name!" she erupted. "Only those crazed and corrupted, screeching and moaning as they killed and scarred our dray have spoken of that place!"

"What place?" Dexius turned toward Tavarian.

"Take them away from here, Kamikal! Take them away at once! I never what to hear it again!" Makilee commanded.

The huntsmen drew their spears, shoving them toward the entrance of the burrow.

They were led outside and to the edge of the woods.

Kamikal sneered. "Do not come back through here again. We will kill you on sight."

Tavarian, Dexius, and Darby walked around the edge of the forest, trying to get back to the brook they had been following.

"What was that about?" Dexius said. "You're not good at making friends. It's no wonder you don't have any."

"I have friends," Tavarian said.

"Well, something you said upset them. You should let me do the talking next time."

"Oh, because everyone loves you so much?"

"The only reason some don't like me is because they're jealous that I do things better than them."

Tavarian laughed. "That's what you think?"

"It's true."

"Is that how you excuse your behavior?"

"I don't need an excuse."

"The fact that so many people don't like you around says otherwise. If you were as great as you think you are, people may actually want to be around you."

"I'm not taking advice from a loser like you."

They walked in silence toward the brook. Tavarian hated that Dexius's words still had any effect on him, but he could not think about anything else. A loser—is that how most people in Rethia thought of him? Someone who would never fit in? A joke to be laughed at? But he had been chosen as a Descender—they couldn't deny that.

Darby grabbed his hand and held on as they walked. She turned to Dexius and pulled Tavarian's arm, leading them closer. Tavarian resisted moving toward Dexius, but she persisted until he relented. Whatever she had in mind, he didn't want to disappoint her.

Darby grabbed Dexius's arm with her other hand so the three of them were walking linked together. It felt silly, like something children would do, but she wanted to be friends with both of them. Did he have to share every friend he made with Dexius? Either way, Tavarian didn't want to be the one causing a problem.

Dexius playfully lifted her arm, pulling her off the ground. Tavarian did the same with her other arm and they began swinging her back and forth over the grass. She giggled as they swung her higher. Tavarian couldn't help but forget his strife with Dexius, if just for a moment.

As they passed under a towering nut-bearing tree, they found the winding brook again. Dexius picked one of the nuts from the ground and peeled its rubbery cover. He popped it on his mouth and started to chew.

Tavarian found one and tried it as well. Soft to the teeth, but not satisfying to eat. They had a weak taste, but at least they didn't taste bad.

Darby ran off toward the brook, prompting Dexius and Tavarian to go after her. She dug into the clay along the banks. As they approached, she showed them two white clumps of sandy rock as they shrugged in confusion. Motioning for Dexius to hold out the handful of nuts, she rubbed the two stones together over them. She did the same for the ones Tavarian had, covering the nuts in a flaky white powder.

After doing the same to her handful, she began eating. Tavarian tried one—the dust from the stones made the nuts gritty to eat, but it gave them a salty flavor, much better than before.

They ate enough to fill themselves, placing as many as they could carry in Tavarian's bag. Tavarian started alongside the brook again, hoping to find Vallohal River soon.

"Where are you going? Strakenbridge is that way." Dexius pointed in the opposite direction.

"What? No, this is the way we were going when we were following the brook," Tavarian declared.

"I'm a hunter. I have a good sense of direction. Yours was thrown off when we walked around the woods."

"I'm sure it's this way."

"You're going to be heading back toward the Grundians if you go that way."

"Or we will if we go your way."

"I'm right about this—trust me this one time."

Tavarian hesitated, but decided to follow Dexius to prove him wrong. Were they ever going to find anything along the brook? Trudging on, they crossed over the soft mossy ground. There were more trees here grouped into clusters and large growths out of the ground. Mushrooms, huge ones, blue and white, were scattered about over the landscape. Some were the same size as Darby.

"I told you!" said Dexius. "We didn't pass by these mushrooms on the way."

"I could have sworn it was the other way," Tavarian said. "I'm not sure how that happened."

"I told you that you wouldn't make it for a day out here without my help."

"Your help? You'd still be in Grunda right now if it weren't for me."

"I would have made it out myself if I had been there long enough," said Dexius. "How long were you there? Months?"

Darby let go of Dexius's hand and glared at him.

"Okay, Darby, fine—he gets credit for getting us out of Grunda," Dexius conceded.

It was the closest thing to an apology he would get from Dexius. As they walked through the mushrooms, Tavarian wondered if they could eat them. He decided not to take the chance since many mushrooms were poisonous.

As they passed the mushroom fields, there were many furred creatures in the distance ahead of them. They were tall, but had thin, frail bodies. Walking on four legs, they occasionally fed on the dark green moss covering the ground. As the three of them approached, the closest of them froze. Their eyes focused on them as they walked closer, and then all at once, they sprinted away, lightning fast.

Whenever they got close enough to more of them up ahead, the same series of events would occur. Eventually, all of them had run off from the path they were taking, and then they settled back into their moss eating spots as they got out of range.

"If I had a bow right now, we'd be eating good," Dexius said.

"You couldn't shoot them," said Tavarian, "They are way too fast."

"Doesn't matter how fast they are, I could hit them." Dexius said.

Tavarian wished he had a bow right now to prove Dexius wrong. He badly wanted Dexius to be exposed as a fraud. Even though no matter what happened, Dexius wouldn't admit it. He amused himself by imagining the excuse Dexius would have when he unable to hit these creatures.

As the day wore on, a light mist filled the air as they walked. A breeze blew through a line of trees along a small forest beside them as the water droplets floated with the wind. A roaring sounded head, but it was not the wind. A cascading waterfall came into view and the brook widened beyond it.

The waterfall reminded Tavarian of the falls on the mountain. The falling water here crashed into the drop below, sending ripples and foam through the stream. Is this what the bottom of the falls on the mountain was like? He never got a good look at them from the bottom of the mountain. The huge, shelled monster had blocked the way.

After standing on the banks in awe of the power of the rushing water, they started up the rise. A mass of water lay ahead of them on the horizon. Tavarian and Dexius picked up their pace, excited to get a closer view of this new discovery. Darby quickened her steps to stay beside Tavarian.

A wide, rapidly flowing river lay in front of them as they approached. This must be the river Cavaros mentioned, Vallohal River. It put the river in Rethia to shame. The thunderous sound of the water flow filled the air. There were forests on the other side in the distance and many trees lined the banks. White crested splashes formed around stones protruding from the water as they stirred along.

A clean, crisp fragrance traveled on the wind as it blew in from the river. Unfamiliar wildlife of all kinds wandered the shallow banks. There were nooks and crannies at the shoreline where the flow stopped and made for suitable drinking spots for the animals.

Small long-armed creatures with black and green fur swam downstream, and then dove under the water to appear upstream again. The thin, fast animals they had encountered earlier were here in abundance. Darby pointed as bright yellow fish jumped from the river and crashed back into the water. Birds with tails on their wings flew overhead and landed on the water. They floated along with the current, feeding on fish near the surface. As though all life in this world had been led here for a common goal, they all came here for this resource, while some were themselves a resource—a nexus of the life and death cycle revealed.

With the speed of the current, it would be unwise for anyone to attempt to cross. As they moved farther on, traversing this close to the water became a hindrance. Big moss-covered stones stacked along their path slowed them as they had to climb them to move forward. They moved back to the higher plains for an easier footing. Tavarian passed around his water container as they snacked on some of the tree nuts while they trudged on.

After hours of river, rocks, and trees, something new appeared in the distance. A group of tall towers stood above the trees across the river. Tavarian's pace increased as his interest grew. A long, sturdy bridge crossed over the wild currents to the other side. The other end of the bridge led to an enormous city in between the soaring towers, larger than any city Tavarian had ever imagined. If they welcomed the people of Muloken, they should welcome them too.

Clanging and racket, voices and shouts came from within. Excitedly, Tavarian stepped onto the bridge. Their footsteps clapped on the wood as they crossed over the water. A few people riding four legged creatures with horns passed by on the other side of the bridge. Tavarian steadied himself cautiously as they came, clunking and shaking the bridge as they went by.

The city itself seemed alive. People and other creatures walked, ran, and hopped in every direction on the brick covered roads between columns and rows of buildings of different shapes and sizes. A huge stone stood at the front of the road with an engraving that read, "STRAKENBRIDGE."

They were here at last.

CHAPTER 8

STRAKENBRIDGE DEFIED EVERYTHING Tavarian had imagined a city could be. Four towers reached into the sky while large white stone buildings surrounded them. Ahead, streets made of round stones stretched out beyond their sight. How could they have enough materials to build such a place? Strange beings passed by—some were abnormally tall and thin, while others walked on four legs. Awestruck, Tavarian gazed at everything around them.

He barely noticed a female with an unusually round head approaching them. "Authentic Lakama necklaces, only two vrupines!"

"No, thank you," said Tavarian.

"Please, we need money to take back to our village. We sell very beautiful necklaces for cheap to help support them. Only two vrupines—that's nothing," she said.

"What's a vrupine?" Tavarian puzzled.

"You know . . . coins . . . money," she said.

Tavarian searched her face for any kind of clue of what she meant. "I don't understand."

"You give me two coins; I give you a necklace," she retorted, beginning to lose patience.

Tavarian turned to Dexius, who glanced back blankly. "How do I get coins?"

"Work for them, steal them—I don't care." The woman flung her hand toward them.

"How do we work for them?" Tavarian inquired.

"Bah! If you don't want to buy, just say so! You are wasting my time!" She huffed and brushed past them.

The woman stopped to speak to another group of people, offering the same deal. Dexius grinned as though he enjoyed seeing Tavarian fail at another social encounter.

The stone buildings on either side of them were filled with windows. Flickering fires made them glow inside with pale orange light. Outside the buildings, smaller merchants peddled various items on wooden racks and stands.

"Do you think we need to earn these coins?" Tavarian asked as they headed toward a street filled with rows of tables and crowds of people making their way between them.

"Sounds like it, maybe it's like a voucher," said Dexius.

"You have to earn more than one voucher just for a necklace? They must in worse shape than Rethia."

The tables were filled with intriguing items. People here wore bright clothing—some were tight-fitting, while others were loose and flowing. They walked between the table stands, pointing at items, arguing over them, and calling others to come over.

"I don't know about that. Look at all the stuff they have here," Dexius said as he moved closer to one of the shop tables.

"There certainly is a lot. I don't know what most of this stuff is." Tavarian picked up a series of metal cylinders that were fused together. The man standing behind the table stared at Tavarian, narrowing his eyes. He set the metal object back on the table and kept walking, uncertain about what had angered the man.

As they continued down the rows of merchant stands, the smoky smells of meat began to enter their nostrils.

"Whatever that is, it's the best thing I've ever smelled in my life," said Dexius.

"Yeah, let's go find out where it's coming from," agreed Tavarian.

As they followed the aroma, they came to a cluster of food stands in the area. The smells of meats and other foods drew them over. Stacks of different meats, cheeses, breads, vegetables, and fruits were piled up everywhere. Tavarian's and Dexius's jaws dropped.

"How do they have so much food?" Tavarian wondered aloud. "And it's already cooked!"

"I think I'm going to spend the rest of my life here," Dexius said, breathing in the delectable blend of scents.

"We have to get back to Rethia at some point." Tavarian reminded him as a man squeezed his way by him.

The people around the food counters did not appear to have manners. They pushed him as they slid in toward the stand operators.

"I don't think I want to go back," Dexius said, moving to the end of the line as Tavarian and Darby moved in behind.

"Don't say that. What about your family?"

The line moved forward and Dexius huddled behind the person in front of him, preventing others from getting in the open space to skip ahead of them in line. "They'll be fine without me."

"Don't you want to see them again?"

"Things are better for me since I left—better than they've ever been."

Tavarian hesitated to remind Dexius about Lirah, but needed to make sure Dexius didn't fall into the same trap every other Rethian did. "What about Lirah?"

"I think she would understand," Dexius replied.

"But we promised her we would return with the stones . . ."

Dexius paused. "We'll bring back the stones for her sake."

The line moved forward, making it finally Dexius's turn.

"How do we get one of these?" Dexius asked the woman tending to some sausages sizzling on a grill.

"Five vrupines," she said.

"Where do we get vrupines?" Dexius asked.

"I'll accept other currency. What do you have? Jun? Kinmet?"

"I don't know what that is," he admitted as the people behind them grew restless.

"What kind of currency do you have, then?"

"I don't . . . none?" Dexius said as Tavarian shrugged behind him.

"Where in the world are you boys from?" she asked.

"Rethia," said Dexius.

"Never heard of it. You will have to find work if you have no money," she said.

"That's how you earn coins?" Dexius asked.

"Yes, get a job doing work for someone, and they will give you vrupines in return. Then you can come back here and trade the coins for sausages."

"Sounds good to me," said Dexius.

They passed a water fountain in the middle of an intersection of roads. Tavarian stared at the fountain. Water bubbled up from a shaft standing above. It cascaded down into the pool like a small waterfall. Intricately carved designs decorated the stone base.

It struck Tavarian as odd to have this in the middle of the street. It had no purpose—it was only blocking the intersection and causing people to have to walk around it. Rethia would never waste resources on something like this.

He couldn't stop staring at it. The fountain brought a bit of the beauty of the natural world into this stone city; perhaps a monument to a waterfall. The flowing water provided a calming contrast to the chaotic activity on the streets. Perhaps its purpose was to bring civility to a place where so many different beings came to interact. Tavarian tried to envision something like this in Rethia. Maybe he could build one when he got back. He had no idea how they made it work, but maybe eventually he could figure it out.

As Tavarian studied the fountain, someone ran by him and snatched the bag from his shoulder.

"Hey! Come back here!" yelled Tavarian. No one tried to stop the thief. They only stared back at him for yelling in the middle of the street.

"Dexius, why didn't you chase him down? I thought you were a great hunter."

"I was keeping an eye on Darby. Why did you let him take it?"

"I need to get my bag."

"Good luck with that—the guy is long gone," Dexius said. "He's lost in the crowd, which is what we need to be. We stand out too much—everyone can tell we are foreigners."

"How do you suggest we do that?"

"Stop looking around at everything," Dexius said. "Walk around like you see this every day."

"I guess you're right."

"You wanted to focus on the mission," Dexius said. "Whatever we are supposed to be doing here."

"Right, first, I need to get my bag."

"You'll never get that stuff back."

"I'm at least going to try."

Tavarian and Darby weaved through the crowd as Dexius reluctantly followed. They passed by some merchants who were very strange—one walked on four legs. The odd creature intimidated Tavarian, so he moved on to someone more like them.

"My bag was stolen. Who might I speak to about finding the thief?" Tavarian inquired.

"There are no thieves around here! Now go away!" said the merchant

"I'm not saying that, I'm just asking—"

"Why don't you go ask that Breghobbin over there? I'm busy!" The merchant pointed toward the four-legged merchant.

"You don't have any customers," Tavarian remarked.

"That's because you're over here talking about things being stolen," the merchant said. "Go bother someone else."

Tavarian turned back to the four-legged merchant he had passed. He slowly made his way over to the creature, unsure how to address it or what it might do when he did. As he approached, the Breghobbin turned toward him, presenting a smile. Its long rounded teeth made for a disconcerting grin.

The long-faced creature had thick pale-yellow skin speckled with blue and violet patches and wore a small brown hat.

"Hello! You find something you like?" it said to Tavarian.

"Uh, no, I just had a question," Tavarian said.

"Of course! How can I be of assistance?" the creature asked. "My name is Taushek, how do you do?"

"I . . . I had my bag . . . my bag was stolen," Tavarian said.

"That's awful!" the Breghobbin said. "That truly is a terrible and very bad thing! I can tell you are a visitor. Let me assure you, thievery is not common in Strakenbridge, and I hope you won't let this experience ruin your visit here!"

"Well, who could I talk to about finding the thief?" Tavarian asked.

"You could check with the guards," Taushek said. "There's a guard station around the other side of the bakery over there."

"Thank you—I will ask them," Tavarian said.

"Do come back and check out my merchandise when you are finished," said Taushek.

"Thank you. I will try," Tavarian said.

"That . . . thing was weird," said Dexius as they walked toward the bakery.

"Yeah, but he's been the most helpful being in this city so far," said Tavarian.

He made his way to the guard station, and found one of the guards there, dressed in a dark green uniform with red markings.

"Hello, my bag was stolen, and I wanted to try to get it back."

"When did this happen?" the guard asked.

"A few moments ago."

"Where at?"

"I was standing by the waterfall thing."

"You mean a water fountain? Which one?"

"Uh, the one right back there." Tavarian pointed back toward the fountain.

"What are the contents of this bag?"

"Um, some flekstones, a saw, a blanket, a sword hilt . . ."

"A sword?" said the guard. "You realize only Strakenbridge citizens are allowed to carry weaponry here. You have to check in any weapons at the gate."

"I wasn't aware, but there's no blade, just a hilt."

"It's part of a weapon, so it has to be checked in."

"Okay, as soon as I get it back, I will check it in."

"Your items have probably already been sold to street merchants. We need a detailed description of each item." The guard took out a piece of paper and a pencil.

"The sword hilt has a wooden handle, metal on the bottom and the top. It also had this circular inlay close to where a blade would be with metal bars spread out from the inlay."

"Okay, got it."

"The flekstones are just that—flekstones," Tavarian said.

"All right, what else?"

"The blanket is burgundy with dark blue circles on it."

"Anything else?"

"A saw about this big." Tavarian spread his hands apart to indicate the size. "And a water canteen."

"Got it . . ."

"That's it—all that's important anyway." Tavarian did not wish the mention the curl of Lirah's hair, he could only hope it would stay inside the bag.

"Very good, we'll get on it." The guard placed the paper with the written report on a shelf under the desk.

"How long does this usually take?"

"You never can tell with these things. Could take a few days; could be a few years. We'll have to search every merchant in Strakenbridge and even then, it may get sold and leave the city before we find it."

"That's not very encouraging."

"Just being honest."

"All right, well, thank you."

Tavarian walked back to Dexius and Darby.

"So now what?" Dexius said.

"I guess we need to find someone who knows about rokenstones," said Tavarian

"How are we going to make it back up the mountain once we get them?"

"We'll have to find someone who can help with that too."

The three started to move on as a man in a long coat came up behind them. Tavarian turned quickly to face him, since his trust in the people of this city was wavering now after the theft.

"Didn't mean to startle you there," the man said as a few travelers moved around them.

"What do you want?" Dexius demanded.

"You were talking about a stolen bag," said the man.

"You were listening to us?" Dexius asked.

"Do you know something about it?" Tavarian asked excitedly.

"No," the man said.

"Oh," Tavarian said, "then what do you want?"

"The guards will never find your bag."

"Yeah, it didn't sound like it," said Tavarian.

"Thanks for the enlightenment," Dexius said sarcastically.

"There is someone who can," the man said. "One who has become famous for finding lost things."

"No thanks," Dexius said.

"Where can I find them?" Tavarian asked.

"Tav, we don't have time for this—let's cut our losses and get going," implored Dexius as he began moving away.

"I really want that bag." Tavarian pressed his lips together.

"This time of day, he is known to frequent Freksley Tavern. It's over by the west gate," the man informed them.

"How will I know them? What's their name?" Tavarian said.

"No one knows," the man replied, walking away.

"How are they famous if no one knows their name?" Dexius inquired.

"Ask the tavern-keeper and you will find them." The man turned back once more as he moved toward the crowd.

"Thank you, sir," said Tavarian, surveying the city for a possible location of the west gate. "We need to find the tavern," he told Dexius.

"No, we don't—a tavern is no place for Darby," said Dexius.

"You and Darby can wait outside if you prefer."

"Why am I even following you? I should be in charge."

"No one is really in charge, Dex—we're both searching for the same thing."

"I'm not looking for your stupid bag."

"It's not stupid," Tavarian said. "You can go ask around about rokenstones while I try to find my bag."

"I'm going to look for a place to earn vrupines," Dexius said. "Maybe I'll ask about rokenstones."

"Fine, whatever. I'll see you soon, Darby."

Darby glanced back at Tavarian as Dexius led her toward the fountain where the streets crossed. Tavarian traveled down a road near the outer edge of the city. It may not be the fastest path to get there, but eventually he had run into the west gate. The shops and merchant tables ended as he continued into a residential district.

The buildings here were tall and compact, and maintained less than the buildings toward the entrance of the city. The bricked roads were dark and chipped, and some of the stones were loosened from their mortar. Tenants in this area wore plainer clothing. It was an odd contrast that didn't exist in Rethia, where everyone had the same things.

Children played in the streets as adults sat in chairs outside their doorways. They stood around the houses openly talking, dancing, and eating where they pleased. There was less decorum here, but they seemed to enjoy themselves more. It was more like Rethia, though in some ways they appeared better off.

Tavarian tried to take Dexius's advice and keep his head straight forward. He grew uncomfortable with the residents staring at him as he walked by the buildings. After making it out of the residential district he came upon a crossing street leading to an open gate.

Along the corner of the street, there was a building wrapped in vines and covered in light pink flowers growing from the roof and spilling out over the outside walls. The vines were well kept and added decoration to the building. A beautifully cut block of wood stood out from the stone walls with the words *Freksley Tavern* carved into it.

The heavy door squeaked, momentarily disturbing the low murmurs of conversation inside as Tavarian tentatively entered the tavern. With no windows to let in sunlight, the interior possessed a somber ambience with only candles lending their faint glimmer. Patrons huddled together around the perimeter in sectioned boxes, allowing for more private engagement than the tables in the open interior. The center of the room featured a square wooden bar lit by torches hanging from the ceiling, making it the brightest part of the tavern.

Tavarian weaved around some of the tables that stood between the booths and the bar, obstructing the path to the center.

"What can I get for ya?" the tavern-keeper asked, setting a glass mug on top of the bar with a clunk.

"I'm looking for someone," Tavarian responded.

The tavern-keeper furrowed his brow as he took a mug off the bar and began cleaning it with a cloth rag.

"Can you be a bit more specific?" quipped the tavern-keeper.

"I'm told there is someone here known for finding things," Tavarian responded.

"Over there," he said, nodding in the direction of one of the candlelit booths behind the bar.

"Thank you." Tavarian tried to sound as polite as he could, sensing some tension from the tavern-keeper.

Three people sat in the booth—a man with a beard and big eyebrows, a creature with a sloped head and dark pink skin, and a figure with a black hood over their shadow-covered face. He was unsure about which one he should speak to as none of them had a friendly demeanor.

Rehearsing what to say in his mind as he approached, he searched for the right words. Their conversation paused as he got close. The three of them glared at him as if waiting for him to speak. He had hoped they would query him first, but they were forcing him to lead.

Lirah always told him to ease into these situations with something light that everyone could identify with, like the weather. He despised this fake ritual of initiating conversation with people and rarely took her advice. With no one saying anything, their gazes grew more hostile by the moment. He had no other choice than to just say it.

"Hello," Tavarian said. "How about this weather?"

"Go away, kid," said the man with the beard.

Unaccustomed to this kind of rudeness, he started to turn and leave. He needed his bag, though, and it would take more than rudeness to make him leave.

"Sorry, I just had a question," said Tavarian.

"Either ask it or be gone!" said the dark pink creature, rubbing the oily skin on its lengthy neck.

"I was told one of you can find things," Tavarian replied.

"That depends on what you need to find," the hooded figure whispered.

"I had a bag that was stolen, and I was told you could get it back."

"Go fetch Blig for me," the hooded one mumbled, gesturing for the other two to leave. They climbed out of the booth, and headed toward the door. The hooded one offered Tavarian a seat in their place.

"What do you have to exchange?" the voice spoke louder this time, and was distinctly feminine. Under the hood, the person wore a mask covering the bottom of her face. The candlelight flickered across her sleek eyes.

"I don't have any vrupines if that's what you mean," said Tavarian.

"What do you have, then? I need something of value," the woman rested her chin on the back of her hand.

"Everything I have of any value is in the bag."

"Then I have incentive to find it, but not to return it to you."

Tavarian's head twitched. "I thought you were supposed to be a good person—someone who helps people—but you're just another crook. Is this entire city filled with thieves?"

"I *am* a good person," she remarked as shadows danced over her face. "Saving this world from darkness requires money and resources."

"Good people don't hide their faces," Tavarian snapped. "Who are you anyway?"

"My name is a mark of death," the woman leaned back in her seat. "Those who hear it are soon to die."

Tavarian's shoulders slumped. "Oh no, not *you*."

"Ah, yes, I thought you looked familiar," she winked.

Tavarian crossed his arms over his chest. "If I had known you were coming here, I would have avoided this place entirely."

"Aw, come now, surely you've missed me after all this time." She removed her mask. "You were so accommodating, letting me sleep next to you in your little . . . shelter."

"That was before I knew you were a thief!" Tavarian growled, surprising himself at how easily the anger flowed off his tongue, unfiltered.

"Thief?" the woman gave him a sly smile. "I'm *so* much more than that."

"You're not doing good here at all. You don't even have any shame about what you did," he said it as though pointing it out would make a difference.

"Shame? What good is shame? You're simply too naive to realize that anything you need will be taken from you unless you take it first. The only real choice you have in this world is to be the hammer or the nail. I prefer being the hammer."

"You shouldn't steal from people—only the worst would do that."

"Wrong." She leaned in. "Everyone steals. The powerful may change the words for it, but they take more than anyone. Then there's the so-called virtuous, a label based on how closely you align yourself with power. As for me, I have no interest in virtues or alignment, only in what must be done."

"And what might that be?" Tavarian slid toward the back of his seat.

"Save the world," she announced. "The cursed town you mentioned before . . ."

"Muloken? I mean, it was strange, but it was just dead crops and run-down buildings."

"My people called it the blight. Whether blight or curse, it's ravaged many more towns than Muloken."

"What other towns?"

"Where I came from, across the sea, it's spread all over. I followed the trail of ghost towns on the other side of the world until there was nothing left. Now it has come here, and I have followed behind it." Her golden eyes were brightened by a reflection of candlelight.

"What is causing it?"

"They call it the Blight Whidge," she said, taking the sides of her cloak in both hands, and bringing it tighter over her face. "A dark figure who travels from town to town leaving nothing but destruction behind. Whatever it is, I will never forget those terrible, red eyes."

"Why would someone want to wipe out all these towns?"

"The Blight Whidge is not of this world. Its intentions are a mystery. But I found a few survivors here that fled Muloken. I've also been getting reports on another town with unexplained disappearances and residents exhibiting odd behavior."

"How are you getting reports?" Tavarian glanced around the tavern at the other tables where people sat silhouetted against the candlelit backdrop. Drinking, eating, laughing, and talking—they were oblivious to the terrors around them.

"This city is a great hub for information, I have little ears everywhere," she said. "I'm not going to remain here much longer, though, so if you want me to find your bag, you had better find some form of payment quickly."

"How about I forgive you for stealing my stuff and we call it even."

The woman cackled. "I don't need your forgiveness. It was only blanket, and I left you one."

"Only because I was lying on it at the time."

"That's not what stopped me."

"And you took the other eibreg I was saving."

"One piece of fruit—I left you with most of your other food."

"Only because you don't like ryberries."

"How about you repair my crossbow, and I will return your bag?"

"You broke it again?"

"What can I say? It gets a lot of wear."

"Okay, fine, I'll repair the crossbow."

The thief whistled loudly and a kid about Darby's size came running into the tavern up to her seat.

"Hey! That's the kid who stole my bag!" Tavarian said.

"Of course," said the woman, "he works for me."

The kid set his backpack on the table, and the woman picked a few smaller bags from inside. She held each of them up until Tavarian found the one with the name *Gadunk* burned into it. He pointed to it, and she tossed it on the table in front of him and placed her crossbow within reach.

The woman motioned for the kid to leave, and he ran back outside.

"I thought you helped people get their stuff back, not steal it from them," Tavarian stated.

"That's the best part." She grinned. "Once I have their items, they come to me to find them. If they're willing to pay more for the items than they would sell for, I return it. It's genius, really."

"You're despicable." Tavarian clenched his lips together, searching through the bag to make sure everything was there.

"These people would give me ten times more than what I take if they knew what I am protecting them from."

Tavarian glanced at her. "Maybe you should tell them."

"They wouldn't believe me. They know nothing yet of the blight. It hasn't hit enough towns around here for the word to spread."

"Maybe it doesn't exist," Tavarian said. "Maybe you are ransacking small towns and calling it a blight so you can come back and be the hero, hoping to get paid for it."

Her left eye began to twitch, and she stood up from the table. "Keep your worthless bag, I'll get my crossbow fixed somewhere else." The thief snatched up the weapon and walked out the door. The tavern-keeper came over to the booth, noticing that she had left.

"That'll be twenty-two vrupines for the drinks."

"I didn't have any drinks," Tavarian said.

"The lady you were sitting with did, so I'll be needing twenty-two vrupines, please."

CHAPTER 9

TAVARIAN SPENT THE rest of the day washing glasses and cleaning tables to work off the debt the thief left him with. Not long after nightfall, Dexius and Darby came walking into the tavern.

"You're still here?" Dexius raised his hands, exasperated.

Tavarian glanced up from the table for a moment before he resumed cleaning it, pretending to ignore Dexius. He dropped the facade when Darby ran up to him and put her arms around his waist. Her face beamed in the glowing candlelight of the tavern, making it impossible not to smile back at her. Perhaps when his baby brother grew to her age, he would be more like this instead of crying all the time. Tavarian wondered if he ever brought any joy to his older sister like this—doubtful.

"You found work already? Let me get some of those coins so I can buy some sausages. There's a lot of other great stuff here too," said Dexius.

"This is just temporary," said Tavarian. "I'm not getting any money."

"What?" Dexius objected. "Then why are you wasting time in here?"

Tavarian didn't want to tell Dexius the whole story. If he knew about the woman pulling this trick on him, Dexius would make fun of him forever. If he had to hear one more time that he couldn't make it out here without Dexius, he would have to punch him.

"I got my bag back." Tavarian lifted it up to show Dexius.

"And you're having to work to get it back?"

"Yeah."

"That bag is wasting a lot of time and money we could be making."

"Why don't you do some work, then?"

"I plan to."

"Did you find anything out about rokenstones?"

"After a lot of investigation, I found out most people around here don't call them rokenstones."

"Okay . . . great job, I guess."

"I'm not finished," said Dexius. "They call them strikens."

"Any idea where to find some?"

"There are lots of them in places underground, but there are some formations that burst through."

"If they're so valuable, wouldn't someone in these shops be selling them?"

"That's just it—they aren't valuable. One person I talked to said it's too dangerous to be anywhere near them."

"If they can give us the power to farm and build faster, wouldn't that be valuable?"

"Well, no one wants them."

"What do you think, Darby?"

A raise of her eyebrows was the only response he got from her.

"Hey!" shouted the tavern-keeper across the room. "If you're not working, you're not paying your debt. Get back to it!"

"I'll meet up with you guys in a bit," Tavarian said. "After they close, I guess. Try to find us a place to stay tonight."

"Yeah, I don't see how with no coins."

"We've seen a few nice people around here, maybe someone will let us stay with them."

"How are you going to find us?"

"Meet me at the fountain after midnight."

As the night wore on and all the patrons had left, Tavarian swept the floors and cleaned down the bar. The tavern-keeper let him have some of uneaten meat, which he wrapped up and placed in his satchel bag. The savory smell of the cooked meat with its hearty seasoning made his mouth water, but he didn't want to stop and eat yet.

Tavarian rushed out the door and headed for the fountain. At this hour, there were few people out on the streets. All the shops and market stands had closed. Guards walked up and down the streets, prompting him to slow down. Running out here in the dark could be suspicious.

When Tavarian arrived at the fountain, no one was there to meet him. Dexius may have been finding a place for them to sleep, he hoped. Tavarian waited and waited. His hunger eventually became too great. He went ahead and ate his portion of the meat. Whatever kind of meat it was, it tasted delicious. Nothing had flavor like this in Rethia. It would be worth going back to the tavern just for this. The night wore on and he picked off a few more pieces of meat to eat.

The streets became foggy as his eyes grew weary. Dexius wasn't coming. Without any other options, Tavarian decided to walk over to an alley behind one of the shops and lie down.

As he made it to the alleyway, a strange man with white hair above his ears and a scraggly beard hobbled toward him.

"This isn't the place for a young one like you in the dark," the man said as he walked up.

"I don't plan to be here much longer," said Tavarian

"Terrible things lurk about in the shadows," said the man, drawing his hands together inside his tattered robe.

Tavarian stepped back, keeping his distance from the old man. "I've had some experience with thieves around here already."

"There are worse than thieves," the man said, "far worse."

"Good thing there are guards all around us," Tavarian reminded him suspiciously.

"Guards can't help you with this," the man said. "Nothing can."

The man's voice began to get shaky as he talked. "I've heard them," he babbled. "The Whisperers . . . I-I saw a glimpse of the dream when they spoke to me."

Tavarian watched the old man cautiously. The man continued to open his mouth before his voice would finally come out.

"It's too late. They will come for you . . ." the man's voice began to screech and crack making Tavarian uncomfortable. "They'll come to take us all!"

Tavarian backed away because the man was clearly mad. He grabbed

Tavarian by the collar and shook him as he talked. "They are the end of everything! What they don't kill, they consume."

Tavarian didn't want to get physical with the old man, but enough was enough. He pried the man's hands off him. The guards nearby paid no attention to the ensuing struggle.

"Behind the stars, the serpent wanders!" the man shrieked.

Finally shoving the man away from him, Tavarian readjusted his tunic. The man continued lunging toward him. "Beware! Don't let them take you! You must die before they take you!"

Tavarian stretched out his arms to keep the old man back.

"What are you talking about?" he asked, even though he knew it was foolish to engage in the man's delusions.

"Beware The Hollow!" the man shouted back.

The words put a chill in Tavarian's skin. The blood seemed to stop flowing through his veins as he recalled the same words scratched into one of the walls in Muloken. Two guards approached. They took hold of the man as he tried to fight them off. Once they brought him under control, they dragged him somewhere away from the street.

Shaken, Tavarian made his way to the wall beside one of the shops. Taking the blanket out of his bag, he unfolded it onto the brick street. He lay down and rolled the blanket over him, hoping he wouldn't be noticed here.

CHAPTER 10

THE MORNING LIGHT awakened Tavarian as crowds of people were already beginning to file into the streets. Getting up quickly, he brushed himself off, rolled up the blanket, and returned it to his bag. A glance toward the fountain revealed Darby and Dexius were standing there searching for him.

Dexius frantically turned in every direction until Tavarian approached.

"Hey! Where were you last night?" Tavarian tried to make his voice sound angry, but he was too sleepy to be mad.

"Darby fell asleep," Dexius said. "I couldn't leave her there, but I didn't want to wake her either."

The way Darby was side-eyeing Dexius indicated to Tavarian that this might not be entirely true.

"So, where were you?" Tavarian asked.

"We stayed with this old woman," Dexius said. "She let us sleep in her house. We were going to come back to get you, but like I said—"

"And I guess waking Darby would be worse than letting me stay out here all night alone?"

"She was sleeping," Dexius said. "She looked like a perfect angel. I just couldn't do it."

"I had some food for both of you," said Tavarian, "but I ended up eating most of it since you never showed."

"That's okay, we had dinner," Dexius said. "And breakfast."

"Oh, well, that's great." Tavarian's head twitched, no longer feigning the anger. "I thought we were working as a team here, but I may as well be on my own."

"You ditched us to go find your dumb bag!" Dexius snapped back, throwing his hands up, "I've done all the actual work!"

"You asked a few questions—that's not exactly work!"

Darby grabbed Dexius by the hand and held it while walking up to Tavarian. She slid her hand in Tavarian's as her innocent eyes moved between him and Dexius. Dexius pulled away from her and put his hands in his pockets.

"We need a plan," Dexius said.

"We need to find someone who knows more about rokenstones, and where to find them," Tavarian added.

They spent the rest of the day wandering around the city asking merchants and shop owners if they needed help. Most of those willing to hire somebody required skills neither of them had. One of the bakeries told Dexius to come back tomorrow when the owner would be in—their only lead so far.

As it grew dark, Tavarian followed Dexius and Darby into one of the nicer residential districts near the eastern gate. Flowers and other plants grew out of wooden containers along the base of the houses. They were all symmetrically lined up, and each had a consistent height to them. Dexius knocked on a door. Muffled footsteps drew closer until the big wooden door creaked open.

"Darby and Dexius, I'm glad to have you back again, and you must be Tavarian," said the silver-haired woman behind the door.

Tavarian glanced at Dexius, surprised he had even mentioned him by name.

"Yes, I'm Tavarian."

"Delighted to cross your path, Tavarian. I am Wynnotha. Please consider this your home while you are here." She ushered them inside.

"Thank you, it's well to . . . cross your path as well," Tavarian replied—an unfamiliar greeting, but useful to learn. Tavarian found it easier to talk to adults than kids his own age. Older people generally had a way of guiding you through a conversation when you were out of place, and unsure of what to say.

"It has been so long since I have had guests in this house, and now I have three. I was just making a late day meal and hoping my helper would be back soon." She rested her hand on Darby's shoulder as they went into the next room.

Tavarian remained skeptical of Wynnotha's generosity. There were many nice people in Rethia, but none would be so happy to share their home with strangers.

"Do you need any more help?" Tavarian called out.

"No, no," Wynnotha said. "Any more bodies in here would just be in the way. You boys have a seat anywhere you like, and we will call when dinner is ready."

Dexius sat down on a big chair made of olive-colored cloth. It appeared much softer than the hard wooden chairs they were used to in Rethia. There were soft places to sit all over the room. How sturdy could they be, though, with all that fabric covering them? Tavarian sat down on a couch with a smooth surface. It had more give to it than wood, but it was much more comfortable.

Should he start up a conversation with Dexius rather than merely sitting here? People normally engaged in some type of conversation when they were in a room with others. With nothing to say, Tavarian decided he would let Dexius start if he wanted to.

His gaze wandered around the room as he grew bored. Long candles on a dark wooden shelf looked intriguing with their shiny silver pieces holding the candles in place. On the other rows of shelves, many books stood upright, packed tightly together.

So many books in one place—how were there enough subjects to read about? Curious, he got off the couch and went over to them. He reached into the shelf and grabbed a book with a red cover. Tavarian tilted it to read the words on the front, *Redemption: The Battle of Strakenbridge.*

He opened the book, thumbing his way through it. There were illustrations on some of the pages; drawings far more detailed than the study books he had read. How could all these people be so much more talented than anyone in Rethia? Rethians never aspired to drawing. Perhaps there wasn't time with all that needed to be done.

Drawings of soldiers wearing heavy armor, carrying swords, and fighting against others filled the section of the book he had turned to. Did people really fight like this? The guards in Rethia carried swords but never used them for anything other than pointing at someone committing an illegal act. The only fighting he witnessed in Rethia were arguments that sometimes led to using their fists, just like he and Dexius had done.

With the number of thieves here, perhaps you need a sword to protect yourself and your property. How did Wynnotha protect her house? Were the guards enough to take care of that? Maybe that was why she wanted them there. If they needed to help protect her and her home while they were here, they should have weapons too. He opened his satchel and peeked in at the sword handle he had found in Muloken. If only he could attach a blade to it.

"Check this out," Tavarian said to Dexius. "It has pictures of soldiers in armor, swords, bows, and some big blades—they're all fighting each other."

"What? Let me see." Dexius got up from his chair and peered over his shoulder.

Tavarian flipped through the book, showing Dexius some of the illustrations. The bows' unusual shapes, compared to the simple ones made in Rethia, caught Dexius's attention.

"As soon as I find work, I'm going to earn enough vrupines to buy a new bow—a curved bow like one of these," he said.

They were so engrossed in the pictures that Wynnotha's call to eat startled them. Entering the room, Tavarian found a wide wooden table beset with tall mugs. Darby placed a pot of stew on top of a cloth mat as Tavarian and Dexius sat down. The concoction of meat, broth, and hearty vegetables instantly made Tavarian's mouth water. Wynnotha set silver bowls in front of each chair, and Darby came back with towels and spoons to hand out to everyone.

Wynnotha filled each bowl with thick brown stew, and Tavarian lifted his spoon. He glanced at the spoon handle, which had small etchings of patterns and tiny flowers. Even the spoons here were decorative. Had everyone in Rootcore grown so bored of basic things that they turned everything into a work of art?

"Dexius tells me you boys came from one of the mountains," said Wynnotha as she took a seat next to Darby. She picked up a metal utensil beside her bowl and dipped it into the stew.

"Yes, this is the first time we have been down in Rootcore." Tavarian peered at the utensil, ready to follow her lead. It appeared like a tiny bowl itself, rounder on the bottom than the spoons they had in Rethia.

"That's what you call the land here? Rootcore?" Wynnotha asked, wiping the corner of her lips with a towel she had placed in her lap.

"Rootcore never made any sense to me," said Dexius as he took the towel that lay beside his bowl and folded it into his lap. "There are no roots to the mountain or anything else."

"No one knew what it was like down here." Tavarian lowered his spoon back into his stew without yet taking a sip. "It was just a guess someone made."

Dexius continued folding his towel, tightening the fold each time. "I could have told you there wasn't a tangled core of roots."

"Then why didn't you?" Tavarian let go of his spoon, leaving it propped on the side of the bowl. He placed his hands on the table in front of him, waiting for Dexius's next ignorant response.

"I did," Dexius said. "You just didn't want to hear it."

"You never said that. You—" Tavarian started.

"We call it Nalacea," Wynnotha interjected. "All the land on this side of the sea is Nalacea."

"That's a nice name." Tavarian picked up his spoon full of stew and brought it to his mouth. The meat didn't have as savory as the meat he had gotten from the tavern, but it was still delicious. It was soaked in a thick gravy-like broth, and green and white vegetables mushed softly as he chewed.

"A lot better than Rootcore." Dexius stopped folding his towel and reached for his spoon.

"I had no idea anyone lived on either of the mountains," she said. "Everyone always says there is no way to get up there."

"A group of us comes down every year," said Tavarian, turning toward her as he gathered another spoonful of stew. He tried to get at least one of each vegetable along with a piece of meat—a balance of everything in one bite.

"Dexius mentioned that, but I have never heard of any of that before," said Wynnotha. "So where did you come from Darby?"

Darby stopped chewing as her eyes drew toward Wynnotha.

"I'm going to ask you every night until you are ready to talk to me," Wynnotha announced, winking at Darby.

"She never talks to us either," said Tavarian as he crunched on something leafy.

"Is she able to speak?" asked Wynnotha.

"I'm not sure," Tavarian said. He smirked as he recalled Darby laughing at Dexius tripping and falling. "She laughs, though. And you can tell by her eyes that she's smart—taking everything in."

"Some have experienced things that change the way we view the world. Sometimes a part of them leaves the everyday behind. It takes times to come back. When she is ready to talk, she will," Wynnotha said.

"She was taken by Grundians," Tavarian remarked.

"Dexius told me about that," Wynnotha said. "He told me all about how you got them out. That was quite clever of you, Tavarian, and very lucky. There aren't many who escape from those fiends."

Tavarian drew in a deep breath, straightening his shoulders as he sat up in his chair. It surprised him that Dexius had given him credit instead of changing the story to favor himself.

"I'm afraid whatever horrors she witnessed may be the cause of her continued silence," she said.

"What do you mean?" Dexius said, shuffling his position in his seat.

"Long before he died, my husband Gerian was in the war." Wynnotha stared ahead as though watching some event play in her mind. "After it ended and he returned, he wasn't the same for a long while. He wouldn't speak much, not even to me. I'm not sure what terrible things he witnessed, but it took him time to get it out of his head, I suppose. Or maybe he just found a way to deal with it. I believe it's the same for our Darby here."

"There *were* some horrible things in that place," Tavarian admitted. Though the other prisoners protected her, Grunda was no place for a young girl such as Darby. It was no place for anyone.

They ate in silence for a few moments before anyone said anything. Darby had finished hers before the rest of them, and Wynnotha filled part of her bowl for a second portion.

"Dexius told me you were looking for strikens," said Wynnotha. "Who would send you to find something like that? If you ever do find any, stay far away from them."

"Why's that?" Tavarian glanced at Dexius, who kept rattling his spoon at the bottom of the bowl, scooping out every last drop of stew.

"You'll get hit by lightning." Wynnotha slapped her palms against the table. "Those things attract lightning whether it's storming or not."

"What do they look like?" Tavarian inquired, leaning over his bowl of stew.

"Black with violet veins going through them—very different from any other stone," she said. "But enough of that, what kind of work are you two planning on doing?"

"I'm going back to the bakery in the morning," said Dexius, turning to each of them as if wanting to see each of their reactions.

"Which one was that? Linan's? Or was it on the west side of town?" Wynnotha stood and filled Dexius's empty bowl with another helping of stew.

"Linan's, I think," Dexius replied and held up his hand to stop her from adding any more.

"Do you have any experience in baking, Dexius?" Wynnotha inquired, offering some extra stew to Tavarian. He shook his hand over his bowl to let her know he didn't need more.

"No, we were asking everyone. The bakery was the only place that told me to come back," Dexius replied.

"You won't get that job, I'm afraid," she stated as she slowly lowered herself back into her seat. "Tell me, what skills do you have? What did you do back home?"

"I'm a really good hunter," boasted Dexius as he cocked his head back.

"Oh? Can you gralloch an animal after a kill?" queried Wynnotha, as she stirred the big pot of stew. She gathered some of the white vegetables with the large spoon and added them to her bowl.

"I sure can," Dexius declared. "Best in the class."

"Go to the butcher and talk to Pevol," Wynnotha advised. "What about you Tavarian? Do you have any skills someone might pay you for?"

"Carpentry . . ." Tavarian said, "and some metalworking."

"You should go ask Ibis—he has a blacksmithing shop and is always needing some help. Tell him Wynnotha sent you."

After the meal, Tavarian and Dexius helped Darby clean up in the kitchen as well as move some tables Wynnotha wanted to rearrange.

"I should have some clothes in storage that you three can wear," Wynnotha said. "Those look like they're about to fall apart. I've been saving them to pass down someday. They used to belong to my son and three daughters. They may not be a perfect fit, but they should be all right."

Tavarian glanced down at his tunic. There were holes worn on the arms and one on the left shoulder. He never really thought about it much before.

At the end of the evening, Dexius and Tavarian slept in one room while Darby slept in Wynnotha's room. It was the most comfortable bed Tavarian had ever slept in, though the conditions at Grunda and sleeping in the woods for last few months may have altered his perception of comfort.

As morning came, they ate their early meal and washed up. Wynnotha fetched some of her children's old clothing and let Dexius, Tavarian, and Darby look through them and try some on. Dexius found a nice cream-colored tunic, and Tavarian found a gray one with black pants that fit the best. He removed his Rethian and Descender pendants from his old tunic and pinned them onto his new one.

Darby came out with her dark hair brushed and flowing over the shoulders of her gray blouse. She wore matching pants, but covering it all was a dark green dress. It was a striking difference—she barely appeared to be the same mud-covered girl he first saw in Grunda. She smiled, spinning around and making the skirt of the dress flare out.

Dexius and Tavarian went back into the commerce district with Dexius going to the butcher and Tavarian going to the blacksmith shop. They decided to meet back at Wynnotha's house when they were done, hopefully after finding work.

Tavarian talked to Ibis, and with Wynnotha's recommendation, the blacksmith decided to give him a chance. Tavarian spent the rest of the day watching Ibis and learning his rules for working in the shop. Once the working day ended, he walked back to Wynnotha's to meet with Darby and Dexius.

Dexius was already there, chatting with Wynnotha and Darby.

"Is that you, Tavarian?" Wynnotha inquired after he opened the front door.

"Yes, it's me," he answered. "I've been working with Ibis all day."

"I knew he would like you!" she cheered. "Dexius found work at the butcher."

"I start tomorrow morning," Dexius informed him.

ꟸ

A couple of weeks went by as Tavarian learned how Ibis ran his shop. He used some different techniques than those Tavarian had learned in Rethia. Eventually, Ibis allowed Tavarian to use the forge to work on the project he had told him about—Tavarian wanted to reforge the broken sword he had found in Muloken.

"We'll try to match the same metals as the bit of sword that's left in the hilt," said Ibis. "The main metal looks like a white metal called lakra. It's an odd choice for a sword, but there's no reason it can't work. I actually have some we can use for this."

Ibis went to the back of the shop and returned with a few bars of lakra that were ready to be melted down.

"The base is silgen with the lakra on top. Based on what I see here, when the blade is sharpened, it exposes the gold silgen. Silgen isn't the best for keeping a sharp edge, but it's durable."

Tavarian melted down the silgen with Ibis's supervision and poured it into one of the casts for a sword blade. As the blade began to cool, they hammered it into shape. Tavarian took out the broken sword hilt to meld the blade onto.

"This is an odd design for a hilt," said the blacksmith. "Where did you come by it?"

"I found it in an old deserted town a ways from here," Tavarian said. "It was the only thing left."

"Must have been a ceremonial sword," he said. "It's not very practical."

"Why do you say that?"

"It's going to be heavy at the hilt," said Ibis. "Poorly balanced. I can make you a better hilt, it just won't be as fancy."

"I really want to use this one," Tavarian said. "It may be impractical but . . . I've had it with me the whole time I've been in Rootcore, uh . . . Nalacea. I've been wanting to reforge it."

"Well, if that's what you want," said Ibis. "I can add some weight to the end of the blade and that may balance it out more."

Ibis added more silgen onto the end of the blade as soon as the two ends were hot enough to melt together. Once the silgen had cooled, they melted the lakra and poured it into the cast. Ibis allowed Tavarian to hammer the heated blade out of the cast and smooth out the inconsistencies. Ibis put the final touches on it, hammering the shape into perfection because Tavarian didn't quite possess the skill yet for techniques like this. The gold color on the edge gave it a nice design that stood out against the odd shiny white metal of the rest of the sword.

Tavarian sharpened the edge of the sword. As Ibis had said, it ground into the lakra and exposed the silgen underneath. The golden edge gave it a nice look against the rest of the white blade. Ibis inspected the blade and sharpened it a bit more, giving it a sharper edge toward the tip and a stronger blunter edge near the base. Ibis handed the sword to Tavarian. He lifted it upright, but it was a bit heavy to comfortably hold. The length of the blade in addition to the heavy hilt was a bit too much. Perhaps Ibis was right about it being just a decoration.

"That's a two-hander, Tav—you'll have to grip and swing it with both," he said.

Tavarian brought his left hand on the pommel underneath his right, making it much easier to hold, but it lacked the flexibility of using a single hand. He held the sword in front of himself as if in a defensive position.

"You never used a sword before, have you?" the blacksmith asked.

"Well, not really," Tavarian admitted.

"That's a horrible defensive position."

"What do you mean?"

"If you're going to carry a sword around, you might as well be able to use it."

The blacksmith stood, taking another sword from the rack. Standing with his side facing Tavarian, he planted his back foot pointing outward. "Back foot like this, body facing out, and head toward the opponent."

Tavarian tried to imitate the stance. The blacksmith kicked Tavarian's back foot farther out until he had it right. "Front foot pointed toward the opponent."

Tavarian turned his foot forward.

"Lift your blade."

Tavarian did so, holding the hilt at his waist and the blade up above his head.

"Too low—you can't counter from that position."

"But I need to be able to defend high and low."

"Dodge the low strikes. If you parry an attack too low, you open yourself to a counter."

"Isn't that risky?"

"Fighting someone with a sword is risky, kid."

"Hopefully, I'll never need to."

"Best way to win a fight is to avoid one. A swordsman who appears to have skill with a blade can be intimidating. You don't want to be carrying that around like a newbian."

Tavarian lifted the sword to chest level. "Is this good?"

"That can work, but point the blade out a bit, toward the opponent."

Tavarian stretched his arms out more and angled the sword toward Ibis.

"There you go—you want to keep them from getting close. Sword fighting is all about measurements; you must learn your reach to the opponent exactly, and you must quickly learn theirs. The winner is the one who closes that distance at the right time. Now, if I strike at you like this, what do you do?" The blacksmith slowly swung toward Tavarian's head.

Tavarian backed away while raising his sword upright and against the slow coming blow.

"You have to block it before this point." He demonstrated for Tavarian. "Keep it pointed toward the opponent, turn your wrists—it's simple. Don't move much from your base stance."

He tried swinging at Tavarian again, and this time Tavarian kept the blade out in front of him and angled the sword to block the blow earlier in the swing.

"There's only four main parries you need to learn, and then I will show you counters and some proper strikes."

"I didn't know you were a swordsman."

"I'm no expert by any means. I do sell blades to some expert swordsmen, however."

Later than usual, Tavarian returned to Wynnotha's house. The others had already finished dinner and were sitting on the couches. Holding small plates, they ate sweet cakes for dessert as they laughed and talked. Tavarian felt like an outsider again. It reminded him of the way Dexius pushed him away from Lirah in Rethia. Dexius had a way of commanding people's attention that Tavarian did not possess. He wished he could change whatever he needed to change to keep this from happening again. What did he have to do to remain close with other people?

Darby leapt from the couch, running to Tavarian. She reached up to give him a hug. That simple gesture made him feel wanted again, part of their group. Maybe she sensed the doubt in him, or maybe just it was part of her nature. Either way, Darby had a knack for dividing her attention between both Tavarian and Dexius. He appreciated that she understood this better than Lirah had.

Tavarian sat at the table, and Darby started bringing cuts of meat and vegetables to him. She placed a plate in front of him. He recounted the day's events while she sat beside him at the table. It was exciting for him to learn swordsmanship, and he had to tell someone, but Dexius wouldn't care. Although she never said anything, Darby listened intently as though it was a fascinating tale. She filled the void of not having Lirah to talk to every day.

"What was your day like?" he asked her. Not surprisingly, she didn't respond; her face only twitched slightly. "Miss Wynnotha!" Tavarian shouted toward the other room. "What did you and Darby do today?"

Wynnotha got up and came into the room.

"Well, we dusted everything in the study, changed all the sheets, cleaned up the kitchen," she said. "We also watched some birds outside the back door. There are two little birds living in a nest in one of the plummery bushes, and they have three eggs they're taking care of."

Darby's eyes lit up as Wynnotha told the story.

"That sounds interesting," he said as Darby smiled back.

As much as he hated to talk to Dexius, he knew it would please Darby.

"What about you, Dexius? What did you do today?"

"Nothing," Dexius said.

"Surely you must have done something."

"I cut up some animals at the butchery."

"Yeah, well, were there any strange or funny things that happened while you were doing that?"

"Nope, just the same thing as every other day."

"Just thought I would ask . . ."

"Oh!" said Dexius, bumping into one of the side tables as he dashed into the room. "There was this kid who came in to exchange currency, and he tried to trick the owner into giving him too much in the exchange."

"Why would he do that?"

"To make money," Dexius said. "After the owner caught on to what he was trying to do, the kid ran out of the shop. He went into another place later and around to some of the stands too. Apparently, he goes all over the city doing this."

Immediately, Tavarian's mind went to the flame-haired girl and her gang of young thieves. How could someone with such a sweet face be so cold? She made this city far worse with her presence. Although, it was impressive that one person made such an impact on a city this large. She truly had become the hammer in her analogy. Could a person have the same impact doing good for the city?

"We could make money a lot faster that way," Dexius proposed. "It would be for a good cause—to help us get rokenstones back to Rethia and keep everyone from going hungry.

"That's exactly what *she* would say," Tavarian blurted. "We're not going to be like that."

Dexius furrowed his brow. "She who?"

"I mean . . . like one of those people. They're no different than the thieves in Rethia that they put in the dungeon for the rest of their lives. If only they did that here, there might not be so many of them around."

"Tavarian is right," Wynnotha said. "What you're talking about is wrong."

"The shop owners have plenty of money," Dexius said. "They won't miss a few coins. We need it more than they do."

"The shop owners put a lot of time, money, and a great deal of risk into opening those shops in the first place. Most of them started out with nothing and it took them years to get rewarded for it. They pay all the people they employ. If they end up losing money, they may not be able to pay their workers. Besides that, it's simply wrong to take from others, no matter what you think they have," Wynnotha stated. "Didn't your parents teach you not to take from other people?"

Dexius's eyes dropped to the ground. He rubbed the side of his forehead.

"What would Lirah think of us if we did something like that?" Tavarian said.

"Lirah probably forgot us already," said Dexius. "We have Darby to take care of now."

"Lirah hasn't forgotten us," Tavarian said, "and yes, we have to be a good example for Darby. She's seen enough of the bad side of the world already."

"It seemed harmless, but I see Wynnotha's point," Dexius conceded.

"Found out anything about Rokenstones yet?" Tavarian asked as he and Dexius headed toward the door the next morning. For Tavarian, it was more something to say than a real question.

"If I had, I would have told you." Dexius wadded up his work apron as he walked out into the street.

"Just thought I would ask," said Tavarian, heading in the other direction. "I'll see you tonight."

Tavarian got back to the blacksmith shop and Ibis assigned him his first unsupervised orders. He had to make twelve chain buckles by the end of the day. He used the forge in the front of the shop while Ibis worked in the back. Ibis promised that if he got those right, he would teach him more about swordsmanship, and show him some proper strikes and cuts.

The first buckle took longer than expected. The importance of the right shape to hold a chain in place superseded anything else. He heated the metal again so he could attempt to hammer it into better shape and correct his mistakes.

As he hammered the edges to form the buckle, a man came in and stood there watching him as he worked. Tavarian didn't need this new distraction right now. It made him hesitant, and he worried about making a mistake.

With a pair of tongs, he dropped the buckle into a tray of water to cool. Tavarian lifted his head and eyed the man—not tall or particularly short, just average height. He had a well-trimmed mustache under his nose, and he wore a small peculiar hat.

"Could you please fetch Ibis for me?" the man said.

"He's busy," Tavarian replied. "He told me not to bother him."

"I'm sure he meant not to bother him with trivial matters—this is business."

"He didn't specify any exceptions."

The man forced an exasperated smile. "I assure you, it will not bother him to hear what I have to say."

"If I go back there, what should I tell him?"

"Tell him Mr. Bradis has a proposition for him. I have acquired some alekserite and need some metal rings cast for it."

"What is alekserite?"

"It's a rare stone everyone in Grettis Falls has been raging for. We'll be the first in Strakenbridge to offer it."

"What's so special about it? Does it have any interesting properties?"

"It's rare and sparkly, and—could you please tell Ibis?"

Tavarian went into the back of the shop to the larger forge. Hesitantly, he called Ibis and told him about the alekserite. He expected Ibis to be annoyed at being disturbed, but he immediately set down his hammer and made his way out front to talk to Mr. Bradis.

Tavarian resumed crafting buckles as Ibis and Mr. Bradis discussed how to split profits of selling rings and other jewelry with alekserite. Once they were done with the conversation and Ibis had returned to the back of the shop, Tavarian put down the buckle he was working on, and ran to catch up with Mr. Bradis.

"Excuse me, Mr. Bradis?"

The man turned around slowly, his mustache twitched, and his eyebrow raised. "What is it? Did Ibis have something else to say?"

Slightly winded, Tavarian tried to slow down his breathing by taking deep breaths. "No sir, I just had a question."

"Oh . . . well, get on with it. I have important matters to get to." Mr. Bradis tapped his fingers on his arm impatiently.

"You know a lot about rare stones—"

"Yes, yes . . . what is your question?" Mr. Bradis waved his hand, urging Tavarian to speed this along.

"Do you know where to find any rokenstones?"

Mr. Bradis's composure brightened a bit as though the question interested him. "Ah, I haven't heard that word in some time. Strikens, I think you mean?"

"Yes, strikens."

"There's no business in strikens, so I don't generally keep up with their locations. I do, however, recall hearing there was an exposed striken vein in Galurigan Swamp, but since no one ever goes through that mire anyway, it shouldn't present a hazard."

Tavarian's head rose. "Where is Galurigan Swamp?"

Mr. Bradis motioned the directions with his hands. "You pass it on the road to Samavere—the road winds around it. It's straight out of Strakenbridge, on the other side of the river."

"Thank you, Mr. Bradis. I'll let you get back to your matters," Tavarian said as he turned back to the shop.

"What interest do you have in strikens?"

"Thanks!" Tavarian purposely ignored the question and ran to get back to working on the buckles.

After the shop had closed, Tavarian had his twelve buckles. He had gotten much better on the last six he made. Ibis spent a little over an hour showing him some attack strikes and how to cut with the sword. He arrived late for dinner again by the time he got to Wynnotha's house.

"I found out where some rokenstones are!" he told Dexius, who was sitting in the main room, turning through pages of illustrations in one of Wynnotha's books.

"What? Where?" Dexius continued studying the book as Tavarian approached.

"Galurigan Swamp," declared Tavarian, watching the cooling embers of the harcha wood in the fireplace.

Dexius wrinkled his nose. "Where is that?"

"It's on the road to Samavere." Tavarian took a poker, moving the wood to give the fire room to breathe. A hundred sparks of orange flew from the blackened logs as they were moved.

"Samavere? That's where Dalson and Reva are from," said Dexius, setting the book down on a wooden table beside him.

"Dalson and Reva?"

"They were in Grunda with us."

"Oh, right—I guess I'm trying to forget that place." Tavarian sat down in one of the soft chairs, trying to relax his stiffened muscles.

"So, I guess you want to go?" said Dexius, staring blankly ahead.

"Of course, that's why we came here." Tavarian could hear the light clanging of Wynnotha and Darby in the other room. She never wanted Dexius or Tavarian to help clean up after a meal, only Darby. It must be to have some time alone to speak to Darby. The thought made him wonder what she talked to her about.

"I hate to leave now," Dexius continued staring at the far wall.

"Why? We're only staying here to find out about the rokenstones." Tavarian's stomach felt uneasy. He didn't like where this was headed.

"I like it here. It's so much better than Rethia."

"Don't tell me you are going to be like all the other Descenders and abandon our families in Rethia."

"They don't want me anyway!" Dexius raised his voice unexpectedly, pausing before speaking again with a calmer tone. "I don't care about going back. I'm only doing this for Lirah."

"I'm not exactly the most liked person either, but we've grown up since we left," said Tavarian. "Imagine how it will be when we return with the stones . . . we'll be heroes!"

"As soon as our mission is over, I'm coming back here—for good, this time."

What lure did Nalacea have on Rethians, so that none of them wanted to return, he wondered. All of them before Dexius had lacked one thing—someone like himself to keep them on course. Once Dexius gets back to

Rethia, he'll remember they've faced far more bad things here than good. Everyone will be welcoming them home and thanking them every time they have extra food on the table. He'll change his mind.

"When are you going to be ready to head out?" Tavarian queried.

"Give me another week to get that bow."

"A week?"

"Hey, you wanted your bag, now I want my bow."

"Okay, fine, we'll leave in a week."

"See you boys tonight! Have a nice day!" shouted Wynnotha from the doorway as they rushed into the street.

"Well with!" they replied, waving back to her as they went their separate ways.

The rest of the week went by slowly as Tavarian finished the details on the sword. He and Ibis polished the blade up to a shiny silver finish and the blacksmith paid him with lessons in swordsmanship.

Ibis made him a custom sheath that strapped on his back to carry the sword. Tavarian couldn't help but to take the sword out and stare at it for a while. It filled him with pride, having contributed to its restoration. He slid his fingers across the side of the blade, careful not to touch the sharp edge. Gripping the hilt, he ran his hand over the notch near the top. The inside of the notch was coated with gold silgen metal where the rest of the hilt had a stretchy cloth material around it. From the notch metal lines led to the handguard.

"Do you know anything about Galurigan Swamp?" Tavarian asked.

"Very little," Ibis said. "What makes you ask?"

"Just overheard someone talking about it."

"Don't let those tales worry you, Tav," Ibis insisted. "There's no such thing as ghosts."

"Wait, what tales?"

"Travelin' folk make up a lot of strange tales to pass the time. It's something to talk about, I suppose. They say the swamp is haunted, that some kind of old evil has taken up residence there of late. No one ever goes in those swamps—no one in their right mind, anyway. It's dangerous, but there are no ghosts or evil."

"If there are no ghosts, what makes it dangerous?"

"Getting stuck in the bogs, and there are creatures in there you would be better off not crossing paths with."

If Ibis had been trying to put Tavarian's mind at ease about there not being any ghosts, his talk of creatures countered it. After putting the finishing touches on the sword, the blacksmith left to turn it over to the Strakenbridge Authority to abide by the laws in the city. Tavarian would be able to pick it up as he left the gates. He continued practicing with one of the blacksmith's model swords, using one of the heavier ones to replicate his sword's weight.

Nearly a week had passed since Tavarian had asked Dexius about the bow. It pleased him to learn that Dexius had bought one, and had turned it over to the Strakenbridge Authority until they left the city.

On the evening before they planned to leave, a heavy thunderstorm broke out nearby. The clouds grew as dark as night, swirling even faster than normal. The rain roared on the roof and in the streets outside. The sound of ten thousand taps played on everything around them. Tavarian and Dexius stood in the doorway of Wynnotha's house watching it. There had never been a rainstorm quite like this in Rethia.

In the distance, streaks of lightning traveled across the sky from cloud to cloud. Some flashes were followed by a clap of thunder. The world around them groaned and grumbled as the noise trailed off. It rained throughout the night. If only he could tell where the lightning was hitting, maybe they would find some rokenstones. It could be hitting the swamps they were heading toward, charging the stones in time for them to find them.

The white noise of rain soothed him to sleep. If it weren't for the occasional booms of thunder nearby, it would have been quite peaceful. The close cracking of the storm frightened Darby, and she snuck into Tavarian's room to climb into the bed with him. It surprised him that she didn't go to Dexius.

"It's going to be all right." He rubbed her shoulder. "We're safe here."

Before long, they were both asleep. During the night, they were awakened twice by loud thunderclaps. Tavarian brushed through Darby's hair with his hand, reassuring her that everything would be all right until she fell asleep again.

CHAPTER 11

THE DAY CAME to leave for Galurigan Swamp. There they could search for the elusive rokenstones Rethians had been after for years. If they didn't leave now, Dexius may grow too attached to this city. Tavarian remained uneasy thinking what to do with Darby. With the stories of dangerous creatures, he decided to leave her with Wynnotha. Darby had gained a familiarity with her by now, so it wouldn't be as hard on her to stay. He trusted Wynnotha to take care of her, and Dexius agreed. Whatever happened to them in the swamp, he couldn't bear for any ill to befall Darby.

Once they had finished their morning meal, he decided to talk to her as she sat on the couch. "Darby, we are leaving. We're heading to what could be a perilous swamp. It's best you stay here with Wynnotha, and then when we find the stones, we'll come back to you."

Darby's eyes grew large as she shook her head emphatically.

"You'll be safe here with Wynnotha." Tavarian leaned over, giving her a kiss on top of her head. He hugged her and stood back up. Darby grabbed his hand.

"Don't you like Wynnotha?" he said as he pulled away.

She signified yes.

"You take care of her too, all right?" Tavarian backed away from where she sat on the couch.

Springs began to well in her eyes as Tavarian and Dexius gathered the few belongings they had.

"I'm going to miss you boys. I made some bread to take with you," Wynnotha said.

"Thank you," said Dexius. "You've been a great host."

"Oh, stop." She laughed. "Hosts don't make their guests work for their stay."

"We were glad to help," said Dexius as he took a wrapped bundle of bread from the table in the middle of the room and placed it in his new satchel.

Tavarian wondered what had gotten into Dexius—being respectful, having manners. Maybe it was all that time he spent dealing with the butcher's customers? The butcher probably didn't take to kindly to his usual attitude.

"You boys don't get near those strikens," Wynnotha said.

"We won't," Tavarian lied. "We just need to find where they are so we can tell our people." He had every intention of taking them once they found some, but he wanted to avoid an argument and lecture from Wynnotha.

"I'll take good care of little Darby here," said Wynnotha.

Tavarian glanced at Darby, who now had tears streaking down her cheeks. It killed him to see her like this, but they had to keep her safe. It would be irresponsible of him to take her into a swamp filled with danger.

Dexius and Tavarian both gave Darby and Wynnotha hugs and headed out the door. Wynnotha took Darby's hand, and they walked out into the alleyway behind them. Tavarian turned as Wynnotha waved to them.

"Well with you both," he called back, taking one last glance toward the house that had been their temporary home. He couldn't stand to look at the sadness in Darby's large brown eyes again. He and Dexius began walking again, heading toward the unknown that awaited them.

A cry arose from behind them. They both turned as Darby broke down into full-on sobbing. It was the first time they had heard her make an actual sound.

"I'm sorry, Tav, but if Darby isn't coming with us, then I'm not going either." Dexius slowly headed back.

What should he do now? He couldn't do this by himself. Tavarian walked back to Wynnotha and Darby. He knelt in front of her, putting him at the same head level. He molded his hand to the shape of the back of her head as he drew her close.

"Do you really want to go with us through the disgusting swamps?" Tavarian asked her as he gazed into her teary eyes. Her face resembled the streets, puddled from the storm overnight.

She nodded her head through the sobs. He peered up at Wynnotha, and then back to Darby.

"I'm sorry, Darby—we only wanted to protect you," he told her. "If you really want to come, we'll let it be your decision."

She grabbed both of their hands, and they headed down the road toward the crowds of people. Still holding Dexius's hand, she wiped her face on the back of her wrist.

"Hey, don't wipe your nose on me!" Dexius joked.

Darby smirked and this time she did wipe her face on his arm.

"Hey!" Dexius playfully yelled, making her silently giggle.

Tavarian waved back to Wynnotha one more time.

"You kids take care and do come back," she returned.

When they reached the gate, Dexius turned in his ticket to pick up his bow. A nice, light brown wood gleamed with a shiny coating. The middle of the bow formed an arch at the handle and the two ends had even more curvature to them. Around the arch were ridged designs carved into the wood. A metal piece above the handle served as a hand guard and guide for the arrow.

Dexius grabbed a tightly wound bundle of arrows and strapped them to his back. He then hung the bow over the quiver.

Tavarian turned in his ticket and the guard checked the storage racks only to come up empty. "There's no 1288. It's been taken already."

"But I have the ticket—how could someone else have taken it without the ticket?"

"Well, it's not here."

"Is this another scam? You take everyone's weapons at the gate, and then keep what you like?"

"Most certainly not!"

"I don't think so, Tav. Otherwise, they would have taken this awesome bow," babbled Dexius.

"Can someone find it? Because I have the ticket right here." Tavarian said.

The guard went to talk to another, and they both came back to the gate station. "Oh, there's your problem," he said. "That's a six, not an eight: 1286."

"Ah, here it is," said the first guard. "Sorry for the mix-up." He handed it over to Tavarian in its backstrap sheath. Breathing a sigh of relief, he unsheathed the blade as they walked toward the bridge, admiring his and Ibis's handiwork.

"I've never seen a sword like that," said Dexius. "What is this for here?" Dexius ran a finger down the metal strips coming from the notch near the blade.

"I'm not sure," Tavarian said. "Decoration, I think."

"It's odd, whatever it is."

Darby stared at the sword as Tavarian returned it to its sheath. "You like it, Darby?"

She nodded her head, and Tavarian strapped the sheath over his neck and across his shoulder.

They moved through the gate back to the bridge they had used to enter the city. The quick water was even closer after the rainstorm the night before.

"How many extra coins do you have?" Tavarian asked.

"Only seven after buying the bow, quiver, and arrows," Dexius said.

"I only have twelve—so, nineteen altogether. That's not going to help us much if we need it."

"Darby has fifty-eight."

"What? How does she have any?"

"Wynnotha was giving her some coins every week for helping her around the house."

"Wow, did you even buy anything, Darby?"

"She just kept the coins because she didn't want to buy anything," said Dexius. "Or maybe she couldn't make up her mind."

"I guess if we come to a town and need some money, that will come in handy."

"As long as Darby is willing to give it to us."

"Yeah, if she saved it all this time, she may not let us spend it."

"If we don't need it out here, she can spend it when we come back."

"Yeah, that's true," Tavarian said, "though I'm rather anxious to get back to Rethia."

"Not me," said Dexius. "Now that I've seen more of Isodonia, Rethia is one of my least favorite places . . . aside from Grunda."

They passed some travelers heading onto the bridge as they set foot on the dirt road heading away from the river off into the distance. The land ahead was similar to the hills alongside the brook—grassy plains with trees scattered about, and red crystals jutting out of the ground.

"I think I've had enough of Nalacea for a while," Tavarian said. "Mostly, I'm ready to get back to everyone again."

"Who is in Rethia that you really want to see so bad? I made more friends in Strakenbridge in a few months than I ever had in Rethia. I don't remember you having any friends besides Lirah."

"Those aren't friends, Dex; they're customers."

"I call them friends. At least they are nicer to me than people in Rethia."

"Besides Lirah, I want to see my sister, my parents, and my baby brother."

"How do you plan to get back up the mountain?"

"I don't have a plan," Tavarian said. "That part hasn't been my focus yet. Once we get the stones, we can figure that out."

"I don't think it's possible," Dexius said. "That's why no one ever returned."

"I'm not giving up yet."

As another downpour came that night, they found shelter under a small cluster of trees. By the time they had put together a canopy over themselves, they were drenched. The cold, wet blanket they shared was not much of a comfort. Yet, something calmed Tavarian out here in the natural setting as it rained.

The panoramic chorus of raindrops called to them like the world singing a lullaby. Tavarian lay on his back, watching the droplets make their way through the mesh of branches and down onto his arm. He didn't mind the occasional drops of water that leaked through their makeshift roof—they were soothing. The wilderness provided a sense of belonging that he didn't experience in Rethia. It made him believe he would find his way, and that he would be more than just the strange kid everyone thought he was.

Once the other two fell asleep, Tavarian drew the bundle of white hair from his satchel. He imagined running his hand through Lirah's curls as he touched it. The sooner they found these stones, the sooner he could get back to her. It was ironic that after spending so much time with her on the mountain dreaming of Nalacea, she was now all he could think about.

As dawn's light reached them through the dome of clouds, Darby returned after having wandered off. She had picked them some small mushrooms. Unlike Dexius and Tavarian, she knew about the plants here in Nalacea. They squished under his teeth in an unpleasant manner. Once the taste hit him, he decided they weren't bad.

After consuming the mushrooms, they put their gear back on and headed toward the road again. Tavarian remained hungry, but the mushrooms made it bearable. They reached the dirt road, now filled with puddles and mud. In the distance ahead, two riders approached. They both rode some sort of furry four-legged creatures with several horns. There had been creatures similar used for transportation in Strakenbridge, but none this fast. As they drew closer, Tavarian, Dexius, and Darby eased off the side of the road. Though wild and fast, the creatures were apparently tame enough for riding.

The two travelers passed, patting the sides of their heads with two fingers extended. Tavarian nodded in acknowledgement, uncertain what the salute meant.

"We have to get some of those!" said Dexius. "Maybe we should have stayed in Strakenbridge a little longer so we could buy some animals like that."

"How many coins do you think that would cost?"

"Must be a lot. There weren't many people in Strakenbridge with riding animals," Dexius said. He was quiet for a few minutes. "If Lirah is all you miss about Rethia, we should bring her down here."

"She's not all that I miss, and besides, Lirah can't breathe down here." Tavarian retorted. "Why do you want to stay in Nalacea so bad?"

"Strakenbridge has so much more to offer," Dexius replied. "Everything about it is better than Rethia."

"Not everything," said Tavarian. "Family is more important than sausages."

"Who needs them?" Dexius said. "Unless you're talking about Darby and Wynnotha."

"But what about—"

"Yes, Lirah—like I said, I'll be her hero. I'll bring back the stones for her."

"Hero? I'm the one doing all the work."

"I got information about the rokenstones."

"All you did was find out they were called strikens."

"It helped."

"Whatever . . . I'm going to be the one who finds them," Tavarian said. "And I'm going to find a way back to Rethia!"

Dexius laughed. "Calm down, I'm only messing with you."

Tavarian walked on with a stern face, not saying anything back.

"If you ever want to get him riled up, just mention Lirah," Dexius said to Darby, but it was clearly an attempt to annoy Tavarian further. Darby glanced at Tavarian, and then back to Dexius.

They made camp among some trees off the road in the late afternoon. Lightning flashed in the distance, but no rain yet. At twilight, Dexius carried his new recurve bow over the next hill. Tavarian and Darby munched on some wild berries as they sat in the soft grass. Tavarian started a fire with his flekstones. Darby gathered handfuls of dry grass while Tavarian gathered an armful of small stones. They placed the stones in a circle in the dirt with the dry grass they had gathered in the middle. Rubbing the flekstones together, Tavarian drew a spark, igniting the grass. Once it turned completely dark, the brightflies lit up the sky in thin bands as they flew in single file, hunting for flowers that only bloom at night.

In the flittering glow of the brightfly light, Dexius dragged a fresh kill down the grassy slope. As Tavarian and Darby watched from camp, Dexius prepared the animal to be cooked. He brought several cutlets of meat over to them. Tavarian and Dexius held cuts over the fire with a knife, making sure they were nice and brown on the outside.

After eating, Dexius placed the extra meat in his bag and covered it in a white powder.

"What's that?" Tavarian asked.

"Preserving salts," said Dexius. "Got it from the butcher."

They sat together under the sparkling brightflies and listened to the sounds of the night. Insects, birds, and other creatures sang together in a chorus of the unfettered wilderness. Tavarian heard a loud snore as he lay down. He moved to Dexius, and was about to wake him when he realized Darby was making all the noise.

Day broke and they packed up, resuming their journey. They found little water in this area other than some puddles left over from the rain, but even those were getting scarce. As much as it had been raining of late, the water surely ran somewhere, but there were no ponds or lakes so far.

Dexius found a group of tiny yellow flowers and picked them to show to Darby. He fixed them into the hair behind her ear.

"There," he said, "now the flowers are pretty."

Darby smiled shyly. Tavarian sighed, annoyed that Wynnotha and even Darby fell for these fabricated charms. He didn't like to make such obvious fetching statements. Real charm should come naturally, not through something you plan and use repeatedly.

By midday, there were two travelers approaching, not from the road but from the grassy plains to their right. The two young men split up. One crossed the road, coming around to flank them on the left side, and the other continued toward them.

"What do you think they're doing?" Tavarian wondered.

"I'm not sure," Dexius grabbed an arrow from his quiver.

"Darby, if something happens, get clear of me," Tavarian said. "I may have to swing this sword."

The two men pulled out daggers as they closed in. Tavarian unstrapped the sheath from his shoulder. Dexius aimed his bow at the man on their left. Unsheathing his blade, Tavarian twirled the heavy sword in his right hand, demonstrating that he had some practice. He brought the spinning blade to a sudden stop and pointed toward the man on their right.

"Whoa there!" said one of the men. "Let's not get feisty."

"Just a game, lads," said the other, putting his silver dagger back into his robe. The two men laughed and walked across the road, continuing through the tall grass.

Neither Dexius nor Tavarian said anything until the two were out of sight. Tavarian held his breath, expecting them to return at any moment.

He exhaled loudly. "You think they're going to follow us?"

Dexius returned the arrow to his quiver. "I think they just happened upon us. We must look like easy pickings."

"So now they're going to find someone else to rob," Tavarian tightened his grip on the sword. "Maybe we should have stopped them."

Dexius wiped the sweat from his forehead. "I'm not interested in getting in a fight with blades and arrows any more than they are."

"I just don't like thinking they're going to rob or hurt someone else because we scared them off." Tavarian eyed the hill the pair had vanished behind.

Dexius wrapped his bow over his shoulder. "What do you think we should do? Kill them? Tie them up? We don't have any rope."

"No, I guess not." Tavarian slid his sword back into its sheath. "I hope whoever they run into can protect themselves."

Dexius stared down the long road ahead. "We should have gotten riding animals."

It neared evening when they came to a sharp bend in the road. The dirt road curved all the way around the forest ahead. Trees and thick underbrush lined the area before them—it was the largest forest they had encountered.

"Is this the place?" guessed Dexius.

"I think so—let's go check it out," Tavarian said. "You okay with that, Darby?"

She nodded with the yellow flowers still lodged in her hair. As they approached the line of trees, a sour odor met them from within. Vines twisted and tangled in the thick woods, while moss hung from the old trees above. A misty smoke hung over the ground and the sounds of strange creatures resonated throughout.

"We should camp for the night," said Dexius. "It's going to be too dark in there."

"I guess you're right." Tavarian said. "I still think those robbers gave up too easily. I'm going to take a walk through the area and make sure they aren't following us."

"I told you, those guys aren't going to come back."

"I just want to be sure." Tavarian marched toward a group of trees at the edge of their sight.

As he finished searching the area, Tavarian met back up with Darby and Dexius at the edge of the woods. They'd already spread out the blanket for the three of them to sleep on. As usual, Dexius retold of his accomplishments for the day—mostly how he scared off the two robbers, acting as though they had not been part of it.

After Dexius's talking slowed down, Tavarian thought about Lirah. He wished she could see him now and how close he was to becoming the first Rethian to find the rokenstones and make it back. When he returned, they would promise themselves to each other. They would have a big family and their family legacy would stand forever.

Tavarian, Darby, and Dexius set foot into the swampy forest the next morning. Tavarian took point, clearing out thick weeds and thorny vines with his sword. The old trees twisted and turned in all directions, some even grew into each other. Black, dark red, and green leaves grew thick on the bushes and trees, long and angular. They came to a green, mossy field. The tall stalks of weeds spread out, making it easy to pass through. Tavarian relaxed, sheathing his sword.

After a few steps over the moss, he plunged down.

Large plants and crossing vines tangled his legs in the water he'd fallen into. Weeds and moss covered the path back to the surface, swallowing him. Panicking, Tavarian flung his arms wildly, struggling to get his head above the thick soup. A hand grabbed him, pulling until the tangled growth began to give way and break. Dexius dragged him onto the muddy ground. Tavarian coughed, taking deep breaths.

"You saved me." Tavarian's soaked hair fell dripping over his widened eyes.

Dexius shrugged. "I guess that makes me your hero."

Tavarian pouted at the remark as he got to his feet. Squeezing the water out of his clothing, he surveyed the mossy substance floating on the water's surface. It was algae, covering the water so thickly that it appeared as solid ground.

"What was that about?" Dexius quipped. "Are you that thirsty?"

"I didn't realize it was water."

Dexius laughed. "I didn't either. I'm glad you found out before I did."

"Maybe you should take the lead the rest of the way!" Tavarian bellowed, embarrassed at his mistake.

"You going to let me have that sword?"

"No, you could have bought a sword instead of a useless bow."

"Useless? This bow has already paid off. It's fed us and scared away those robbers."

"It was this sword more than your bow that intimidated them."

"I doubt they were afraid of engaging you in a fight, but they didn't have a chance to get close enough with me and this bow."

Darby began tugging at the back of Dexius's shirt.

"We better get moving if we're going to find those stones and get out of this place before nightfall," Dexius said.

Tavarian turned and rambled through the clearing, testing any mossy ground with his sword. Water covered the entire area, forcing them now to wade through it. They kept to the shallows, stepping on roots twisting beneath the water. Tavarian hit a deep spot, and scrambled to find a place to stand up in.

Dexius shifted his quiver so that it rested on his chest and kneeled to allow Darby to climb on his back because her legs were too short to step over some of the deep pools. The marsh deepened as Tavarian moved farther, raising the water level to nearly up to his knees. The tall reeds sticking out of the water deceived him, making it look shallower than it was.

Stepping onto the next set of reeds made him sink more than knee-deep into the marsh. Tavarian faltered. "Maybe we should go back and find a way around this."

"We're just following you," Dexius said.

"I didn't think it was going to get this deep." Tavarian's eyes caught some movement under the marsh behind Dexius. A long black creature swam from the deeper mire, nearly camouflaged in the dark water.

"Go! Run!" Tavarian said as he began jumping swiftly to each patch of reeds and grass he could find. There was no time to test the water's depth now.

Dexius spun around as the creature opened its long, toothy mouth. With Darby still on his back, Dexius leapt across the reeds. Without paying attention in front of him, he collided with Tavarian, knocking all three off them into the deeper marsh.

Tavarian immediately swam toward a line of trees ahead of them. He checked back for Darby, unsure if she could swim. As he turned, she swam past him. Fortunately, the water here appeared deep enough that there were no plants tangling up their arms and legs.

The creature grabbed Dexius's leg in its mouth, flipping him over and pulling him beneath the water.

"Dex!" Tavarian dropped back to the spot where Dexius had gone under. Climbing to a clump of reeds he could stand on, he grabbed his sword, waiting for the creature to expose itself. Tavarian kicked at the water, hoping to distract the swamp beast.

Finally, Dexius sprang to the surface, swimming toward Darby, who was already on the shore. Tavarian sheathed his weapon, and swam the shortest distance he could to the shoreline. He expected the monster to grab him at any moment. Dexius and Tavarian climbed onto the muddy bank, catching their breath.

Patches of red stained Dexius's pants. He rolled up the cloth to reveal several small puncture marks just below his right knee. He cleaned the algae and mud from the wounds with marsh water—not ideal, but options were limited.

"Just when I was beginning to like this place," Dexius joked.

"I can't believe no one wants to come here," added Tavarian sarcastically.

CHAPTER 12

AFTER RESTING FOR a while, they proceeded into the murky forest. They found drier ground there, but it was dense with tall grass, weeds, and vines.

"I'm not going near water ever again," Tavarian muttered as they stepped through an ever-thickening fog hanging low along the ground.

Dexius smirked. "You may want a drink at some point."

"Not if I can help it," Tavarian said.

They reached a line of trees with wide trunks. Their limbs began near the ground, and crookedly reached high above them. Canopies of dark foliage emanated from everywhere. Flora of all kinds formed together in organic pandemonium. Rust-colored moss hung from the trees above while yellow and white mushrooms protruded from rotting wood along the ground. There were nearly as many dead trees here as there were living ones. Some still stood while others had fallen, becoming part of the spongy turf beneath their feet.

The farther they trudged through the swamp, the stranger the foliage became. Fibrous stalks, tall and pale yellow, formed into ridged shapes that defied gravity. Tavarian sliced through the stalks as he made his way through the swamp.

As he cut a trail through, several eyes turned toward him from the ends of the stalks. Tavarian jumped back. The tall reeds had orange eyes that peered around at him as he approached. Tavarian lowered his blade, apprehensive about cutting any farther.

He brushed the stalks aside with his hands. The eyes turned as their stalks were bent, remaining fixed on Tavarian as he made a temporary passage through them. Surrounded by moving eyes, Tavarian shuddered as he hurried to make it out of the field of stalks.

"Why did you stop cutting these down?" Dexius said.

"I don't like this," Tavarian replied. "They're staring at me. It feels like . . . I'm killing someone."

"They're just plants," Dexius said. "They'll grow back."

"What if their eyes don't grow back?"

"They probably do," said Dexius. "I guess . . ."

Darby poked her finger toward the eyes of the plants. Their lids closed whenever she got too close. Darby and Dexius played with the eye stalks, unnerving Tavarian all the more. This whole place creeped him out.

He reminded himself they were just like any other plant as he sliced through a cluster of stalks in front of him. Eyes continued to roll in his direction as he cut them down.

"Did I tell you how much I hate this place?" Tavarian announced.

"You're the one who wanted to come here," Dexius said.

"Doesn't mean I can't hate it," said Tavarian.

Dexius picked up one of the cut stalks from the ground. Its eye was wide open, but no longer moving. He dangled it in front of Darby, who seemed both entertained and freaked out.

"Don't play with those," said Tavarian. "It's gross."

"I'm keeping it. It will be great to show people."

"It'll be shriveled up by tomorrow."

"Then I'll have a shriveled-up plant eye to show off."

Tavarian advanced through the stalks until they came to an area with pockets of deep, dark water. Old trees grew around the pools, exposing their gnarled roots out of the muddy banks into the water below. Gelatinous creatures scurried, hopped, and slithered away as they neared the trees. Tavarian avoided the pools, but one huge pond required them to find a way to pass around it.

Dexius found an old fallen tree crossing between the smallest gap of the pond, motioning for them to come over. Darby followed, and Tavarian hesitantly crossed the thin trunk behind them. The deep water sloshed under the tree bridge as they carefully crossed. A stream flowed nearby, leading out of sight behind the maze of trees and brush. Did this stream flow into Vallohal? If they got lost, they could follow the stream back.

After treading across the dried mud terrain through scattered leaves, limbs, and vines, the sounds of insects and birds had gone silent. They had passed into an area starkly different from the rest of the forest. The trunks and limbs transformed, resembling vines more than branches. Hanging limp and sinewy against one another, they formed a chaotic web. Strings of thick ooze formed from the plant life. As if melting, the plants dripped slowly into puddles on the ground.

Like Muloken, all the flora had turned dark as ash. The air was abnormally still, as though dead. Tavarian stepped on something. A large dead bird lay beneath his foot. Ahead of them, several dead animals littered the area. His throat tightened as he moved through the carcasses. Surprisingly, they emanated no smell. Surrounding many of the corpses were the lifeless husks of insects that normally fed on the dead.

Rising out of the blackened ground stood an enormous gray boulder. The rock rose taller than Tavarian. The three of them gathered around the stone as Dexius touched its rough exterior.

"This doesn't look like a rokenstone," Tavarian asserted.

"Not the way Wynnotha described it," said Dexius.

"Well, there aren't any other stones around here."

Dexius walked behind the stone. Patterns in the dirt spiraled from the boulder and under their feet toward the rest of the black forest. As Tavarian moved closer, a pale green light flashed across the face of the stone. It quickly vanished and the dull gray surface returned.

Tavarian backed up, trying to regain a glimpse of the effect. After a few attempts, he caught it again. He took a few steps toward the boulder, kneeling where the green glare emerged.

The exterior of the stone became translucent. The green glow pulsed as he stared into it. Tiny metallic bits were floating inside, silhouetted by the pale light, but blurred out of focus. Tavarian's head grew numb. His mind bent, twisting into the faceted crystal, and splitting into different planes.

He traveled along the edge of a path outside his present reality. The other side of the fractal tunnel gave way to another world. Light gray and orange dunes lay across the horizon under a twilight sky. Passing farther into the twisting mindscape, he came to a place with long red feathery leaves hanging from the trees ahead. The red trees opened to a large pool of still water. Its glassy surface mirrored the starry skies above.

"Hey, come over here!"

Tavarian's mind snapped back into his head. His eyesight returned to normal as Dexius pointed out a spot of inky black in the midst of the dead land around them. There was something wrong here—the dark spot seemed too uniform in color to be real. Dexius lowered the eyeball plant he had kept toward the spot. As the orange eyeball breached the darkness, it vanished. When he pulled it out of the spot, the eyeball remained missing. Every part of the stem that had passed into the hole had vanished. Dexius jumped back from the spot, dropping what remained of the stalk.

"Did you see that?" Dexius said in disbelief.

"We have to find at least one stone," said Tavarian, his mind too cloudy to process what just happened. "I'll be a failure. We'll both be failures."

"There's still plenty of swamp left to search," Dexius mumbled. His eyes were still fixed on the puddle of void.

Tavarian collapsed near the stone. An unnatural despair washed over him.

"Are we ever going to find these rokenstones? What if Marvus was right, and they don't exist? We've come all this way for nothing."

"Why did we ever come with you?" barked Dexius. "You're still a loser, always whining."

"I'm too tired to fight with you right now," Tavarian admitted. "I'm going to take a walk."

Tavarian stood back up and moved toward a thicker part of the forest.

"What are you telling me for?" Dexius said as he stood up.

As Tavarian walked, something unnatural flew toward him. A whisper slithered its way into his mind. Like the voice inside his head, but different . . . foreign . . . invasive.

That's it, keep going, it told him. *We will lead you to the stones you seek. Everything you have wanted. Every thought, every breath has led you to this moment. You were chosen because you are the only one in Rethia capable of finding them. You were destined for this because you are the best among them.*

You only need the power of the stones to show them. You don't need their help. You will use the stones to build great things. Not only will you be welcomed among them, but you will also be praised. These companions hold you back; they only want to steal your glory. Come and reach out to us; let us feed you. Then all . . . will see your greatness.

Tavarian rubbed his forehead, shocked by his own thoughts. This voice reached deep down into his psyche, raking the dark, recessive corners of his soul. Buried emotions were dredged. Thoughts he never allowed to fully manifest boiled to the surface.

The voice guided Tavarian until at last he came upon something that should not exist. It lingered before him—a shapeless void floating over the ground. Its form was in constant motion, ebbing and flowing, twisting and turning, as he approached. The outer edge of the shadow scintillated and flickered as if the air itself burned in its presence. The dark object emanated a vibrating, buzzing sound as it moved toward him. The images of trees and foliage warped as it passed in front of them.

"You're just like my father!" Dexius yelled as Tavarian turned to find a bow aimed at him. "Determined to tear our family apart!"

Dexius had not drawn back the arrow yet, but appeared mere moments away from it.

"What are you talking about? I'm not tearing up your family! You need any excuse so you can take the rokenstones for yourself, so you can be the hero." Tavarian seethed as he brandished his white blade.

Dexius pulled back the arrow with the bowstring.

"You won't kill me without getting sliced open in the process," Tavarian declared.

An awful scream tore through the air—a piercing sound that shook Tavarian and Dexius. It dissipated the whispers in his mind. The sustained cry eventually paused, inhaled, and quickly resumed.

Tavarian and Dexius turned around to face the source of the screams. Darby stood behind them with tears pouring from her face. Screaming without abandon, she could barely catch her breath.

"No! No! Nooo!!" she breathlessly voiced in between howls.

Adrenaline rushed like mad through Tavarian, but his attention shifted to the moving shadow.

The shadow hung in the air, anomalous and out of place. Reaching toward them, it oozed and flowed like a drop of oil in water. Tavarian and Dexius bolted toward Darby. She didn't move as she continued to scream. She kicked and swung at them as they tried to get her away.

"Nooooo!!" she cried.

Tavarian grabbed her arm forcefully. He couldn't keep her still. Dexius grabbed her other arm. They both dragged her away as the shadowy entity crept closer.

The decayed logs and trees stretched unnaturally toward the shadow as it passed close by. Branches and vines were sucked into it, vanishing completely. The aura around the dark form flickered as it swallowed nearby debris. It began to close in on them as their legs buckled. They all went splashing into another deep marsh. The shadow suddenly stopped. Hovering at the edge of the marshy water, it watched them from the bank.

Tavarian and Dexius swam farther away from the edge of the mire, pulling Darby along with them, making sure they kept her head above the water.

"Mama! It ate them! It ate them!" Darby screamed and began to struggle against them again.

"What is she talking about?" Dexius said.

"Breathe, Darby—take a deep breath," said Tavarian. "You're all right. Everything is all right." He snapped his fingers in front of her face. "We're both here."

Her distant eyes began to focus. She grabbed on tightly to Tavarian and didn't relax her grip until they had made it to another spot of dry ground.

As Darby and Dexius started running, Tavarian scanned the forest for the shadow. There was no sign of it. Dashing through tall reeds, Tavarian rushed to catch up with Dexius and Darby. They came upon an enormous old tree. It stood near scattered pools of marsh. The tree's roots were exposed at its base like bent legs of insects standing in the mud. In all directions, its branches spread out, jagged and crooked.

Climbing over its roots, they made their way around the old tree. Tangled masses of vines and brush impeded them. Tavarian took point, running as he slashed his sword through the clutter. As they wandered on, they were greeted by gloomy light. The road reappeared. Finally, they were out of the swamp. Here, the road curved around the marshlands. Covered in cuts and prickly thorn needles, they made their way back on the road.

Lights from a nearby town were visible on the horizon. After what they just experienced, none of them wanted to camp close to the swamp tonight. Without saying anything to communicate what they planned to do, they all began walking along the road toward the town.

"What was that thing?" Tavarian asked, his aggression toward Dexius all but faded.

"How would I know?" said Dexius. "You were the one that heard about this place."

"They said it was haunted, but they didn't mention anything like that."

"Haunted? When were you going to mention this?"

"It was just stories. Nothing is really haunted."

"After seeing that, you don't think it's haunted?"

"Whether it's haunted or not, I don't think I want to go back."

"Me either, forget the rokenstones."

"No, there has to be some other place we can look."

Tavarian glanced over at Darby.

"Darby, are you all right?" he said, kneeling down so their faces were level.

She nodded.

"What were you saying back there?" Tavarian questioned.

She rubbed her nose and turned away.

Tavarian touched her elbow gently. "I wish you would speak to us, Darby."

"That thing probably just scared her," Dexius said. "Don't tell me it didn't scare you."

"It was horrifying, but . . ." Tavarian said. "It was almost like staring into . . . myself."

Darby chewed on the back of her knuckles while they talked. A light breeze lifted her hair and dropped it down over her eyes. She was lost in her own world.

"I think it was more than being afraid. She said, 'Mama,'" Tavarian said.

"Little girls cry for their mother when they get scared." Dexius shrugged. "My little sister would always call for Mom. Even when our mother wasn't there."

"Your sister can barely walk yet. Darby probably isn't more than a few years younger than us," Tavarian said. "The whole thing creeps me out. I just wonder if she was remembering something."

"It would be nice if she would tell us."

Tavarian turned to Darby. "Where is your mother, Darby?"

Darby frantically shook her head and her face collapsed into her hands. Tavarian timidly rested a hand on her shoulder for a moment, and then lifted it away. Something about initiating contact or affection remained foreign to him, even though he had witnessed others putting their arm around someone or touching their arm or hand during a conversation. He wasn't sure it would be as welcomed from him.

The road carried them to a V-shaped fork where the road from Strakenbridge met with a crossing road that went winding off alongside another forest. The two roads melded into a singular path through a small market area.

They passed a wooden sign at the front with a word carved into it that read, "Samavere." There were people in separate stands selling crafted goods, but mostly food. Farm-grown fruits and vegetables like they had in Rethia lined the tables, but these were larger and brighter.

Voices blended together as a few other travelers browsed the various stands. Tavarian, Darby, and Dexius walked on through, weaving past the crowd. The pleasant smells of dried grasses and tilled soil greeted them as they came to the center of the town. It reminded Tavarian of home, walking with Lirah on the roads along the farm district. He imagined the view from the edge of the mountain, wondering what mysteries lay beneath the clouds. It seemed so long ago.

A few shops, a tavern, and an inn were located here, but the inn caught their attention the most. They made their way to the inn and walked inside.

"You kids need a room?" said the innkeeper, a well-dressed older man with a brown hat and a gray mustache. He smoked on a pipe made of a hollowed-out plant. "Aren't you a little young to be traveling around by yourselves?"

"We're older than we look," Dexius said.

"Hey, that's a nasty cut on your leg," the innkeeper said.

Tavarian checked his leg, and then remembered the creature that bit Dexius in the swamp.

"Let me call the nurse—have a seat over there," said the innkeeper.

"It's fine, there's no need—" started Dexius.

"No, you need that wound cleaned. Just sit down there and we'll get you fixed up."

They waited in the den for a while until the nurse finally arrived. She carried a large black bag and wore a clean beige jacket. Her long black hair had a touch of gray spilling down over the collar. She lifted the leg of Dexius's pants and cleaned the dotted wound with a wet cloth.

"This looks like an animal bite—what was it?" she asked.

"It was something big and dark," Dexius answered.

"Was it near the swamp?" the nurse asked.

"Yes, it was."

"I hope you'll stay away from that swamp from now on," she said. "All sorts of nasty creatures in there."

"Where did you folks come in from?" the innkeeper asked.

"Strakenbridge," said Tavarian.

"Any news from those parts?" the innkeeper said.

"Nothing I heard about," said Dexius. "Ow!"

Tavarian winced as the nurse stitched the holes in Dexius's leg closed.

"Any signs of Grundians?" the innkeeper leaned forward and took the pipe out of his mouth as if it helped him to hear better.

"Not in a long time, thankfully," said Tavarian.

"Good—we were raided by Grundians some time ago. They stole ale from the tavern, a lot of wood from the mill, and five of our residents."

"That's awful," Tavarian said, not wanting to get into their time in Grunda.

"Did your residents ever make it back?" Dexius asked. The needle stuck him again. "Ouch!"

"Funny you should ask—it's rare that anyone comes back alive," said the innkeeper. "But two of them escaped and came back here. From what they told us, the other three had died months before they got out."

"Are their names Dalson and Reva?" said Dexius, grimacing as the nurse continued.

"Yes—you know them?" the innkeeper raised his eyebrow.

"You know who rescued them?" Dexius asked.

"Dexius, let's not bother the man anymore. We're here for a room," said Tavarian, unsure of where Dexius was going with this.

"Must have been a small army," the innkeeper said.

"No, it was this guy right here." Dexius slapped Tavarian's shoulder.

The innkeeper laughed. "Is that what he told you?"

"Saw it with my own eyes," Dexius said.

He continued to chuckle. "Sure ya did."

"How much for one night for the three of us?" Tavarian asked, trying to change the subject.

"For the Grundian slayer? Seventeen vrupines," the innkeeper snickered.

"And twenty for the leg," the nurse said.

"Twenty!" Dexius worriedly exclaimed. "Uh, Darby?"

Darby reached into a pocket and produced a handful of coins. Tavarian took some and added a few of his own and gave them to the innkeeper and the nurse. A young girl came and led them up the stairs to their room. Inside, a large bed filled the middle of the wooden floor. The fluffy pillows and billowing folds of blankets were a welcome sight. Ornamental wooden posts with carved designs adorned each end. Citizens of every town except Rethia seemed to put time into beautifying the wooden furnishings they had.

They let Darby have the bed, and Dexius and Tavarian clumped together some extra blankets for themselves. The candlelight on the nightstand cast long flickering shadows over the walls of the room, making it creepier than complete darkness. The shadows put the image of that horrible entity in the swamp back into Tavarian's mind. He got up to peer out the window. The night revealed nothing but the lantern lights on the road through town.

Although unseen, he knew the swamp loomed on the horizon. That thing was out there. Tavarian wished now that they had traveled to a town farther away, but they were so tired. There were guards with torches below patrolling the road, but it made Tavarian no less fearful.

The earlier events played over and over in his mind. Logic told him that it couldn't be real. Maybe he had misinterpreted the actual events, but he couldn't shake the uncomfortable thoughts.

There was something more than just the horrifying shadow—a disturbing echo his mind buried deep within. The monster found something inside him; it touched part of his soul and revealed a darkness unknown. Was he really a good person? What had he really done to help anyone?

Tavarian stared at the lantern lights on the street outside. The glow flickered, making the shadows dance. He helped his family when they made him. He fixed or built things for people, but had his motivation been to help them or to show everyone his worth? To prove to himself and others that he was more clever, more intelligent than most of the people in Rethia and perhaps anywhere else. He wanted to find the rokenstones and to bring them back to Rethia—the first person to do so. Where did that desire come from—to help the people of Rethia or to glorify himself?

Perhaps both were true. There were people he cared about in Rethia that he would do anything for: Lirah and his family. As much as he wanted to fit in, Tavarian remained indifferent to most of those he didn't speak to on a regular basis. They didn't seem to particularly care about him.

If he needed incentive to do good, did that still make him a good person? Was it the same way for others? Tavarian did not recall many citizens of Rethia going out of their way to help others that often. There were too many needs for yourself and your family.

Lirah befriended him even while the other students found him odd. Some of her friends didn't understand why she spent time with him. She did the same for Dexius. If anyone deserved to have a better life by bringing back the rokenstones, it was her. Despite the traits he found less than perfect, she exemplified good.

As much as Valea and his parents annoyed him and did not understand him, they wanted the best for him. They rarely were that interested in his inventions, but they pushed him to improve. They deserved a better life too. What other glory did he need? He would dedicate this triumph to them. Then perhaps, other Rethians would view him differently and welcome him.

His attention diverted to a dark figure moving oddly along the road. Its stride had no pattern or rhythm as it walked, lurching forward and falling back. A guard stood in its path, not noticing the stranger as it closed behind him.

As it reached the guard, he turned around and caught the figure lumbering toward him. The guard then propped the man up on his shoulder and walked him toward one of the buildings. Tavarian realized it must have been a drunkard staggering out of the tavern. The guard walked him home. The world had taken on a different tone; everything was now suspect.

Flickers of lightning in the distance highlighted the trees on the horizon. Beyond those trees were the marshlands. He couldn't tell if the lightning struck in the swamp or not. If there were rokenstones in the swamp, it made sense for lightning to be attracted to them. Maybe they could find someone here who knew more about them. He had come too far to be stopped this close to the end. Weariness set in, outweighing Tavarian's uneasiness. He undressed to his underclothes and crawled into the nest of blankets on the floor.

Dawn came, and Darby had already gotten up. With no sign of her in the room, Tavarian hurried through the hallway and down the stairs.

An older woman sitting at the front desk smiled as he rushed to the door. The woman gestured toward a window at the back of the room. "She's right out there."

Darby had taken their clothes to the stream behind the inn. The girl who had led them to their room was washing some bedsheets nearby. Tavarian watched from the window, resisting the urge to scold Darby for going out alone.

A small waterwheel carried bundles of clothes under the swift current of the stream and back up and over to do it again. The girl placed small pebbles in with the clothes as they went around the wheel. She allowed Darby to use it, though Darby hesitated to get very close to her. When she came back to the room, she placed the wet clothes by the window to dry.

"Thank you, Darby," Tavarian said, "but please be careful going out by yourself."

Her face changed into a bit of a frown.

"But we do appreciate it," he reiterated.

"You're the best, Darby," Dexius said, making her eyes light up and her lips curl into a smile.

They got dressed in their still wet clothes, and walked to the tavern in hopes of finding breakfast. Several tables, more than half of them occupied, were spread around the room. At the end stood a wooden bar where a man and three women worked, cooking over a large fire pit.

Three men sat around the bar, but most everyone else sat around the small tables, eating. All of them were wearing worn clothing except for one person hooded in black leaning their head against the wall in the corner. The tavern offered one choice for breakfast, but they were treated to a plentiful meal of some type of meat, eggs, bread, and juice—all for the cost of fifteen vrupine coins for the three of them. How did this small town have so much food to offer anyone who came in here?

As they began to eat, they noticed a sign on the wall near the table. It was a drawing of three men, and itmentioned a reward of three hundred vrupines.

"Three hundred? What do you have to do to get that?" Dexius wondered, mixing the meat and eggs together on his plate.

"Maybe those people are hiring," said Tavarian, referring to the drawing of the men.

The clanging and clattering of metal utensils on plates filled the interior of the place. Puffs of smoke occasionally wafted from the fire into the open space. The burning wood smelled good enough to eat.

"What are we doing now?" asked Dexius. "We should head back to Strakenbridge."

"There was some lightning that hit near the swamp last night," Tavarian said, scooping up a bite of eggs. "We could scout around the edges of the forest, maybe find some stones."

"I'm not going anywhere near that swamp," Dexius said. "Find some other place to look for those stones."

"Not *in* the swamp, just around it," Tavarian said.

"That would be near it," said Dexius. "I'm not going, and neither is Darby."

"Well, I suppose we could ask people here in Samavere."

As they continued eating, one of the tavern maids came out from behind the bar, carrying food and drinks to one of the tables. Amid all the commotion of the people talking, the stranger in black sat motionless in the corner.

"Hey, there's Reva!" Dexius said, waving to one of the maids as she went to deliver another group's order.

"Well, I'll be . . ." she said as she finished setting down the plates. "Dexius, what brings you to Samavere? Surely you didn't come just to see me." Reva picked up a few used empty plates and set them on the table next to them.

"And Darby!" she said. "You still with these two?"

Darby nodded as she sipped on her glass of yellow juice.

"Tavarian, I can't thank you enough for helping us get out of that awful place."

"I'm just glad we all made it out alive," Tavarian said.

"You need to be careful where you go," said Reva. "The Grundians are looking for you."

"Looking for me?" The blood rushed from Tavarian's face.

"They hit Tiramark," she said. "Tore up the place pretty good—said they were searching for a boy."

"How far away is that?" Tavarian asked. He wanted to get up from the table and run instead of wasting time sitting here eating.

"It's a few towns over. You should be safe here. We've been preparing for another Grundian raid," she said.

"We don't plan on being here long," said Dexius, eating the last bit of his eggs.

Tavarian glanced back to the stranger in the corner. Their face was concealed by shadows of obscured light. Unmoving, they merely sat there watching the room.

"What brings you over this way?" Reva asked, glancing toward the bar.

"We were looking for rokenstones. Know where we can find them?" Dexius asked, picking up a piece of bread from his plate.

"There aren't any right here, I can tell you that. It would be foolish to build a town near rokenstones." She held up a finger toward the bar to ask for another minute.

Dexius pointed at the sign. "What do you have to do to get those three hundred vrupines?"

"Oh, if you catch those three bandits, you get the reward," Reva said.

"How would someone catch three bandits?" Tavarian asked.

"I couldn't tell you. I imagine it wouldn't be easy—that's why they are offering three hundred for their capture," said Reva.

"Do you think they're all that dangerous?" Dexius asked.

"They beat up a couple walking outside the town one night, and took all their coins and belongings. Their willingness to attack the vulnerable makes them a threat, I'd say, but that doesn't mean they would be good in a fight," Reva said.

"I wonder if we could take them," said Dexius as he sipped a bit of his juice.

"Are you crazy? You boys shouldn't get involved in that. There's three of them, and you never can tell what desperate men like them will do. They'd be willing to do anything to avoid being killed or taken in," said Reva.

"We were told there could be rokenstones in the swamp," Tavarian mentioned, steering the conversation to something more productive.

"Oh, I suppose there could be some in the swamp—lots of lightning around there," she said. "No one goes near it; too many stories about strange things happening there. That place gives me the creeps."

"There's something in there. I didn't believe in ghosts before, but after being in that swamp, I don't know if I can say that now," said Dexius.

"You actually went in the swamp?" Reva asked. "What made you go in there?"

"Rokenstones, but we didn't find any," Tavarian said.

"You're talking about those strikens right? Why would you even want those?" she said.

"That's what our people sent us here for," said Tavarian.

"The only folks I've ever heard of who went looking for strikens was the Roken Order, but that was long ago. They aren't even around anymore."

"Roken Order?" Dexius perked up. "What's that?"

"Honestly, I don't know," she said. "Those days were before my time. I only hear about them every now and then when some old traveler comes through here."

"What have you heard?" Tavarian spoke earlier than he planned, causing a bit of egg to roll out of his mouth. He put a hand over his mouth, hoping no one noticed.

"They were the only ones who could touch strikens without dying. They gathered all they could find for some kind of dangerous magic."

"What happened to them?" Dexius asked.

"If you ask me, they probably all got burned by lightning," Reva snickered.

"But you said they were the only ones who could touch them—" Tavarian started.

"Just making a joke," said Reva. "What did you see in the swamp?"

"A shadow that moved through the forest . . ." Dexius began. "A spirit of some kind. It was somehow reading my mind, or maybe I was reading its mind."

"This is freaking me out." Reva leaned in. "Then what happened?"

"It spoke to me inside my head. It was like my thoughts were getting mixed up with its voice," said Dexius.

"Yes, that's exactly what happened to me," Tavarian said, turning his attention back to the corner of the room.

The stranger had left. Tavarian turned toward the bar, but only the same three men and one woman were there.

Someone walked into the tavern—a man who seemed familiar. He wore a tunic made of thick material and an old worn hat.

"Dalson, look who's here!" Reva turned toward the man.

"Dexius, didn't expect to see you again. How you been getting on?" Dalson said, lifting the side of his hat to scratch his head.

"Good, yeah, been doing good," Dexius said.

"And Tavarian, yeah, good to see you too." Dalson avoided eye contact with him.

He recalled Dalson punching and spitting on him as he curled up in the corner, trying to defend himself. They didn't beat him up that badly, but he could not easily put it aside. After all their talk of the prisoners sticking together, they cast him out when he tried to help them.

Tavarian merely nodded back at Dalson. He didn't want to be rude, but at the same time, he couldn't force himself to be friendly either.

"Oh, and Darby too. You keeping these guys out of trouble?" Dalson said.

Darby smiled shyly at him.

"What brings you over here?" Reva asked Dalson.

"Had a short break at the mill, and I wanted to run over and see you for a minute," said Dalson as his eyes wandered around the tavern.

Reva gave him a quick kiss. "That was thoughtful of you."

"Brek's not here today?" Dalson asked, scratching the side of his head again.

"He's in the back," Reva said. "Did you need to see him?"

"No," said Dalson as he took his hat off to rub an area above his ear. "Just thought it was strange that he wasn't at the bar."

"He's not always here in the mornings. He'll be around later," she said.

"Oh, right, I wasn't thinking," he said.

"Is everything all right?" she asked him.

"Yeah, yeah, everything is fine." Dalson brushed his hand across his head.

"You keep rubbing your head," Reva mentioned.

"Oh, yeah, a little bit of a headache, I guess," he said. "Nothing to worry about."

"Hey, Dalson, you know anything about rokenstones?" Dexius asked.

"Only to stay far away from them, why?" he replied.

"Right," Dexius said. "But not where to find any?"

"Can't say that I do," Dalson answered.

Tavarian, Dexius, and Darby finished eating and started heading out the door.

"Come back tonight," Reva said. "We're having a special on roast yillah, crushed tomtins, and fresh piloa. It will be my treat."

"That's kind of you, Reva, but unnecessary," Dexius said.

"Please, it's the least I can do," she said.

They left the tavern and walked along the street, passing small stores and shops along the way. Tavarian hoped to find someone who could tell them anything about rokenstones in the area. After walking by a few buildings, they came to the corner of the road near a gate guarded by two men with bows on their backs. Tavarian turned around, crossing the street to the shops on the other side.

"Silra's Jewelry." Tavarian read one of the signs aloud. "A whole shop with nothing but jewels?"

Dexius moved up to the window, peering through. "I see drawings of gemstones."

"Oh, maybe they would be able to tell us something," Tavarian said.

"Like everyone else, they'll probably just tell us to stay away from rokenstones," said Dexius, still peeking through the glass.

As Tavarian reached for the door, he heard something rustle behind them. The hooded person from the tavern brushed past Dexius and rushed at him. The cloaked figure put a cold blade to his neck and pointed a crossbow at Dexius. Dexius pushed Darby behind him and drew his bow. He reached for an arrow, but stopped, pulling the quiver around to check inside.

"Oh no! Did you lose your arrows?" said the cloaked woman. "What awful timing." It was the voice of the flame-haired thief.

"There were just . . ." Dexius shook the quiver as if he didn't trust his eyes.

"Show me where you saw the shadow," the thief demanded.

"I'm not going back in that swamp!" Tavarian tried to loosen himself from her grip, but froze when she poked the knife firmly against his skin. "You can't kill me. You'd lose the information I have."

"Your two friends here can tell me," she said. "If you won't show me, I'll just move to the next one."

Tavarian glanced at Darby and Dexius. "Neither of us is going in there!" Dexius said.

"It seems an introduction is long overdue, Tavarian," the young woman said. "My name is Malidora."

Tavarian froze. Was she saying he was marked for death? If she was truly willing to kill him, he didn't want it to happen in front of Darby. More than that, he didn't want to die. If she killed him, she may drag Darby into the swamp. Where were the townspeople right now? Surely someone should be passing by to help them.

"All right, I'll show you where it is," Tavarian said. "But I'm not sticking around beyond that."

"I knew you would come around eventually," she said, pulling Tavarian around and nudging him ahead.

"After this, stay away from us. I don't ever want to see you again," Tavarian said.

She kept the blade to Tavarian's throat as they walked off the road between two shops, and through the grassy underbrush toward the forest. Dexius and Darby followed behind them.

"I don't mind you coming along," she told them. "But do keep your distance."

"Dexius, don't bring Darby out here," Tavarian said.

"You think she'll listen to me?" Dexius said. "Darby, go back to the room and wait for us."

Darby ignored him and kept walking.

"See? She won't do it," he said.

"Well, you go back to the room, and she'll follow you," Tavarian ordered.

"Enough! The only sound coming out of any of you should be telling me where to find this place," Malidora said.

Tavarian sighed as he continued walking toward the forest on the horizon.

CHAPTER 13

"HOW ARE YOU going to kill a shadow?" Tavarian asked as he tilted his neck away from Malidora's blade.

"It's not a shadow," she replied. "They're called Nulthereals."

"They? There's more than one?" Tavarian inquired.

Their feet swished through the tall grass as they moved farther from Samavere. The tall dark forest surrounding the swamp stood ahead of them, waiting. As Tavarian anticipated entering the swamp again, horripilation formed on the tops of his arms.

"He has a host of them, but they don't all follow him." Malidora directed Tavarian to the right, avoiding a series of thorn-covered vines.

"Follow who?" Tavarian stumbled, forcing Malidora to right him back on course.

"The red-eyed man . . . the Blight Whidge."

"Blight Whidge?" Tavarian's heart beat faster. He feared that he would go insane if they encountered one of the shadows again.

"The source of all the blight. He travels from town to town, killing everything. It is he who summons the Nulthereals; he who holds all the power."

"How did you know they were going to attack this town?" He tried to turn toward her, but she pressed the blade harder until he returned to face the forest ahead. His rubbed his hands together as they began to tremble, unsure if it was the shadow he feared or the darkness within himself.

"I used to think he randomly selected their next location, but I think I'm starting to learn his pattern. This is the first time I have successfully predicted where he would hit next."

As they approached the edge of the dark forest, the haunting calls of raptors echoed through the trees. Vibrating pulses of insects swelled, and the sour smells of wet decay enveloped them.

"So, where do we go?" Malidora asked, grasping his arm with her free hand.

"We didn't enter the forest from this side. I can't tell how to get there going in like this," Tavarian said.

"Where did you enter?" She nicked the side of his chin with the blade.

"On the other side," he said, wincing. "Near the bend in the road."

"We'll go to the other side, then," Malidora grumbled. "Let me just say, if this is a stalling tactic, you are making a big mistake."

"I can get us there," Dexius said from behind them. "Tavarian has a terrible sense of direction, and I don't feel like wasting more time than we have to."

"Well, by all means, lead the way." Malidora stopped Tavarian while allowing Dexius and Darby to move ahead.

Malidora withdrew her blade long enough to remove her hood, letting her hair down. As much as he despised her, Tavarian couldn't deny her wild beauty. Like a magnet, she pulled his gaze, and he hoped for any glimpse of her and her mesmerizing hair. It appeared as beautiful and dangerous as she was.

Pretending to look at something out in the forest, he stole another glance. Her eyes locked onto his from the side of her face as a knowing smile crossed her lips. Tavarian's cheeks burned with embarrassment, and he directed his eyes to Dexius walking ahead of them.

She put the blade against Tavarian's back, allowing him to walk more freely through the forest. At times, Darby stopped to wait for them to move closer as though checking on Tavarian.

"Who is the girl?" Malidora asked.

"What do you care?" said Tavarian.

"Is she a sister?"

"Not that it's any of your concern, but no."

"You're protective of her. How did you come to travel together?"

"She was held captive," said Tavarian, "and I helped her escape."

"What made you risk your life to help her?"

"I was in the same mess she was. I got myself out, and helped some others."

"But you keep her with you," Malidora said. "You could have taken her to another town to be cared for."

"She trusts me, and I don't want to break that trust."

"So, you take her along on your quest despite the potential danger."

"I didn't ask her to come—I let her make that choice," said Tavarian. "Don't try to criticize me after everything you've done!"

Malidora continued walking. "Don't get so defensive. I was the same way at her age. I hated sitting around the house all day. I wanted to get out in the world and discover new places, new people. She knows you are on some kind of quest, and she wants to be part of it."

Tavarian huffed. "She's nothing like you."

"Things have changed a lot since then . . . I've changed," Malidora said. "The world turned out to be very different than I imagined. I've had to adapt to survive in it."

"That's what you call it? Surviving? Stealing and using others to get what you want?"

"If you want to change the world you have to take some . . . shortcuts," she said. "I could go through this brief life following all the rules while watching Isodonia slowly die, never making a dent. Or I could do what it takes to stop this. A nail can hold a board, but a hammer can build a wall."

"There was only one shadow, one town abandoned, one dead spot in the swamp—it's far from destroying the whole world."

"You've haven't seen the things I have. There's nothing left of Varkandor, the continent across the sea," she said. "The complacency you hold is exactly what the Blight Whidge thrives on."

"What are you saying I should do?"

"Whatever it takes," said Malidora. "By doing nothing, you are helping it. This is how it passes from one town to the next, unchallenged."

"Dexius and I have got a job we were chosen to do. If this is your quest, then good luck in it, but it's not part of our mission. We haven't been trained to deal with spirits or shadows."

"What greater mission is there than this? I don't know much about your town, but they are all the same. Powerful people wanting more control. Hammers that need nails," she said. "If you were chosen to do something, it was so you could take the risk while they get the reward."

"I'm helping my community," said Tavarian, "my people. I was chosen because I am among the few who can go where others can't."

"That's what they always tell people like you," Malidora said, "that you're sacrificing for the greater good."

"Rethia isn't like Strakenbridge," said Tavarian. "Thieves get punished. Everyone gets the same amount of food and clothing. We care about each other and make sure everyone has what they need."

"If they have all that, then why are you here?" said Malidora. "Try to look past the illusion."

"You haven't been there," Tavarian noted.

"Every city begins as an organization of people, designed to protect one another, and to serve their needs. It's a living organism, breathing life into everything. Over time, the organism grows until it takes more effort to keep it alive. The bigger it becomes, the more it must be fed. Its processes and functions become the focus, while those it is supposed to serve are ignored. It changes from an organism into a machine controlled by those who keep its processes running, and who keep feeding it. They gain all the power while everyone else loses it."

Tavarian clenched his teeth. He wanted to tell her how wrong she was about Rethia, but nothing he could say would dissuade her. At least she had stopped pressing the blade so tightly against his skin—perhaps he should keep her distracted. "Who set you on this path to stop the curse?"

Malidora paused for a moment, glancing down at her feet. "It's by my own choice." She lifted her head. "As much as I would like to say that I am only doing this to save every person in Isodonia, the truth is, I just want to kill *him*." An expression of hatred crossed her face for a moment—an expression Tavarian hadn't noticed from her before.

"The man with the red eyes?"

"Yes, the Blight Whidge."

"Why do you want to kill him so bad? It sounds like more than trying to save the world."

"Because he ruined my life," she said. "He killed everyone I ever cared about—my family and friends. He destroyed my homeland, the beautiful steam forests that were once alive with amazing creatures, and the rest of my kindred. The only reason I keep going is for the satisfaction of watching the life slowly ooze out of him."

"Oh . . . I-I had no idea."

"I'm not sure why I'm telling you this," said Malidora. "But it was nice to say it out loud for once."

"How long ago was that?" Tavarian asked.

"Nearly fifteen years ago—I was younger than your friend Darby at the time."

"I'm sorry that happened," Tavarian said. "That's too crazy to even imagine."

"If I've learned anything about life," said Malidora, "it's that you have to take what you want before it snuffs you out."

They came upon a different side of the marsh than they had encountered the day before. Green film covered the surface and crawled up the surrounding trees, covering them in spongy growth. Dexius and Darby stopped before the tall reeds along the bank.

"We should walk around this. There was a large, hungry creature in these waters," said Dexius.

"No, we'll go through—I'll cover anything that comes near you," she said as she readied her crossbow.

"I-I don't really want to go in that water," Dexius said.

"Stand aside, then. Tavarian, go! We don't have time for this!" Malidora put the blade to his back, increasing the pressure through his clothing.

Tavarian tepidly waded into the slimy water, and then began to swim. There were large flat plants here, floating on the water. He swam around them, hoping to avoid getting tangled in any weeds or roots. Relieved, he finally reached the thick, muddy bank on the other side of the pond.

Malidora took a running start and leaped out over the marsh. She landed on top of one of the floating plants, and surprisingly, it supported her weight. Leaping up into the branches of an old tree nearby, she swung her legs up and over the limb, coming to a standing position long enough to jump out again. Catching hold of a group of vines, she swung out to land on another plant floating farther out in the marsh.

She continued to do this across the marsh, never pausing, as if it were a normal stroll down the road.

"That's how you do it," Malidora crowed as she reached the bank.

"If I hadn't hurt my leg, I would do that," Dexius said, pointing to his bandage.

Malidora grinned. "You're good at excuses. You must get a lot of practice."

She trained her crossbow on them as Tavarian crossed through the marsh. He used the floating plants as much as he could, but did not attempt swinging through the trees as Malidora had. Following behind, Dexius and Darby swam across the green water, catching up with them as they continued through the swamp, passing through tangled vines and thick underbrush until they reached another field of eyeball plants like those they had walked through the day before. Not far ahead stood the dead forest with the enormous stone standing up from the blackened dirt below.

The familiar dread at the sight of the fleshy, sinewy vegetation sent chills down his back.

"This is it . . . we're not going any farther," Tavarian said.

"You weren't lying," she said. "This is definitely the blight. It hasn't corrupted much of the swamp yet. They will attack before it gets to the point where most would notice it."

"We got you here, so now we're leaving," said Dexius.

"Fine," Malidora said. "Go wherever you wish. I'm going to end this once and for all."

Tavarian and Dexius hurried away from the area, leading Darby back the way they had come. Tavarian checked back once more as Malidora ran off through the blighted area. As they came to the edge of the marsh, Tavarian hesitated.

"I think I would rather go around this time, I don't like getting in that slimy water," he said.

"Neither do I—let's find a way around," Dexius agreed.

As they wandered along the bank, a thick growth of enormous roots from a cluster of trees blocked their passage. They would have to move farther away from the water to get around them.

As they moved deeper into the forest, the colors of the trees suddenly vanished as a bolt of lightning ripped through the area to their right. The birds scattered in all directions as the thunder sounded immediately after. It was the most concentrated form of power Tavarian had ever witnessed. Each individual hair on his body stood straight up. He turned to check if Dexius and Darby were all right. They were shaken, but otherwise fine.

He began walking in the direction of the lightning blast.

"Tav, where you going?" Dexius incredulously asked.

"Just wanted to check it out," Tavarian replied.

Weaving through the trees, Tavarian hurried toward the spot.

"That's probably not the best idea, Tav!" Dexius said.

As he passed through the old twisted trees, one stood out. It had nearly split in half. A small flame still burned at the point where the lightning had struck it. Near the base of the tree, a stone formation protruded through the dirt among its knotted roots. Red crystal formations grew everywhere in Nalacea, but they were nothing like this. The twisted black crystals pulsed with a violet filament within them.

Tavarian's eyes widened. They matched Wynnotha's description of a rokenstone. He ran toward it, retrieving the hammer from his satchel.

"Don't!" yelled Darby unexpectedly.

The voice caught Tavarian off guard. Hers was probably the only voice that could break his focus in this moment. Darby ripped a piece of cloth from the bottom of her tattered trousers. Tavarian paused, waiting for an explanation.

She brought the piece of cloth over to him, holding it out for him to take.

"Wrap this around the handle," she said quietly. "Metal will activate it, and your skin touching the metal will activate it."

Tavarian rolled the cloth around the metal handle of the hammer as Darby instructed. Checking her eyes for approval, he knelt near the black crystallized formation. As he hit the ends of the rokenstone with the hammer, red sparks jumped out from the impacts.

After several hits, it gave way, and pieces broke off from the stone formation. Tavarian reached out for one of the small stone bits on the ground until Darby's wincing startled him.

"Don't touch it with your skin either. "

He tore pieces of cloth from his own trousers and picked up five pieces of the formation, wrapping each one in cloth and placing them in his satchel.

"Safe," said Darby.

"We've got it!" He held his bag toward Dexius.

"I don't think I believed this would really happen," Dexius said. "You found it."

"We both did," Tavarian said. "It took both of us to get here."

"I guess you're right," Dexius said, "and neither of us could have done it without Darby."

"That's for certain," Tavarian said. "Thank you, Darby."

As they moved toward the water, Tavarian became disoriented. The trees of the swamp stretched out before them, making the distance to the marshy water much greater than it should be.

"Which way is it, Dex?" Tavarian asked.

The wind whistled through the trees, and then settled as insects chattered around them. The world spun and then righted itself as they walked on. The sounds of the insects came to an abrupt stop. The whistling wind grew loud once again. It's pitched changed to a screech. Tavarian quickened his pace. He wanted to leave this swamp forever. They still had to walk around the slimy water to get out.

"Dex, which way?"

He had to get of this swamp right now. Tavarian crept toward the edge of terror. He tried to calm down. *Slow breaths, deep breaths*, he told himself. The more he tried not to panic, the more he exhausted himself. His heartbeat was quickening, and his chest grew tight. The treetops reached downward as he moved toward them. The screeching wind buzzed. The chattering insects vibrated. He could feel them. Their vibration erupted inside him, crawling under his skin. They tried to get out, but escape eluded them. They were all trapped together in this madness.

"Ta-Tav'rian . . ." came a soft quavering voice.

Tavarian sought the source through the twisting trees stretching forever into the sky.

"Tav'rian," said the voice again. His frantic mind slowed. The vibrating stopped, there were no insects. The sounds of the murky forest had died.

Darby stood still, pointing at something. The silence grew frightfully loud. Tavarian's eyes traced the direction she pointed. He found Dexius, whose eyes were closed as if he were standing there asleep. The forest widened. Something stood close—a presence; an object his mind could not interpret. As if his brain's sense of logic masked it from view.

The dark blur came into focus. Towering over them, the thing held Dexius in its grip. Shrouded in smoky, dripping darkness was a being formed of shadow—the shape of a person with a dark hollow body. Its eyes burned like red, glowing flames.

Bristling energy surrounding the silhouette-like form as it reached toward Dexius. The color faded from Dexius as a bright mist reached toward the red-eyed man. The shadow man turned to Tavarian. Its red eyes glowed brighter.

A swift, winding sound pierced the air. Flashing across the sky, a dark red streak tore through the forest. The arrow protruded from the shadow fiend's head. Stunned, it dropped Dexius. The mist spilled back into Dexius's body giving color once again to his skin. The dark being brought its hand to the arrow in its head. The arrow faded into smoke, dissipating into its shadowy fingers. It turned back to Dexius, raising its hand toward him again. Another arrow struck. Two more quickly followed. The shadow man lifted his hand to the arrows as another barrage slammed into him, causing him to lean forward before dropping face-first into the mud below with a hard splat.

Tavarian and Darby pulled Dexius away from the fallen shadow. Malidora walked toward the dead man, triumphantly reloading her crossbow.

"Remember me?" she announced, kicking the shadow man and turning him over with her foot. "Enter the twilight with the name Malidora burned into your soul!"

She fired another bolt into its head. His glowing eyes faded, while his features became more human.

"Your trail of blight has come to an end!"

Bubbling from the wounds erupted a thick dark liquid. Malidora reached down to pluck the arrows embedded in the man's head. The fluid poured from his nose, ears, and mouth. It continued to flow out, more than could have been contained inside the shadow man's body. Malidora took a step back, watching until the liquid had accumulated a sizable puddle on the ground nearby.

A retching suction came from the ooze as it solidified. It formed into various shapes as it rose from the pile. A whispering chorus of unintelligible words escaped from the horrid mass as it continued to grow. Malidora backed up farther, eyes narrowed—the first time her face presented anything other than complete confidence.

The shape rose, forming into an unnatural monstrosity. It towered over them in height with long arms nearly touching the ground. It stood on a tripod of misshapen legs. Dark fibrous bands weaved together from its head casting a webbing above the area. The white energy flowing around it formed a series of glowing tendril arms that extended outward.

Malidora aimed her crossbow and fired. Her arrow streaked red as it flew toward the thing, and then sizzled as it disappeared inside. She drew another arrow from her side quiver, firing again with the same result. Dexius, Tavarian, and Darby ran from the tendrils until they were out of their reach.

Malidora jumped, backflipping as one of the appendages lunged at her. The nightmarish beast vanished from its spot, materializing at another part of its web, closer to Malidora. Before her feet hit the ground a second tentacle grabbed her.

The monster brought her close, siphoning the life from Malidora into the gaping void of its shadow body. Tavarian unsheathed his sword and ran at the monster. One of its unoccupied tentacles leapt toward him. Tavarian swung, hacking into the attacking tendrils. After several cuts, he chopped through one of them as another grabbed hold of his leg. He slashed into it until his sword freed him. Unlike the void body of the monster, these bright appendages could be damaged.

Tavarian made his way through the gauntlet of tentacles, rushing to Malidora. She struggled to move as some of her arrows spilled from her quiver onto the ground. Swinging his sword into the arms holding her,

Tavarian moved closer to the beast. Dexius ran into the fray. He picked up a handful of arrows Malidora had dropped, firing at the tendrils with his bow. Malidora was finally loosened from the creature's grasp. As Tavarian helped her up, she ran with the rest of them away from the monster.

The monster shook with fury, but did not move to attack them. It extended its remaining tendrils outward. The creature vanished and reappeared again at the edges of its web, but it could not reach. It began teleporting itself to every possible position within its web, as if out of frustration.

The creature did not move its legs to walk—it only seemed able to teleport along the path of its webbing. The severed tendrils slowly regenerated, but remained out of range. Malidora fired another arrow at the monster to no effect.

A vibrating sound came up from their left as foliage twisted and warped, making a sizzling sound as it flew into two nearby Nulthereals coming toward them.

"Head to the water!" Malidora shouted. They immediately followed as she ran to the marsh, diving into the thick green muck.

The two Nulthereals floated to the edge of the water.

"We've got to figure out a way to destroy that thing," said Malidora.

"Don't look at *me*," Dexius said, turning away.

"What is it about water?" Tavarian wondered. "Does it hurt them?"

"No, it doesn't do anything to them," said Malidora. "But they never float over water."

"This swamp water could kill anything," said Dexius.

The group swam farther into the marsh. They moved deeper into the murky water, several ripples headed toward them. Near the surface were the scaly backs of large creatures.

"Meligiles! Climb on the kekri plants," Malidora said.

The names were unfamiliar to Tavarian, but he assumed that kekri plants were the floating swamp plants scattered about on the water.

Malidora loaded her crossbow and fired. The bolt hit the closest meligile. It stopped moving, leaving a bloody patch in the water. As she quickly loaded another arrow, Dexius fired a shot, hitting another. The group of swamp creatures drew closer as Malidora hit a third.

Before Dexius could get his next shot off, one of the meligiles burst from the water near Tavarian. Its long slender snout of razor-sharp teeth pushed its way through the plant toward him. Tavarian plunged his blade into the meligile's head. Its body slid off the kekri plant and into the opaque marsh. Dexius switched targets, firing a shot into the next closest creature.

Malidora had taken out two more, but they were still coming. One of them began tugging on the kekri plant Darby was standing on, causing her to fall into the water. Dexius immediately redirected his aim and shot the reptile that had pushed her in. Tavarian reached for her hand and dragged her onto the kekri he stood on.

The meligiles surrounded them as Malidora and Dexius continued pumping arrows into as many of them as they could. Tavarian stabbed and slashed the creatures that came close to him. Finally, there was nothing left moving in the water. A mass of meligile bodies floated on their backs, exposing their pink and white underbellies.

Malidora led them across the marsh as they jumped from kekri to kekri as fast as they could go. Finally, they had found solid ground again. They climbed out of the marsh and into the thicket of reeds and vines. Leaning against a group of trees, they took a rest. As they caught their breaths, a vibration sounded through the trees. Nulthereals were coming toward them. They had gone around the marsh.

The buzzing and vibration gave way to a strange chatter. Several rodents leapt at them from high in the trees. The small furry creatures landed hard on the ground, some not moving afterward. One landed on Tavarian, biting his neck. It drew blood until he grabbed it and slung it against one of the nearby trees.

They all ran to edge of the swamp as the rodents chased them, jumping, clawing, and biting them. Swatting and grabbing the creatures from themselves and each other, they at last made it to daylight. Malidora seized one of the rodents from Darby's hair and slammed it into the ground.

Once they were out of the forest and back on the road, the rodents stopped and scurried back among the trees. They stood bending over in the middle of the road, breathing heavy and fast. Dexius sat down, touching the red scratches covering his arms.

"That wasn't so bad, was it?" Malidora quipped as she gasped for breath.

A large lump in the back of Dexius's shirt started moving. Malidora smacked the lump and it started running across his back toward the right sleeve. Dexius frantically removed the shirt. He began stomping on the shirt where it lay on the ground. Grabbing the rodent by the tail, Malidora flung it into the trees.

They walked until they had reached the farms outside the small town. Malidora led them into an old abandoned building near one of the farmhouses outside Samavere. They collapsed into the rickety chairs inside a small kitchen area. After searching the cellar, Malidora returned with a few bottles of ale and a pan of water. She poured the ale onto the cuts and scratches on Darby's arms and neck. Darby grimaced as the alcohol reacted to her wounds, but she made no sound. After fetching more clean water, she treated her own wounds and then offered to do the same for Tavarian and Dexius.

CHAPTER 14

CHILDREN PLAYED IN the distant fields as Tavarian watched through the window of the dilapidated building. The kids were oblivious to the dangers and fears of the world that he now knew. Their shadows grew long as the sun fell low behind the haze.

Malidora found some stained drinking glasses and set them on a gray table sitting in the corner. She poured what was left of the clean water into three of the glasses.

"Meligiles don't typically behave that way," Malidora collapsed into a dusty chair and poured some of the ale into her glass.

"They don't typically try to eat people?" Dexius picked Darby's chair up with her in it and moved her in front of the table in reach of one of the glasses.

"They never attack in groups like that," Malidora stated, eyeing Darby as she picked prickly burs out of the thick material of her dress.

"Forget meligiles, what was that . . . monster thing?" Tavarian inquired, turning away from the window.

Dexius took a sip of water. "I was hoping no one was going to mention it."

"I've never seen anything like it," said Malidora, downing the contents of the glass in one swift gulp. "I thought this would all be over once I killed the Blight Whidge."

"Maybe it is," Tavarian said. "It couldn't follow us. It only moved where those web things were."

"It's been walking all across this world until now," Malidora ran her fingers through her black and red hair, rubbing her temples.

"Maybe it could when it was inside a man," Tavarian's nose bent slightly against the back of his knuckles as he attempted to make some logical sense of this. "But outside of him, it can't."

"Yes." Malidora turned up the rest of the bottle. "But I'm not sure why."

"So, we can just leave it there and never have to worry about it again. Sounds great to me," Dexius said.

"If it is immobilized," Malidora said, "all the more reason to finish it off. Besides that, there are still Nulthereals out here. They may still be a threat to this town."

"What was it doing to you, Dex?" Tavarian moved closer to the table, grabbing his water.

"It was trying to kill me," Dexius remarked, taking a sip from the glass in front of him.

"It was consuming you," Malidora stood and removed the battle dress she wore over her other clothing. Folding it on the back of the chair, she went back to her seat.

"It felt like a lot of pressure." Dexius finished the glass of water and set it down on the table, staring at the wall as if it were miles away. "Like I was folding up inside myself."

Malidora set her crossbow and quiver on the table. "There are some whose minds are broken by the shadow's sway. They rant and rave about a dark realm the Nulthereals came from. They say it is better to die than to be consumed by The Hollow."

"The Hollow?" Tavarian shivered. "I keep hearing that. What is The Hollow?"

"I have no idea." Malidora slid one of the arrows out of her quiver. "But I don't think I want to find out." Many of the arrowheads appeared stained with a red powder, but there were some that were longer with a shiny silver point.

Tavarian glanced at her as she inspected the other arrows. "There was this crazy man in Strakenbridge yelling about something wandering behind the stars."

"What's a star again?" Malidora lifted an eyebrow as she pushed the arrows back inside.

Dexius examined a puffy scratch on Darby's forehead, rubbing the skin around it. "You don't know what a star is?"

"She's never seen the sky." Tavarian propped his head on his fist, remembering that she had never been above the obscuring clouds like they had.

Dexius stiffened his shoulders. "A star is like the sun but really far away."

"So, patches of cloudy light?" Malidora picked up the crossbow. She pulled the trigger, making a faint clicking sound, and narrowed her eyes as if there was something she didn't like.

"Sort of, but there are no clouds way up in the heavens." Dexius stretched his hand up into the air.

"So, what is there?" Malidora glanced up from the crossbow.

"Just empty space, I guess," Dexius peered through the window.

Malidora narrowed her eyes at him again. "Empty space?"

"And stars," Tavarian added.

Malidora closed her eyes. "Well, that certainly clears everything up. I don't see how any of this is relevant to killing this thing,"

"Are you sure it can be killed?" Dexius motioned for Malidora to pour some of the ale in the bottle she held. She rolled her eyes and took another drink.

"If it can exist in this world, you can kill it." Malidora wiped the corner of her mouth. "Or at least send it back to wherever it came from."

"Your arrows went inside of it," Dexius remarked

"Everything did," she said. "Trees, rocks—it's like a hole."

"I cut one of its arms." Tavarian rose from the chair.

"Yes, those can grab and hit," Malidora said. "I suppose normal rules apply to them, but the body does not seem to be a physical object. Perhaps it really *is* a hole."

Dexius shook his head. "How do you destroy a hole?"

"You fill it," she leaned over the table. "Or seal it shut."

"Those shadows swallowed whole trees," noted Tavarian, pacing the floor. "I don't think filling it will work. We should leave it alone; leave it there immobilized in the swamp."

"Yes, we found the stones," Dexius said. "We need to get back to Rethia."

"He's right." Tavarian quickly opened his bag. The rokenstones were still there, wrapped in torn cloth. "We have our own mission to complete, and we aren't equipped to handle something like this."

"You three are the only other sane people I know who have witnessed this." Malidora leaned back in her chair, closing her eyes. Shadows of the trees outside fell over the house, dimming the light shining through the window. "No one else will believe me."

"We've nearly died in that swamp twice." Dexius stood up from the chair, grabbing his bow. "I think we've pushed our luck far enough."

"We're not warriors." Tavarian stopped pacing. "Why don't you take some of that money you steal and hire some?"

"It's not enough to buy an army," Malidora said. "Mercenaries don't appreciate abstracts. They prefer to fight things that bleed. I'm not sure that they will stay around when they're faced with something that defies combat skill, strategy, and general logic. Besides, I like to remain inconspicuous. If I go offering large sums of money to soldiers, people will start asking questions."

"Are you really a thief?" Dexius asked.

"I wouldn't say 'thief.' I fancy myself as more of an opportunistic adventurer," Malidora replied, resting her chin on her hand as she braced her elbow against the table.

Dexius drummed his fingers on the table. "You don't look like a thief. Tav is always blowing things out of proportion."

"I blow things out of proportion?" Tavarian retorted. "You realize why your quiver was empty earlier, right?"

"I found some of them in the woods," muttered Dexius.

"Show him, Malidora," Tavarian nodded toward her quiver.

Malidora glared at Tavarian before turning to Dexius. "I took them to protect myself. I couldn't risk being shot while you led me to the blight's location."

"Could you go ahead and give them to me now?" asked Dexius.

"Of course," she said, picking up the quiver from the floor. She reached inside and counted out seventeen of Dexius's arrows, handing them to him.

"They're too long to fit in my crossbow," Malidora said. "There's no reason for me to keep them."

Tavarian grabbed the back of the chair. "Besides selling them?"

"You're very distrusting," she said, resting her foot on the table. "At least you are learning the nature of the world."

"It's not the nature of the world," Tavarian said. "It's you."

"I'm simply a product of the world. The world needs repair, much like my crossbow." Malidora patted her crossbow sitting on the table.

"Again?" said Tavarian. "Can you go one day without breaking it?"

"You used to be a lot nicer," she replied. "This time, it wasn't my fault. I had to do some quick loading to get through those meligiles."

"What do you plan to give in trade for my services?" Tavarian asked.

"How about your life?" She tapped her hand on the barrel of the weapon. "This crossbow saved you and your two friends here quite a few times back there."

"All right, fine," he groaned. "I'll look at it, but we would not have been in danger had you not forced us in there."

Tavarian sat in one of the chairs and began tinkering with the crossbow. Darby kneeled up in her seat, watching Tavarian work.

"But now you realize how important this is," said Malidora. "If we don't stop it now, the last of us will be huddled in a corner wishing they had acted sooner."

Tavarian removed a frayed tension spring from the crossbow and began bending it back into shape.

"I liked the world a lot better when I didn't know this thing existed," Dexius said, staring out the window.

"So did I . . ." Malidora said.

Once he had the spring in a form that could provide resistance, Tavarian worked it back into the firing mechanism.

"Like Tavarian said, we have no experience fighting. We'll help spread the word, but that's all we can do."

As he pulled the unloaded crossbow's trigger, the firing mechanism released the spring with a clicking sound.

"I had plenty of experience by the time I was your age, but I suppose my life has been far from typical."

Tavarian pushed the crossbow toward Malidora. "It's ready to go now," he told her.

"Excellent." She moved her feet back to the floor. "I suppose I'll see you boys around then."

"I'm sure I speak for everyone when I say well be with you." Dexius got up from the chair, putting a hand on Darby's shoulder.

"I suppose I should thank you." Malidora smirked. "Even though the assistance had to be dragged out of you. For your sakes, you better hope I find a way to destroy these things, so you have a home to go back to."

"Well with, Malidora. Be safe out there," said Tavarian.

"You would wish a thief well?" Malidora quipped.

"Not a thief, but maybe an opportunistic adventurer," replied Tavarian.

Malidora smiled, giving him a wink as she continued drinking what was left of the ale. Tavarian got up from the table. Darby sat for a moment eyeing Malidora, then rose from her chair to follow them.

"Take care of her," Malidora said, glancing at Darby. "She's been through enough in her short life already."

"That's one thing I can promise," Tavarian said.

"She's our family now," assured Dexius.

❧

Tavarian, Darby, and Dexius went back to the tavern. Even though Tavarian hated to let Reva treat them to a meal, they really needed to save all the coins they could. After finishing their dinner and talking to Reva for a bit, they walked back to the inn and checked back into their room using some of Darby's coins. They spent the remaining few hours of the evening sitting in the room and talking.

Tavarian wiped down his blade with a scrap of cloth while Dexius bragged about how many meligiles he brought down during the frenzy.

"Roken," Darby said, watching him clean the red and black stains from what used to be a shiny white and gold sword. Tavarian paused at the rare sound of her voice.

"It's not broken, just a bit dirty," he told her.

Before long it turned pitch black outside and they crawled in between their sheets to rest.

As the night wore on, they were awakened by loud voices outside. Tavarian rushed to the window to find several people gathered in the middle of town. Some of them were standing around talking, while others were frantically pacing back and forth.

"What's going on out there?" Dexius whispered.

"I'm not sure—something must have happened," said Tavarian.

"Let me see." Dexius got off his pallet on the floor and joined Tavarian by the window.

Guards were beginning to come out. Some of them were talking to a group of people near the tavern. Others were controlling the crowd, keeping them off the streets, and trying to calm the commotion.

"What do you think is going on?" Dexius said.

"I'm going to go down and find out," Tavarian said.

"I'll go with you."

"You better stay and watch Darby."

Darby sat up in the bed with terror on her face in the faint, flickering glow of candlelight.

"Yeah, I'll stay with her," said Dexius. "Don't stay too long. Come back and tell us what's going on."

Tavarian made his way out of the room and down the stairs. No one attended the door in the entryway. He opened it and went outside into the cool night air. A crowd of people were gathered not far away while across the street, a man and two other people talked to a few of the guards. Tavarian moved toward the crowd, intent on finding out the cause the disturbance. He couldn't yet make anything intelligible out among the murmuring of the group.

When he reached the first group, he stood close enough to make out what some were saying.

"She was out picking perecots last time we saw her," said a voice in the crowd.

"Who are they looking for?" asked another.

"Marigol—such a troubled girl."

"Probably ran away; her father is always drunk."

"They keep her sister locked in a room most of the day."

"They think she went into the swamp."

"What in the gloom would drive her in there?"

"They're wanting to go searching for her tonight."

One of the guards walked over to the crowd. "Any volunteers to search the edge of the forests tonight?"

"Don't go out there," someone said. "Don't go anywhere near that swamp."

"Sorry miss, but unless you want to volunteer, you are free to go back inside now," said the guard.

"There's something unnatural in those woods," she replied. "There will be more missing if you go out there."

Tavarian turned toward the direction of the voice he now recognized as Malidora.

"All the more reason to find her, if there's anything out there," someone said.

"I'll go," a young man said as he stepped forward. A woman also stepped up to go, and they walked back toward the smaller group across the street.

"This is becoming all too familiar," Malidora said after spotting Tavarian in the crowd near the inn and making her way over to him.

"I thought you wanted someone to go out there," Tavarian said.

"Not like this," she said. "Definitely not at night."

"You didn't set all this up?" Tavarian asked skeptically.

"You think I kidnapped a girl, and made everyone think she is in the swamp just so they would go out there and help me fight that thing?" Malidora said.

"It sounds like your style," Tavarian said.

"You really are quite annoying, but I suppose it's something I would consider," said Malidora. "I almost wish I had thought of it, but this wasn't my doing."

"What do you make of it, then?"

"I think you should get back inside, rest up, and be ready to leave this town in the morning."

"Why do you say that?"

"The Blight Whidge is beginning to draw people toward the swamp. Unless you want to witness what happened to Muloken firsthand, I suggest you don't stay a moment longer than you have to.

"All right, what are you going to do?"

"I may go back out there in the morning. You go on back to sleep."

"Don't do anything crazy."

She smiled. "Crazy is what I do best."

Tavarian made it back to the room and recounted what he had learned to Dexius and Darby. Once they settled back in their beds and got past their initial restlessness from the excitement of recent events, they finally got back to sleep.

ණ

The next morning, they packed up and made their way downstairs. Darby pointed to a string that Tavarian had neglected to tie in his tunic. He stopped and corrected his oversight while Dexius went over to the desk.

"Was the missing girl found?" Dexius asked as he offered the key to the maiden at the desk.

She angrily marked on a piece of cloth paper with an ink pen. "How should I know?"

"There was a lot of commotion last night—thought you may have heard some news." Dexius held out the key, but the maiden kept scribbling, beginning to tear a hole in the paper.

"It's not my fault!" said the girl.

Dexius jerked his head back. "Did I say something wrong?"

"Don't blame the noise on me!" the maiden continued tearing the paper apart with the pen as if oblivious to her actions.

Since she wouldn't take the key, Dexius placed it on the desk. "I wasn't blaming you. Thank you for the room."

Tavarian glanced at Dexius as he started out the door. Dexius's face bore the same confusion he suspected crossed his own. They decided to stop at the tavern for breakfast and discuss the best path back to Rethia. After sitting at the table for a while, no one had come to take their request. Some of the maids came by to certain tables and the tavern-keeper stood behind the bar wiping down the wooden surface.

Dexius got up and went to talk to Reva. "Hey, we've been waiting for a while, could someone take down our order?"

"You want special treatment? I'm trying to do my job!" she said. "If you'll get out of the way, I can do it."

"I just—we're leaving soon, if you could stop by our table before we leave—" Dexius said.

"When I get to it!" she snapped.

Dexius sat back down.

"That didn't go so well," Tavarian said, pleased that Dexius had failed so badly in a social interaction.

"Must be on edge with the girl missing. I'm going to check with the tavern-keeper," Dexius said, getting up from his seat again.

Tavarian glanced at Darby, who followed Dexius with her eyes, clearly interested in hearing more about the missing girl too.

Tavarian strained to listen to the conversation across the room.

"Did they find the missing girl?" Dexius inquired.

The tavern-keeper stopped wiping down the same spot of wood he had been cleaning for the past few minutes. His eyes focused on Dexius. "What girl?"

"The one they were trying to find last night," said Dexius. "There was a lot of commotion outside our room."

"I haven't heard anything about a missing girl. Now, what can I get ya to drink?" he asked.

"I'm surprised you haven't—you of all people." Dexius said.

"I don't keep up with everyone around here, kid. Now, what'll it be?" he said.

Dexius returned to his seat, squinting his eyes as if replaying the recent conversation in his mind.

"That was odd," said Tavarian. A loud thud sounded on the other side of the tavern as a man burst into the room.

"There you are!" said Dalson, stomping loudly into the tavern. Everyone inside paused for a moment and turned to look at him. Some continued to stare, while others went back to their food or drink.

"What can I get ya?" the tavern-keeper replied, directing his attention back to the bar he was wiping down with a cloth.

"Don't act surprised." Dalson slowly walked to the bar, patting his side as he did. "You know good and well why I'm here." He walked with straight posture, not appearing to be drunk.

"Could I get ya a measure of brew?" the tavern-keeper did not glance up this time, continuing to wipe a small area of the shiny wood.

"That won't get you off the hook," snapped Dalson as he stopped just before coming to arm's reach of the bar.

"What'll it be today?" said the tavern-keeper as he continued to wipe the same spot in a circular motion. His responses did not seem to fit Dalson's actions—maybe he was trying to calm the situation down.

"Reva told me everything." Dalson remained in front of the bar, feet slightly spread apart. "I know why you keep her working late."

Dexius and Tavarian glanced at each other, uncertain what this would lead to. The tavern-keeper kept rubbing the same spot on the bar with a towel. Dexius brushed through the hair resting on Darby's forehead, making it stand up more than helping. Darby pushed his hand away and brushed through it herself.

"I didn't tell you anything! What are you going on about?" shouted Reva, coming out of the back room. "You know exactly why I have to work late. If you made more money at the mill, I wouldn't have to!"

"Oh, don't you try to blame me for this!" Dalson snarled. "Whatever you two have going on, it's over!"

The tavern-keeper did not glance up at all.

"You hear me?" Dalson pounded his fist on the bar, close to where the tavernkeeper continued to wipe it.

Dexius huddled up close to Darby, still messing with her hair.

"What can I get ya?" the tavern-keeper had no reaction to Dalson's behavior.

Dalson rushed the bar in a rage, leaping over it and onto the tavern-keeper. They both landed on the floor at the backside of the bar area, rattling a stack of plates that rained down all around them, a few of them breaking on the floor in the process.

Tavarian stood up from his chair, unsure what to do. Dexius sat with his feet squeezed up onto the chair as he covered Darby's eyes with his hand.

Grabbing one of the plates, Dalson hit the tavern-keeper over the head, breaking the plate into splintered pieces. With nothing left of the plate but a shard of glass in his hand, Dalson stabbed the tavern-keeper in the chest. He pulled the piece of the plate out of the wound as a red stain spread across the tavern-keeper's apron. Dalson struck him again as he gasped for air, doing little to defend himself.

Tavarian moved toward the door, glancing back to find Dexius still holding Darby and keeping her eyes covered. He motioned for them to get up, and Dexius grabbed Darby, carrying her to the door.

"What . . . will . . . it be . . . today?" the tavern-keeper wheezed as though unaware of what was happening.

As they dashed out of the tavern, many of the patrons continued eating as if this happened every day. Tavarian turned back as Reva ran over, pounding her fists into Dalson's back. Most of the diners remained seated, but some ran over to join Reva in attacking Dalson.

Tavarian searched for a guard outside, but the only one nearby was yelling at a kid lying on the ground, while another kicked at him. Smoke rose from behind the buildings at the center of town. Fights broke out outside of nearby buildings, and continued in the streets.

"We have to get out of here!" Malidora said, running up behind them. "Focus on my voice! Don't listen to the whispers!"

A familiar vibration grew loud. The numbing in his head made Tavarian dizzy.

In the ear of his mind, a voice whispered, *Your friends conspire against you. Do you know what they say when you are not around? They want the stones. If you don't abandon them now, you will have to kill them later.* Tavarian put his hands tight over his ears, but it did not stop the voices. *You know she is a thief. She has already stolen from you. If you follow her, she will take everything.*

Seeds of doubt, already planted, began to blossom. Why should he follow Malidora? What did Dexius talk to Darby about when he wasn't around? Had he tried to turn her against him? How could he trust them? A dissonant voice joined the chorus, its volume overtaking the whispers.

He wandered out of the daydream as Malidora shouted at him. She held his face between her gloved hands as his focus returned. Tavarian grabbed hold of Darby's hand. Malidora turned and dashed after Dexius.

What were these thoughts? Were these really the shadows manipulating him? It felt so true, like they told him secrets he desperately needed to know. Tavarian remained unsure of how much he should trust any of them.

He moved toward Malidora as she grabbed Dexius by the arm. The door of one of the nearby shops burst open as a man tumbled outside onto the street. A woman ran to the fallen man and knelt beside him. She laughed at him, taunting him rather than helping him. Had everyone in this town gone mad?

"Dexius, whatever thoughts you are having, they aren't your own," Malidora said. "Remember how it felt when we were in the swamp, the numbing feeling . . . the buzzing? Recognize the weakness in yourself; don't let them exploit it. If you concede your flaws and move past them, they have no power over you."

Darby ran over and grabbed his hand. His focus changed to her, making him smile for a moment. Then his face changed. His eyes glazed over, staring off as if at something distant. His brow furrowed.

"I wanted a family," Dexius lamented, "but I'm never good enough. If everyone likes Tavarian so much, just go and leave me here. It's where I belong,"

Darby tried to pull him forward, but he pulled his hand out of her grasp.

"If it helps, I don't like Tavarian that much! Now move!" Malidora yelled into his ear and pulled him with her to get him walking. Even though she may have only been trying to snap Dexius out of his stupor, Tavarian couldn't help but feel backhanded by the remark.

Darby grabbed Dexius's hand again and he squeezed back and let her guide him.

"This escalated faster than usual," Malidora said.

They crossed the center of town as complete chaos broke out. Fires had started in several buildings. Guards were cutting people in the streets. Large groups of people threw stones or anything they could find into windows and at other people.

Fortunately, Tavarian and the others moved through the center of town largely unnoticed. Most of them were engaged in attacking someone or defending themselves. As they passed the town's center, there were several people slowly walking past the shops to a grassy area. Something dark strode toward them—a shadow in the form of a human, its red eyes burning as it headed toward the town. It was the Blight Whidge they had fought before, but this time in the form of a human female. Flanked by four Nulthereals, they marched to the city.

"It found a new body," Malidora said.

The group of people continued their approach. The Nulthereals pulled them with some invisible forces as they got close enough. They dragged people into their bodies, and swallowed them into the void. Some woke from their stupor as they were pulled in, unable to resist.

Darby closed her eyes. "They're eating them!" she said, holding Dexius's hand as they ran.

Tavarian slowed for a moment as the shadow girl walked onto the road behind them. She moved toward a large group of people engaged in a fight. There were some in the mob trying to break it up but having little success.

Stretching out her hand toward them, the shadow girl drained them as their skin grew pale and their forms began to blur. It was the same thing the Blight Whidge had done to Dexius. A blur of their bodies stretched toward her hand until they became nothing but a shapeless mass of energy in front of her.

The shapeless energy writhed and fluttered as black liquid poured into it—the arrival of a new Nulthereal. It pulled in the rest of the people in, swallowing them into the new abyss.

Something tugged at his arm as he turned to find Malidora urging him to run. As they reached the gates, two guards with spears came and blocked their path. Malidora grabbed her crossbow and a single fluid motion, she fired at the first guard, and then reloaded and shot the second one as they ran through the gate, arrows streaking with red trails. Dexius flung open the latch on the wooden gates. They leaned into the gate with their shoulders, moving it enough to pass through and out of the city.

CHAPTER 15

THE FOUR OF them ran until they reached the bank of a river. Though not as wide as Vallohal, it would be difficult to cross it safely. The waters were rough, moving swift and steady downstream.

The dirt path they were on curved around the water to a nearby boat launch. Wooden boxes sat close to the edge. Discarded parts of fish lay scattered about around them. A few birds had gathered, and were busy cleaning them up. There were more birds circling overhead, as if waiting for the next fisherman. It struck Tavarian that it may be a while before anyone comes to this area to fish again.

There had been a symbiotic relationship between the people and birds here. The birds were cleaning up what the fisherman didn't want, and they had an easy, dependable supply of food. It probably went beyond even that as insects likely cleaned up bits that even the birds missed.

Perhaps now the fish in this area would live longer. What would it mean for the birds? Would they have to move on to survive? Maybe the tables would turn. The fish would now win, while the birds would lose. Which was it supposed to be? Which was the better outcome, he wondered. Who should be the winner? Maybe that's why the shadows had come—to change the course of nature, and to shift the balance away from people.

Perhaps Malidora was right—it is all one big machine. She referred to towns and civilizations, but maybe it went beyond that. What if nature itself ignored the struggles of organisms within it to achieve its own purposes? Even as doubt crept along the edges, something deep within his soul stirred—someone had chosen him to accomplish a task for Rethia. He refused to believe life had no meaning. Every obstacle that had been put in his path, he had overcome. In spite of his weaknesses, his strengths had taken him this far.

Initially, Tavarian questioned the council's judgment when they chose Dexius as a Descender. Yet, he wouldn't have made it this far without him. How much easier would this task have been if all the Descenders had survived and worked together?

"So, what now? Why did we go this way? We should have gone back out the way we came," Dexius said as he paced chaotically in the hard wet sand.

Darby stood close, watching him.

"Because of the river, genius. Being near water is the only protection we have right now," said Malidora as she removed her skirt armor and lay it over a nearby bush.

"We should go back to Strakenbridge." Dexius was still frantically moving about. "It's much safer there."

"You can do whatever you like; I was trying to get us to safety." Malidora took off her quiver and placed it and her crossbow on a tuft of grass. "I need to regroup and prepare for the fight ahead."

"You're going after that thing again?" Tavarian brushed off a moss-covered log before sitting on it.

Malidora sat on a large rock, staring toward Samavere. "I've been chasing it all my life—of course I am."

"I can't take this anymore. This is making me crazy. I feel like I'm . . . like I'm . . ." Dexius rubbed his head as he continued to walk in circles, unable to remain still.

"Losing yourself?" Malidora finished, leaning back and propping herself up on her arms.

"Yes . . . how are you not affected by those things?" Dexius stopped his hectic movements, glancing at her.

"I am," Malidora replied. "Their words are in my mind as well."

"But you don't seem to be," said Dexius.

"They affect me, but I don't allow them to control me," said Malidora. "They can be resisted. Look at Darby—she got through it."

Dexius turned to Darby. "Are you saying it doesn't work on girls?"

Malidora laughed.

"Did you not see the women in Samavere? Inciting men to fight each other, joining in the fights themselves, taking torches to buildings," said Tavarian. "The Blight Whidge is now in a woman's body."

"I guess I was focused on getting out of there," Dexius admitted. "So how do you resist it, Malidora?"

"I know myself." Malidora sat up straight on the stone. "We all have a dark self, but few recognize it. Even fewer accept it. I know my weaknesses, my temptations, and selfish desires. The Nulthereals know them too. They draw out your worst traits and exaggerate them. You must know your way around before you go walking in the dark. Otherwise, you'll end up lost forever. You have to understand your aggression, the evil thoughts inside that you normally restrain.

Allow some of that darkness in, but only as much as you can control. You are still trying to find out who you are and what you want to be. You doubt yourself and seek acceptance in others . . . that makes you vulnerable."

"Wrong," Dexius said. "I don't care what anyone thinks about me."

"But you do." Malidora slid off the rock, setting her feet on the ground. "You are full of jealousy and insecurity. That is what Nulthereals prey on."

"You don't know anything about me!" Dexius bellowed, turning away from her.

"How is Darby able to resist?" Tavarian said.

"She has encountered her dark self," Malidora said. "A lot has happened to her at such a young age. Perhaps she's encountered Nulthereals before."

"She's seen them as many times as we have," said Tavarian.

"Are you certain?" Malidora asked.

Tavarian kneeled to speak to Darby at eye level. "Darby, did you see these shadow things before we met you?"

She closed her eyes and tilted her head in affirmation.

"You did? When? What happened?" Tavarian questioned.

Darby tightened her eyes and turned away.

"I wish we could get her to talk to us," Dexius said.

"She's seen more than her mind can process," Malidora said. "Give her time."

"So, what are you going to do now?" Dexius said, raising his eyebrows.

"Try and predict its next move," Malidora said. "I think I've figured out the pattern now—I was right about Samavere."

"There's a pattern?" Tavarian said.

"I believe so," Malidora said. "They never move into a populated area brazenly. They use subtlety and cunning, never hitting targets in close proximity. If they did, word would spread faster. I believe it chooses a large radius and hits small communities within it first, choosing those that have enough distance from one another. What little news that does come is disregarded as ghost stories or crazy."

"Why would it do all that . . . if it can't be killed?" Dexius was half asking and half making a statement.

"You're right . . ." said Malidora. "It must have a weakness!"

"We need to figure out what it is," Dexius said.

"First, I think you should bathe in the shallow water here, relax, and calm yourself," Malidora said.

"You think that will help?" Dexius asked.

"If it doesn't, at least you won't stink anymore." Malidora grinned.

Dexius frowned and sniffed his shirt. "How do you know it's me? Could be you."

"It's definitely you—I'm familiar with your scent," she replied.

"My scent? Wow, I mean . . . I know it's me and all, but let's not get obsessive here," said Dexius playfully.

Tavarian couldn't help but crack a smile; it was the first time he had been amused by one of Dexius's remarks.

"I have a keen sense of smell. It's how I track people." She winked.

"Just what an obsessed person would say," said Dexius with some extra swagger. "If you wanted to bathe with me, all you had to do was ask."

"No, you boys go first and us girls will set up camp," said Malidora.

"I'm not going in with you out here," Tavarian said. "You'll take all our stuff."

"Darby needs someone to go with her when it's her turn, and it doesn't need to be either of you. Besides, you don't have anything I can use," said Malidora. "Darby is the one with the coins."

"How do you know that?" Tavarian and Dexius both eyed her skeptically.

"I have ears," Malidora said. "Giving all the coins to her may be the smartest thing you've done. I wouldn't take them from Darby."

Tavarian and Dexius glanced at each other.

"Do you think we can trust her, Darby?" Dexius asked.

Darby looked uncertain, but signaled she did.

"Don't worry, I'm close to stopping the Blight Whidge; there's nothing you have right now that helps me do that," Malidora mentioned.

"Call us if she tries to do anything—we'll be watching," said Tavarian.

Tavarian and Dexius bathed in a secluded shallow spot in the river, and then Malidora and Darby took their turns. Dexius caught sight of a wild treg not far away and killed it with his bow. Tavarian gathered some tree branches and made a fire by rubbing the flekstones he had in his satchel together. When Darby and Malidora returned, Malidora helped Dexius clean and cook the animal. As night settled over them, they gathered around the fire to sleep.

"You still have my blanket," Tavarian said as he took the one he still had from his bag.

"And I appreciate it," said Malidora, removing the blanket wrapped in her vest. She unfolded it beside Darby as she stared at the cracking fire.

"I never said you could have it," said Tavarian as he watched Malidora offer Darby a place to lie down.

"Think of it as an unintentional donation to the cause." Malidora smirked.

Tavarian sighed. "I want it back eventually."

Darby crawled over to where Tavarian sat on his blanket and lay down beside him.

"I'll share the blanket with you," Dexius said, walking around the fire toward Malidora.

Malidora let out a quick raspy laugh. "No thanks, I'm not offering to share it with you."

"It's Tavarian's blanket. Tavarian, can I sleep on your other blanket?" said Dexius.

"Very well," said Malidora before Tavarian could answer. "You're at least smart enough to know better than to try anything."

"What would I try?" Dexius said. "If I decide to do something, I do it."

"If you need any help making a good decision . . ." Malidora tapped her fingers on the crossbow beside her.

Dexius grinned uneasily and wrapped himself up in the other side of the blanket next to Malidora. Unsurprisingly, he didn't get that close to her. Soon Darby's rhythmic breathing next to Tavarian and the chorus of nocturnal creatures remained the only sounds in the world.

Dexius put out the fire as morning came, and cut some pieces of cooked meat from the treg. After they had finished eating, they buried the fire with the sandy dirt.

"I need to get moving. I'm headed to Grenova. If you aren't coming with me, this is where we part," said Malidora as she sat on the blanket. She rested a tattered piece of cloth on her bent knee, studying it. Tavarian moved around behind her, curious to see what was looking at.

"Wait . . ." said Tavarian. "You have a map?"

"I'm using it to predict their movements," she said, keeping her eyes on the cloth.

"How long have you had that?" Tavarian stood over her, trying to make out the words.

"A while," Malidora said, peering up at him. "What does it matter?"

"You could have shown me how to get to Strakenbridge."

"You were already going the right way."

"Is Grunda on there?" Tavarian inquired, kneeling beside her for a closer look.

"There are many things on here," stated Malidora. "What of it?"

"I guess I wouldn't have known what Grunda was at that point anyway," Tavarian resigned.

"Are you coming with me or not?" Malidora prompted. She folded the map up, placing it in a vest pocket.

"I haven't changed my decision," said Tavarian, grabbing his satchel from where it lay on the blanket. He took a quick look through it, making sure nothing had been taken. "We have our own mission, and I don't think we are capable of helping you with this."

"I can't shoot shadows," said Dexius. "And apparently, I'm too insecure to resist them. Besides, I don't think it's going to work out between us. You kick too hard in your sleep."

"What makes you think I was asleep?" Malidora grinned.

"We'd better start heading toward Rethia," said Tavarian, staring at the horizon. "Any advice on how to climb a mountain?"

"No, I've never needed to climb one," Malidora said. "What direction is Rethia?"

"Uh, that way I think." Tavarian pointed back toward Samavere.

"Actually, it's more that way," Dexius corrected, motioning in another direction.

"I would suggest you go southeast around Samavere and then cut west," she said.

"I completely agree," said Dexius.

"You can come with me around Samavere if you want," Malidora offered.

"I can't believe I'm saying it, but that sounds good," said Tavarian. "If we run into any Grundians or shadows, I definitely want you around."

"Couldn't get enough of my scent, could you?" Dexius teased as he stood beside her.

"Don't make me change my mind." Malidora marched toward the forest ahead.

"You okay with that, Darby?" Tavarian asked.

She seemed to approve.

Dexius, Tavarian, and Darby moved behind Malidora into the forests covering the area behind the small stream flowing near Samavere. Many of the trees here were short compared to the old ones in the swamp, allowing a good amount of sunlight to filter through. Light gray stones covered the landscape, enveloped in golden grass. The uneven ground made for an ankle-twisting hike.

"What are you doing?" Dexius asked as Malidora kneeled to plunder through the grass and dirt along the way.

"Checking if anyone has been through here of late," she replied.

"Has there been?" asked Tavarian.

"Not in this area," she said.

"Do shadows even make tracks?" Dexius asked.

"The Nulthereals don't, but the Blight Whidge does," Malidora said, rising to her feet.

As they passed around the town, dense smoke rose behind the trees. The hazy gray smoke indicated the fire itself had burned down to embers and was smoldering.

"Do you think anything is left?" Dexius asked.

"Very little," said Malidora.

"Can we get closer?" he wondered.

"No, we shouldn't risk it," she said. "There's nothing left you would want to see."

They continued through the forest, leaving the smoking remains of Samavere behind them. Malidora appeared interested in something she found on the ground, and led them on a different course, into the thicker parts of the forest.

"What did you find?" said Dexius.

"When I know, I'll be sure to tell you," she replied.

The afternoon wore on and it began to rain. The thick foliage they were under provided decent shelter from the drops that fell lightly. At times it came down steadily before returning to a light mist. They followed Malidora as she made a path through the trees, and then curved around back in the other direction, stopping occasionally to examine the ground.

"Are you sure you know where you're going?" Dexius said.

"Would it help if I said yes?" Malidora peered up at him.

"I think we're going around in circles now," Tavarian said.

Darby continued as if the walking had not tired her at all. Though shorter than the rest of them, she kept pace with ease, sometimes running off to investigate a new insect or to pick a wildflower.

It grew darker and Malidora picked up the pace. Tavarian began to tire out. He had not had a good night of sleep since the first encounter with the shadows in the swamp.

Something alerted Malidora. She gestured for them all to keep quiet and stay put. Crouching behind stones and ducking under trees, she moved ahead of them. She snuck through the underbrush, vanishing within.

A little while later, she returned. "There's a group of bandits over there. I believe it is the same group who were wanted in Samavere. As soon as it gets dark, we're going to take them out."

There was a tingling in Tavarian's chest. "What? We're not attacking bandits!"

"Come on, it'll be fun." Malidora cocked her hip. "They have a docimare I really want."

"Docimare? What is that?" Dexius perked up.

"Tall, four legs, strong back," said Malidora. "You can ride them, or they can pull a cart."

Tavarian let out an exasperated breath. "We're not risking our lives for that."

"Of course not—I have a plan." Malidora pulled the sleeves of her battledress, making it tight around her shoulders.

Tavarian rubbed the back of his neck. "I think this is where we part ways."

"You haven't even heard my plan," said Malidora, folding her arms across her chest.

Heat flushed into Tavarian's face. "I don't care what it is! There's no plan I'm going to follow that involves stealing from bandits."

"We could get where we are going so much faster." Malidora stepped up to Tavarian, giving him a hard pat on the shoulder. "I need to get to Grenova before the shadows do."

Dexius leaned toward her. "What is the plan?"

"Dexius!" Tavarian glared at him.

"There are three of them are in a camp over there." Malidora swept her hair back. "Actually, four, but one of them hasn't seen much action." She waved a finger at Dexius. "You will take one of them out with your bow. I'll take the second and third. Tavarian will take out the unseasoned one while that is going on."

Tavarian shook his head. "You really think the three of us are going to take out four bandits?"

"I could do it myself," she said, turning a palm to them, "but I was trying to include you guys."

Dexius raised an eyebrow as he peered at her. "Your plan involves a lot of vague statements like 'take them out'—can you elaborate on those parts?"

Malidora put her hands on her hips. "I'm allowing room for creativity. You wouldn't tell an artist how to paint. I can teach you how to fight if you wish."

"It doesn't matter." Tavarian's head twitched. "We're not doing it."

"Very well." Malidora twisted a strand of her hair between her thumb and forefinger. "But you can't ride on my cart once I get it."

"I'm in," Dexius said, taking the bow off his shoulder. "These bandits have probably done some terrible things. They deserve to die more than the treg I shot yesterday."

Tavarian grabbed both sides of his head in his hands. "Are you crazy, Dex? They'll do bad things to us . . . they could be killers. She's not even after them for any kind of justice, she just wants a faster ride."

"So she can stop the shadows." Dexius ran his fingers across the fletching of his arrows, straightening them out.

"I'm glad someone is beginning to understand this." Malidora strutted to a patch of soft grass and sat down. "I thought your friend would have come around by now."

"Tav?" said Dexius. "We're not friends."

Malidora laughed. "You guys are definitely friends. You're just too jealous of each other to notice it."

As night began to fall, Tavarian sat with Darby while Dexius and Malidora snuck through the brush toward the bandit's camp. He put a hand on Darby's shoulder, hoping she didn't completely understand the situation.

He thought about killing the fourth bandit, and how it would have been his part of the plan. What if the bandit hurt Dexius, would he be able to live with himself? He hadn't forgiven him for punching him in front of Lirah and nearly ruining his plans to escape the Grundians. When it came down to it, why did he even team up with Dexius?

Dexius saved his life a couple times—he couldn't forget that either.

He worried about Darby. How could he face her again if he let something happen to Dexius?

"Darby, I'm going to make sure they're okay. Let's find you a hiding place," he told her. They found a spot by a rock surrounded by short bushes, and had her sit up against the stone.

"Stay hidden," he said as her eyes grew large. "It'll be all right. I'll be close by and won't be gone long."

Tavarian spotted Dexius behind a tree, but he couldn't locate Malidora. He crouched in the underbrush, watching as Dexius drew back his bowstring and aimed at one of the bandits sitting by the fire. A red streak flew into the camp. One of the men was leaning against a tree, talking to the others. The arrow hit the tree, missing him by inches. The bandits jumped to their feet. Two of them drew swords while the one sitting by the fire grabbed a bow. Dexius stood there in position with his bow drawn.

The bandits all took cover in the trees surrounding the camp. The bowman aimed, seeking any sign of movement. Dexius remained still. The bowman signaled to one of the men, who ran off into the thicket, flanking their position. The other swordsman circled around the other way. As the bowman crept from behind the tree, a red, streaking bolt hit him in the chest. Dexius still had his arrow in position, all he had to do was release.

Malidora burst from the bushes and ran straight toward one of the flanking swordsmen, loading her crossbow as she ran. He turned toward her, but her arrow found him before he realized what hit him. The other swordsman slashed at her from behind. Tavarian drew his blade, and without thinking, broke his cover in the tree line.

Malidora ducked away from the swing, sweeping the bandit's legs out from under him, and then firing a bolt into his shoulder. She stood over the swordsman as he grabbed the bolt that was stuck in him.

"In case you are wondering," she said. "The name's Malidora." She shot him with another bolt to the heart and the swordsman's limbs fell limp. The fourth bandit backed toward the thick underbrush, armed with a knife. Tavarian ran at him as Malidora loaded her crossbow. The man turned to run.

"Don't!" shouted Tavarian. "Unless you can outrun an arrow."

The man froze and turned around. He dropped the blade and bowed his head sheepishly as if expecting a death blow at any moment. Malidora rushed over with her crossbow aimed at him. Dexius still had not moved.

"Dexius, go check on Darby," Tavarian suggested.

"On it," Dexius replied as he rustled through the bushes.

Tavarian inspected the man's pockets and patted down his clothing, checking for hidden blades. He found nothing, satisfied the man was unarmed. The man eyed Tavarian curiously.

"I'm not here to take prisoners," Malidora said.

"Please! I only drive the shippy," said the man.

"The what?" Tavarian inquired.

"The shippy," he said, "th-the cart the docimare is tied to."

"You're a criminal," Malidora retorted. "There was a reward for bringing your group of bandits in either dead or alive in Samavere."

"I've never committed any crime," he said. "As I said, I only drive the shippy."

"You're complicit," Malidora said. "You were aiding them."

"I don't know what they did," he stated. "They said they were gambling on tallor."

"What's tallor?" Dexius asked as he walked up with Darby following behind him.

"They were wanted in several towns across Isodonia," Malidora said. "They beat men and women, even a kid in one case. They robbed people, stabbed a few, and then as soon as the local authorities made connections, they left town."

"Dex! Don't bring Darby over here!" Tavarian snapped, realizing there were bodies of bandits lying on the ground nearby.

Dexius put his hand over Darby's eyes. Tavarian rubbed his forehead, hoping Darby had not seen the bodies. He tried to avoid them himself.

"I wasn't aware of anything criminal going on," the man said.

"Come on," Tavarian said. "You must have suspected something."

"I knew something wasn't right," he said, lifting his head to look him in the eye for a moment before gazing off. "But I didn't ask questions. I need money to get away from here, to start a new life."

"What's your name?" Tavarian asked, returning his sword to its sheath.

"Amateurs," Malidora sighed. "We don't need his name."

"Yarvik," he said, glancing toward the docimare as it huffed and bellowed, pulling against the rope that tied it to a nearby tree.

"What kind of life were you planning for, Yarvik?" Tavarian asked, hoping to find something that would keep Malidora from killing him.

"We don't need information from him." Malidora wiped the sweat from her forehead.

"Hopefully, I'll find a place far away from the Grundians and start a family," Yarvik said.

"I'm not taking prisoners, so either I shoot you in the head, or you provide us with some kind of value."

"Don't shoot him, Malidora." Tavarian moved in front of Yarvik. "I believe him."

"That doesn't change anything," she said.

"I can drive the shippy for you!" said Yarvik. "It takes skill and familiarity with the animal—otherwise, you are not going to get very far. It's why they kept me around and paid me. I'll give you a nice, friendly discount."

"Discount? You think I'm paying you?" Malidora said, her weapon still pointed at his head.

"One hundred percent discount?" Yarvik said.

"That's more like it," Malidora relented. "I'm not dealing with prisoners, so if you require too much attention, we're back to the original plan."

"Thank you for your mercy! Y-you won't regret it," Yarvik cried out. "Where are you headed?"

"Thank *him*," she said, motioning at Tavarian. "I fully intended to drop you."

CHAPTER 16

DARBY'S FACE EXPRESSED excitement as they bounced along on the shippy. They came out of the forest and into the grassy fields ahead. Dexius seemed to be having fun too, as they had nothing like this in Rethia. Though not a smooth ride, it was faster and much less tiring than walking. Having cleared enough distance from the town, Malidora had Yarvik drive them back onto the road. The smoothness of the dirt pathway made for a much more comfortable trip. Parts of the road were nothing more than worn grass in two lines through the meadows, perfectly fitting the spacing of the wheels of the shippy.

Yarvik hadn't said much, which was not a surprise with Malidora watching his every move.

"What happened to you back there?" Malidora asked Dexius. "You never fired a shot."

"I-I . . . it's different than shooting a treg," Dexius said.

"They would not have hesitated to kill you," Malidora said. "Why give them leniency? If you want to get anywhere in this world, you have to be the one doing the pushing. Just like this mission you two are on—someone sent you on this quest and you are out here doing their bidding, giving them more power."

"We were chosen—it's an honor," Tavarian said.

"We'll be the first ones to bring them back. We're going to welcomed like heroes," Dexius added.

"You'll be forgotten within days. Whoever you give those stones to, whatever they are for, you are handing them more power, more control. When you go back, keep the stones for yourself. Keep all the power," Malidora advised.

"It's not about power, it's about helping everyone in Rethia," Tavarian retorted. "The world isn't as callus as you think. The people in Rethia don't care about control. They just want to feed their families."

"It may not be about control for the common people, but they unknowingly serve those who crave it. You'll come to understand this as you get older, but until then . . . enjoy your blissful ignorance," said Malidora.

They rolled on down the road, passing a couple small towns along the way. Even with the obscured blue moonlight through the clouds, not enough light remained to continue their journey. They found a stretch of trees that made for a good place to park the shippy—hidden away from the eyes of thieves who may try to take it while they slept.

"Who would walk around in the dark just to steal?" Dexius asked as they sat around the campfire, eating some cooked meat they had bought in the last town they had passed on the road.

"There are some that do," Yarvik said.

"Like the bandits you were with?" Malidora said.

"Or sometimes bounty hunters like yourself," Yarvik said. "And then there's the mawlons—we don't want to attract them."

"Mawlons? What's that?" Tavarian asked.

"A myth," Malidora said. "Supposed to be furry beasts that walk upright. Sharp claws, long snout, big teeth—they are said to wander through the plains and forests at night, attracted to certain rare metals. Supposedly, they will kill for them."

"It's not a myth," Yarvik said. "I've heard them."

"Heard them?" Malidora questioned. "How do you even know what they sound like?"

"When I was young and had no real home, I stayed in a small town by a lake. It was a good place to earn some coins. We fished in the lake for pere and gabbils, which I could either sell or keep for myself. I lived with an elderly couple in their barn house. They raised docimares and trained them for riding. I and a few outcasts rented the empty space to sleep.

"They had two daughters staying in the house with them. The daughters had children of their own in the house as well. For about a week, every evening around dusk, a strange sound would come through the forest. It was like an animal call, but one that we hadn't heard before." Yarvik tried to imitate the bellowing sound.

"It was unnerving for those of us sleeping in the barn, but with no signs of anything being out there, we tried to ignore it." Yarvik glanced around at their faces in the moonlight as if making sure they were still listening. "The next week, the sound comes again as it starts getting dark, but we think nothing of it. A few hours later, after we had all fallen asleep, there was knocking against the walls of the barn house.

"I got up, as did one of the others, and found nothing unusual. As we got back in our beds, the call started again, much louder this time. Then, there was a scream, a woman's scream. We shot out of bed and went outside and the old lady was screaming her head off.

"We asked her what happened, but she wouldn't tell us. We found out later that one of her daughters was missing, along with the daughter's children. We questioned the old man about it, and he told us to stop asking. Things never were quite the same around there after that, and eventually, the old man wanted us gone."

The fire flickered on their faces as Tavarian tried to read them. For a moment, the only sounds were pops and crackles as firewood reacted to the flames.

"That doesn't mean it was mawlons," said Malidora. "There are many things that could have happened."

"You're going to give Darby nightmares," Dexius said.

"Darby already has nightmares," said Tavarian.

"Well, she doesn't need any more," Dexius explained.

"I swear it is true," Yarvik said.

"Even if it is true," said Malidora, "are you sure it wasn't something going on within the family? Maybe it was the old man."

"The old man? No, everyone I have told that story to has said it had to be mawlons," said Yarvik.

"So, assuming your account is correct," said Malidora. "Your proof is that the people who heard this story of something you never actually saw confirmed it was mawlons."

"Look, you don't have to believe it, but that's what happened," Yarvik said.

The five of them sat around the heat of the fire, gazing at the flames as they made shadows dance around them. Darby pointed overhead as the twinkling patterns of brightflies glittered across the skies. Tavarian grew weary, and he and Darby joined the others in lying down for the night.

"If anyone makes that sound during the night," Dexius said, "be prepared to pull an arrow out of your chest."

"What sound?" Tavarian asked.

"That mawlon sound," said Dexius. "Darby won't be able to sleep . . ."

Tavarian and Malidora chuckled. Tavarian glanced at Darby and she met him with a wide smile on her face.

"You're concerned about Darby," said Tavarian, snickering.

"Yes, do you really want to upset her?" Dexius said.

"You shouldn't have even mentioned it." Malidora smirked. "Now I almost have to do it."

Malidora began practicing making the bellowing sound that Yarvik had done earlier.

"Stop! You really want Darby to be frightened all night?" asked Dexius.

"I'll stop this time, but only for Darby's sake," said Malidora.

As the others began to fall asleep, Tavarian peeked into his satchel, and pulled the cloth wrappings open on one of the five rokenstone pieces that he had taken from the swamp. He caught a glimpse of the shiny black stone with pulsing violet crystals inside. Once he made sure the stones were still there, he carefully wrapped it back up and closed his satchel again.

They slept soundly until dawn came and began to wash away the darkness of the night. Malidora buried the fire with the dirt around it, and they gathered up their blankets into the shippy. Yarvik fed the docimare with some of the strange jellylike growth forming on the nearby trees as Darby watched.

"His name is Neris," said Yarvik, noticing Darby smiling at the animal as it ate. "Would you like to feed him?"

Darby nodded and Yarvik motioned for her to come over. He handed her a few pieces of the pale red plant.

"Break it up into smaller pieces," he told her.

Tavarian watched as she happily broke up the strange plant into smaller bits. He realized Darby probably had not felt like part of the group lately, and he had been a bad friend to not try and include her in some way.

They mostly chatted as they traveled, something Darby didn't do. He needed to find something she could participate in that didn't require talking. She put her hand up near the docimare's mouth as Yarvik instructed, and the docimare sniffed her.

The animal stuck out its long, thin tongue toward the small bits of plant in her hand. She giggled as the plant pieces stuck to its tongue and then were pulled into its mouth. He wondered if she had ever seen an animal like this, and wished he could talk to her about her life leading up to her getting caught by the Grundians.

Once they had all climbed into the shippy, Yarvik slapped the rear of the docimare to encourage it to start moving. They moved along the path through a small forest of rust-colored trees. These trees were different than any they had known in Rethia. Their leaves were like long fingers, gesturing in the swift morning breeze.

After they had been on the road for a while, Tavarian recalled his realization earlier in the morning about including Darby. "Why don't we play a game?"

"How about we don't?" Malidora said.

"I'll play . . . what kind of game?" Dexius said.

"Darby?" said Tavarian, waiting for a response.

She motioned yes, probably pleased to be able to do something besides listen to the rest of them drone on about nothing the whole trip.

"Yarvik?" asked Tavarian.

"You all go ahead—maybe I'll join in if it's something I can do while driving," he replied.

"Okay, so we each take turns asking a question, just any random question you can think of," said Tavarian.

"Oh, this could get ugly," Malidora said. "Be glad I'm not playing."

"And Darby has a special job," Tavarian said. "She will point to the person she wants, and they will have to answer that question."

"What if Darby wants to ask a question?" Dexius said.

"She can if she wants to," said Tavarian.

"Okay, I'm ready when you are," Dexius stated.

"All right, I'll start," Tavarian said. "What is your favorite food?"

Darby pursed her lips and pointed to Dexius.

"I'd have to say those trouder sausages back in Strakenbridge," Dexius replied.

"What is trouder?" Malidora asked.

"It's good, whatever it is," Dexius said.

"It's a big ugly bird. Doesn't fly much," Yarvik said. "Trouder meat gets made into all kinds of things."

"Okay, my turn," Dexius said. "How many wild beasts have you successfully hunted and killed?"

Darby pointed at Tavarian since he was the only other player in the game.

Tavarian exhaled loudly. "Uh, none."

Dexius beamed. "If anyone is wondering, forty-seven for me." He glanced at everyone as if to get a read on their expressions.

"Oooh, so impressive," Malidora remarked sarcastically. "I'm dying to share a blanket with you again."

Tavarian smiled internally at Malidora's sarcasm. She may not have intended it, but it felt as though she came to his defense. Finally, there was someone immune to Dexius's supposed charm. Dexius started to open his mouth, but apparently had nothing he deemed worthy of voicing. He had to hand it to Malidora, rarely did anyone leave Dexius without words.

"All right, my turn," Tavarian said. "How many people have you freed from the Grundians?"

"Okay, guys," Malidora said. "This is going nowhere. We get that you are both amazing at whatever it is you do. I suppose I'll play just so this doesn't devolve in some kind of man flex contest."

"Good," said Tavarian. "It's your turn then."

"All right, now for a real question," Malidora said. "If you could have anything you wanted in this world, what would it be?"

Darby paused for a minute, and then pointed at Dexius. He took a few minutes to think about the question. Tavarian had never really contemplated the possibilities of a question like this and he suspected Dexius had not either. He only thought in terms framed within the goals of Rethia. Tavarian's mind wondered how he would answer this, and at first, he considered his dream of being able to build new things and improving what had been already built. But what if he could go beyond what seemed possible and come up with ideas to build something the world has never seen? He could help Rethia, and improve everything in Nalacea as well—something that would change people's daily lives for the better. He now carried the power to save them. Perhaps he shouldn't give them to the council, as Malidora had suggested.

"Maybe have my own town. It would be nothing like Rethia. Everyone in the town would help each other like one big family. There would be plenty of food and . . . beautiful girls," said Dexius.

"I like how you started with the town nonsense and ended with what you actually wanted to say," quipped Malidora.

"No, the town family is the main thing," Dexius insisted.

"That sounds just like Rethia . . . except the food part," said Tavarian. "You said it wouldn't be anything like Rethia."

"Rethia is nothing like that," Dexius stated. "It's nothing like what a family is supposed to be."

"What do you think a family should be, then?" Tavarian prompted.

"Helping each other, caring for each other," Dexius said. "They're proud of you when you accomplish something, and supportive when you mess up. They don't punish you for things that aren't even your fault."

"I don't have that with everyone in Rethia," Tavarian said. "But there are people like that. What about your family?"

"I think it's my turn," Dexius said, ignoring him. "What is the strangest thing you've ever seen?"

Darby chewed on her tongue and then pointed at Malidora.

"Ah, good choice, Darby," Malidora said. "I know far more of this world than any of you."

"So, stop boasting about it and tell us," Dexius said.

"How about I sew your ears shut while I tell everyone else?" Malidora said.

Dexius laughed, and a reassured expression crossed his face as if he enjoyed getting these types of responses from her.

"Some years ago, when I was . . . maybe a little younger than Tavarian looks to be now, I traveled with a group across some of the unsettled parts of Varkandor. We came upon a barren, red wasteland as far as you could see. The dirt was made up of small pebbly pieces about the size of my thumb. So, this dirt rolled around under your feet as you walked on it, which made it hard to walk up the hills and mounds. Anyway, we came across this region called Haskar, and these beings living there were almost people like us, but they were of smaller build and had slender arms and these bladelike hands with no fingers on them.

"They burrowed into the red dirt, deep down, and made homes in these tunnels. There was water under the ground that they had discovered, and they had made an entire city down there. They allowed us to come and drink and offered us food to eat. The food they ate was mostly this sticky goo they made from plants growing in the some of the natural caves near the rivers and lakes.

"Once we got down there, they told us we had to serve them and work our way up through their system before we could be treated with any kind of respect. We had to walk for miles through the network of tunnels to cut down plants, and then haul them back to where they were stored. We had to have a pile that was a certain height by the end of the day, or we would get punished.

"After several weeks had gone by, there was a massive creature on the surface that had crossed through the wastelands and died. We all had to go up through the tunnels to the outside and cut parts off the creature to carry back down to the city. When everyone was preoccupied with doing that, we made a run for it. So, yeah, that was the strangest thing I've ever seen."

"Mawlons are more believable than that," Yarvik said.

"The difference is, I actually witnessed this with my own eyes," said Malidora.

"So you say . . ." Yarvik retorted.

Darby pointed at something in the distance. There was a fence stretched out between the trees around a settlement of some sort.

"Is there a town here?" Dexius stared intently beyond the fence. "I could really use something to eat."

"I think we all could," Tavarian said.

Malidora retrieved the map from her vest, searching it for answers.

"There isn't anything here on the map," she said as her eyes narrowed.

Yarvik turned the shippy, veering off onto another road between two sections of the fence. A large open gate stood down the road ahead.

CHAPTER 17

AS THEY PASSED through the gates, the odor of animal manure conflicted with the pleasant aromas of dried grasses and flowers. A huge house sat in the center of the cleared land, adorned by several smaller buildings behind it. On either side of the road were pens containing groups of various furry animals.

It wasn't quite the kind of town they were expecting. Like Rethia, there were no taverns or inns here. Two men approached them as Yarvik slowed the docimare's pace.

"We weren't expecting any buyers today—what can we do for you?" asked one of the men. He appeared very clean for someone who worked with all these animals, wearing a fitted leathery vest over a bright white shirt. A tightly shaped brown hat adorned his head, and he had a thick but trimmed beard. He smoked a sweet smelling weed from a cylindrical wooden piece he held in his mouth.

"We were searching for a place that had food," Malidora said. "We spotted the fence and thought there may be a town here."

"You could almost call it a town," the man said. "We're ranchers. We train and sell livestock for any purpose you need. We do quite well out here without the restrictions of a city."

"Sounds like my kind of place," said Malidora.

"If you need food," the man said, "we do eat around here. I'm sure we could arrange some kind of trade."

"Thank you—we do have some coin," she said.

"What kind of coin?" he asked.

Malidora prodded Darby to hand her a coin. Once Darby had given it to her, she handed it to the man in the leather vest.

"Strakenbridge currency," said the man. "That'll work; most anyone will take that around here."

Malidora smiled and the two men began walking down the road. "C'mon inside. Lakara should have something hot for you to eat."

Tavarian climbed down from the shippy and picked Darby up to set her on the ground. She could've jumped, but he wanted to help her, and she didn't appear to mind.

Malidora leaned over to Yarvik and whispered, "If you think I won't shoot you here in front of everyone, test me and learn."

The house they entered was made of dark wood and had high angled ceilings. Shadows rounded the corners, out of the candlelight's flickering reach. The smell of old wood permeated the interior. It smelled good—obviously well maintained and taken care of. They passed a room with a big glowing fire and went into a larger room with a long table. Trophies of fierce animal heads adorned the walls of the room. Some of the animals were new to Tavarian.

"Please, have a seat wherever you like," said the man. "Most of us ate a while ago, but Lakara always has something on the fire. My name is Rekil. If you don't mind, I'll keep you company while they bring some food out."

"Thank you, Rekil," Malidora said as she guided Yarvik to sit at the end of a long bench that appeared to be made from a tree trunk cut down the middle. She sat down next to him.

"Yes, thank you, this is most gracious of you," said Dexius, sitting next to Malidora.

Tavarian pointed for Darby to move to the other side of the table, wondering if he should say something too. It was redundant to repeat everyone else's words, but awkward or perhaps mildly rude to say nothing. He opted to say nothing anyway as it was a far easier decision.

"So, are the five of you all related? Can't say I see any resemblance," Rekil said, plopping himself down next to Dexius.

Malidora removed her gloves and set them on the bench between her and Dexius. "No, we're all just going to the same place."

"And what place might that be?" Rekil dropped his heavy arms on the table, shaking it slightly.

"A town up ahead." Malidora glanced at the wall as if she could see through it. "Called Grenova."

"Grenova . . ." Rekil moved his hand to his face, making a chin rest. "We just had a visitor from Grenova. Not sure there's much work up there."

"We were told there was," Malidora said. "I suppose it doesn't hurt to check."

Tavarian appreciated that Malidora did all the talking. There were some things best not to divulge to strangers, but you don't want to outright lie to them either. Some people could detect dishonesty. It would start suspicions. She did a good job of walking that line.

"Pardon me for being forthcoming, but I've never seen anyone like you before," he said to Malidora. "Is that your natural hair?"

"Yes, I'm Arkanthian," she said. "My homeland is across the ocean on the continent of Varkandor."

"Ah, I can't say I know much about Varkandor," said Rekil. "Never heard of anyone that has been there."

"There's not much left now but black vines and sand," she said. "The vegetation has withered away. Hopefully, there were others who crossed the sea before I did. Maybe there will be more of us passing through these parts as time goes on."

"That's a terrible thing to have happened to your land," he said. "I hope you find a home in Nalacea."

"I'm sure I will eventually," she said, peering past Dexius at Rekil.

Rekil rubbed the hair on his chin. "Are they all like you?"

"Arkanthians?" Malidora moved her eyes toward the table. "We all have similar traits, I suppose."

"You have such lovely features," Rekil said, eyeing her.

"Agreed, but she kicks pretty hard in her sleep." Dexius said, smirking at Malidora.

Everyone at the table turned and stared at Dexius. His face went from confident to confused to red with embarrassment. Malidora's eyes pierced him as if she wanted to shoot him right then and there.

"It's not what you think." Malidora cleared her throat. "He tries to embarrass me, but embarrasses himself instead."

Tavarian struggled not to laugh as Rekil glanced from Dexius back to Malidora.

Rekil smiled. "What about the rest of you?"

"Dexius and I are from Rethia," Tavarian spoke up.

Rekil narrowed his eyes. "Rethia? Is that on Varkandor as well?"

"No, it's on this side of the sea, on the mountain," Tavarian said.

"There's a mountain near Grenova, Mount Kravaka," Rekil said, "and there's Mount Laroken, but there's no one living on either of them. There's no way to get up there."

"Must be another mountain," said Tavarian.

"I'm not familiar with another mountain anywhere around here," Rekil said.

"It must be farther away than we thought," Dexius said.

"Interesting . . . I'll have to inquire about other mountains sometime," said Rekil.

A woman came out of the other room carrying a big pot, and the other man from earlier carried a stack of bowls that he placed in front of each of them except for Rekil. She poured stew from the pot into each of the bowls.

The smell of the stew made Tavarian even more hungry. There was a variety of chopped vegetables and something that smelled like spiced meat. He sat there waiting for someone to bring out spoons, but no one ever did. Rekil and Lakara stared at them as though waiting for them to start eating.

Tavarian glanced at Malidora and Yarvik, hoping to get direction on how they were going to eat.

"Eat up, we've already had some so there's no need to wait for us," Lakara said.

This stew smelled even better than the one Wynnotha had made for them. His hunger was becoming too much to bear. Finally, Tavarian plucked a chunk of the meat out of the stew and started eating it. Lakara and Rekil didn't say anything about it, so the rest of them followed suit.

After they all had pulled out pieces of meat and vegetables, Lakara commented on their eating style. "Interesting way to eat a stew," she said. "Doesn't bother us though, people do things differently in other places."

"How do you eat it?" Dexius asked.

"Out of the bowl," Rekil said. "Just tilt it or lap it up."

Dexius tried it, but he tipped the bowl too far and the broth started running down both sides of his mouth, spilling into his shirt and lap. Most of them chuckled, especially Rekil and Lakara.

"I guess it takes some practice," Rekil said.

There was a knocking somewhere inside the house—a sound of thunking on hollow wood. Lakara got up from the table and walked into another room.

"So, what kind of work do you do?" Rekil asked, turning to Malidora.

"Various things—whatever I can find," said Malidora. "Most recently I helped track down the location of a group of bandits."

"That's quite interesting," said Rekil. "How does one go about tracking down people who don't want to be found?"

"I have a keen sense of smell," Malidora said. "All of my kind does."

"That's a handy thing to have," Rekil remarked.

"It serves me well," said Malidora. "Then I read signs. The way grass is lying once it has been disturbed, cloth pieces on vines and branches—there's always signs when someone has passed through an area recently."

"I wonder if you could track down missing animals," Rekil said.

Tavarian shaped his hand into a cup and attempted to get some of the broth out of the bowl. The stew had cooled enough that it was just warm to the touch, but he had only minor success with this method. He stopped as footsteps came briskly toward the room.

Lakara went over to Rekil, and whispered into his ear. A pained expression came over his face and he muttered something back to her. Lakara left the room again and Rekil got up from his seat.

"Excuse me, it seems our visitor is a bit restless," he said.

"Oh? What's wrong?" Malidora asked.

"It's nothing to concern yourself with—please keep eating."

"Please, I would like to know," said Malidora. "If he is from Grenova, it may suit my interests."

"It's nothing like that," Rekil said. He lowered his voice into nearly a whisper. "The man has lost his mind to be quite honest. Lakara thinks we should act as though we believe him, but I think we should just call it what it is: crazy."

"Could you elaborate?" she said.

"He's been saying a lot of crazy stuff; something about whispers being after him."

Malidora got up from her seat immediately. "Could they already be there? I need to speak to this man!"

"I don't think that's a good idea," Rekil said. "It may get him more riled up."

"It's important," said Malidora as she began walking out of the room after Lakara.

"Wait!" said Rekil, getting out of his chair. "Don't go back there!"

He went after her. The rest of them exchanged glances until Tavarian slowly got up from his seat. He walked down the hallway hesitantly in the direction they were headed. Rekil was standing in the doorway of another room, and Lakara and Malidora's attention was on a man sitting on the floor against the wall.

"They're coming for us," the man said, his voice trembling. "They're coming for us all." He paused. His eyes wandered around the room, though not focusing on anyone. "It sent them upon us as it dreams in The Hollow. Its dreams shall become our dreams. Its will shall become our action."

"What sent them?" Malidora knelt beside him, speaking in a soft, calm voice.

The man turned to her and squinted his eyes, and then his stare went blank again.

"What were you trying to say?" she asked.

"The serpent on the other side," he said. "It knows our thoughts. It needs our energy."

The man closed his eyes for a moment and then opened them wide.

"Don't let them be taken to The Hollow!" he said, grabbing her vest. "You must kill everyone you can to stop what is coming!"

"No, we must fight them," Malidora said.

"No!" said the man. "It's too much to risk!"

"Where did you hear them . . . the whispers?" Malidora inquired.

"I don't want to hear them anymore," he said. "I don't trust them."

"Can you tell me where the whispers came from?" Malidora asked, placing a hand gently on his shoulder. The man sat quiet and still for a moment before jerking violently, startling Malidora as she withdrew her hand.

"In the shadow of the mountain," he said. "The forests near Mount Kravaka."

"I'm going to stop them," she said, placing a hand on his knee. "For all our sakes."

"They can't be stopped!" the man said. "You mustn't go near them. They whisper when you get close. They make you do terrible things!"

"Thank you for your help," she said, rising to her feet. She turned toward the doorway to see everyone standing there and moved out of the room.

"Don't go near them!" he yelled to her. "DON'T GO NEAR!" he screamed in a horrid broken voice.

Malidora froze and closed her eyes. She didn't turn back, resuming her path out of the doorway. Tavarian backed up out of her way, bumping his head on something hard. He turned to Dexius peering over his shoulder.

"Don't stand so close." Tavarian rubbed the back of his head.

Malidora strode past them with purpose. She entered the dining room and grabbed her battledress, putting it on as she started for the front door.

"We've got to hurry," she said. "They're already there."

"Who is?" Yarvik said, getting up from the table. "Who was screaming at you?"

"The Blight Whidge is there," said Malidora. "Now, let's move!"

Tavarian went over to Darby.

"You ready to go?" he asked her.

She shrugged.

"I guess we're going to have to," said Tavarian. "Did you get enough to eat?"

Darby affirmed she did.

"Good . . . all right, let's run, Malidora is in a hurry." Tavarian started running ahead as Darby smiled and ran after him. He hoped that by making it a game of sorts, it would calm Darby's nerves after hearing the delirious man. Yarvik stroked the fur on the docimare's head, and then climbed into the driver's seat. Malidora was already sitting in the shippy and Dexius jumped in just before Tavarian and Darby ran up.

Soon, they were back on the road. Tavarian regretted rushing off like that without offering to help Lakara clean up the bowls. Perhaps one day, he could return and make it up to them. The idea expelled some of the guilt at least.

As they rode farther into the wilderness, Malidora took a deep breath and sat up straight. "If you are heading home, we'll stop long enough to drop you off. Have your things ready."

"All right, we will." Tavarian brushed a loose strand of hair behind Darby's ear. "We need to give Darby a real home."

Malidora pursed her lips. "Good, she deserves that. I'm glad you guys are taking care of her."

Yarvik turned around "What is going on?"

"We're going to drop them off." Malidora rubbed her gloved hands together. "As soon as they are clear, speed us to Grenova. Don't ask—just get me there fast, and you'll never have to deal with me again."

"I will get you there, then," said Yarvik.

Malidora glanced at Darby, then Dexius and Tavarian. "I'm not one for goodbyes," she said, "but if anyone has any parting words, criticisms, or name-calling, now is the time."

"Yarvik, you seem decent." Dexius gave him a quick knock on the shoulder. "I hope you find your fortune out there, without bandits."

"Yes, thank you for your help," Tavarian said. "Well be with you."

"You are welcome. I don't know how you got mixed up with this bounty hunter." Yarvik pulled the reins tight, slowing the docimare. "Hope you both find what you are looking for as well."

"I'm not a bounty hunter." Malidora grimaced.

"And you too, Malidora." Tavarian searched for something to say. "Even though you steal and, well, murder, I'll kinda miss your company. I felt a lot safer with you around."

Malidora laughed. "That's a better farewell than I usually get."

"Be careful." Tavarian warned as the shippy slowed to a stop. "Please don't take those shadows on by yourself."

"We'll see what happens." Malidora rubbed Darby's head as she began to stand up.

"I guess you can keep the blanket," Tavarian said as he grabbed his sword and satchel.

"That blanket has my scent on it," Dexius said to Malidora as he reached for his bow and quiver. "Something to remember me by."

Malidora rolled her eyes and chuckled. "Just when I was beginning to tolerate you, you decide to leave—that's the way it goes."

Tavarian climbed out and helped Darby as Dexius jumped down. "One question before we go." Dexius tapped on the side of the shippy near Malidora. "How do you get that red smoke that trails behind your crossbow bolts?"

Malidora grinned. "I'm afraid that's a trade secret."

"I'll find out one day," Dexius said.

"Darby, I hope they give you a good home," Malidora said as Darby stared back at her. "Don't let the world change you. Keep good people around you." She tapped Yarvik on the back. "Let's go!"

The docimare started up its trot again. "Well with, Malidora," Tavarian shouted as he watched them leave. Malidora bumped her fist above her heart in some sort of salute.

"Be careful out there!" Dexius yelled.

Yarvik gave one last wave before he turned around to steer the docimare. Darby, Dexius, and Tavarian watched until no trace of them remained on the horizon.

"Well, I guess it's down to just us again," said Tavarian, reaching out to rub Darby's shoulder as she glanced up at him.

"What's your plan for getting up the mountain?" said Dexius as they began walking toward what they hoped was Rethia.

"First, we need to check around the base of the mountain," Tavarian said. "Maybe there is another way up."

Dexius and Darby followed Tavarian over the grassy plains for the rest of the day, but the mountain didn't appear much closer than when they started. They came to a rocky dry valley. Signs that water sometimes flowed over this area could be seen in the lines carved through the rock. New grass blades had begun to break through the stone, and small fishlike creatures swam around in puddles of what remained of the last rain.

Walls of rock overlooked them on either side. Orange reflections tinged the mingling clouds as the sun set ahead of them. It signaled that it was time to camp for the night. This valley served a good enough place for it. They laid out their blanket under an alcove. Without wood in the area to build a fire, they huddled up together for warmth. Strange noises echoed through the night air. A low howling off in the distance made them nervous, but at least they could hear how far away it was.

Darby murmured in her sleep as she turned and tossed in the wrap of the blanket. It appeared to be a nightmare. Tavarian decided to wake her. She jumped as he put his hand on her small shoulder.

"Were you having a bad dream?" he asked.

She nodded while breathing heavily.

"What about?"

Darby shook away the question with her hand. Tavarian hated to ask, but wanted to find a way to help her.

They had a strong bond, even though she rarely spoke. Her expressions and actions told a lot about her. He hoped she could live with them in Rethia and meet his parents, sister, and especially Lirah. Lirah would take her right under her wing. She could start school and learn a trade and see the sun for the first time.

The renewed world lit up as they gathered their blanket and weapons for the next part of the journey. Tavarian cupped his hands together into the water that was trapped in crevasses of rock. It contained a strong taste of a mineral, likely embedded in the stone. Soon they were off again. The weariness of sleep wore off as they came out of the valley into a small, wooded area—a scenic place, where many birds gathered among the abundant flowers surrounding the trees. Red, gold, and violet blooms dotted the area, setting Tavarian's mind in peaceful ease. He focused on the environment around him instead of dwelling on how to get back to Rethia.

The mountain drew nigh, growing at an increasingly rapid pace the nearer they came. Now that they were almost there, a nervous excitement filled him as he realized how close Lirah was. Today could be the day he sees her again for the first time in several months. How long had it been exactly? The Grundians had held him up for too long.

How close was it now to the next Descension? It surely wasn't too far away. He needed to get back and warn them about the road collapse. Thunder sounded off in the distance behind them. Tavarian turned back toward the other mountain. How were things going for Malidora? He hoped she had not tried to go up against the shadows, while still not admitting to himself that he cared about her. There were signs she had the right intentions. She wasn't pure evil, at least. There were good deeds that came with the bad. What might she have been like if she hadn't witnessed her family killed and her homeland destroyed? Could it all be blamed on that, or was it her nature regardless of the circumstances? Either way, only she was responsible for the choices she made.

Even though she could resist the shadow's influence, her whole life had been consumed by them. Is this what Darby had experienced? Is she what Darby might become? He hoped not. He had to do whatever he could to ensure that didn't happen. If Darby grew up like Malidora, he may lose all hope in the world.

The mountain finally towered above them. They had made it. Now the real work began—figuring out a way to ascend it.

"I never thought I would be back here again," said Dexius.

Darby gazed up at the mountain, eyes widening. She turned away from it, looking at the surrounding trees and moss-covered dirt, and then back toward the top of the mountain.

CHAPTER 18

"HAVE YOU EVER seen a mountain like this before, Darby?" Tavarian asked.

She continued staring at it while Dexius walked on around the mountain's base. Tavarian followed, searching for any places they could reach that may allow them to climb all the way up. They come across a path leading upward to a large gap. The rest of the path was obscured by the hanging clouds making up the lower atmosphere.

They could climb up the small rise to get to it, but the gap in the middle would be far too much to overcome. Dexius continued around the edge of the mountain's base. He stopped, bending down to check something on the ground.

Tavarian went over to investigate a skull embedded into the rock. It appeared to have been there for a long time—too old to be one of the Descenders from their group. They searched the uneven edges at the foot of the mountain. More bones were scattered about, most barely sticking up out of the dried mud and rock. There were complete skeletons along with singular broken bones.

Darby gripped Tavarian's hand as they walked around the bones.

"This should have been us," said Dexius.

Tavarian wiped his forehead, as if doing so would clear the images of that day, and the Descenders who fell—how close he had come to dying. What a depressing end that would be, with his only glimpse of Nalacea briefly happening as he fell toward it.

His ears roared as they neared the large, cascading waterfall. He believed it was the same one they watched fall into the cloudscape and disappear so many times over the years. A deep pool caught the water as it crashed down, flowing on to a stream leading into a lush meadow. Nothing they could use to climb emerged around the falls.

Crossing the swirling pool or the stream appeared quite dangerous. Any hope of climbing the mountain faded rapidly. What if Lirah gazed down from the top of the falls right now, not realizing they were here? The image made him even more resolute in finding a way up.

A rumbling in the trees on the side of the mountain shook the ground they were standing on. Across the stream stood the enormous creature Tavarian had encountered on his first day in Nalacea. Its front legs perched on the side of the mountain while its back legs remained on the ground. Its enormous shell sat atop its back as it munched on trees.

Dexius stared in disbelief and Darby gripped Tavarian's hand even harder. They ran back around to the other side of the mountain, and fortunately, the creature didn't pay them any mind. They made it back to the broken mountain pathway.

"Crossing that gap is the only option," Tavarian said.

"Only we can't cross it," said Dexius.

"If I could build something," mumbled Tavarian, "like the bridge at Strakenbridge crossing the river. It wasn't as big of a gap as this, but—"

"Yeah, how you going to do that?" Dexius said.

Tavarian said, "I have a saw, but it would take weeks to cut down enough trees to build what we need."

"I'm not sure how strong these trees are," said Dexius. "And you'd have to contend with that forest eater back there."

"Yeah . . ." Tavarian groaned, realizing the depth of the task ahead.

Darby loosened her grip on his hand. Before he knew it, she sprinted away from the mountain.

"Darby!" he shouted. "Where are you going?"

Dexius called to her as they both chased after her.

She had boundless energy as Tavarian and Dexius ran out of breath trying to keep her in sight. The scattered trees obstructed their view as they tried to keep up. What had they done that made her leave? Had he been too absorbed in his own goals to give her enough attention? Did he misinterpret something?

After running across the thicket, a familiar sight came into view. It was the old town that had been wrecked by the blight, Muloken. After what Tavarian had seen, no doubt remained that the Nulthereal shadows did this. Darby stood in front of one of the remaining buildings as they caught up to her.

"Darby, why did you run off like that?" Tavarian said in an almost scolding tone.

Her brow furrowed as though she didn't like his question.

"What did we do wrong?"

She shook her head, pointing toward the broken houses and buildings.

"This place gives me the creeps. Do you really want to stay here for the night?" said Tavarian.

She shook her head again adamantly and pointed to the buildings again.

"What's she trying to say?" Dexius wondered.

"I'm not sure," said Tavarian.

She continued pointing all around at the buildings.

"Oh!" Tavarian said excitedly, "Darby, you're a genius!"

"What?" Dexius asked.

"We can use the wood from these buildings!" said Tavarian.

"Oh . . . yeah, we could do that," Dexius said. "But should we? That's the real question."

"Of course we should," Tavarian said.

"How did you find this place, Darby?" Dexius wondered.

Tavarian went to work on the buildings, using his blacksmith hammer to knock the planks and logs loose from all the long spikes in the frames. Much of the wood had been broken loose already from the destruction that had taken place here, which made his work much easier.

After a few hours of breaking up the wood, they started moving it closer to the mountain. Darby helped Dexius drag some of the planks and logs across the woodlands to Tavarian, who moved them the rest of the way to the mountain path. Once Tavarian had gathered a few logs, several flat boards, and many spikes, he went to work.

Tavarian sawed the flat boards into shorter sections. Once finished, he walked up the path to the gap in the road. Taking one of the long spikes, he hammered the flat board into the rock of the mountainside. Standing on that block of wood, he pounded more nails into the mountain rock. Leaving the nail heads sticking out enough, he used them as a foothold.

Once he had enough spikes in place for one log, he walked back down the spikes and Dexius help him push the log down on top of the nails. Tavarian hammered the long nails down onto the flat board pieces at each end.

This whole process would take days, and he couldn't wait that long. Aside from yearning to see Lirah again, the next Descension approached. It could be any day now for all he knew.

"It's going to take too long to do it this way and make it safe enough for Darby," Tavarian said.

"What are you saying?" Dexius asked.

"I could just make steps out of these spikes all the way across and one of us could get up there. After that, whoever goes up can tell the council about the road being out, and they could give us supplies to finish the bridge, and maybe even test more Rethians to see who can breathe in the lower atmosphere to help us."

"I'll stay down here with Darby," Dexius said. "You go on up."

"Really? I'm surprised," Tavarian said. "I thought you wanted to be the hero."

"No," remarked Dexius. "I'd rather not see that place again."

"You don't want to see your family?" Tavarian prodded. "Wouldn't they be proud of you?"

"They've never been proud of me," Dexius replied. "They're better off without me. And I'm better off staying here."

"So, you're never going back?" Tavarian ran his hand through his hair.

"I only came with you this far to help you bring the stones," Dexius stated. "For Lirah."

Tavarian had not planned for this. He wanted to bring Darby up the mountain to live with them in Rethia. This would force her to choose who she wanted to go with. What if she chose to go back to Strakenbridge and live with Wynnotha and Dexius? Tavarian closed his eyes and took a deep breath. Now was not the time to worry about it—they would have to discuss all of this later.

"All right, I'll come back as soon as I can, and let you know what the council says."

"Darby and I will go back to that old town and wait for you."

"Well with."

"You too."

Tavarian began hammering spikes into the rocks one at a time, each one a little higher than the one before it. He leaned on the mountainside as he stood on top of the spikes out over the ground below. The spikes were digging into his feet through his shoes. His back began to tire out and his arm began to ache from all the hammering. It was slow and tiring work, but he had to put in enough nails to keep a safe distance between each one.

After working on it all day, he accidently caught a glimpse downward, making him dizzy. Settling himself, he resumed. He had to finish before it grew dark. Passing into the clouds of the lower atmosphere, Nalacea was now hidden from view. Climbing up on a small plateau, he went on foot as far as he could before having to return to knocking the nails into the rock. Below him was the tree he had fallen into, growing out near the wall of stone.

He finally pounded in the last spike needed to get to the broken edge of the mountain road. Taking a precarious step off the spike onto the path, he found the courage to lift his other foot and place it on the path as well. He took another step and then another. After three more steps, he slipped on the smooth rock of the steep incline.

He slid backward toward the edge of the path. As he continued to skid, he whipped his sword from its sheath and stabbed it into the stone below. The sharp end of the blade stuck into the rock just enough to slow him. He brought all his weight down on the sword, grinding it deeper into the stone.

Regaining leverage, he pulled himself up. Plunging the sword into the stone ahead, he climbed, using the weapon for traction. Eventually, he made it to a flatter surface where he could easily walk his way up the road to Rethia.

Catching his first glimpse of the sky in months, he saw the setting sun dipping below the horizon of clouds. Tavarian paused to take it in—he had taken the clear sunlit sky for granted for most of his life. Moving ahead, he hurriedly stepped up to the top of the plateau.

He reached the top at dusk, exhausted. Two Rethian peace control officers stood talking to each other with their backs facing him. As he got close enough to speak to them, one of the officers turned to him. Tavarian had anticipated the moment they saw him, calling for everyone to see that Tavarian had returned with the rokenstones.

"Intruder!" said the officer, unsheathing his sword. The other peace control officer turned and brandished his weapon as well.

"You are not welcome here," said the other. "Turn back at once!"

"No, wait! It's me, Tavarian." He waved his hands frantically at them. "I am one of the Descenders . . . I have the rokenstones!"

"Turn back now or you'll be jailed," the first control officer said.

"Don't you recognize me?" Tavarian pointed to his Rethian pendant. "Go get one of the council members or the teachers—they'll tell you."

"I said turn back!" the officer replied, moving toward him in an aggressive manner.

Tavarian held up the satchel. "I did it! I have them! I have to get these rokenstones to the council."

"Take him, quietly!" said the second officer as the two of them grabbed his arms.

Tavarian tried to yell out as one of them put a gag in his mouth. They put a piece of cloth over his head, and dragged him across the dirt street. The voices of others passed by, whispering that the officers had caught another thief. How had they not understood? How did they not know who he was? After the ceremony announcing the Descenders, the peace control officers should know him. Once the councilors realized what the officers had done, they would be furious. He wondered how he should react when they released him. Should he tell them to forgive the control officers? That it was an honest mistake? He grew angrier by the moment. At this point, he would be glad to see them punished.

They took Tavarian across a wooden floor, then down a set of stairs. The officers' footsteps echoed through the wide hall. Loose gravel scraped beneath his shoes as they dragged him across the stone floor. The peace control officers pushed him into the far wall and took his sheathed sword. As they removed the gag and blindfold, the dreary darkness of the cell greeted him.

The dancing flame of the candles in the hall brought the only life to this place. The officers removed his satchel and dumped the contents onto the floor. The clothed covered rokenstones scattered in different directions as they hit the hard ground, some of them rolling out of their safe covering. The peace control officers took the saw and hammer, slamming the barred metal door behind them.

"Could you please get the council to come down here? They'll know who I am!" Tavarian pleaded.

They ignored him, rushing back up the steps and out of sight. The crash of a door at the top of the stairs slammed behind them. Tavarian surveyed the dark room. Across from him were four other barred cells like the one he was in.

"Why would the council come down to see you?" queried a voice in the dark.

Tavarian tried to focus on the darkened corner of the cell across from him, but found nothing. The voice was a man, older than him, with a practiced tongue.

"They would care about me because I'm not a thief like the rest of you," Tavarian stated.

"They call everyone they put in here a thief," the man said. "I assure you, I am no thief any more than you are."

"I was one of the Descenders," Tavarian said, "but they didn't recognize me. I came back with the rokenstones."

"Oh, they recognize you . . ." the man said. "A Descender who returned? They wouldn't like that at all. You are a threat to them."

"What do you mean?"

"The same reason I am here. It's—" the man started.

"How would I be a threat?"

"I'm getting to that. You'd best learn some patience, kid. There are long days ahead."

"Sorry, go ahead."

"It's your knowledge. You and I . . . we know too much."

"That doesn't make any sense. Why would knowledge be a problem?"

Another voice from across the room sounded out, "Be quiet! I can't think!"

"Knowledge is a threat to their control."

"I don't know anything that would be threatening."

"You know quite a bit—perhaps you just haven't put it all together yet," the man said. "If the council allowed you to talk to anyone, they could lose control of everything."

"What control? The council serves us."

The man forced a laugh. "They tell us how many trees we can cut for wood, how much metal we can use, how many crops we can grow. They tell us what kind of classes we can take, what jobs we can have. If that's not control, tell me what is?"

"So? They do it to help Rethia. Someone has to figure all of that out."

"Each person can figure those things out for themselves. If they gave each family a stretch of land to do what they wanted with it, we would never be low on food. We could build houses whenever we wanted."

"That would never work," Tavarian said. "What if we had too many carpenters, then what would I do?"

"If no one ever needed your services as a carpenter, you could do something else. But it would be your choice instead of theirs. What if you are the best carpenter in Rethia? We'd never know it because the council took that decision away from you. Now all the carpenters are the same because there's no reason to do better. Their job is guaranteed."

"Yeah, there are carpenters down there who are so good, they build works of art."

"Was it better than this place?"

"In most ways, yes," said Tavarian. "Food was overflowing there, but they had thieves in the streets and no one seemed to care that much."

"I guess no town is perfect, but right now, I would take the thieves with the abundance of food, instead of the mindless farmers we have."

"Our farmers aren't mindless. If they didn't work, we would've all starved."

"Like everyone else, they only do what they are told to do. If they wanted, they could plant more, harvest more often. There are ways to increase production and take better care of the crops."

"Quiet!" said the voice from the darkened corner of the prison.

"Pay him no mind," said the man.

"Why don't they do that, then?"

"Because there's nothing to gain. There are other things to do, and they have families. They get the same voucher we all get either way."

"So, only some should get a voucher?"

"If we all traded among one another, it would all be just fine, or at least better than this. The more you produce, the more you can trade for, depending on how much you want or need. Rethia would be a much better place."

"Even if that is true, I brought back rokenstones," said Tavarian. "We can make machines that will produce much faster."

"The council—"

"Stop talking!" said the other voice. He continued yelling over and over, hitting the bars on his cell as the sound of metal clanking against metal echoed through the room. There were footsteps sounding through the clanking and yelling. Three peace control officers entered the room and walked over to the noisy man's cell.

One of the officers took a chain of metal keys from his belt and unlocked the door of the cell. The officers entered the cell, and the blunt slaps of fists against flesh echoed in the hall as they beat the man making all the noise.

"Bind his hands!" said one of the officers. "And gag him!"

After the rustling subsided, the officers' steps echoed back up the stairs and they were left with nothing more than the sounds of dripping water.

"That will make things a bit quieter in here." The man continued, "The council is not interested in rokenstones."

"Rokenstones are what all of this is about."

"Ah, you're so close . . . so close to making the connection," said the man. "There is only so much space on this mountain for everything the population needs—at least the way the council has divided it up. You need the forests for wood and wildlife to hunt. You need rivers for fish and buildings for everyone to live and go to school in. And every week there isn't enough food, so they must cut everyone's share. Everyone gets a voucher no matter what. Everyone must be fed . . . at the same time . . . crops get ruined, fish spoil, and wood isn't properly treated. It's an endless cycle that never works. On top of that, the number of people grows, but the supply does not. The council doesn't know what we need. They can only react to changes after they happen."

"Which is why I got the rokenstones . . ."

"Who knows if the rokenstones can be used to power these machines they mention?"

"If not, what's the point of doing this every year?"

"They say they want rokenstones so we can increase the supply to meet the demand, but their real solution is to simply lower the demand."

"Meaning what?"

"The Descension is their way of reducing the demand. To reduce the demand, you must reduce the population. You all leave the mountain searching for the stones and never return, leaving fewer people here to consume resources."

The images of the Descenders falling off the mountain replayed through Tavarian's mind. The broken body at the foot of the mountain he refused to look at. The scattered bones he and Dexius found.

"I don't believe that," Tavarian scoffed.

"Why does no one ever return?" the man asked. "Maybe you are the first, but maybe not. Maybe there were others, but they all ended up in here like you and me."

"As I said, there is plenty of food out there . . ."

"So what happened to the rest of your group?"

"They're all . . . they're dead," said Tavarian. "The mountain path is broken. We all fell, and only two of us made it."

"So, that's it—that's how they ensure no one returns. They march the outcasts to their deaths to reduce the population so they can maintain control."

"Outcasts? We're Descenders."

"Same thing. They choose those who don't get along with others, or don't fit in. Descenders are those with the least chance of being a productive minion, and the least chance of coupling with another and having children."

"If they want to reduce the population, why would they want to keep people who are more likely to have children?"

"I suppose they still need children. They need someone to replace the older ones that they've work to death well past their ability to do it."

"You may think I'm an outcast, but Lirah and I are going to be coupled once I get out of here."

"You won't be getting out. You're like me now. You know too much."

"All I know is some crazy story you told me."

"You know about the collapsed road. You know that most of the Descenders fell to their deaths."

"We were chosen because we can breathe the air in the lower atmosphere. It had nothing to do with being an outcast."

"Anyone can breathe that air. There's nothing different about the lower atmosphere. It's merely another lie to maintain control."

"But there were others who came out of the testing rooms coughing."

"Some of the rooms get smoke while others get vapor. It's all controlled."

"You have an answer for everything."

"Because it's the truth."

"If it's the truth, how did you learn all this?"

"I used to work cleaning the council hall. Sometimes councilors would come in the hall for private conversations. There were times they didn't know I was there. I would stop cleaning and hide. I was curious about what councilors did and what they talked about. On one occasion, I was wiping down the wooden seats in the council chamber and two councilors came in to have a private meeting. They were discussing reports on students from the teachers on which ones were the most expendable. The teachers had reported who were the least obedient, socially developed, and like I said before, least likely to be coupled with another. That got my curiosity going even more. I wanted to know who they were talking about. I started looking through papers on desks and in drawers. The more I found, the more daring I became. Eventually, I got too bold and they caught me."

Tavarian's mind rushed through everything he remembered about his life in Rethia. How he didn't get along with some of the teachers in certain classes. How he wasn't that well liked and was labeled as awkward. He considered Dexius; he was disliked for different reasons. He was good at hunting and other survival skills, but his arrogant attitude put people off.

Dexius had outwardly changed a lot in the past few months. He still had that same attitude, but Tavarian understood now that Dexius didn't really believe he was better than anyone. What he needed was validation from others.

Tavarian had similar flaws that were made worse by trying to be something that he wasn't. He made excuses when he lost confidence in himself, desperately trying to cling to an image he wanted everyone to see. Maybe all those things that Lirah told him were finally sinking in. All he really wanted was to fit in. He thought he had to be the best at everything to overcome what others thought of him in order to be accepted.

Did Rethia really intend to cast them out just because of these minor issues? Everyone has flaws. His heart sank while his blood began to boil. He didn't want to believe this was true, but it all added up.

"I have to get out of here," Tavarian said.

"There's no getting out, and no one lasts too many years in here with as little as they feed us."

Tavarian bent down and grabbed the pieces of cloth used to cover the rokenstones. Two of the stones were on the floor inside the cell while the other three had rolled into the hallway. He grabbed the two stones with the cloth and wrapped them up. Carefully, he placed them back into his satchel.

The peace control officers had taken his saw and hammer—they wouldn't help get through these metal bars anyway. What could he use possibly use to get through metal? If he had enough heat, he could bend the metal bars, but then he would need a hammer. It didn't matter because there was no source of heat that intense here. He missed that hammer already. His dad gave it to him when he left Rethia. Breaking pieces of rokenstones from the formation and pounding spikes into the mountainside would remain the last things he used it for. Recalling Darby's reaction when he went to strike the rokenstones, Tavarian wondered what would have happened if she had not wrapped the handle with cloth. Would he have been struck by lightning?

One of the flekstones sat near the edge of the cell, but the other one lay out of his reach. They were useless by themselves. The tied bundle of Lirah's white hair floated in a puddle of murky water. Tavarian reached down and picked up the soggy curl and placed it in his bag. It would dry eventually. His blanket was beside the bag—he took it and spread it on the floor to lie on.

As he tried to sleep that night, all he could think about was how much he despised the people of Rethia. All the skeletons of the past Descenders at the foot of the mountain were kids they had purposely killed. The teachers who didn't like him, the ones who didn't try to get past his so-called awkwardness—they were complicit in this even if they weren't completely aware of the council's doing. Could the fight he and Dexius had gotten into in front of a teacher have caused the two of them to be chosen as Descenders?

Everything he had dreamed of, it had all been a lie. The only thing worthwhile about his existence was Lirah and his family. He had to get out of here. He had to get to Lirah. If everyone could breathe the air in the lower atmosphere, then he could take her away from here and start a new life. Other than the people who cared about him, he trusted no one. He respected no one here anymore.

Tavarian awakened the next morning as the peace control officers were coming around to give each prisoner bits of a thin, pliable metal. They were to bend and shape the metal into small pendants. Some parts were already cut into hands like the ones given to everyone in the Rethian Community. Others were the raised fists that the Council wore and had given to him and all the other Descenders.

Even though Tavarian had some blacksmithing skill, working on these tiny metal pieces made a difficult task. They gave the prisoners food based on the number of acceptable pendants that were made. The slow, monotonous work made for a long day. He started getting the hang of it, little by little speeding up his progress.

That evening, a guard came and inspected each pendant and decided if they passed or failed. Officers came around to each cell and set plates through the bars of the cells as well as cups of water. Tavarian received only a small piece of bread and only a quarter of a cup of water.

With little to eat, Tavarian finished quickly while the other prisoners continued eating their larger meals. He drank all of his water in one gulp. This was not enough. Grabbing the cup, he banged it against the bars of the cell.

"I didn't get enough food!" Tavarian yelled.

"I wouldn't do that," said the man in the cell across from him.

"More food!" he continued to yell, clanking his rusty metal cup against the bars.

"They're not going to give you more food—stay quiet or your night is going to get a lot worse," the man said.

Tavarian continued yelling and hitting the cup until he heard a door open, followed by footsteps coming down the stairs. He pulled one of the wrapped rokenstones from his satchel, and removed part of the cloth that covered it. Inside the stone, its violet crystals pulsated. On the crossbars of the cell, he placed one stone, careful to touch only where the cloth covered it. The echoes of footsteps sounded in the hall as he removed the cloth completely from the stone.

Two officers walked over to his cell.

"Gotta teach the new guy how this works," the guard muttered, seemingly annoyed to have to come down to do any work. He took the chain from his belt and put a key into the lock of the cell.

As soon as the metal key went into the lock on the door, a bright flash erupted through the dark. The guard began convulsing as sparks flew from the key. The guard's stiff body toppled to the ground. The other guard ran over and grabbed the key still in the door. The same affliction struck him.

Commotion rose in the hallway as Tavarian watched in amazement. He took a piece of cloth and removed the rokenstone from the crossbar. Wrapping it up, he placed it back in his satchel. Reaching between the bars of the door, he grabbed the key still inside the lock and turned it. The door sprang open.

Tavarian walked over to the man in the cell across from him, and after trying two different keys, found the one that unlocked the door. The man was wide eyed as if excited and scared at the same time. He handed the man the chain of keys.

"Whatever happens next is up to you," Tavarian said. "Well with."

He bent over to grab the three rokenstones that had rolled just out of reach of his cell the day before, grateful that the guards hadn't paid them any attenion. Tavarian ascended the stairs, quickly but quietly. When he reached the top, he came to a small room with armor on a stand and a set of swords. His white blade stood propped against the sword rack. Apparently, no one else wanted to use the heavy two-handed sword with a strangely designed hilt.

He grabbed his sheathed sword and strapped it on his back. A nearby officer drew his blade as he ran toward him. Tavarian unsheathed his weapon and assumed a defensive stance like the blacksmith had taught him, keeping his weapon high and angled toward the guard. The peace control officer looked nervous. Perhaps he had no experience fighting an armed opponent.

"How did you get out of your cell!" the officer demanded. "Get back in there and I won't report you."

"I don't belong in here," Tavarian said. "I was one of the Descenders!"

The guard swung at his head, and Tavarian tilted his blade to block the attack to his left. He tried to remember his counterattack moves as the guard swung at the same side but lower. Tavarian dropped his hands to parry the blow and quickly tilted his sword to stab the guard in the chest.

The blow knocked the guard off his feet, through the doorway, and into a larger room with several seats. This room was more ornately decorated than any place he had been in Rethia. Red cloth adorned each seat and part of the flooring.

The guard stood, examining the dent in his chest plate with his hand. Tavarian slowed his breathing and focused—this was a real sword fight, and losing could mean death. His trepidation was mixed with excitement as the adrenaline shot through him.

The guard attacked again, twirling his blade with a flourish. Nearly fooled, Tavarian barely brought his sword to his left to parry the blow in time. The readjustment caused him to overcompensate—a mistake that left him open for the next attack to his right. Tavarian couldn't get his blade in position in time. He dove to the floor on his left to avoid the strike.

The guard rushed toward him. Tavarian jumped to his feet. Swinging his sword horizontally, he parried the guard's downward slash. Pushing against the guard's blade, he slid his feet into a proper defensive stance. He reminded himself what the blacksmith had said about not wasting motion, using slight changes in hand positioning or simply tilting the blade to easily get to his base stance and not leave himself open to counters.

The guard unleashed a flurry of attacks as Tavarian turned his blade back and forth to block them. The guard slashed from left to right as Tavarian guided the blows away. Disengaging from the guard's reach, the torrent of attacks ceased. Ibis was right about his heavy sword. He couldn't move as fast as the guard could with a smaller blade.

Tavarian lunged and closed with an attack of his own. He struck at an angle toward the right side of the guard's upper body without thinking about the armor the guard had on. The guard quickly blocked it, but the weight of Tavarian's sword caused the guard's sword to recoil from the weight of the larger blade.

The weight of the sword could be an advantage if he used it. The guard's attack quickly resumed. Instead of merely absorbing the blow, he swung into the path of the attack. When the swords hit, he knocked the guard's blade back. It took the guard a second longer to get his sword back into a defensive position.

Tavarian let the guard attack again. As soon as he recognized where the attack was headed, he swung at the guard's sword even harder. The recoil knocked the guard's arm back again. Tavarian quickly lowered his blade to thrust it under the guard's armored sleeve.

The sword went into the guard's side high under his arm. Shouting in pain, the guard switched to his nondominant hand and tried to ready himself to defend another blow. Blood poured down the side of his armor. The amount surprised Tavarian. The adrenaline kicked in harder now.

The guard suddenly dropped his sword while staggering away from Tavarian, and then crumpled to the floor. He no longer moved. Tavarian kicked the guard's sword away and turned the guard over on his back.

If anyone came into the chamber with the guard lying here, they would all be searching for him. He dragged the guard back into the smaller room with the sword and armor racks. The wounded guard was less visible here. Footsteps sounded up the stairs behind him. It was likely the man in the cell across from him with the rest of the prisoners he released, but there wasn't enough time for Tavarian to stick around and find out.

Tavarian moved back into the open room. The bloodstains fortunately did not show up on the red cloth lining the floors. Watching for peace control officers at each doorway he came to, he eventually made it outside. The sun had recently set behind the clouds. Tavarian made his way through the deserted town.

CHAPTER 19

ONLY PEACE CONTROL officers walked the streets of Rethia after curfew. Tavarian decided to sneak through the small wooded areas bordering the mountain edges. After ensuring the area was clear, he left the trees and went closer to the main road.

He turned onto the road where Lirah lived, speeding up his pace. The area was dark by the time he got there. Only a few lights remained on inside her house. The small Rethian houses seemed so plain to him now. They were nothing like the grandeur of the buildings in Strakenbridge and even the smaller towns. As he opened the gate, he recalled putting the swinging latch on it—the same kind of gate he made for the Grundians on a larger scale. That seemed like a lifetime ago.

Tavarian silently crept into the darkness behind the house to Lirah's window. He tapped on the glass, but she didn't respond. Risking a little more volume, he tapped harder. Someone began to stir inside.

As soon as she opened the window, he grabbed her cheeks and kissed her. The way he should have kissed her the night before he left. She jumped in surprise. For a moment she relaxed and returned his kiss. Suddenly, she started pushing him away from her. "Who—"

As Tavarian drew closer to the light from inside the house, her blue eyes grew big.

"Tavarian! Is it really you? How? You seem so different! You've grown. I can't believe how strong you look now," she said.

"It's me!" he said, and went to kiss her again.

She backed away. "Tavarian, I . . . I didn't think I would ever see you again."

"I told you I would come back."

"But no one ever comes back," she said, still in shock.

"I need to tell you something," he said. "I found out why no one ever returns."

"What is it like down there? Is it everything we dreamed of?

"Nothing like what we imagined," he said, smiling. "There are red crystals growing up from the ground, giant mushrooms, a spooky swamp with plants that have eyeballs . . ."

"Wow, that's amazing! Tell me everything! Let me run and get Mom!"

"No! No, don't tell her I'm here. Just listen for a second," he said, his smile fading. "When we walked down the mountain, everyone fell. There's a big gap in the pathway down." Tavarian glanced at the small sprouts of grass beneath his feet. "Everyone is dead except, oddly enough, Dexius and me. We are the only ones who survived."

Lirah's mouth dropped open slightly before she spoke. "What? That's awful. I'm so glad you two are okay! So, you really took care of each other like you promised?"

"We did, but there's something I need to tell you," he said, peering down at his feet again as if he would find the right words there. Lirah believed in Rethia and the community. What would this do to her? Would she even accept it? "The council is aware of the broken road. They want the Descenders to die, or at least not be able to come back."

Lirah narrowed her eyes. "What makes you think that? Why would they?"

"Because I found some rokenstones . . ." He glanced back up to view what her eyes told him.

"You found them? You saved us!" she said loudly, making Tavarian scan the moonlit road for peace control officers.

They were the words he had longed to hear. It was the moment Tavarian had dreamt of, soured by the context of this new reality.

"They don't even want them." He turned around, leaning up against the side of the house. "When I came up the path, the peace control officers grabbed me and threw me in the dungeon. I told them I had the stones, and they didn't care."

"Why would they throw you in the dungeon?" Her words breathed warm on the back of his neck as she leaned out the window.

Tavarian faced her again. "Because they don't want me to tell anyone that most of the Descenders died falling through the gap in the road. They *wanted* us to die."

Lirah brushed her fingers across her lips. "Why would they want you to die?"

"They don't want the rokenstones to increase production." Tavarian stared deeply into her eyes. "They want to decrease the population."

She blinked rapidly. "But the stones were supposed to help us."

"The stones do have power, but they're dangerous. No one in Rootcore uses them." Tavarian gripped the sill of the window, shifting his weight toward her.

"They don't use them to power the machines you were talking about?" Lirah lowered her head as she withdrew from the window.

"I didn't find anyone who does," said Tavarian before pressing his lips together.

Her pretty eyebrows drew together as she closed her eyes. "It's all been a lie?"

"I'm afraid so," Tavarian breathed the words out, wondering if he did the right thing. The pained look on her face was more than he could bear, but he had to get her out of here. The only way to get her away from this place was to know the truth. Lirah moved from the window, sitting on her bed to process the news.

"Where is Dexius?" she said as she walked back to the window.

"He's waiting for us at the bottom."

Lirah glanced at the floor. "I guess I shouldn't be surprised that he wouldn't want to come back. How did you get up here?"

"I found some metal stakes and hammered them into the rocks and used them for steps to cross the gap."

"You always were the most inventive," she said with a glimmer of a smile.

"There are so many stories I need to tell you."

"Is that a sword?" She leaned farther out the window, peering at the white blade on his back. "It looks bloody."

"Yeah, that's a story of its own."

"What will you do now?" Lirah peered down at him, grabbing the window frame. "If they want you in prison, how can you go back to classes again?"

"I can't," he said. "Even if I could, I wouldn't want to. They choose the biggest outcasts to Descend. They don't want me here, and I don't want to be part of this place anymore."

"You're not an outcast, Tav!" she said. "Most people like you. They just don't know how to talk to you, but they will. You've changed a lot since you've been gone. Everyone will see that."

"I don't care anymore. I have no desire to waste another minute of my life with these people."

"Tav . . . don't blame everyone . . . I just wish—"

"I came here to rescue you from this place—to take you back with me."

"But Tav, I can't." She shook her head. "I can't breathe the air."

"Yes, you can," he rested his hand on hers. "Everyone in Rethia can. It's another lie to control you."

"I'm not sure I could climb down."

"I'll help you. We'll take it slow."

"But my home is here. Everyone I know is here." Lirah moved her hand from under his, bringing it to her neck. "I can't just leave them."

"I won't be here. I thought you wanted us to be together."

"Tav," Lirah covered her face with her hand. "I . . . I promised myself to someone."

Tavarian recoiled. "What? What do you mean?" All warmth fled from his body. "I thought . . ."

Lirah withdrew the hand from her face, revealing the chaotic storm in her eyes. "I do! I do love you, Tav. I always have. But not in the way you want me to."

"What do you mean? You said—" he started. "You said you would be waiting for me when I came back."

"I'm so sorry, Tav," she grabbed the back of her head with both hands, straightening her curls. "I thought I would never see you again. I thought it was a perfect way for us to end things—for you to remember me."

"By leading me on? By lying to me?"

Tears began to rain onto her cheek. "Oh, Tav . . . I never should have said that. I'm a horrible person. I thought . . . It was a stupid thing to do. I just wanted you to be happy and give you confidence to make it in Rootcore."

"Coming here was a mistake." Heat returned to Tavarian's face, now overflowing beyond control. "All the time in Rethia—what I thought was home—it was just an empty worthless joke. Every single thing I ever believed was a lie. I've never been special or chosen for anything, just trash to be tossed away.

"Tavarian, don't talk that way," she said as her eyes grew. "I hate when you do that."

"I don't care what you hate!" Tavarian snapped. "You're just like everyone else. Everyone here is a liar. I wish I had never met you. I would have been better off without you. Go find another hopeless outcast to help—I'm done with this place!"

Her eyes quickly narrowed. "If that's how you feel, go ahead and leave!"

She slammed the window shut and blew out the candle. Tavarian turned and walked around the house to the gate, opening it for what would likely be the last time, and started down the road.

Out of habit, he walked in the wrong direction, but he didn't care. He didn't want to go back and face Dexius or anyone. If Dexius found out what happened with Lirah, he would make fun of him forever. Tavarian couldn't deal with that right now. Once that happened, his tolerance of Dexius would be gone. They would be back to hating each other again.

He despised the thought of forcing Darby to choose which one of them she would go with. His number of friends dwindled by the minute. Soon he may not have any left. Tavarian wandered down the dirt road they used to walk, toward the farm district and the woods leading to the waterfall.

Where was there left to go now? What was left for him anywhere? Maybe he would just wander aimlessly, avoiding any contact with other beings. The whole world had been laughing at him all his life.

Tavarian walked through the trees and to the edge of the mountain, the falling water cascading into the clouds below. He now knew what the bottom of the falls was like, but it didn't matter anymore. Things were supposed to be so different when he returned to this spot again. He should be triumphant after conquering Nalacea and bringing back the rokenstones. Instead, it was the worst day of his life.

He stood near the edge of the plateau, leaning against the wooden fence. Tavarian could almost hear the shadows, whispering to him like the forked tongue of a serpent flicking at the hollow places in his weary mind. Tempting him to lean over the edge. It was what Rethia had chosen for him. One leap was all that separated him from the intended destiny of a Descender.

More than temptation, the thought of doing what the council wanted burned a fire into his soul. Rethia would come to regret casting him out. He imagined becoming greater than anyone in Rethia ever dreamed of being. They had no idea what he could accomplish. Tavarian wasn't entirely sure himself, but it stirred his heart. Thoughts of revenge flashed through his mind, but he didn't have the will nor desire to put any of them to action. Whether healthy or not, he enjoyed the idea, the fantasy of it.

The situation with Lirah hurt and embarrassed him, but if anything, he had a lot of practice in dealing with embarrassment. He had recovered before, and he could do it again. For the first time, he had no idea what he wanted out of life. He never dreamed beyond this, of being chosen to descend, or of Lirah liking him. He had accomplished every challenge set before him, whether it paid off or not. If he could set his sights on something true, something worthwhile, he may achieve something great.

"Tavarian . . ." said a voice behind him. He quickly turned to see Lirah standing there among the trees. Her white curly hair was glowing in the blue moonlight. As much as he despised her right now, he couldn't deny her beauty. It made the anger wane, if only a little.

"What?" he answered defensively. Unsure of her intentions, he put his guard up, preparing for more hurtful words.

"I can't let things end like this," she said. "If I never see you again, please don't let my last memory of you be *this*."

"There's nothing left to say," he said.

"You don't have to say anything. Just know that you *are* important—never forget that. You're special to me . . . and I'll never regret our friendship for a single day."

"Lirah, let's not do this."

"No, listen," she said. "If you need to hate me, I understand. I probably deserve your hate. I only hope that someday you'll forgive me and remember our happy times."

"I don't hate you," he said, lowering his tone.

"You're important to a lot of people, Tav," she said. "All you have to do is let them in; allow people to see you for who you are. Don't try to be who you think they want you to be. If you must return to Rootcore, make it a fresh start. Let them see the real Tavarian, the one I know and love."

"I thought of you every day," he told her. "It got me through some difficult times."

"You may not believe me right now, but I thought of you too . . . constantly," she said. "Since you left, I've come out here to the waterfall and looked over the clouds, hoping they would allow me a glimpse of you and Dexius. I worried and hoped that you both were okay. I dreamed of what you were experiencing out there, what you were doing. I missed talking to you and seeing you after classes. I even missed that head twitch you do that annoys me." She giggled a little.

"Head twitch?"

"When you go like this." She demonstrated cocking her head to the side, three times in a row.

"I don't do that."

She laughed. "You do it all the time!"

"Well, you're always bouncing your hair with your hands," he said.

"Oh, that's annoying?"

"Well, no, it's actually kind of cute. Let me think of something else."

She snickered. "Okay, if you must."

"The thing that annoyed me the most about you were how you act better than everyone. Well, not everyone . . . mostly me, talking down to me."

"Oh?" she said. "I never thought I was better than you. I guess telling you what you're doing wrong would give you that impression. I'm sorry. It was only because I wanted to help you. I wanted everyone to see through the things that prevented them from knowing you the way I do."

"I know, I just thought . . . while we're being honest."

"Yeah, that's good to know. You seem more confident now—more determined. Whatever happened down there, it did you some good."

"You were right about me . . . most of the time. All I ever wanted was to fit in. Like you always said, I was trying too hard. When everyone ignored the quiet, awkward kid I was, I thought I had to be the best at everything to overcome that."

"And now you don't seem too afraid of what people think."

"I suppose that's it," he said. "So, who is this guy that you promised yourself to?"

"It's Neylin."

"Oh," said Tavarian. "He always seemed like a good person. I guess I can see why you would like him."

"He is. He's a great guy . . . like you. It's just . . . I don't know how these feelings work, Tav. I had different kinds of feelings for you."

"I didn't mean what I said earlier about wishing we had never been friends."

"I understand."

"I should probably go. I can't be seen by the peace control officers. Please don't tell anyone I was here. I'm not sure what they would do if they knew that you saw me. I shouldn't have risked your safety, but at the time I thought you would . . . be coming with me."

"I'm glad you came back, and that I was able to see you again. I'm not sure what I'm going to do knowing all this about Rethia, especially when the next Descension comes."

"Don't risk your safety if you are going to stay. Tell no one what I told you tonight."

She reached out, wrapping her arms around him, and he returned her embrace. She squeezed him tight and kissed him on the cheek. Her small wet lips touched sweetly on his skin. He cupped the curls of her hair with his hand, bouncing them the way she always did. She smiled even as the moonlight revealed the sparkling diamonds forming in her eyes.

"You'll always be my best friend, Tavarian," she said as he started off.

A lump formed in the back of his throat that he had to clear before opening his mouth again. "Well with, Lirah."

Tavarian walked back to the edge of the woods, watching her until she moved out of sight. The best thing to do would be to go now, but he couldn't leave without making one more stop. Over the crooked shadows, he ran down the road toward his old house.

Sneaking around the side of the home, he approached two windows faintly glowing by lantern light. He tapped lightly on the left window, increasing the amount of force until the floor thumped on the inside. Valea's face moved close to the glass, lit by contrasting red and blue. The window opened.

"Is that you, Bryas?" she whispered. "You know I could get in big trouble sneaking out this late."

"It's Tavarian," he said quietly.

"Don't joke . . ." she scolded.

"No, Valea, it's me," Tavarian said.

She leaned through the open window, squinting.

"Tav! I can't—" she started loudly.

"Keep it down!" he said. "I don't want anyone else to know I'm here."

"What are you talking about?" Valea said. "Why not?"

Tavarian explained what happened to him when he returned with the rokenstones. He told her the real reason for the Descension every year and how they selected the Descenders, picking the ones that fit in the least in the community.

"Tav, are you sure?" Valea said, still leaning out the window, hair gently blowing in the breeze. "I mean, you wouldn't joke about something like this would you?"

"I wish I was joking, but it's all true."

"The council must pay for this! When this gets out—"

"Wait . . . don't tell anyone about this. This information is dangerous. Anyone who knows about this will be thrown in prison."

"They can't throw us all in prison!"

"I shouldn't have told you," said Tavarian. "I'm endangering you just by being here. I just wanted you to know why I'm not coming back for good. I'm going back to live in Rootcore."

"You did the right thing by telling me," Valea said. "If they want you dead, then leave. I don't know what I'm going to do, but somehow I'm going to help make Rethia a place where you can come back and not have to worry about being jailed or killed."

"Please be careful," he said. "If you become their enemy, you'll be in the same position I am."

"I'll be careful."

"If you ever need to leave, I nailed several stakes into the side of the mountain," said Tavarian. "It will still be dangerous. The road is steep before the drop off."

Valea leaned farther out the window frame and gave him a hug. His head hurt from the emotional pain of the past hour. This could not be a last goodbye. He couldn't bear the thought. If he had to climb the mountain and sneak past the peace control officers in the dark to see her again, he would do it.

"Well be with you, Tavarian," she said, rubbing her eyes.

"Well with . . ."

Tavarian backed into the shadows as Valea pulled the window down.

"Oh, one more thing," Tavarian began before the window shut. "Who's Bryas?"

Valea smiled. "No one that you need to worry about." She closed the window, stepping out of the glow of the lantern.

Tavarian stood there a moment, taking in one last glimpse of his old house. It was like looking back at his old self. The part he had outgrown and left behind. Suddenly, the window opened again.

"He's a good friend, Tav," said Valea. "I like him, but I'm not sure if I want to promise myself to him—at least, not yet. I don't know if I'm ready for that right now."

"I hope it works out for the best," he said. "Whatever you decide."

"Thank you," said Valea. "Maybe you'll get to meet him one day."

"I hope so." Tavarian headed back to the moonlit road.

He tried to focus on the good things about Rethia: the farmland, the waterfall, the forests, the modest river, Lirah, Valea, and his family. It had not all been worthless. He made it back to the lower part of the road without incident. He barely noticed stepping down the spikes he had nailed into the side of the mountain. The moon and stars were gone now, behind the veil of the lower atmosphere. A blue haze in the clouds was the only sign of the moon.

As he started the walk to Muloken, the emotions of what had recently transpired began to hit him. It was such a different result than he had expected, like he had been transported to a new world, another reality where everything turned against him. He wiped a tear from his cheek, hoping Dexius wouldn't notice once he got back to him and Darby.

CHAPTER 20

AFTER WALKING BETWEEN the scattered trees and moss-covered fields in the dark, Tavarian could make out the jagged silhouettes of the ruined town of Muloken. As he stepped through the chaotic remnants of a place many families once called home, he called out to Dexius and Darby to alert them of his approach. He didn't get an answer.

Cautiously, he entered one of the broken houses. He investigated each room with only a bit of blue moonlight to show his surroundings. There was nothing in the first building, so he moved on to the next. He called out again, but got no response.

Tavarian anxiously checked the remaining buildings until he found them in one of the wrecked houses, lying together. Thankfully, they were only asleep.

"It's a good thing I wasn't a bandit," Tavarian said. "You're supposed to be protecting Darby."

"I am," Dexius said, turning over to a sitting position on the floor. "I would have shot you if you were a bandit. I'm just used to your sound."

Darby woke up and sat up on the blanket when she realized Tavarian returned.

"My sound?" Tavarian asked, propping him arm against the leaning frame of the wall.

"The sound of your walk." Dexius rubbed his eyes.

"And what does my walk sound like?"

"Like pat, pat, pat, pat, slide . . . pat, pat, pat, slide."

Tavarian laughed. "Whatever . . . so Malidora has scents, and you have sounds."

"We're both hunters, we've got to have keen senses," said Dexius. "Are they going to fix the gap in the mountain path?"

"No," said Tavarian, eyeing the floorboards as the hurt returned. "No, they are not."

"Why not? What are they going to do, then?"

Tavarian's heart was drained. He couldn't bear to speak of everything that happened in the last few days. Where would he even begin? He breathed deep, recalling the images of the prison, the fight with the guard, and most of all, Lirah's disappointing words.

"Tavarian, what are they going to do to get us up there?" demanded Dexius.

Tavarian put his head in his hands as he sat down on the blanket beside Darby. Shaking his head, he exhaled a sigh that escaped through his nose.

"What happened?" Dexius pressed.

Darby edged toward Tavarian, leaning against him. Everything that happened recently stormed though his mind. She pulled his hand away from his head as he allowed her to squeeze her fingers between his.

"It's okay, Tavarian," she said.

"It doesn't feel okay," he responded, sweeping the stray hairs away from her eyes.

"Mama used to—" Darby started, but turned away.

"What? You wanted to say something. Tell me Darby," Tavarian implored. "What about your mother?"

Darby's eyes moved back to him for a moment and then toward the weathered floor. She took a deep breath.

"Please . . ." Tavarian urged.

"She would say . . ." Darby took another breath, her voice slightly raspy. "That the real journey is not out here in the world, it's within yourself. You may not always make it to where you want to go, but that doesn't mean the journey is over. Stay on your path, and you will eventually make it where you need to be. The place we are needed most is the place where we belong."

Tavarian blinked rapidly as he eyed Darby. It was the longest sentence she had uttered in his presence.

"Your mother sounds like a wise person," said Tavarian.

Darby agreed, meeting his eyes.

"Tav, you gotta tell us what happened," Dexius reminded him.

There were no insects in the dead town, but the distant chirping signified there was still life all around Muloken. The night showed through the holes in the ceiling. Streams of brightflies moved through the dark sky on their way to and from the nocturnal blossoms they craved. Despite everything that happened in Rethia, the world kept on going. Was the world indifferent to his pain? Or was it reminding him that everything would be there when he was ready to return to it? Nothing had really changed. He was alive, and he still had Darby and Dexius.

Tavarian finally mustered the fortitude to give them the details about being imprisoned, his escape, and the truth about the Descension.

"So, we're not honored—we're outcasts." Dexius loosened his Rethian pendants from his tunic as he stood and went to the doorway of the rundown house. He tossed them as far as could over the rooftops of the ruined buildings. "I told you we should have stayed in Strakenbridge."

"I did see Lirah, at least." Tavarian said, recalling the last image of her, gleaming in the moonlight with a sweet, sad smile. He couldn't bear the thought of never seeing her again. Though her words, and her betrayal, oddly helped to heal the blow. It was almost like cauterizing a wound.

"What did she say? Did you tell her about all this?"

"I told her."

"And she didn't come with you?" Dexius said. "You told her she could breathe the air here, right?"

"She's promised herself." Tavarian stared at the floor. He wanted to say it without appearing hurt by it. "She's going to be coupled with Neylin."

"Neylin?" Dexius furrowed his brow. "But all he does is read and study . . . what does she see in him?"

"He's smart and friendly—everyone likes being around him. He's everything I'm not. I think he'll treat her well, and she seems happy."

"Everything you're not? Do you think Neylin would have saved us in Grunda? Would Neylin have made it through the swamp with all the . . .

you know—all that bad stuff? Would he have found rokenstones and brought them back?"

"A lot of good that did. I'm not sure I'm such a good person anyway," said Tavarian, standing and moving toward the broken window. "When we were in the swamp, the shadows whispered to me." Tavarian stared out at the darkness, the faint blue moonlight reflecting off the drooping stems in the withered garden. "They told me I couldn't trust you, that you wanted to take the rokenstones for yourself so you could come back and be the hero, and that I needed to leave you and Darby in order to be the hero I wanted to be."

"But the Nulthereals were trying to control you," Dexius said. "It doesn't make you a bad person."

"That's the thing," said Tavarian. "They weren't controlling me. The Nulthereals didn't put those thoughts in my head—they were already there. It made me realize how selfish I was or maybe still am. I didn't want to bring the stones back to help the community. I wanted to get the stones so I would be praised. So I would be welcomed back, and I would fit in with everyone at school. I'm sorry I ever threatened you, because of my selfishness."

"They told me you only cared about the rokenstones," Dexius said. "That as soon as you had them, you would convince Darby to leave with you. When we were staying with Wynnotha, we felt like a family—a family like I always wanted, like everyone else had. I wanted to stay with Wynnotha with Darby and . . . even you."

"Why don't you like your own family?" Tavarian half turned toward him, keeping his eyes on the blighted garden.

Dexius leaned against the broken wall. "Every time I ever thought we were finally going to be a real family, my father left us. He'd run off somewhere, and my mom would chase after him. They'd leave me and my sister alone for days, and then come back like nothing happened. But when my father came back, he seemed to hate us. He would punish me. He'd always find something I did wrong as an excuse to bruise me up."

Tavarian turned to him. "I'm sorry, Dex, I had no idea."

"Don't be sorry," Dexius said. "Lirah was the only person I ever told before now. That's why I drew my bow on you in the swamp. I thought we could be like a real family, but I thought . . . The whispers told me that you were going to be like my father and ruin it—leave me alone just like he always did."

"Does that mean none of us are good? That we're no better than the darkness within us? None of us except Darby." Tavarian turned back toward the window.

"The shadows told me to burn this town and everyone in it." Darby remained still on the blanket. Her voice took them by surprise as much as the words.

Tavarian tilted his head to the side and Dexius narrowed his eyes as they both glanced at her. "Where's the temptation in that?" Tavarian said.

"Like you said, it was already on my mind." Darby stood and moved through the torn wall of the wooden house, outside into the night air. Dexius and Tavarian followed her past the blighted gardens in the middle of the town. She entered another wrecked house, slowly wandering through the remains of its rooms. They found her in one of the chambers in the back. She stood in front of a bed that was mostly intact. It had a dark wooden frame with two large flowers carved into the footboard. Between the two flowers was a word carved in fancy cursive letters.

"What are you trying to tell us?" Dexius asked, studying the room.

Darby moved to the footboard, and traced the carved writing with her finger. Tavarian could hardly read the word imprinted into the wood because the style of writing was illegible to him.

"What's she trying to show us?" Dexius watched as Tavarian bent down to examine the carving.

Tavarian squinted at the footboard of the bed. "Wait, does that say Darby?"

Darby nodded emphatically. Dexius and Tavarian glanced at each other.

"You lived here?" Dexius asked, rubbing the back of his neck.

Darby affirmed again.

"Why would you want to burn this place down if you lived here?" Dexius stroked the skin underneath the collar of his tunic.

"Mama was the gardener." Darby sat down on the bed. "Strange things began happening. Everyone started arguing; fighting all the time over every little thing. One day, the flowers Mama planted in the garden turned black. A few days later, the crops next to the garden got the same disease and died. There wasn't enough food for everyone. Some left for other towns to get food and seeds to bring back. Many blamed Mama for what happened. She couldn't leave the house without someone saying mean things to her, so she stopped going outside."

Darby lowered her head, closing her eyes.

Tavarian rubbed her shoulder. "You don't have to say anything you don't want to."

"The well dried up . . ." Darby continued with her eyes shut. "My brother and I had to walk to the brook to get water. I ran ahead of my brother and his friend to fill my bucket first. Before they got to the brook, the shadow—" Darby began to shiver, producing stuttering breaths. "It ate them! I stayed by the brook until it left. I ran home to tell Mama." Darby squeezed her eyes tight, the skin wrinkling around them. "She wouldn't say anything when I told her. She wouldn't move."

Dexius sat beside her on the bed, putting an arm around her. She leaned her head against his chest for a moment, and then sat up straight, moving away from him.

"The same thing that happened to the flowers happened to her. I tried to get someone to help me move her body to bury her, but no one would help. They said she deserved it; that all of this was her fault." Darby started coughing. She turned away, clearing her throat and then continued, "Her body lay on the floor underneath the lidradary vines that she grew inside along the walls." Darby slid off the bed to her feet, moving to the doorway of the room. "I hated everyone in this place for killing her—for leaving her there to wither."

Darby slid down the frame of the door to the wooden floor. "Then the whispers came. They found dark thoughts inside of me, wanting to set fire to everything. They told me to destroy this place and anyone who remained." She rested her head on her knees as she drew them up. "I found a bottle of oil that we used in the lanterns. There were candles I lit at night in Mama's bedroom."

Tavarian and Dexius remained still as she spoke, their faces wearing expressions ranging from sadness to horror and back again.

"When I walked past her body to the other room, a white lidradary bloom had opened on the vines. White with small pink spots on the petals—Mama's favorite kind. It was like," Darby rubbed her eyes. "Like a message from her. Telling me to stop. I ignored the whispers and ran back to the brook."

After a few moments of awkward silence, Tavarian finally spoke up. He had no idea what he should say, but he knew he should say something. "I'm so sorry, Darby, that's horrible."

"That's not the point," Darby stood up in the doorway. "You said we're no better than the darkness within . . ." She took a deep breath. "There's darkness within everyone, but it's not the darkness that defines you, it's your rejection of it. When you ignore the selfishness inside to help others, that's where the good is. The shadows . . . they don't give you that chance. They take away the part of you that would normally resist the bad thoughts."

Tavarian leaned against the wall, trying to bring order to the thoughts running through his head. "Don't disparage your weaknesses, rely on your strengths. My sister told me that before I left Rethia."

"I would not have been about to do any of that if it weren't for the voices. I still struggle with how much was the shadows and how much was me. Whoever killed Mama would not have done what they did. No one would have ignored me when I asked for help. Either way, we have to take responsibility for our actions. I can't forgive myself unless I forgive those who hurt me."

"So you're saying we need to forgive ourselves, forgive each other, and move on?" Dexius stood up from the bed.

Darby nodded. "Yes, we can't carry these dark burdens forever. We have to learn, forgive, and move forward. It's that simple and that difficult. I'm telling myself this as much as I'm telling it to you."

"Well, I for one, am willing to forgive you all for everything you've done," Dexius said with a bit of feigned impudence, putting his hands on his waist.

Tavarian snorted out a laugh, caught off guard with the joke after sharing their harrowing stories. "You're an example for us all," he sarcastically replied. "I suppose I can forgive everything you've put us through as well."

Darby slept in her old bed through the rest of the night while Dexius and Tavarian lay on the floor beside it. Tavarian worried about the unknown future facing him. Perhaps he could go back to Ibis in Strakenbridge and become a true blacksmith apprentice. He could be a carpenter like he had always wanted to be. They had been able to make it out in the wilds on their own—maybe they could explore more of the world and find another place that could be home.

As he considered of all the possibilities, something in the back of his mind lingered. It bothered him—disturbing memories of the Nulthereals' destruction of Samavere. They had wiped out Malidora's homeland and her family. They had destroyed Darby's home in Muloken and her family.

The shadows were a much bigger problem than Tavarian wanted to admit. Malidora was right—the blight could actually take over Isodonia. Could she really stop it on her own? Most of the world around them knew nothing of this growing nightmare. Even though he knew about it, he had not done much more to stop it than anyone else. As Malidora said, there are two kinds of people in the world. He didn't completely share that belief, but in this instance, perhaps she was right.

When morning came, Tavarian gathered his bag and sword. Darby ate some of the tree nuts they had collected during the journey, while Dexius sat up on the blanket.

"I've been thinking about what to do next," Tavarian said, standing by the tattered doorway. "We need to start a new life here, obviously, all three of us. Like Dexius said, we're family and I will always stand by you. I hope we will all do that for each other."

"The only loyalty I have left is to us," said Dexius.

Darby signified her agreement.

"There's something I need to do," Tavarian announced. "The Blight Whidge has to be stopped. I don't know if Malidora can stop it by herself. I'm going to find her and help in any way I can."

"If you are going, we are going," said Dexius, rising to his feet and grabbing his bow that stood propped against the wall by the bed.

"First, listen," said Tavarian. "There was a message here in Muloken saying they left to go to Strakenbridge. Malidora talked to some of those refugees there. Take Darby back to Strakenbridge and find them—they should recognize her. Get as many as you can to spread the word about the Nulthereals. Find others willing to investigate Muloken and Samavere. When I find Malidora, I'll have to convince her we can get people to believe the blight is real and to stand against it. Once I convince her, we'll meet you back in Strakenbridge."

"This could work." Dexius took a deep breath. "Imagine *us* . . . bringing an army together to save the world. That's way better than finding some stupid rocks."

"Darby, I know you won't like this, but we need to help save Isodonia before it's too late. For Muloken and most of all, for your family. We need Malidora's help to win this fight."

Darby pursed her lips. "Okay, we'll go."

"Hopefully, we can stay with Wynnotha again," said Dexius. "Just don't keep us waiting too long."

Tavarian smiled. "You mean like how you kept me waiting all night at the fountain?"

"More like how you kept us waiting while you went to get that stupid bag." Dexius snickered.

"I'll get there as quickly as I can." Tavarian grinned and walked out the door, surveying the horizon.

Darby stood misty-eyed in the gloomy morning sun.

Tavarian reached down and gave her big hug. "Take care of Dexius."

He put a hand to her cheek and leaned down to give her a kiss on her forehead. Tavarian moved toward Dexius, giving him a hug too. Dexius hesitated, but relaxed and hugged him back.

"The world has turned upside down," said Tavarian. "You've been one of the best friends I could have."

"You're not as much of a loser as I thought. I guess being around me for a while helped," Dexius said, smiling.

Tavarian laughed. "Be safe on the way there. Don't go anywhere near Grunda . . . or those woods with the black-eyed creatures."

"We won't," Dexius said. "Tell Malidora I said hi."

Darby ran off suddenly to one of the other buildings, and Tavarian and

Dexius followed, wondering what was going on. They caught up with her inside, and found her standing next to a small metal wheel and a turn crank.

"What is it?" Tavarian asked.

"You still have the stones?" she inquired.

"Yes," Tavarian replied. "I suppose I should bury them since they're useless now."

"Turn it," she said, gesturing toward the crank.

Tavarian began turning the crank and the thick metal wheel started spinning.

"Let me see one of the stones," Darby said.

Tavarian stopped turning the crank to reach into his satchel. Making sure it remained wrapped in cloth, he carefully lifted one of the rokenstones from his bag. He hesitated to hand something so lethal to Darby, but she had proven to have far more knowledge about the rokenstones than anyone else.

He turned the crank again, and while holding on the cloth, Darby brought the stone close to the wheel. Sparks flew as the stone touched the spinning metal. Darby rotated the stone as the spinning wheel smoothed it.

"That's good," she said. "Now I need your sword."

Confused but intrigued, Tavarian unsheathed the sword, and then she took the wrapped stone and held it up to the socket carved into the lavishly crafted sword hilt. She tried to fit it inside the socket, but found it was slightly too big.

Darby returned to the wheel, and Tavarian turned it for her. She filed down the stone a bit more and then held it to the socket again. This time, it snapped into place, touching the thin metal lines inside. She pointed to a small piece of metal on the hilt. When he touched it, the metal slid and clicked into place.

The blade instantly came to life, flashing like lightning. It hummed and vibrated in his hand. The sword was now much lighter as he swung it easily with one hand. The rokenstones somehow powered the sword. Its blade became nothing more than a blur, vibrating so fast it couldn't be clearly seen. Darby walked over, and he lowered the sword. She pulled the switch back and the humming sound went away.

"How did you know about this?" Tavarian asked as his heartbeat slowed to its normal rate.

"Rokensword," she said.

"Who told you that?" Tavarian wondered.

"Members of the Roken Order lived in Muloken," Darby said.

"I thought they didn't exist," said Tavarian.

"They live in secret," Darby said. "There aren't many left."

"Why so secret?" Dexius inquired.

"They study valekrum," Darby answered. "If their knowledge went to the wrong people, it could change Isodonia forever."

"What's valekrum?" Dexius asked.

"The power of lightning," said Darby.

"So, you had machines powered by rokenstones?" Tavarian asked.

Darby shrugged. "A few."

"Darby, for someone so young and quiet, you may be the smartest person I know," Tavarian said, sheathing the sword. "I suppose this sword belongs to you," he said. "I found the hilt here in Muloken."

"No, you keep it," she said. "You fixed it."

"Thank you," Tavarian said. "I promise I'll only use it if I have to."

"Hey, are there any rokenbows?" Dexius asked.

"I don't know much about weapons." Darby tilted her head.

"Hold on to these." Tavarian held out one of the wrapped rokenstones to Darby. "You know how to handle them better than either of us. Maybe we can figure out a way to use them later."

She took those he had left, checking their covering, and distributing them between both pockets of the leggings she wore under her dress.

Tavarian gave Darby one last hug and Dexius a pat on the shoulder, and set off on his new journey. It had been a while since he had been alone. From the time he had wandered into Grunda, he'd had companions. He already missed having Dexius beside him and Darby running off the path to pick flowers. The conversation with them the previous night had relieved him from an enormous burden he didn't realize he carried.

Sharing the same experiences as others fulfilled him—his excitement and even his despair. But he enjoyed the solitude as well. It gave him time to think and solve issues in his head. He could reflect on deeper emotions he wouldn't allow to come to the surface with others around.

Now there was nothing but time to reflect as he crossed over a field covered with huge spikes of obelisk-shaped rocks sticking out from the ground. Tavarian wondered how he could convince Malidora to hold back. Even as the other mountain moved closer, he had not come up with an answer yet.

This mountain had to be the other island in the sea of clouds they had seen from Rethia. He never imagined a situation like this would one day lead him there.

For one of the first times in his life, he stepped with confidence. Though he had been treated as a reject by those who controlled Rethia, this was the first time he was truly free. He was on a quest to help all of Isodonia, not something Rethia had sent him to do to maintain its control.

He had a group of friends he fit in with now. After everything he did to try to earn other people's respect, he found it in unexpected friends.

At the turn of night, Tavarian camped under a group of trees with nothing but the nocturnal spirits of nature to keep him company. So much filled his mind that it barely let him drift off to sleep.

When he did sleep, he dreamt of Lirah with her white hair glowing blue in the moonlight, waving in the soft breeze. She knelt beside him as he lay on his blanket under the sparkling of brightflies. He sat up to catch a strand of hair flowing over her face and brushed it away from her eyes. The weight of her curls faded away under the palm of his hand.

Tavarian woke as the emptiness of her rejection returned. He reached in his satchel and found the curl Lirah had given him. It was no longer white, having been stained by the grime and dirt of the dungeon. Though the lock of hair had lost much of its meaning, he could not bring himself to part with it.

Putting the bundle of hair back into the tight corner of the satchel, Tavarian prepared for the new day's journey. The mountain he was headed to was not so distant now. For a moment, a small breach opened in the lower atmosphere giving a glimpse of the bright blue sky above. He blinked and the opening vanished, leaving him to wonder if he'd only imagined it.

The mountain now rose above him as he came up a small rise on the hardened dusty path. A bright forest nearly surrounded a small lake near the base of the mountain. A cave nearby tunneled into the side of the mountain. As Tavarian moved around the lake, a burst of water and steam rose high out of the ground. He had never encountered anything like it. It rained large drops of water around the area and then stopped.

A large waterfall tumbled down the mountain into the lake, even bigger than the one in Rethia. Tavarian stepped toward the place where the water had burst from the rock. There was a fissure deep in the stone. The hardened mud and rock had eroded around the hole in a mixture of different colors flowing into strange patterns.

Tavarian peered into the hole in the ground. There was nothing inside but darkness and the echoes of water trickling deep within. As he moved on toward the cave, another jet of water burst up from the hole. Scalding mist touched his arm and Tavarian backed away from it with haste. He was fortunate it had not erupted while he'd been standing closer to it, and was equally fortunate that the wind was not blowing in his direction.

Tavarian moved farther around the base of the mountain, toward a small village on the other side. A wooden fence bordered the edges of the village. No one noticed as he passed through the open gate. There were many beings here walking between the huts made of stone and mud. They resembled people, but the men and women were completely devoid of hair. Their heads formed into an unusual point at the top. A thick, hardened horn protruded from their temples and curved around the back of their heads, following the contour.

They all busily walked back and forth. Some were working, carrying bowls filled with water and pouring it into a well near the center of the town. Others were shopping in market areas selling various fruits and plants. Tavarian weaved through the unorganized crowd unnoticed. He passed a display of ornate jewelry strung together to wear around the neck, wrists, or horn in their case.

A multitude of pottery of all shapes and sizes were on display as he continued through the pathways. He wondered if Yarvik and Malidora were still here or if she had already left to fight the shadows. If they were here, they shouldn't be too hard to find as they would stand out, although there were some among the crowd who were more like them.

Passing through smells of cooked meats, Tavarian began to wish he had coins to buy food. The market area gave way to clusters of living communities with smaller huts housing the residents of the village. Children played in the tall grass that grew between the blue crystal stones and rust-colored dirt that defined this region.

There must be someone he could inquire about Malidora's whereabouts. Everyone here moved about, busy and determined, preoccupied with whatever business they had in the village. He did not know how to approach anyone.

As he passed through the living communities, the stern faces of the villagers were less welcoming. Perhaps he should get back to the market where they seemed more accommodating to strangers. As he was about to leave, he noticed an area where people were sitting on stone benches around a large structure not too far away. People were crowded together talking, drinking, and eating, but otherwise not busy.

Making his way over, Tavarian followed a group who walked up to a larger building, poured drinks into ceramic cups, paid someone at the front, and then walked back to their seats. It was quite different from the taverns in Strakenbridge and Samavere, but much the same concept.

"Tavarian!" It was Malidora. Two large, horned, local men were sitting with her. Tavarian hesitantly moved over to where they were sitting.

"What are you doing here? You miss me?" She held a ceramic vessel close to her chin, using her elbow on the table to prop her arm. She held it delicately as though it could slip through her fingers at any moment.

"Miss you?" Tavarian said. "Hardly . . ."

As Malidora focused her attention on Tavarian, the two horned strangers turned to talk to each other.

"So you weren't able to climb the mountain," said Malidora as she leaned back in her chair. Her eyes squinted confidently, as though she knew everything.

"I climbed it," said Tavarian.

"And yet, here you are," she said.

"Things didn't go as planned," he said. "They lied to us . . . it was all a lie."

"So, your precious community is the same as the rest of the world." Malidora took a sip of her drink. "I warned you. The systems of the machine are the same wherever you go. It's the one constant I've found everywhere I have traveled. You're nothing but an asset to be used." She took another sip. "Every system has vulnerabilities. Seek them out. Exploit them. Make it work for you." Malidora turned the vessel up and finished the drink, setting the container on the table. "Now that you've seen what's behind the veil, what do you think? Did it change you?"

"Not really—I still want the same thing. I want to build something that matters. I want to do something that makes a difference, for myself and for the people I care about," Tavarian said. "For once, I want to be the hammer."

"Yes! That's what I've been waiting to hear." Malidora leaned over the table toward him. "I knew you had it in you. Where are those two friends of yours?"

"They are heading to Strakenbridge to find all the refugees from Muloken. They're going to try to convince people to go and visit the remains of Muloken and Samavere, and hopefully, they will believe them. If they do, then maybe we can make a stand against the shadows."

"A valiant effort," she said. "I don't think it will work. They won't find anyone to travel there based on their story. Even when the word gets back to Strakenbridge about the destroyed towns, they won't believe that a force from another universe caused it. By the time anyone believes them, it would be too late. Why didn't you go with them?"

"I'm supposed to be here to convince you to wait until they have an army to help you," said Tavarian. "But I know you aren't going to wait. So I want to help you fight the shadows in whatever way I can."

One of the strangers at the table laughed. "You believe in her shadows?"

"As will you, soon enough," Malidora said as the two resumed the conversation between themselves. "Yes, they're in the forest on the other side of the mountain. There are no signs their influence has taken hold here yet."

"Who are your new friends?" Tavarian asked Malidora.

"Part of my plan," Malidora said. "They claim they don't believe there are shadows in the woods out there, but they aren't as convinced as they would lead you to believe. They are warriors and they're familiar with the old ways their people used to vanquish evil."

"And what ways are those?" Tavarian asked.

"When I kill the shadow girl containing the Blight Whidge, they're going to burn the body before it can emerge. That should take care of it,"

Malidora said. "It may be able to move over land and sea in that body, but it is also vulnerable in it. If we destroy the body while it inhabits it, it will either die with it or be forced back to wherever it came from."

"That makes sense, but what if it doesn't work?" Tavarian asked.

"We've got backup plans," Malidora said. "Ulok and Gomere are going to cover their blades in grulik blood and stab the body with it as well. He says the blood is like poison to unnatural creatures."

"Unnatural creatures?" Tavarian said.

"Mawlons and other unsettling things," Ulok said.

"Seriously? Mawlons? And you laughed at me about the shadows." Malidora sighed. "Anyway, when this all goes down, we can only hope that you can resist their conditioning."

"How are they going to be able to resist?" Tavarian asked.

"Nothing is going to control us," said Ulok.

Tavarian grimaced; there was probably no one who believed they could be controlled.

"I've been training them," Malidora assured him.

"I hope it works," Tavarian said.

Malidora groaned. "We're running short on time. I was training a third, but if you can beat their control we should start tomorrow. You guys good?"

"The sooner we go, the sooner we get paid," Gromere said.

"We'll meet at the gate at first light," said Malidora.

"Okay . . ." said Tavarian. "Is there anywhere I can stay?"

"Can't you be a little more resourceful?" muttered Malidora. "I suppose you can stay in my hut, but you'll sleep on the floor."

"That's fine, but I'm getting the impression you are annoyed with my being here—I thought I was helping you," Tavarian said.

"I don't need help," Malidora said. "I'm letting you contribute."

She must have noticed the sour expression on his face.

"Don't take everything so personally. I'm glad you're here," she added.

The day went on, and Tavarian killed time walking around the village. He wandered through the shops again. It surprised him that Malidora handed over enough coins to get food, even though she wanted him to bring something back for her. The coins were no doubt stolen, but he was too hungry to care.

In what could be his last day alive, he experienced the tastiest smoked meat he had ever eaten—even better than the trouder sausages in Strakenbridge. Tavarian wasn't sure what animal it came from, but if he survived this, he would have to find out.

He wished Dexius and Darby were here with him. If he ever were to see them again, he would surely have a great story to tell. Without Dexius here, he and Malidora didn't talk much. Those days and nights traveling with Dexius, Darby, Malidora, and even Yarvik were some of the most fun times he'd had in his life. It's funny how you never recognize how good things are until they have passed.

CHAPTER 21

THE NEXT MORNING, Tavarian awoke to Malidora moving about in the room. With her back to him, she slipped off her loose nightshirt and picked up a thicker black top. Tavarian turned away out of respect, but couldn't resist turning back for a moment. Her shoulders and back were smooth but tightly shaped with muscular tone. Soft, delicate curves rounded out her waist and hips. Several long scars across her back could not diminish her beautiful form.

Tavarian wondered what caused such wounds, but decided it was best not to ask. That would only reveal that he had looked. Malidora put on her thick battledress and filled her quiver with bolts. He pretended to just begin waking up, grabbing his sword and sheath, and then putting on the rest of his clothing.

He followed her out of the hut and through the village toward the gate. The villagers had not fully woken up yet as few residents were walking about. Ulok waited at the gate along with Gromere as they practiced twirling their spears to finish in a defensive stance.

"Prepare your minds for the assault you may face," Malidora warned as she strutted past them. Metal pieces tied together around their necks clanged against each other as Ulok and Gromere started after her.

Tavarian rushed alongside her. "I didn't do so well the first time the whispers got to me."

"No one does. I'm hoping my preparation will help these guys snap out of it," said Malidora as she strode toward the forest.

Tavarian lifted his head to the clouds covering the top of the mountain. "What happened the first time you heard them?"

Malidora's golden eyes moved beyond the rows of trees ahead. "There's not enough good to make up for what I've done."

"What happened?" Tavarian inquired before noticing her distant stare.

Malidora turned to him. "Perhaps I'll tell you tomorrow."

"Maybe it will give you some peace to talk about it." Tavarian glanced back.

"It's too late for that." Malidora lifted her hood over her head. "But if we are here tomorrow, this will all be over."

"It's not too late—there's more ahead than there is behind," Tavarian said, reminding himself as much as her.

Malidora laughed and quickened her pace.

"What?" Tavarian sped up to stay with her.

"Listen to yourself, all this positivity and inspirational drivel. What happened up on the mountain?"

"Nothing positive." The warmth drained out of him for a moment, leaving him feeling the emptiness left by a dead dream. "I guess I'm reassuring myself as much as anyone else."

"You're a good kid, Tav—I mean, you're a good guy," she said. "I get what you're trying to say. If things go bad here, save yourself. I won't think less of you if you run. Go back to Darby and Dexius and tell them I wouldn't wait."

"No, this is it," Tavarian said. "I'm here to the end."

"Very well, but if you change your mind . . ."

The geyser erupted behind them as Malidora ran to the edge of the small lake under the waterfall tumbling down over different levels of rock in the mountain.

"This lake will be our safe zone. If we need to regroup, get in the water and meet here!" she shouted so Ulok and Gromere could hear. She glanced at Tavarian and dashed toward the forest ahead.

Soon after passing the thick green brush of the forest, they came to a place of death and decay. The grass on the ground had turned black, spindly, and thin. Dead trees filled the area, dark and limp as though made of rotten flesh. Stiff dead animals littered the ground—a smaller version of the dead spot in the swamp. Through the limp hanging trees, a gray boulder stood. It was the same large stone Tavarian had seen in Galurigan.

"I call this Blightwood." Malidora came to a halt. "Keep your eyes open and your mind closed."

Gromere lit a torch to carry with him as he crept into the black dripping foliage. "What happened here?"

Ulok reached out to one of the fleshy trees. As he touched one of the branches, it tore loose and crumbled into ash. Some of its pieces were small and light enough to vanish on the air. "This is not natural." Ulok rubbed the residue between his fingers.

Malidora stepped over to him. "You beginning to believe me yet?"

"Something isn't right here." Ulok turned to Gromere.

Malidora pulled the crossbow from her battledress, snapping it into shape. "You're about to get more than you can comprehend."

Gromere began to walk in a different direction—he seemed confident, purposeful.

"Gromere? You see something?" Malidora watched him as he trudged ahead.

He moved faster, ignoring her question.

"Get him back here!" Malidora shouted, heading after him.

Tavarian was closest as he ran after Gromere, tackling him to ground once he caught up. His torch lay burning on the blackened surface, but did not ignite the dead foliage. Gromere threw Tavarian off him and got back to his feet. Grabbing the torch, he turned and resumed walking.

As Tavarian chased him, a familiar buzzing disrupted the air. An invisible force pressed on him as his head grew numb. Whispers seeped into his thoughts. *You know what it's like to be betrayed. Take your sword. Kill this one before he has the chance. It will be easy to stab him from behind. Eliminate the liability. Imagine the satisfaction as his flesh bows and gives way to your avenging blade. It is the only choice.*

Tavarian grabbed Gromere from behind, trying to pull him to the ground.

"Don't listen to the voices—they're controlling you! Clear them out of your mind!" Tavarian yelled, ignoring his own whispered thoughts.

Gromere struggled as Tavarian continued pulling him down. As they wrestled, Tavarian lost leverage and Gromere shoved him to the ground. He rolled through the wet, black grime, dodging Gromere's boot as he tried to stomp on him.

Suddenly a red arrow flashed by, hitting Gromere in the arm.

"Ow! Why did you shoot me?" Gomere demanded. Perhaps the pain distracted him enough so that he awakened from the Nulthereals' control.

"Get out of here! Give me the torch and get back to the lake!" she yelled.

After staring at her for a moment, he tossed the torch to Malidora and ran toward the lake, clutching his bleeding shoulder. Tavarian breathed a sigh of relief and got back to his feet. As he did, Ulok came charging at him. Tavarian slid his sword out of its sheath just in time to redirect Ulok's thrusting spear.

Malidora turned, aiming her crossbow in their direction. Ulok lunged with his spear again as Tavarian jumped sideways to dodge the attack. He didn't want to hurt Ulok, but Ulok displayed far more combat experience than the guard he fought in Rethia. He slid the switch on the blade, activating the rokenstone. The vibrating of the sword echoed through the dead forest. The blade sparkled and flashed as he twirled it, ready for Ulok's next attack.

Ulok stabbed at him again. Tavarian swung his blade to parry and the rokensword sliced through the metal spear as if it were nothing more than a twig. Ulok stared at the half of spear he held before slashing at Tavarian with it.

Tavarian now had the range advantage and Ulok did not have much to defend himself with. It did nothing to stop him as he spun the halved spear at Tavarian. Tavarian easily deflected the slash attempts as he backpedaled to keep Ulok at a distance.

Ulok waited for an opening. Lowering his head, he charged at Tavarian to ram him with his horns. Tavarian lifted his blade toward Ulok as he closed in on him. A flash of light lit up the forest as Ulok smashed into the sword, knocking him to the ashen ground. Smoke wafted up from the wound on his chest as Ulok lay motionless on the ground.

Malidora kept her crossbow trained on Tavarian. Did she think he was being controlled? She tossed the torch to him and fired. The arrow streaked by his head, close enough that he could smell the chemical she used on her arrows as it passed by.

Tavarian caught the torch and turned to Malidora in shock. She stared right past him. He spun around, and saw a girl rising out of the dark blight covering the ground, her face twisted and deformed. This was not a normal girl—it was a being shrouded in supernatural darkness. It was the Blight Whidge. Malidora's arrow remained embedded in her forehead. The shadow girl brought her hand to the arrow and siphoned it into her fingertips like it was made of smoke.

Tavarian dove out of the way as Malidora shot a handful of arrows, firing in quick succession. The shadow girl raised both hands and the bolts stopped in mid-air. Tavarian could no longer move as he tried to stand. Malidora froze while loading another bolt.

His senses stopped. The world around them faded away, leaving only the three of them there facing one another. As he tried to reason what was going on, a series of voices approached him from all directions.

These were different than the subtle whispers of the Nulthereals. They were powerful; they punched into his head, shaking his soul and pounding his brain. The voices melded together in unison, forming a singular reverberating utterance.

"Your interference is tiresome," the voice came from the shadow girl, but it was not a girl's voice. It pressed through his mind like a change of wind dissipating a billowing smoke. "We will not allow you to destroy this body. This world has been marked. Impedance is no longer possible. Go to the town and wait. If you do not resist, you will be rewarded. You may join the great dream of the Nulvain Gaith. Shed your constrictive material mind and body. The collective knowledge and power of the Gaith will be yours."

"I don't know about Tavarian, but I prefer to remain myself," Malidora thought.

Tavarian realized his mind connected not only to the shadow girl, but also to Malidora.

The shadow said, "You can either be useful or your matter can be ripped apart and scattered across the Everance."

White energy emanated from the girl, pulling on him, not on his physical body, but on his consciousness. The catalog of his memory opened as if it were being observed. He tried to push back, but this force was too strong. A string of events from younger days passed by. All those thoughts and feelings shot through him chaotically at the same time.

There were other visions he did not remember. He sat on a small raft floating in a massive, craterous lake. The land surrounding it sloped with iridescent rock. Hot steam rose from the water as they traveled from the lake to a river to another lake. Beyond the sloping rock were thick, tall forests. The trees were enormous, never ending as they reached up into the mist covering the sky. Tavarian extended his hand out of the boat to touch the water—hot, but not scalding hot.

"Go faster, Mal!" said a voice.

He turned to find a male sitting in the back of the raft. His hair black was streaked with patterns of white stripes. Tavarian sensed Malidora's resistance to him experiencing her memories like this. They were buried deep in her subconscious, and she did not like them being stirred up, especially in front of someone else. Tavarian knew how violating this felt to her, like naked shame. The sensation from her was so strong, he wished he could turn it off.

He instinctively knew the male was her brother, and one of her older sisters sat in front of her on the wooden raft.

"Why don't you paddle some?" a young Malidora proposed in the memory.

"Because you're too weak," said her sister. "We're helping you get strong."

Malidora wasn't fond of her siblings; they always treated her like the lowest form of life. She hated being the youngest.

As they came to the next river, Malidora recognized the trees growing along the banks of the steamy water. They were home.

"You were supposed to be back hours ago!" her father shouted as they were unloading the containers of plants and seeds.

"They wouldn't help paddle!" Malidora said, hoping they would be in trouble.

"Ha! You expect him to believe that? If we let you paddle, we would've never gotten back," said her sister.

"We're late because Malidora kept running off. We had to stop and find her," her brother said to their father. "I don't know why you insist we take her."

"Malidora! How many times have I told you not to wander off!" her father said. "I'm not letting you leave here until you can learn to stay with your elders."

"I don't want to go with *them*!" she shouted back.

She loved leaving their village nestled near the river, sprawling across a patch of land like an island between the rivers and the large round lakes surrounding them. She enjoyed exploring new places and observing new people. There was so much to see out there in the world, but she hated having to go with her siblings. They resented having to take her and did everything they could to show their father it was a bad idea.

Her father nearly always believed them over her, but this time she wasn't going to take it. She ran off into the forest, unsure where she headed.

"Malidora, get back here!" her father yelled.

For hours, she walked deep into the Arkanthian forests. The loud calls of predatory fowl echoed under the canopy of leaves. A light rain fell on her as the milvek trees sweat from their branches. The steam and mists swirled toward a spot ahead as she ran over to investigate.

As she moved closer, her senses told her to leave this place. The forest in this area was bathed in unnatural shade. All the trees were dark and soft. Their branches were barely strong enough to support their weight. She rubbed her hands to stop the tingling. Her mind raced as thoughts twisted in her mind, offering comfort in this dreadful place.

A whisper on the air made her turn, searching for its source. The whispers drew closer and louder. She sniffed the air, but there were no scents at all. The whispers came again, closer and closer. Malidora dropped to her knees and covered her ears as the voices surrounded her. They continued to move closer until at last they were inside her head. The whisperer understood why she ran from home. It believed her about her siblings.

"Get out of my mind!" Malidora shouted, breaking through the vision.

Tavarian realized they were back in the dead forest near Grenova. Malidora remained frozen beside him. The arrows she had fired still hung in the air. His head began to grow numb as he slipped back into the vision again.

As it grew dark in the Arkanthian forests, Malidora hid. If she stayed there, they would come after her. Her father would send someone to fetch her and bring her back to the house; they would be quite angry with her by now. A few hours later, there were footsteps through the misty trees not far from her location. Her two oldest siblings called out for her.

Before long, her brother came upon the strange dead part of the forest she had found earlier. He tilted his head as if reacting to something. Maybe the whispers were speaking to him too.

He headed straight to the trees where Malidora hid, as if he could see through the underbrush to her exact location. She tried to make a run for it, but it was too late. He grabbed her by the arm and started pulling her back into the wet, steamy forest.

As he dragged her over the slippery ground, Malidora was convinced he was going to hurt or even kill her. Even though he grabbed her roughly, she knew he was taking her back home. Her body, however, told her differently, shaking as her heart beat rapidly. Her mind stormed into chaotic fractures. She clenched her fists. She'd never experienced emotions so intense.

As Malidora struggled to free herself, everything told her she faced certain death. She pulled a carving blade from her belt and slashed down on her brother's wrist. Stunned, he let her go and fell to the ground, his arm bleeding profusely.

Malidora ran back toward the dead forest. She hadn't gotten far before her sister spotted her. Her sister chased her down and grabbed her from behind. Without hesitation, Malidora stabbed blindly behind her. The knife hit firm and then gave way.

"Malidora . . . what have you done?" Her sister crouched in the mud as she clutched her stomach while blood stained her clothing and hands.

Conflicted in the moment, vindication blended with nauseating guilt. It had not been the red-eyed man who killed her family. Malidora killed them. Tavarian experienced her shame as she sensed his shock and condemnation.

But Tavarian had experienced this event as if it happened to him—the influence of the shadows on her, the undying remorse she carried with her now. His condemnation turned to sympathy as he recognized that it had not been her fault. The shadows played on her negative emotions and twisted them to an infinite degree. He shuddered to think what he and Dexius might have done to each other if it had not been for Darby screaming that day in the swamp.

"You were right—it was the Blight Whidge who killed your family. He was controlling you," he communicated to her.

"I was weak, I should have been able to resist," she said.

"You didn't even know what it was at the time. You wouldn't resist what seemed like your own instincts."

Malidora's memories cycled to a gathering of people in a darkened room.

"If I hadn't been such a brat and ran off."

The dark room faded as pressure surrounded Tavarian. Malidora pressed against the shadow's control of her mind.

"They should not have treated you that way. It was a normal reaction," Tavarian assured her.

The pressure then released, and the dark room returned, this time mixed with other visions of fearful and angered faces.

"Did you see it? Did you see its thoughts as well? It wanted you to experience my memories, to turn us against each other," she said. "The Blight Whidge is toying with us. It enjoys controlling us, turning life against itself. Are you still with me?"

"I'm with you."

"Then help me push against it," Malidora said. "We'll do it together."

CHAPTER 22

TAVARIAN STRAINED TO resist the paralyzing force, sensing the same from Malidora. The pressure was like pushing on a door while a hundred people held their weight against it. Malidora started to move again in slow motion. Able to wiggle a toe, then his eyes, Tavarian shoved harder. A terrible ripping sound fractured the world around them as they broke free.

As the forest reappeared, two Nulthereals shielded the shadow girl. The motionless arrows Malidora had fired at the whidge resumed course but flew harmlessly into the void of the Nulthereals. Protected by the two shadows, the whidge girl strode past Tavarian and Malidora.

Malidora fired more arrows as the shadow beings left the forest, as if hoping to get a shot by the Nulthereals and hit the girl. Tavarian's heart weighed heavy, sinking into his chest. He realized their interference might have caused these Nulthereals to accelerate their attack on Grenova, the way they had with Samavere.

Malidora bolted toward the lake as the Nulthereals headed toward Gromere, who stood in the shallow water. The warrior gazed at the shadow girl, as if in a trance. He walked out of the water toward her.

"No! Stay in the water!" yelled Malidora.

The warrior ignored the order as he walked up to the shadows floating along the shore.

Gromere fell to the ground as two arrows went into him.

The three shadow beings paused for a moment, and then resumed their path around the mountain. Tavarian turned to Malidora, wondering why she killed the warrior. With her twisted mind, she must have meant to prevent the shadows from turning Gromere against them again.

The shadows passed over the geyser. What a perfect time it would have been for it erupt right now. Unfortunately, it didn't happen.

"Wait!" Tavarian yelled. "Don't leave me here! I want to join you!"

The shadow girl stopped for a moment and its voices returned in his mind. He recognized how stupid and desperate this idea was. The whidge probably wouldn't believe him, but he knew how much it delighted in influencing people to do its bidding, whether it be to follow it or kill other people. It regarded organic life as ignorant and inferior, nothing more than pieces with which to play their game.

Kill her then . . . kill her and the rewards are yours, bring vengeance to all she has wronged, for all she has murdered, it whispered.

"I don't know if I can do it."

You enjoy the feeling of the weapon you wield. It gives you power over life and death—the power to avenge the innocent.

"But she has a crossbow, how will I ever get close enough to kill her?"

That is our condition! Do it or perish. It matters not how—

The geyser erupted; water and steam shot a mile high into the air. The quaking of the blast knocked the Blight Whidge on its face as scalding steam sizzled over its shadow girl body. Hatred burned through her red glowing eyes as she climbed to her feet. A salvo of arrows streaked into her body as the two Nulthereals raced to cover her. She dissolved the arrows with a lift of her hand just as another volley went into her. Her hand twitched as another arrow went through her shoulder. The shadow girl's mouth drooped open as her body went limp, collapsing onto the wet rocks.

Malidora rushed toward the water as the Nulthereals moved after her. "Torch it!" she yelled to Tavarian. The Nulthereals chased Malidora until she careened into the water. Tavarian dragged the torch over the body of the shadow girl. The body and clothing were still wet from the geyser, and did not immediately catch fire, but as the oil from the torch rubbed across her, the blaze ignited. The dark supernatural shadowy visage faded, and her sharp, fierce features began to change into the soft, sweet face of a young woman.

Tavarian questioned his actions now that a person appeared before him. The sight of the girl burning disturbed him. He recalled the monstrous creature that nearly killed them in the swamp and destroyed Samavere. This thing only used the girl as a shell to inhabit.

As it burned, Tavarian rushed into the water with Malidora. The body was completely engulfed in flames now, topped with thick black smoke rising above the trees, bathing the water in a bright orange glow.

Amid the cracking and popping of the flames came a sizzling, hissing sound. A dark webbing rose from the burning mass, stretching above them in all directions. Knee deep in the water, Malidora ran from under it as fast as she could.

The monster materialized at the edge of the lake. One of its appendages caught her. It pulled her through the water to the horrid body of the whidge. The monster's vile maw waited as if ready to drain the life from her.

Tavarian leaped at it, slicing through the tentacle in one swing. The powered rokensword vibrated through the appendage with ease. Malidora broke free of its grip. The whidge turned its attention to Tavarian.

Tendrils coiled around him, trapping his arms to his body. As it pulled him in, Tavarian struggled to get his sword free. Pelted with arrows, the fibrous appendages loosened their hold long enough for Tavarian to liberate his sword. Slashing through the tangle of tendrils, he was able to escape. More appendages seized him, dragging him again toward the fiend.

Tavarian turned to face the Blight Whidge. Two more tendrils flew toward him. He cut through them, training his sword at the monster's head. The end of the blade went through the darkness as he swung. When the sword came out the other side, the blade's tip was gone, erased. It was the same way Malidora's arrows vanished into the monster's void.

The two Nulthereals moved toward Malidora as she stood in the shallow water. She jumped farther in as they waited at the edges of the lake.

Tavarian cut through the remaining tendrils holding him, dropping them to the ground. The shadow monster extended its remaining tentacles toward him. The appendages wrapped around his body, squeezing the air from his lungs. The flat part of the sword pressed into a cluster of tendrils. As the blade continued to touch the appendages, it began to flash and sizzle. Lightning from the sword fired through the entire network of appendages. The tentacles fell away from the whidge, landing in a smoldering heap around it.

The monster raised its two long shadowy arms, pulling Tavarian to it by some invisible force. Using its power seemed to be weakening the whidge as the bright aura surrounding it faded. The gripping force paralyzed Tavarian. The shadow heaved on his soul while his body came along for the ride.

Negative emotions flooded his mind, dredging up feelings from recent events. Part of him wanted to stop resisting and let himself be taken inside the hellish mouth. At least it would end this poison in his mind. He pictured Lirah, Dexius, Malidora, and Darby. Maybe they would be better off without him.

Deep down, he knew it to be a lie. The shadows twisted dark emotions beyond reason. Like Malidora had said, if you travel in the dark you had better know your way around. If he could make it out of the Grundian's prison, he could make it out of this.

As it pulled him closer, he sensed a familiar energy surrounding the whidge—the thin, bright disk outlining its alien form. Though it had grown dim, it had the same pulsating connection when his mind had been tethered with Malidora's. Reaching toward the energy, it emanated back at him, connecting to some common essence they both shared.

He pushed on it, hoping to repel himself from the whidge. Suddenly, everything stopped. It affected Malidora too. Their minds connected again. All movement stopped in this dimension they had collapsed into. Visions of Malidora's memories, and his own, passed by at light speed. The memories slowed as she attempted to regain her thoughts.

Tavarian understood what she meant to do. She pushed past the visions of their own memories to peer into the mind of the whidge. Tavarian focused on the energy the same way she did. A strange set of thoughts streamed in the distance.

Mountains of nonsensical imaginings drifted into their minds. It countered by attacking Tavarian's mind, playing through some of his memories, but too many to focus on. He relaxed to slow his thoughts as Malidora had done earlier.

Alien memories raced through their minds again. Most of them incomprehensible—images of fearful and angered faces, shadowy arms crawling across a blue diamond surface, a billion stars scattered across a nebulous galaxy, worlds crumbling into dust funneled through a tempest.

Beyond the flow of memories gushed focused thoughts. The whidge grew concerned. It had drawn too much of its energy in this material space. If the energy field became too weak, its aethrial body would spill into this material universe. If aethrium and matter collided, it would tear open reality. It could destroy the whidge, but may also have dire consequences for Isodonia.

Malidora threw caution to the wind. She focused on the energy disk. With some common force inside her, she pushed on the energy field. Life essence, soul, whatever the whidge attempted to drain from them, she now used against it. Reluctantly, Tavarian joined her.

A tiny separation grew within the field, a crack as on a sheet of ice. The break expanded as a dark, dusty substance spilled from the whidge. Their connection broke and the surreal timeless state collapsed. The dark substance fell to the dry ground, burning holes deep into the dirt and rock. Some of it landed in shallow pockets of water, forming into stone. The substance had also hit Tavarian. Instantly, the water on him and his sword sizzled and turned to shiny, crystallized, black stone.

The break in the energy disk stabilized. The whidge raised its long shadowy arms to siphon life energy from Tavarian. It seemed to strengthen its energy field. In desperation, Tavarian swung his blade. The black crystal blade made contact with the void body of the whidge. Its left arm crumbled to the ground as the sword went through.

The whidge crystallized into black glassy stone, its body transforming into a physical form. Now able to interact with the physical universe, it struck Tavarian with its remaining arm, knocking him into the lake. The whidge furiously dashed toward him. Before it could reach him, a barrage of streaking, red arrows penetrated the monster's stone body.

The weakened crystallized form cracked and then shattered, exploding into rock and dust. Malidora waded through the water toward the remains of the shadow monster. She bent down and plucked a stone from the water. As she tilted and turned it, an iridescent sheen reflected as the sunlight hit it. The Nulthereals remained on the dry banks near the lake, unmoving.

The hardened shadow substance still covered Tavarian. He tried to wipe it off, but it wasn't working. He attempted to dissolve it in the water of the lake, but it clung to his skin and clothes. Its contact disturbed him; he wanted it off—now. He swam to the waterfall rushing down the mountain, hoping its force could remove the substance.

The holes that had burned into the ground from the substance expanded. They widened and formed together, reaching the edge of the lake. Water trickled into the open cavity, crystallizing the void on the walls it touched.

The dark untouched by the lake continued expanding, eroding the ground beneath the water's edge. The drip turned into a gush as water surged into the gaping darkness. Tavarian climbed onto a group of boulders, heading toward the mountain. The massive waterfall crashed over the rocks surrounding the pool ahead.

Something caught his eye as he stepped toward the cascade. One of the Nulthereals stirred. It rapidly headed toward Malidora from behind. Though the flow of water had hardened the edges of the void and stopped its expansion, the lake continued to pour into the abyss. The waist-high water she once stood in now shallowed to ankle deep.

"Malidora!" Tavarian called out.

She glanced up from the curious stone she held, spotting the approaching Nulthereal. It was already close enough that it tugged her body with its powerful force.

"Malidora!" he shouted again, diving into the lake.

Tavarian swam as fast as he could. The Nulthereal yanked her into its shadowy void, swallowing her whole. The Nulthereal's outline shimmered violently. As the aura stabilized, it remained at the water's edge, waiting for Tavarian to leave the safety of the deep water. The second one lingered too, on the bank to his left.

A flurry of whispers exploded in his mind. *Breathe in the water. Fill your lungs with its suffocating reprieve! Take your weapon! Drain the lifeblood from its useless husk.*

Tavarian rushed to the shallows, charging at the Nulthereal.

"Malidora!" He held out his now blackened sword. As he closed in, the shadow's gripping force took hold. Raising his sword as it drew him in, he slashed at the whispering shadow.

Hit by the shadow-stone blade, the Nulthereal split, shattering into five pieces that fell to the wet sand. A painful buzzing ran through him as the other Nulthereal enveloped him. Its force took hold, pulling him toward it. It positioned itself so that its drawing force took Tavarian toward the deep chasm.

Tavarian had no way to reach the shadow as it slowly dragged him to the edge of the abyss. Adjusting his grip on the sword handle, he hurled the blade at the Nulthereal. The black blade accelerated at the Nulthereal as its force pulled it in. It stuck on impact. The shadow began to crack around the sword. Fissures grew deeper until the shadow crumbled into pieces. The pulling force stopped.

Tavarian stood over the Nulthereal's broken remains. Knocking bits of dust and rock away, he reclaimed his sword. There was no sign of Malidora among the rubble. This time he was too late. She was gone.

He kicked at the piles of shadow stone, unsure what to do next. The last few moments replayed in his mind. It was uncharacteristic that Malidora dropped her guard, but he should have stayed with her while the Nulthereals roamed about. Despite the ill things she had done, and all those she had taken advantage of, she gave her life so Isodonia could endure. Possibly the greatest feat anyone had ever done in this world. Maybe her final act did enough good to make up for the bad, but maybe not. Either way, he couldn't believe she really was gone.

As he stared at the broken Nulthereals, his arm began to itch. It grew worse until he couldn't bear it any longer. The alien substance still covered him. Tavarian moved to the falls, climbing on the large stones. He thrust his sword into the soft rock, steadying himself on the slippery surface.

Once stable, he let go of the sword, stepping underneath the barrage of water. The dark substance on his hands and clothing separated as the water washed over him. It seemed to work, until everything went dark.

No longer sensing the ground beneath his feet, Tavarian floated through the sheets of water. The roar of the falls had stopped even as they continued to flow. Silence overwhelmed him until something in the distant darkness stirred. Thousands of voices, speaking at once, grew closer. The unintelligible calamity thundered until at last the voices merged and spoke as one.

A foreign object in our domain . . . Obstructing the gateway . . . Too miniscule to see but we sense . . . consciousness . . . Yes, a living soul. Come closer, living one. Shed the weak confines of your material body. Step from the waters of this perennial vortex.

The voices had a peculiar wavering quality and seemed to have a power of their own. They tugged at Tavarian's mind. A force far greater than the whidge cycled through his thoughts at blurring speed. Emotions ran through him as if being sampled. As the assault continued, his thoughts clouded.

There is no need for life filled with pain and regret. You wish to find a place where you are accepted. Where you matter and have purpose. That place is waiting for you. Merge with the Gaith mind collective, the future masters of the Everance. There is no purpose greater than this.

Tavarian contemplated the words. He had achieved his mission. Although he lost Malidora, Dexius and Darby were likely safe in Strakenbridge. His desire to be greater than anyone in Rethia, to make them regret casting him out, remained raw in his heart. Uncertain what this offer truly meant, it sounded well beyond anything Isodonia could offer. In the end, as much as this world had its downsides, he would miss it—the beauty and curiosity of Nalacea, the rivers and trees, the strange animals and creatures, but mostly, Darby and Dexius.

Tavarian wanted to realize what he could become in this life. He wanted to discover what Darby and Dexius would become. The multitude of voices crept closer.

He continued through the cascading water. His mind became foggy. The thing that tampered with his thoughts had done something to his mind. Its power was too strong.

The sound of the voices faded, and the roar of the waterfall returned as he kept going. A storm of blue clouds churned ahead. Tavarian tried to shut the voices out as he moved through the blue tempest. Ground returned beneath his feet. He ran over the rocky surface, tripping on the uneven ground.

A light shone down on him from above, casting a shadow over the rocks. Behind him, the waterfall danced down a wall of solid stone. The spray gleamed near the beam of light. The air was thick and moist here, and contained a strange musty odor. He must have passed through the waterfall into a cave. Something happened when he entered, but his thoughts were scrambled. He had no recollection of it.

A bit of light cast onto a large machine. By its dirty appearance, it hadn't been used in a very long time. Not far from the machine was a wall of perfectly formed white stone. He jerked back his hand when he touched it as a shocking vibration jolted him. Along the wall were meticulously carved shapes and forms; it could have been writing, but it was no language that he knew how to read.

He moved farther into the cavern until he reached an area that was obviously not naturally formed. A long hallway was carved and shaped into a decorative ceiling with straight walls and a level floor. More carvings surrounded a row of lit torches lining the walls. Grabbing one of the torches from its stand, he moved through the dark hall. His footsteps echoed through the large space as he passed a junction.

His footsteps were joined by others. He turned and began to walk back the other way until some shapes and shadows filled the hall ahead of him. More beings appeared in the hall behind him.

"See? I was right—it's an intruder!" said something just beyond his torchlight.

"I didn't mean to intrude," he said. "I've lost my way and can't remember how I got in here."

The footsteps slowed and four hunched creatures covered in fur cautiously approached.

One of them gasped as they got close. "What manner of creature are you?"

Tavarian had never seen anything like them. "I'm . . . I'm having trouble remembering anything."

"What are you doing here?" another demanded.

"I don't know. Please, I'll leave if you will show me the way," he said.

"He's not Kavekkian," said one. "No claws . . . no weapons . . . he looks harmless enough. Who are you?"

"I-I can't remember. I can't remember anything!"

One of the creatures reached toward him, moving his shirt away from the satchel strapped on his shoulder.

"What does it say?" it asked. "Ga . . . dunk."

"Gadunk? Is that your name?" another said.

"Gadunk?" he repeated. "I think—no, that's not quite it."

"Is something wrong with you? How do you not know your own name?" said one of the furry creatures.

"Gavrian . . . I think." he said.

"He needs help, let him rest for a while. I'll take him to one of the beds. Come on, Gavian," said one who appeared to be female.

"Gavrian," he repeated.

She flipped the strand of braided hair on the side of her head. "That's what I said. I'll take care of you, Gavian. I'm Taragris. Let's get you some rest, and you'll feel better by evening."

"Yeah, I just need some rest." He took a deep breath.

"We've got a lot of work that needs to be done around here, and we can use all the help we can get. You look to have some strength to you. I'm sure Medigrin will let you stay if you can help us. We have a world to save."

"I can help. I know how to build things."

"Perfect. You'll fit in with us nicely!"

EPILOGUE

GAVIAN PAUSED, AS he had caught up to what Ambrielle already knew from their adventures on Anatharia.

"Wow! That's an amazing story!" Ambrielle rocked back in the wooden chair, lifting its front legs off the floor.

"Amber, please be quiet!" the librarian whispered loudly as she took another book from her cart, placing it between two others on the shelf across from the study area they were seated at.

Ambrielle shook the pencil back and forth in her hand, twisting her lips together to one side of her face. "That's why we have to be quiet."

"Oh, I was expecting something a bit more . . . dangerous," said Gavian, peering at the woman.

"Well, that was only the first warning. You haven't seen the scary side of Ms. Bracklin yet," Ambrielle said, stifling a laugh.

Gavian studied the woman as she continued to roll her cart to each aisle. She didn't appear particularly scary, but he had learned appearances don't always tell the whole story. He glanced back at Ambrielle, who grinned as she rocked back in her chair. Gavian smiled back as he realized she wasn't completely serious.

"I really thought you were human," whispered Ambrielle as she stared blankly ahead. "I can't believe I've kissed an alien."

"Alien? Does that bother you?" Gavian's mind went back to the night on Anatharia where they first kissed by the waterfall.

"No, it's awesome," Ambrielle said quietly, but with excitement. "I'm so glad you remembered everything."

"Why did you not come back?" Gavian inquired, unable to hold back the question any longer.

"Gavian, I'm so sorry I was gone so long . . . or should I call you Tavarian now?" She set her hand on his.

Gavian turned his hand over to hold hers, rubbing her soft skin with his thumb. "Stick with Gavian. I'm done with that Rethian name."

"Okay, good, I'm too used to Gavian now. But to answer your question, I knew there was something I had to do when I came back. Once I got here, I remembered what happened before I left. My mother . . . died before I ended up in the desert. I realized I had alienated the friends who wanted to be there for me. I ignored my family when they needed me most. I guess I thought if I hid away from everyone, I could work through it on my own. But that didn't help anyone. I had left everything in such a mess that I couldn't go back to Solsellion until I had fixed everything here. You came at a perfect time. I started to doubt you were real. I couldn't believe someone like you would really be out there waiting for me."

It hurt to know Ambrielle experienced such pain, and he wished he could have been there to help her in some way. At the same time, it relieved him to know her absence had nothing to do with him.

"I'm deeply sorry about your mother," said Gavian. "Now I understand."

"Thank you, I'm doing pretty okay now, I think . . ."

"I'm glad." As pleased as it made him, the statement didn't seem to fully express what he felt, but he wasn't sure what else to say. As he peered into her big brown eyes, Gavian thought about how fortunate he was to have met her. How incredible it was that they met in a world light years from either of their homes. They had faced tribulation, both together and apart, and the connection between them felt stronger than ever. He hoped it was the same for her.

"It's scary to think Nulthereals are on another world," she said as her chair rocked back too far. Ambrielle quickly leaned forward, stomping her feet to the floor to catch herself. She glanced over to Ms. Bracklin, who gave her a stern stare. Gavian paused, lifting his eyebrows until he was sure it was okay to continue.

"Yes, I wonder if any others are going through what Isodonia and Solsellion have," he added.

"Did you destroy all of them on Isodonia?" Ambrielle leaned over the table, resting her chin on her folded knuckles.

"I don't know," said Gavian. "The Blight Whidge always had Nulthereals with it, but I don't know if they were the same ones. Malidora mentioned a host of them."

"I wonder how she is doing now." Ambrielle's eyes wandered as if searching for something.

"Malidora? You think she's alive?" Gavian queried. Could there actually be hope?

"The same thing happened to me and I'm still here." Ambrielle's focus returned to Gavian.

"Yes, but I thought that was just luck. Sidaire said when she and her people were swallowed by Nulthereals, they were taken by a monster. That's what she called it anyway."

"I think that monster spoke to me, but it couldn't see me," said Ambrielle. "I guess I *was* lucky. We can only pray she can escape like Sidaire did."

"Sidaire doesn't even remember how she got out, but I guess if anyone can do it, it's Malidora."

Ambrielle opened her mouth as if to speak and then paused, her eyebrows drawing together. "What about Darby and Dexius—you never saw them again?"

"No, but I'm sure they made it back to Strakenbridge," he said. The mention of their names brought images to Gavian's mind. He pictured what they might be doing now. How many years had it actually been now since he last saw them? Would he even recognize them now?

"Maybe they actually did gather an army and finish off the rest of the shadows," Ambrielle said, sitting straight up in her chair.

Gavian smiled. "Wouldn't that be something? But at least the source is destroyed."

"The Blight Whidge? That makes me wonder." Ambrielle's nose twitched as she rubbed the side of her face. "There must be a whidge on Solsellion somewhere. How are things going there?"

"Things are going well," said Gavian. "Maetha and Fegrin returned to Anatharia. It's mostly run by Sidaire and the sentinels now. We never came across a whidge there."

"Everyone has done such a great job," Ambrielle said.

Gavian closed his eyes for a moment. As much as it made him happy to imagine what Dexius and Darby were doing now, it also greatly concerned him.

"You want to go back, don't you?" Ambrielle seemed to be studying him. "That's why you came here, isn't it? To tell me you are leaving."

"I . . ." Gavian began. "Yes, I wanted to make sure you were safe and happy, but I do feel compelled to check on Darby and Dexius too. They must think I'm dead by now."

"I understand. You should go." Ambrielle pursed her lips.

"Oh, just like that?" His heart sank. Had all this time apart changed their relationship? He wasn't sure he could bear this again. "I thought you might object a little bit."

"What? Why would I object?" Ambrielle raised her head.

Gavian gritted his teeth. "I thought maybe you cared. You disappeared without a word. I went to a lot of trouble to find you, and now that I'm leaving, you're all like, 'Okay, go ahead.'"

Ambrielle laughed. "Are you kidding? I'm not letting you out of my sight again. And I would hate to miss what could be one of the greatest adventures of all time!"

"Amber!" said Ms. Bracklin as she stormed closer to their table. "Must you be so loud? This is not the place for conversation! You should leave if all you are going to do is talk."

"There you go again," Gavian whispered with a bit a sarcasm. "Always getting me in trouble."

Ambrielle snickered, cupping her hand over her mouth. "C'mon, let's go. I've got some things I need to take with us."

Gavian picked up his satchel and jacket from the chair beside him and followed Ambrielle as she strolled through the open room toward the main door. Ms. Bracklin eyed them the entire time until the door slowly closed behind them. They had somehow copied his automatic closing gate idea.

As Ambrielle ran ahead, he searched his satchel, making sure everything he needed for his return to Isodonia remained intact. Digging through the smaller items surrounding the silbrace Avo'Doria had given him, he touched something soft in the corner pocket—the banded curl of Lirah's hair.

Though stained with grime, part of it was still as white as the day she gave it to him. No longer holding the meaning it once had, he loosened the string keeping the individual strands together. He let go as the gentle breeze took them from his hand.

"What did you see, Gav?" Ambrielle stopped as he watched the hairs scatter into the wind.

"Nothing," he told her, turning to catch up. "It's nothing."

THANKS FOR READING!

I would love to know what you thought of Shadowsphere. Please leave a comment in the review section.

JOIN MY NEWSLETTER AND GET A FREE BOOK!

Get my short story, Elyravess, free when you sign up to my newsletter at *https://bewildernessseries.com/*

The newsletter will give you monthly updates on upcoming books in the series, behind the scenes, and artwork!

Four hundred million years before the events of Bewilderness: Book One, a group of miners on the world of Elyravess accidently discover an ancient ceremonial chamber containing an object they have never seen before: A glowing blue rift within a great column of stone. Young Hegane joins his father as a Cereveshian archaeologist arrives to study the strange anomaly. Given the seemingly tiresome task of keeping the archaeologist's daughter, Lyleth, entertained, Hegane quickly finds her to be the most interesting being he's ever met.

Becoming fast friends, the pair are allowed to observe as the breach is studied, but what happens next will change their lives forever.

COMING IN 2023

Neverscape (Bewilderness Book Three) will tell the story of Malidora as she attempts to escape the clutches of the five Gaith of The Hollow.

ABOUT THE AUTHOR

When author Kevin Cox decided for fun to write a single chapter a few years back, he ended up writing another and another until finally a novel was born. He was hooked and has been writing ever since, feeling as if it were something he should have been doing his whole life.

Inspiration for Kevin's writing comes from the world around him - while driving, showering, reading, or listening to a conversation. He enjoys listening to music while he writes, playing songs whose tempo aligns with what he is writing at that time.

Kevin believes that a good story is made up of great characters - ones with struggles and motivations and overcome obstacles in their path. He hopes that his young adult readers of his books learn that we are all going through struggles that perhaps aren't visible to all and that his stories inspire his readers to reach out to someone experiencing challenges and to also open up to others who will listen to their own troubles.

Kevin lives in southwest Georgia in a small town called Leesburg.

When he isn't writing thought-provoking science fiction fantasy stories for young adults, he enjoys playing guitar, video games, and traveling.

Please contact or follow on social media for the latest news and info on the next book in the series.

Email: authorkevincox@gmail.com

Instagram: @kevincoxauthor

Twitter: @authorkevincox

Facebook: *https://www.facebook.com/authorkevincox/*

OTHER WORKS

Bewilderness: Book One

Available on Amazon.com *https://www.amazon.com/dp/B09J3Z9J2F*

"This meticulously crafted YA journey will challenge readers' expectations until the last page."

— Kirkus Reviews (starred review)

When a young girl wakes up in an unknown world and encounters dark forces that threaten the universe, only she can change its destiny.

Accessing portals to other realms, Ambrielle journeys across multiple worlds as she searches for answers to find her way home.

Sixteen-year-old Ambrielle has no memory of her life. In fact, she doesn't even know if her name is Ambrielle, the name her new alien friend gave her when she woke up mysteriously stranded in a desolate world with no humans. As she slowly cobbles together bits and pieces of her life, Ambrielle tries to fit in with the many alien species she encounters and settle their divisive conflicts, all while eluding shadowy entities from a realm beyond the universe as she seeks a way to return to Earth.

www.ingramcontent.com/pod-product-compliance
Lightning Source LLC
Chambersburg PA
CBHW020258030826
48979CB00026B/1384/J

* 9 7 9 8 9 8 6 6 3 6 8 0 1 *